Professor Bernard Knight, CBE, became a Home Office pathologist in 1965 and was appointed Professor of Forensic Pathology, University of Wales College of Medicine, in 1980. During his forty-year career with the Home Office, he performed over 25,000 autopsies and was involved in many high profile cases.

Bernard Knight is the author of twelve novels, a biography and numerous popular and academic non-fiction books. *Fear in the Forest* is the seventh novel in the Crowner John series, following *The Grim Reaper*, *The Tinner's Corpse*, *The Sanctuary Seeker*, *The Poisoned Chalice*, *Crowner's Quest* and *The Awful Secret*.

D0092822

Also by Bernard Knight

The Sanctuary Seeker
The Poisoned Chalice
Crowner's Quest
The Awful Secret
The Tinner's Corpse
The Grim Reaper

FEAR IN THE FOREST

Bernard Knight

POCKET BOOKS

LONDON • SYDNEY • NEW YORK • TOKYO • SINGAPORE • TORONTO

First published in Great Britain by Simon & Schuster UK Ltd, 2003
This edition published by Pocket Books, 2003
An imprint of Simon & Schuster UK Ltd
A Viacom company

3 5 7 9 10 8 6 4

Simon & Schuster UK Ltd
Africa House
64–78 Kingsway
London WC2B 6AH

www.simonsays.co.uk

Simon & Schuster Australia
Sydney

A CIP catalogue record for this book is available
from the British Library

ISBN 0–7434–4990–8

Typeset by Palimpsest Book Production Limited,
Polmont, Stirlingshire
Printed and bound in Great Britain by
Bookmarque Ltd, Croydon, Surrey

Acknowledgements

Over the years that the Crowner John stories have appeared, many people have provided invaluable advice about various aspects of life and law in the late twelfth century. In this book, once again the staff of the West Country Studies Unit at Exeter have been as helpful as usual, as have Professor Thomas Watkin and the staff of the Law Library of the University of Wales Cardiff. My good friend Susanna Gregory, author of the well-known Matthew Bartholomew series of historical mysteries about Cambridge, kindly gave me some more information about medieval dress. Finally, I would like to acknowledge the unfailing interest and encouragement of both my publisher, Kate Lyall Grant and script editor, Gillian Holmes.

Author's Foreword

In medieval times, much of England was appropriated by the kings as Royal Forest, a practice reaching its peak in the twelfth-century reign of Henry II, when almost a third of the country was taken over. Though much of this land belonged directly to the King, the rest did not – but still the monarch wielded his forest regime over it, to the increasing resentment of the barons and other landowners. In fact, this was one of the factors which led to Magna Carta being forced on King John in 1215. Three of its clauses were concerned with limiting the oppression of the forest laws; three years later there was even a separate Charter of the Forest.

In those days, the word 'forest' did not necessarily mean wooded land – it meant areas, including open country, where certain wild beasts and the greenery they fed upon were protected so that the King could have sole hunting rights, to the exclusion of even the owners of the land where the animals roamed. These beasts were carefully classified, the main ones being the 'venison' – the hart and the hind (red deer), fallow and roe deer, the hare and the wild boar, lesser game being the fox, marten, wolf, coney (rabbit) and squirrel. All the vegetation, the trees, coppices, bushes and pasture, was known as the 'vert', an important distinction from the 'venison'.

Apart from the enjoyment of the hunt, which was the main sport of those times, the King gained much financial profit from the forests – from the sale of meat, timber, rights of pasture, building permits and the establishment of forges, tanneries and brew-houses. He could also give, rent or sell these profitable amenities to others, including religious houses.

To enforce his rights, the monarch established a separate

system of forest laws, courts and officers, which was harsh and oppressive. The penalty for killing a deer was mutilation or death, and even gathering firewood could attract a fine or imprisonment. The foresters who policed these lands were notorious for their rapacity and corruption; they usually received no salary and some even paid to hold their jobs, as the opportunities for extortion were so great. In 1204, the landowners of Devon paid a huge sum to King John to give up some of the Royal Forest outside Dartmoor and Exmoor, but at the time of our story a considerable part of the county was still under this iron rule.

Coroners, established in September 1194, had many legal and fiscal duties involving dead bodies, wrecks, royal fish, fires, assaults, rapes, etc., but could also be given any special investigation on an ad hoc basis, by means of a royal commission, charging them with a particular task on behalf of the King, as happens in this story.

Apart from a few rare gold coins, the only money in circulation was the silver penny, which was often cut into segments for use as lower denominations. The shilling, mark and pound were not coins, but nominal values, the shilling being twelve pence (equivalent to the present 5p), a mark two-thirds of a pound (about 66p) and a pound 240 pence (100p).

The language spoken by the common folk in Devon at that time was mainly Early Middle English, unintelligible to us today, but some retained their Celtic tongue, similar to Cornish, Welsh and Breton. The speech of the ruling classes was Norman French, but the Church used Latin, as did virtually all written documents – though only about one in a hundred people could read and write.

Many of the main characters in this story actually existed in history, such as the sheriff, bishop, archdeacons and burgesses of Exeter – though the coroners were unrecorded until the middle of the next century. The remaining names are authentic for the period and place, almost all being taken from the court records of the Devon Eyre held at Exeter in 1238.

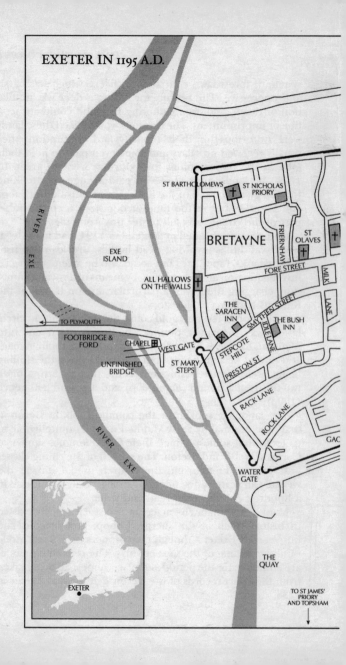

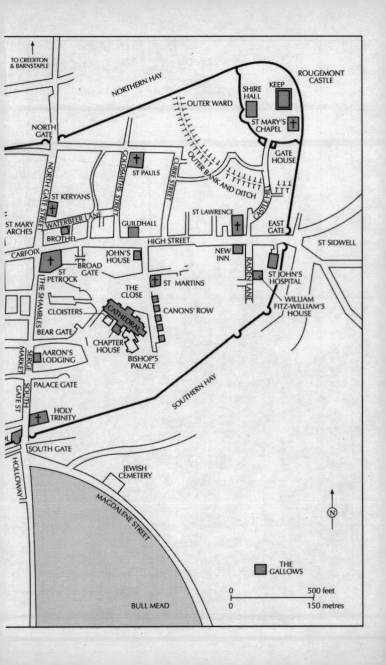

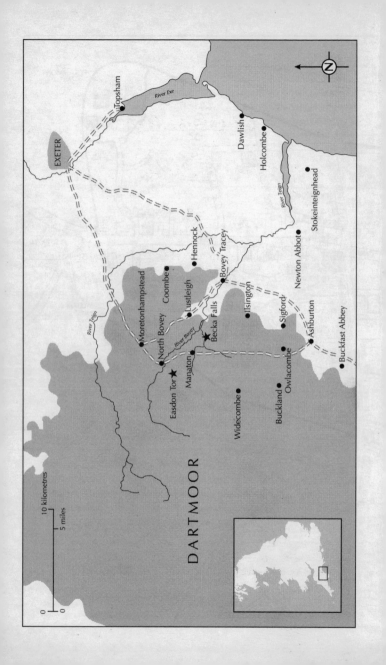

GLOSSARY

AGISTERS
Officers who regulated the use of forest land for 'agisting' – pasture and forage for cattle and pigs, for which live-stock owners were charged a rent.

ALE
A brewed drink, before the advent of hops – derived from an 'ale', a village celebration where much drinking took place.

APPEAL
Unlike the modern legal meaning, an appeal was an accusation by an aggrieved person, often a relative of a victim, against another for a felonious crime. Historically it preceded (and competed with) the Crown's right to prosecute and demanded either financial compensation or trial by combat or the Ordeal.

AMERCEMENT
An arbitrary fine on a person or community by a law officer, for some breach of the complex regulations of the law. Where imposed by a coroner, he would record the amercement, but the collection of the money would normally be ordered by the royal justices when they visited at the Eyre of Assize.

ATTACHMENT
An order made by a law officer, including a coroner, to ensure that a person, whether suspect or witness, appeared at a court hearing. It resembled a bail bond or surety, distraining upon a person's money or goods, which would be forfeit if he failed to appear.

BAILEY
Originally the defended areas, sometimes concentric, around a castle keep ('motte and bailey') but later also applied to the yard of a dwelling.

BAILIFF
Overseer of a manor or estate, directing the farming and other work. He would have manor reeves under him and himself be responsible either directly to his lord or to the steward or seneschal.

BAILIWICK
A division of the forest, of which there were four in the Dartmoor forest. Each was under the jurisdiction of a Verderer.

BOTTLER
A servant responsible for providing drink in a household – the origin of 'butler'.

BURGESS
A freeman of substance in a town or borough, usually a merchant. A group of burgesses ran the town administration and in Exeter elected two Portreeves (later a Mayor) as their leaders.

CANON
A priestly member of the chapter of a cathedral. Also called a prebendary. Exeter had twenty-four canons, most of whom

lived near the cathedral. Many employed junior priests (vicars) to carry out their duties for them.

CHAPTER

The administrative body of a cathedral, composed of the canons (prebendaries). They met daily to conduct business in the Chapter House, so-called because a chapter of the Rule of St Benedict was read before each session.

COIF

A close-fitting cap or helmet, usually of linen, covering the ears and tied under the chin; worn by men and women.

COMPLINE

The last of the religious services of the day, usually in late afternoon or early evening.

CONSTABLE

Has several meanings, but could refer to a senior commander, usually the custodian of a castle, which in Exeter belonged to the King – or a watchman who patrolled the streets to keep order.

CORONER

A senior law officer in each county, second only to the sheriff. First formally established in September 1194, though there is a mention of the coroner in Saxon times. Three knights and one clerk were recruited in each county, to carry out a wide range of legal and financial duties. The name comes from *custos placitorum coronas*, meaning 'Keeper of the Pleas of the Crown', as he recorded all serious crimes, deaths and legal events for the King's judges.

COVER-CHIEF

More correctly 'couvre-chef', a linen headcover, worn by women, held in place by a band around the head, and flowing down the back and front of the chest. Termed 'head-rail' in Saxon times.

CURFEW

The prohibition of open fires in towns after dark, for fear of starting conflagrations. Derived from 'couvre-feu', from the extinguishing or banking-down of fires at night. During the curfew, the city gates were closed from dusk to dawn – one thirteenth-century mayor of Exeter was hanged for failing to ensure this.

DEODAND

Literally 'a gift from God', it was the forfeiture of anything that had caused a death, such as a sword, a cart or even a mill-wheel. It was confiscated by the coroner for the king, but was sometimes given as compensation to the victim's family.

DESTRIER

A large war-horse able to carry the weight of an armoured knight. When firearms made armour redundant, destriers became shire-horses, replacing oxen as draught animals.

DORTER

The dormitory of a monastery, abbey or priory.

EYRE

A sitting of the King's justices, introduced by Henry II in 1166, which moved around the country in circuits. There were two types, the 'Eyre of Assize' which was the forerunner of the later Assize and latterly Crown Courts, which was supposed to visit each county town regularly to try serious cases; and the General Eyre, which came at long intervals to scrutinise the administration of each county.

FARM
The taxation from a county, collected in coin on behalf of the sheriff and taken by him personally every six months to the royal treasury at London or Winchester. The sum was fixed annually by the king or his ministers; if the sheriff could extract more from the county, he could retain the excess, which made the office of sheriff much sought after.

FLETCHER
A maker of arrows.

FOREST
Strictly, a wild area, with or without trees. The Royal Forests were areas sequestered by the king, whether he owned the actual land or not, where only he could hunt and take the profit from various activities, such as wood-felling, forges, brewing etc.

FOREST EYRE
The higher court enforcing forest laws, dealing with all offences against venison and those of vert worth more than four pence. Usually held every three years, after being summoned by letters patent from the king. The sheriff summoned all nobility, forest officers and four members of each township to attend.

FORESTER
An officer, similar to a gamekeeper, directly responsible for enforcing the harsh forest laws and taking offenders to the forest courts. He had a groom or page to assist him. He was nominated by the Warden of the Forest, but received no salary – sometimes paying for the privilege of the job, because of the opportunities for extortion. His badge was a horn.

HAUBERK
A chain-mail tunic with long sleeves to protect the wearer from neck to calf; usually slit for riding a horse.

HUNDRED
An administrative division of a county, originally named for a hundred hides of land or a hundred families.

JUSTICES
The king's judges, originally from his royal court, but later chosen from barons, senior priests and administrators. They sat in the various law courts, such as the Eyre of Assize or as Commissioners of Gaol Delivery. From 1195 onwards, 'keepers of the peace' were recruited from local knights, who by the fourteenth century, evolved into 'justices of the peace'.

KIRTLE
A lady's gown.

MATINS
The first service of the religious day, originally at midnight.

MARK
A measure of money, though not an actual coin, as only pennies existed. A mark was two-thirds of a pound i.e. thirteen shillings and fourpence (sixty-six decimal pence).

MUTILATION
A common punishment as an alternative to hanging. A hand, foot, or genitals were amputated or blinding carried out.

ORDEAL
A test of guilt or innocence, such as walking over nine red-hot plough-shares, picking a stone from a barrel of boiling water or molten lead; if burns appeared, the person was judged guilty. For women, submersion in water was the ordeal, the guilty floating!

PALFREY
A small, docile horse suitable for use by a woman.

PAPAL LEGATE
An official emissary of the Vatican.

SECONDARIES
Young men aspiring to become priests, thus under 24 years of age. They assisted canons and vicars in their duties in the cathedral.

TERCE
The fourth of the nine services of the cathedral day, usually around nine in the morning.

TRIAL BY BATTLE
An ancient right to settle a dispute by fighting to the death. Usually, an appealer (qv) would demand financial compensation from the alleged perpetrator or be challenged to battle. Women and unfit persons could employ a champion to fight for them.

VENISON
The wild animals of the forest which were hunted, protected by the forest laws. They were divided into the 'beasts of the forest' – hart, hind, hare, boar and wolf, the 'beasts of the chase' – buck, doe, fox, marten, roe and the 'beasts of warren' – hare, rabbit (coney), cat, badger, pheasant, partridge, woodcock and squirrel.

VERDERER
An administrative forest officer responsible for holding the Attachment Courts every forty days and committing serious offences to the Forest Eyre. He was responsible to the sovereign, not the Warden. There were usually four in each royal forest, one to each bailiwick. His badge was an axe.

VERT
The vegetation of the forest – trees, bushes and pasture, the use of which was also subject to the forest laws.

VICAR
A priest employed by a more senior cleric, such as a canon, to carry out some of his religious duties, especially the many daily services in a cathedral. Often called a 'vicar-choral' from his participation in chanted services.

WARDEN OF THE FOREST
The senior forest adminsitrator, appointed by the king, who was responsible for organising the Forest Eyre and who nominated the foresters, but not verderers, who were individually responsible to the king.

WIMPLE
Linen or silk cloth worn framing a woman's face and covering the throat.

WOODMOTE
An alternative name for the lowest level of forest courts, usually known as the 'Attachment Courts' or the 'Forty Day' courts. Sometimes incorrectly called 'Swainmotes'. Only offences against the vert amounting to less than four pence could be dealt with by these courts; offences against the venison or larger vert offences could only be recorded and referred to the higher court, the Forest Eyre.

WOODWARDS
Employed by private landowners to protect the vert and venison, but outside the royal forests. Although they were servants of the landowner, they still had to adhere to the same oaths and codes as the foresters. Their badge was a bill-hook.

PROLOGUE

June 1195

The hamlet dozed in the afternoon sun. The dappled shadows of a few fleecy clouds glided slowly across the green woods that rose on either side of the small valley. Most of the two score men and boys of Sigford were working in the strip-fields that lined the track through the village: a few more were scything hay in an enclosed part of the meadow land beyond the fields. The ragged idiot boy was hiding from the sun under a hawthorn bush, keeping an eye on a dozen goats cropping the summer grass along the verge of the dusty road that led to Owlacombe and distant Ashburton.

The smithy was silent, as the blacksmith was squatting outside the wall of the alehouse a hundred paces away, restoring his sweating body with a quart of Widow Mody's indifferent brew. At least it was cool and wet, he thought – though he regretted the death of the widow's sister from the yellow plague last year. By God, she used to brew a good ale!

The smith drank slowly, spinning out the time before he must go back to his forge, where the flames from the furnace and the labour of his hammering convinced him that Hell itself would be a relief from working in this summer heat. The only sound was the distant smack of mattocks as the labourers hacked at weeds in the furrows between the rows of beans, turnips and oats. This quilted patchwork of crops was all that stood between the people of Sigford and starvation next winter.

Much nearer, he heard the buzzing of a couple of bluebottles as they hovered over his boots, attracted by the dried blood of a chicken he had killed that morning. He felt himself nodding off and pulled himself together with a jerk. Sigford was too small to have either a church or a manor house and it belonged to the manor of Ilsington, a mile away. Their lord, William de Pagnell, had a nasty habit of sending his servants on unexpected visits to check on the village. Though the smith was a freeman, it would not be politic to be found in mid-afternoon dozing against the alehouse wall with a jar in his hand. He struggled to shake off his lethargy and stared out over the green hills in front, the outriders of Dartmoor, the grim plateau that lay high beyond the dells and coombes west of Sigford.

As he gathered the will to finish his ale and get back to work, a new sound began to insinuate itself into his consciousness. Faintly at first, then more clearly, the sound of hoofs reached his ears. Well used to horses from his trade as a farrier, he could tell that the rider was in a hurry. In case it was de Pagnell's steward or manor-reeve, he gulped the rest of his ale, put the pot on the ground and hurriedly rose to get back to his smithy. But before he went five paces, his keen ears told him something else – this horse was running wild, without a rider.

A bend in the track hid the approaching animal until the hammering of its hoofs was all too clear. As a cloud of reddish dust swirled around the bend, he was aware of the men in the fields shouting in alarm.

Abruptly, Morcar, the village reeve, and a couple of good-wives appeared from their cottages opposite, as a tall brown mare materialised through the dust, its eyes rolling wildly as it charged down the track between the dwellings. Wary not to get trampled, both the smith and the reeve ran into the roadway, waving their arms and yelling. At the last minute, just as they were about to throw themselves out of its path, the mare shied, pranced and finally skidded to a stop, trembling and frothing, a foam of sweat mixing with the grime on its flanks.

Only then, as the dust settled, did they see what was being dragged from the left-side stirrup. With a foot trapped in the iron hoop, the rider was face down, and when in desperate haste the two villagers lifted him up, they looked in horror at his ravaged features, dragged an unknown distance on the flinty surface of the unforgiving road. His clothing was ripped to shreds, but two things were all too obvious to Morcar and the smith.

On his breast was an embroidered badge depicting an axe – and from the centre of his back protruded the broken shaft of an arrow.

CHAPTER ONE

In which Crowner John holds an inquest

As Sigford lacked a church or even a tithe barn, the coroner's inquest had to be held in the open air on what passed for the village green. Where the Bagtor lane came down from the moor to join the main track, a triangle of beaten grass lay between the alehouse and the smithy. Here the villagers gathered to eat, dance and get drunk on saints' days and the occasional chapman or pedlar set out his ribbons, threads and trinkets for the women to paw over.

This Tuesday noontide, however, saw a unique gathering on the dusty greensward. For the first time in history, a coroner's inquest was to be held in the village, a happening beyond the comprehension of anyone other than Morcar, who had a vague notion of this new-fangled process.

The previous autumn, he had been told by William de Pagnell's bailiff that henceforth all deaths, other than those from old age or disease, must immediately be reported to himself or the manor-reeve, so that the King's coroner in Exeter could be notified. This obscure command had gone in one of Morcar's ears and out the other, and as no unnatural deaths had happened in Sigford since then the matter had been forgotten until yesterday, when a battered corpse had been dragged into the village.

Now the sleepy hamlet had been invaded by three men from the great city of Exeter. Although it was barely sixteen miles away, only two villagers had ever been there, and these awesome officials were as alien as if they had come from the moon. The whole population, ordered by the bailiff to congregate on the green at midday, stood silently as the coroner and his companions rode into the village. At their head was a great black destrier, a former warhorse, carrying the lean and forbidding figure of the coroner himself. Dressed in a long tunic as black as his steed, he hunched in his saddle like some great bird of prey. Hair of the same jet colour was swept back from his bony forehead to the nape of his neck. Heavy eyebrows hung over deep-set eyes, and a long hooked nose added to his eagle-like appearance. The dark stubble on his lean cheeks gave further credence to his old nickname of 'Black John', given to him by the soldiers of campaigns from Ireland to the Holy Land. His wide leather belt and diagonal baldric carried a formidable broadsword.

Sir John de Wolfe walked his horse to the centre of the grassy patch, watched in silence by the small crowd as the reeve came forward to take the reins. Behind him, a giant of a man with wild ginger hair and a huge straggling moustache of the same colour halted his brown mare and slid to the ground. The third visitor was a complete contrast, a little man with a slight hump on his left shoulder, riding a grey pony side-saddle like a woman.

The coroner dismounted and the reeve and two other villagers led their mounts away to be fed and watered, whilst the three men stood in the centre of the green and looked about them.

'God-forsaken bloody place!' muttered the dishevelled redhead under his breath, as he looked around at the handful of dwellings that made up the village.

They were all shacks built of cob, with roofs of thatch in varying states of dilapidation, most surrounded by a small plot containing a vegetable patch and a few scrawny fowls. The only larger building was the alehouse, and from its door now strode a man in a fine yellow tunic, followed by a pair in more sober clothes. He marched up to the trio on the green and smacked his forearm across his chest in greeting.

'Sir John, welcome! I am William de Pagnell, lord of the manor of Ilsington – which includes this miserable vill!'

He had a sharp, foxy face, and the coroner took an instant dislike to him.

However, he managed to conceal it, as the man was trying to be civil in the face of what could only be an unwelcome visitation. The arrival of the county's second-most senior law officer could never be good news, especially as one of his major functions was the imposition of fines for the King's treasury.

'Before you begin your duties, you must eat and drink something. You must have been a few hours on the road from Exeter, in this damned heat.'

De Pagnell perfunctorily introduced the other two men as his steward and bailiff, as he led the way across to the alehouse. In the single large room, which stank of stale urine, spilt ale and of the calves mewling behind a hurdle at the other end, they all sat around the dead fire-pit on a collection of rough benches and a few milking stools. Widow Mody and a snivelling waif brought them pottery mugs of ale and a tray of fresh bread and slices of boiled pork, which, in spite of the cloud of flies settling on it, tasted surprisingly good.

The coroner gruffly matched William's introductions by poking a thumb at his own companions as he spoke.

'Gwyn of Polruan, my officer and right-hand man.'

Gwyn grinned, his bright blue eyes twinkling in his

red, knobbly face. He was as tall as the lanky coroner, but built like a bull, his wide shoulders emphasised by the boiled-leather jerkin that he wore whatever the weather.

'And this is my clerk, Thomas de Peyne, who works wonders with a pen and parchment.'

The little fellow, who was dressed in a patched black cassock like a priest, smiled shyly at the compliment, a rare thing from his usually taciturn master. Thomas had a thin, pinched face, with a long pointed nose and a receding chin. His looks were further marred by a slight squint and the sparse, mousy hair that was cropped into a parody of a clerical tonsure.

'This is a bad business, Crowner,' said de Pagnell. 'I wish to God it had happened on someone else's manor, not mine!'

'It may well have, from what I've been told,' snapped de Wolfe. 'The body ended up here, but who knows where the death took place?'

'Does that make any difference to your findings?' asked the lord hopefully.

John de Wolfe shook his head. 'The new law says that the coroner investigates where the corpse lies. If someone drowns off Dover, but is washed up on the shores of Devon, then the burden is on me.'

They ate and drank hurriedly, as the Exeter men wanted to get on with their task and get back to the city. Gwyn finished first and ambled out with the bailiff from Ilsington, the person who, the evening before, had ridden to Exeter to notify the coroner. By the time de Wolfe and the others had ducked out of the low doorway into the blinding sunlight, Gwyn was standing within the circle of villagers, beckoning the bailiff as he pushed a handcart out of a nearby shed. As he trundled the cart to the centre of the parched grass, the crowd saw that it bore an inert shape under a couple of sacks. The coroner strode to stand alongside it, followed by Thomas de Peyne, who had brought a pair of stools from the alehouse. He sat himself down unobtrusively behind the coroner and delved into a shapeless pilgrim's pouch to pull out a parchment roll, a quill pen and a stone phial of ink, which he set on the other stool.

As de Pagnell and his servants joined the ring of villagers, Gwyn stepped forward and bellowed in a voice that echoed across the little valley.

'All ye who have anything to do before the King's coroner for the county of Devon, draw near and give your attendance.'

Having formally opened the proceedings, the Cornishman turned to his master.

'The village reeve has rounded up all the men and boys from here, apart from the idiot. He didn't attempt to get any from farther afield.'

John nodded resignedly. Although the rules demanded that all males over the age of twelve be summoned from the four nearest villages, it was a physical impossibility and would have left the countryside denuded of workers in the fields and those who herded the livestock. He took a step forward and glared around the throng.

'I am Sir John de Wolfe, our sovereign King Richard's coroner for this county. We are here to enquire as to where, when and by what means this man came to his death.'

He slapped the edge of the cart with his hand to emphasise the point.

'The King's Chief Justiciar, in his wisdom, last year set out certain formalities for dealing with violent and suspicious deaths – if these have not been complied with, then the law prescribes certain penalties.'

There was a subdued groan from some in the

gathering. Unfamiliar though they were with this new system, long experience warned them that the ever-grasping authorities would fleece their thin purses once again.

'So who was the First Finder?'

Reluctantly, the blacksmith stepped forward, the reeve a pace behind him.

'We were the ones who stopped the horse, sir.'

'And did you then raise the hue and cry?'

The smith looked at Morcar, who shrugged.

'I suppose so, Crowner. At least, the whole village came running at once, but there was no one to chase after – that bloody mare just galloped in unbidden!'

De Wolfe had some sympathy with them. For centuries, going back to Saxon times, it had been the rule that when a crime was discovered a hue and cry should be started, the four nearest households being knocked up and a frantic hunt begun for the culprit. But in these circumstances, where the horse may have come from five or more miles away, it would have been a pointless exercise.

'Before seeking how and when he died, I have to be certain of the name of the deceased.'

Immediately, William de Pagnell spoke up, his tenants and serfs all looking warily at him from under lowered brows.

'As you already know, Sir John, there's little doubt of that, even though his features are so ill used from being dragged along the highway.'

The smith nodded and spoke up boldly.

'I knew him as soon as I saw his garments, Crowner. The badge on his breast, that yellow axe, marked him as a verderer – and I knew from his size and that brown moustache that it must be Humphrey le Bonde. I've often seen him riding through the village.'

De Wolfe grunted, a favourite response of his. He

turned to the cart and motioned to Gwyn to pull off the sacks over the cadaver.

'We need to make quite sure. You men are now the jury and you must view the body with me.'

He motioned to the nearest dozen and Gwyn marshalled them past the cart, where they stared with morbid interest at the battered corpse lying face up on the boards. The cheeks, forehead and chin were ravaged by deep lacerations and covered in streaks of dried blood and grime, but the eyes were open and stared up sightlessly at the blue sky. Although he had been dead less than a day, the remorseless June sun was already generating an odour and bluebottles were buzzing enthusiastically around the open wounds.

His shredded clothing consisted of the remains of a thigh-length fawn tunic held tightly round the waist with a thick leather belt, which carried a long dagger in a sheath over one hip and a purse on the other. The legs were covered in torn brown worsted breeches tucked into stout riding boots. John pointed a finger at the prominent badge sewn on to the breast of the tunic, depicting a yellow axe on a green background.

'Undoubtedly the emblem of a verderer, one of the senior officers of the Royal Forest. But which one? We have four in Dartmoor Forest alone – and others elsewhere in the county.'

William de Pagnell looked impatient.

'I've told you, Crowner, there's not the slightest doubt! I know the man, it's Humphrey le Bonde, the verderer for this south-eastern bailiwick.'

There was a growl of assent from the village men, but the coroner was stubborn in his desire for certainty.

'The face is unrecognisable, so can you be quite sure?'

'His build is stocky, he has that short thick neck, middling brown hair, a full moustache and no beard.

It must be him, for the other verderers would have no occasion to be in his part of the forest.'

'Where is he from?'

'He lives in Ashburton, he has a wife and three children, to the best of my recollection,' answered de Pagnell. 'He must be in his late thirties, a freeholder with a few acres. He was once a retainer of Reginald de Courcy, but bought out his knight-service some years ago.'

Though women and girls were legally excluded from the judicial process as being of no account, they had all congregated behind their men, determined not to miss any of the drama that so rarely visited their hamlet. Now one of them raised her voice from the back – John recognised her as the dumpy ale-wife who had served them.

'Look at his left hand, Crowner!' she yelled. 'I've given him meat and drink more than once when he was passing through and I noticed he had a finger missing.'

Before the coroner could declare a woman's evidence inadmissible, Gwyn had grabbed the corpse's hand and held it up, breaking the stiffness of rigor mortis.

'She's right, Crowner – an old amputation,' he said triumphantly.

John rumbled in his throat, his usual response when he had nothing to say, and the manor lord gave a smug smile as the coroner finally gave way.

'Very well, I will accept that this is Humphrey le Bonde.'

Though not a vindictive man, de Wolfe felt mild satisfaction in delivering his next declaration. 'So he is undoubtedly of Norman stock and no possibility of Presentment of Englishry can apply. I therefore amerce the village in the sum of ten marks.'

There was a groan from the few men who understood what was implied. Since the Conquest, anyone found dead was assumed to be a Norman and thus the victim of Saxon assassination, unless the community could present evidence that the dead man was himself a Saxon. After well over a century, this rule was cynically out of date, especially since intermarriage had blunted the distinction between the races – but it was still a useful source of revenue for the Crown. However, the coroner's next words blunted the severity of the potential fine.

'This will be recorded on my rolls to be presented to the Justices at the next Eyre, for them to decide if it shall be enforced.'

As the Eyre had only just been held in Exeter, it was likely to be at least a couple of years before it returned, so the villagers had a long breathing space. If the murderer were found in the meantime, then the amercement would lapse.

With the eyes of the audience glued upon him, de Wolfe turned back to the corpse and groped in le Bonde's money pouch. He took out a handful of silver pennies, together with a small ivory charm crudely carved into the shape of the Virgin Mary.

'That didn't bring him much luck,' murmured de Pagnell sarcastically.

The coroner scowled, his dark eyes glittering angrily from under the bushy black brows that crested his long face.

'Neither was the poor man killed for his money – for murdered he certainly was!'

He gestured to Gwyn, who turned the burly corpse over as if it were a feather pillow and laid it face down on the rough boards. Though they already knew the circumstances, there was a subdued hiss of dismay and concern from the encircling jurors as they saw the stump of the broken shaft sticking from between the shoulder-blades. Dried blood discoloured the tunic over a large area of the back.

Well used to the routine, Gwyn unbuckled the belt and began undressing the deceased man, removing the ripped tunic and undershirt, but leaving the breeches in place. He slid the upper garments over the stump of the arrow and held them up to display the slit made by the steel head.

De Wolfe grasped the missile and waggled it about in the wound.

'It's in deep, by the feel of it,' he said, half to himself. With a few experimental twists, he lined up the barbs with the wound between the ribs, close to the spine. He pulled and with a sucking sound some four inches of willow shaft came out, along with a gout of clotted blood.

He bent to wipe it in the grass at his feet, then examined it closely, before handing it to Gwyn.

'Well, what d'you think?'

'Serviceable, but not a professional job,' said his officer critically. 'The sort of thing a bowman would make up himself.'

'Like an outlaw?' suggested de Pagnell. 'There's plenty of those in the forest hereabouts. But he wasn't robbed.'

'The horse may have bolted and carried him away before they had a chance to rifle his purse,' said de Wolfe. He took the remains of the arrow back from Gwyn and dropped it on to the cart.

'Men of the jury, you all need to pass by the cadaver and look at the fatal wound and the instrument that caused it.'

As the villagers shuffled past, their expressions varying from sheepishness to avid curiosity, John de Wolfe checked with his clerk to make sure that his roll had captured what had been said. Though the coroner could read and write little more than his own name, he was trying to learn and made a show of looking over Thomas's shoulder to see how much Latin script was on the parchment. When the jury had seen their fill, Gwyn herded them back into line and John began to wind up the brief proceedings.

'Have any of you anything useful to tell me about this matter?' he growled, scanning the guileless faces as if daring them to say anything.

'There's little they could know, as this poor fellow was dragged into their village from God knows where!' objected William de Pagnell.

De Wolfe ignored the interruption, though he would dearly have liked to have put his boot up the backside of the lord of the manor.

'Then I require you to consider your verdict – though it can be no other than that this man was slain by someone as yet unknown.'

He fixed the village reeve with a stony stare. 'You are the foreman, so speak with your fellows.' The coroner's tone suggested that he defied any man to challenge his conclusions. It took only a few seconds of heads being put together and rapid whispering for Morcar to turn back to de Wolfe and meekly agree with his suggestion. Clearing his throat noisily, the coroner closed the proceedings with a few words.

'I find that the deceased was Humphrey le Bonde, a Norman of Ashburton and a verderer of the Royal Forest. He died at a place undetermined within the County of Devon on the fourteenth day of June in the year of Our Lord 1195. He was unlawfully slain by an arrow in his back, murdered by a person or persons as yet unknown.'

With a final glare around the assembled villagers, he turned away to indicate that the performance was over.

'Cover him up and put him back in that shed,' he commanded Gwyn. 'But keep that arrowhead.'

His officer picked up the missile and looked at it dubiously, as the reeve pushed the cart away. 'It's no good as a deodand, surely?'

Any object that caused a death could be seized by the coroner and declared deodand, then sold for the King's treasury or sometimes for the benefit of the deceased's family. A good sword, a horse or cart and even a mill-wheel might fetch a decent price, but a broken arrow was worthless.

'No, but maybe we'll come across another exactly the same somewhere.' De Wolfe turned to William de Pagnell. 'I've finished with the corpse – what's to become of it?'

'My steward sent a message to Ashburton. Le Bonde's brother is coming with a cart later today to take it home for burial.' The manor lord looked genuinely troubled for once. 'There'll be sadness in that household, with a widow and little ones to care for. Why slay the fellow, if it was not for robbery?'

De Wolfe shrugged his shoulders, towering above the shorter man.

'The forest officers have never been popular – he wouldn't be the first to take an arrow in the back.'

'Foresters, maybe – even woodwards. But verderers only run the forty-day courts, they're not involved in the everyday rough and tumble.'

The coroner, anxious to get away, edged around the manor-lord.

'That's one of the matters I have to look into. When I get back to Exeter, I'll call on the Warden of the Forests, to see what he says. But now we must go back towards Ashburton and see if there are any signs of where this attack took place.'

Minutes later they were back in the saddle and, with

a feeling of relief, the villagers of Sigford watched them vanish around the same bend from which the trouble had galloped in the day before.

Going back to Ashburton meant riding away from the direction of the city and then retracing their route by a different road, using the main track from Plymouth to Exeter, so it was early evening before they splashed through the ford on the River Exe to reach the West Gate. The detour had been a waste of time, but one which John de Wolfe felt had to be made.

A number of horses and oxen had passed along the way from Sigford to Ashburton in the day since the murder, so there was no chance of finding where the scuff marks from the dragged victim began on the hard, dusty road. With no assault from staff or sword, there would be no bloodstaining or crushing of undergrowth on the verge – just a swift, silent arrow whistling out of the trees at a passing horseman.

It should have been the sheriff's job to hunt for the killer, as Sir Richard de Revelle was the supposed enforcer of law and order in the county – but from bitter experience John knew that his brother-in-law was more concerned with raising taxes and creaming off as much as possible for himself, through the many devious schemes he had in operation.

Though de Revelle was sneeringly contemptuous of the new office of coroner, which had been established only the previous autumn, he was already content to let de Wolfe do much of the hard work of investigation, as long as he could claim the credit for any successes.

The thought of his brother-in-law led John's mind to his wife Matilda and his habitual scowl deepened as he rode through the gate and up the slope of Fore Street to the centre of the city. The streets were narrow and crowded, so the coroner's big horse often had to nudge people aside to make any progress. As they passed Carfoix, the crossing of the four roads from each main gate, he reined up in the congested high street to wait for Gwyn to pull alongside. Their clerk was still far behind, saddle-sick on his long-suffering pony.

'I'll have to call in at my house to say I'm back or I'll get the evil eye,' de Wolfe growled. 'But in an hour I want to talk to the Warden, Nicholas de Bosco. You know where he lives?'

'I thought he had a manor out at Kenn.'

'He has, but since his wife died and his daughters married away he spends much of his time in his town-house in St Pancras Lane. So get yourself there, tell him one of his verderers is dead and that I'd like to speak to him at his home in an hour or so.'

The Cornishman pulled his mare around and pushed his way through the crowd into a side street on their left, anxious to get this errand done so that he could visit the Bush Inn to satisfy his insatiable appetite for food and ale.

De Wolfe plodded slowly up the narrow main street, lined by houses and shops of all shapes and sizes. Many of the original wooden buildings were being replaced in stone, as the city dwellers became more affluent. Exeter was now a rich city, the revenues from wool and tin, as well as the agricultural produce for miles around, filling the coffers of its many burgesses. John himself derived a good income from trade, as he had ploughed his spoils from foreign campaigns into a wool-exporting partnership with one of the city's two Portreeves, the men elected by the burgesses to administer the city. He had no salary for being the King's coroner – in fact coroners were forbidden to take any profit at all and must already have a private income of at least twenty pounds a year, the theory being that rich men had no need for graft and embezzlement. Though John stuck rigidly to this rule, he was the exception, as most officials – especially the sheriffs – were notorious for their greed and dishonesty.

As he walked his horse Odin past the new Guildhall, he nodded and grunted at many passers-by who knew him – there were few in the city who did not recognise the tall, grim ex-Crusader. People struggled past handcarts, porters with huge bundles, pedlars, priests, beggars and urchins, all so massed on the rubbish-strewn cobbles that the big stallion had to tread carefully to avoid crushing someone. Most of Exeter's streets were hard-packed earth, but High Street was roughly paved, with a central gutter that carried the sewage downhill to the river.

Some way farther up, he reached a narrow opening and turned into one of the narrow passageways into the Cathedral Close. This was Martin's Lane, where he had his own dwelling. Two tall, narrow houses stood together on his right, opposite the pine-end of an inn, behind which was a livery stable. Here John dismounted and left Odin in the care of Andrew the farrier, before crossing the lane and pushing open his heavy front door.

He dropped with a sigh of relief on to a bench along the back wall of the small vestibule, dragging off his riding boots to put on a pair of soft, pointed house shoes. On his left was the planked door to his hall, firmly closed. With a sinking feeling, he opened it and stepped through into the space behind the screens that helped to block the winter draughts. Beyond them, the high, bare main room of his house stretched up to the exposed rafters of the roof. Even in this sultry summer weather, it felt cold and unwelcoming, the timber walls hung with dismal tapestries. The only redeeming feature filled the far wall, a large stone fireplace with its conical chimney, which John had built to replace the usual fire-pit in the centre of the floor. At the same time, Matilda had insisted on covering that floor with flagstones, insisting that the usual rush-covered beaten earth was beneath the dignity of a sheriff's sister and a coroner's wife.

He looked towards the empty hearth, expecting to see Matilda filling one of the cowl-backed chairs, but for once the room was empty. He glanced up at the slit window high to one side of the fireplace, which went through into the solar, the only other room in the house, which doubled as his wife's boudoir and their bedroom. There was no sound or movement, and he turned and went back into the vestibule.

From the covered passage that led around the side of the house to the yard behind came a handsome, dark-haired young woman, a smile of welcome on her face. A large hound ambled after her.

'I thought I heard the door slam, Crowner! The mistress is at her prayers in St Olave's.'

'Thank God for that, Mary! I need food and drink.'

As he followed her back down the alleyway, he placed an affectionate hand on her bottom, but she skipped a pace ahead of him.

'Now, Crowner! I tend only to the needs of your stomach these days, remember?' He grinned wryly, remembering nostalgically the times when their cook-maid had been more accommodating – until the suspicions of her mistress, aroused by her nosy French maid Lucille, had decided Mary that her job was more valuable than flirting with the master.

In the yard were the shacks that housed the kitchen, where Mary lived, the woodshed and the privy. Beneath the outside wooden stairs that led up to the solar, Matilda's maid dwelt in a large box-like cabin, but at the moment she was with her mistress at church.

John sat on the kitchen's only stool and drank a quart of ale while Mary made him a meal of fried bacon, eggs and onion, with a small loaf and butter. As he ate, she squatted near by and listened while he told her of the day's events and the strange killing of the verderer. She was an attentive audience – John often felt the better for unwinding his tension by talking to her. Mary frequently had intelligent comments to make and her fund of local gossip gleaned at the market stalls of the city was sometimes very useful to him.

'I heard from a carter from Moretonhampstead, who comes in with geese for the poulterer, that the foresters up there have lately become even more oppressive than usual,' she reported. 'Though what that can have to do with this, I can't see.'

De Wolfe mused on this as he ate. The complicated structure of forest law had always been a matter of exasperation to both landowner and peasant alike. The cruel and punitive measures for any transgression of the strict rules of the Royal Forests had been a scandal for centuries, but had worsened under old King Henry. Yet, like Mary, he could see no connection with the slaying of Humphrey le Bonde, as the most hated men were the foresters and woodwards, not the higher judicial officers – though even they were hardly popular figures.

'So what's to be done about it?' asked Mary, as she refilled his ale-pot and cleared away the iron pan from which he had eaten.

'I'm off to see the Warden now – he's the immediate superior of the dead man, he must be told at once.'

Rising to his feet, he stretched and jerked his head up towards the solar.

'What sort of mood was she in?' he asked glumly.

'As usual – no better, no worse. She seems more

settled these past few weeks. You haven't done anything
particularly terrible lately, I suppose.'

John grunted, then gave the maid a quick peck on
the cheek.

'Pray for me that it will continue, Mary. I'll be back
late, I expect.'

Hands on her hips, the cook smiled and shook her
head in resignation.

'No doubt you'll find the need for a mug of ale at
the Bush,' she murmured under her breath, as the tall
figure loped off up the passage.

CHAPTER TWO

In which Crowner John talks to the Warden of the Forests

Nicholas de Bosco lived in a quieter part of Exeter, between the North Gate and Rougemont Castle, the fortress that occupied the highest ground in the north-eastern corner of the city walls. St Pancras Lane took its name from the nearby church, one of twenty-seven in a town of four thousand inhabitants. The Warden lived in a narrow dwelling similar to that of John de Wolfe, with a stone-tiled roof and a blind front, with only one shuttered window and a door facing the street. It was but a few minutes' walk for the coroner from Martin's Lane, and his rapping on the front door was answered by a wizened old servant whom he took to be de Bosco's bottler.

John was shown into the hall, a gloomy chamber hung with swords, shields, spears and other paraphernalia of past campaigns. A woman's touch was obviously lacking as the room contained only the bare necessities for living, with no gestures to comfort. A pair of oak settles stood either side of an empty fire-pit in centre of the floor, and a long table bore a few pewter cups and a flask of wine. Yet the man who rose to greet the coroner was a minor lord, with three manors in the county. A knight since his youth, like John he had fought in several campaigns in Ireland

and France and had been to the Third Crusade, though their paths had never crossed outside Devon. Nicholas de Bosco was almost two decades older than de Wolfe's forty years and he looked every day of it. He had a thin, gaunt face and his sparse hair was white. He had no beard or moustache – nor a single tooth in his head. However, his grey eyes were bright and sharp and his grip was firm as he grasped John's forearm in greeting. He used his left hand, for the right was crippled from an old spear wound sustained in battle in Normandy years before. Nicholas motioned the coroner to a seat opposite and beckoned to his servant to serve them wine.

'We have met briefly several times, Sir John, in some of the burgesses' functions in the Guildhall. I have long known of your reputation as a fighting man in the service of our King.'

As with de Wolfe's coronership, Nicholas owed his appointment as Warden of the Royal Forests of Devon to his faithful adherence to Richard the Lionheart – and to his father King Henry before him. They exchanged a few memories of campaigns long past, but after they had drunk each other's health in good Poitou red, John got down to business.

'My officer told you that yesterday one of your verderers was murdered?' he asked bluntly.

De Bosco nodded sadly. 'I find it hard to believe. Humphrey le Bonde was a good man, solid and dependable. Why should anyone wish to kill him? I understand it was not a common robbery.'

'It's unlikely, though we can't be sure. His purse was not taken, nor was there any sign of a struggle along the highway. I hoped you might be able to shed some light on the mystery.'

Nicholas shook his head in mystification. 'I was not all that close to him, but I know of nothing that would cause anyone to wish him dead. The relationship of Warden to verderers is a loose one, though we are all officers of the Royal Forest.'

The hovering bottler refilled John's cup as the other man explained further.

'As you will know, each of the forests has a Warden, appointed directly by the King – or in reality by the Curia Regis or Chief Justiciar on his behalf. It's supposed to be an appointment for life and I have been overseeing Devon since Richard put me here in '91.'

He paused to sip his wine, staring pensively into the cold ashes of the firepit. 'In the last year there has been some agitation to remove me. No one will come forward openly, but I have had anonymous letters telling me to resign – and even a couple of threats on my life.'

John sat up straighter – this might have some bearing on le Bonde's killing.

'Do you know if the same happened to the verderer?'

De Bosco shook his head. 'Not that I know of – and I would be surprised if it were so. I'm sure this is a political matter, which would not affect a mere verderer. I don't wish to sound patronising, but there is considerable difference between our ranks. Wardens, like coroners, have to be men of substance – at least manor lords or even a baron. Verderers are drawn from the ranks of lesser knights or even just freeholders.'

De Wolfe, who had spent much of his adult life out of England, had never before needed to understand the hierarchy of the forest officers and sought some explanation.

'So are verderers also appointed by the Crown?'

De Bosco exhaled through his bare gums. 'It's complicated! There are four of them in every forest, one to each quadrant. They are recommended by a sheriff's writ and elected by freeholders in the County

Court. But at least in theory they are responsible directly to the King, not to the Warden. It's a strange system.'

John had pricked his ears up at the mention of the sheriff. Anything that involved his brother-in-law needed to be looked at very carefully.

'So the nomination comes from the sheriff?'

The Warden nodded. 'No doubt Richard de Revelle already has someone in mind, if he knows yet about the death of Humphrey le Bonde.'

'What's the difference in the functions of these officers?'

Nicholas drained his cup and waved it at his servant to be refilled.

'I'm just an administrator – it matters not whether I ever set foot in the forest. With my clerk, I compile the records of all income to the Treasury from forest activities and of all court cases, to send to the Justiciar each year.'

He stared rather glumly into his wine cup. 'It's hardly an exciting task, but our king was minded to give it to me, so I do the best job I can. I have to organise the Forest Eyre, though that court is rarely held more often than every three years. I am supposed to deal with all complaints relating to forest law and exercise discipline over all the other forest staff, though in fact the verderers cannot be dismissed except by royal command.'

'And these verderers – what do they do?'

'Their main function is to deal with the lower forest courts – the Attachment Courts, where most of the everyday offences are heard.'

De Wolfe rubbed his black stubble.

'Are they the same as these 'forty-day' courts?'

'That's the common man's name for them, though some call them 'woodmotes'. The verderers can deal with minor offences at these courts, mainly those against the vert of the forest. Anything more serious, such as accusations of venison, has to be referred to the Forest Eyre – which means that many poor bloody miscreants spend a few years in prison, where they often die before their case is even heard.'

Though John might be vague about the administration of the forest, he knew very well that 'vert' referred to the trees, vegetation and indeed trade in the royal demesne. 'Venison' concerned the creatures of the forest, though even these were strictly categorised from roe deer down to rabbits.

'So who does the actual supervision of the forest, if verderers are really only concerned with their local courts?'

A sour expression clouded De Bosco's lined face. 'The damned foresters, that's who! Though they're rough, common men, they rule the forests as if they own them! I'm supposed to be in charge of them, but they go their own way almost unchecked.'

'You don't sound over-fond of them, Warden.'

Nicholas scowled. 'Their name is a byword for greed and corruption, Crowner! They have too much authority and they misuse it to terrorise the forest folk. They take full advantage of their power, especially when the verderer is weak and lets them get away with it.'

'Was Humphrey le Bonde weak?'

De Bosco shook his head. 'Not particularly. He did his best to control the worst excesses, and we sometimes spoke of finding some way to curb the misrule of the foresters. But they always had some excuse and recently claimed that they had the backing of the sheriff in some of what they did.'

Again, an alarm bell clanged inside John's head at the mention of Richard de Revelle's possible involvement. He declined another measure of wine and stood up ready to leave, thanking the Warden for his help.

'I may need to call on you again, when more facts are known. But at the moment, you have no idea why anyone should want to murder a verderer?'

Nicholas de Bosco walked the coroner to his street door.

'It's a complete mystery to me, de Wolfe. But there are strange things stirring in the forest, and I don't mean wild boar! Recently, some of the foresters are becoming even more strict and oppressive than usual, and the reaction from both the peasants and the barons is hardening. True, the income that I send to Winchester has increased lately, but I suspect that it is but a fraction of what is being extorted from the forest folk.'

His tired face looked even more unhappy as he finished his tale of woe. 'I wish I knew what was going on myself – though I can't see how this death can be connected with it.'

After he had left the Warden, de Wolfe loped along the streets towards Rougemont, trying to make sense of the death of le Bonde, who seemed an unlikely candidate for assassination, if robbery was not the motive. A large part of Devon was designated as a Royal Forest, where irrespective of the ownership of the land all hunting and many other aspects of the rural economy were reserved to the King. He had recently heard that many landowners, from cottagers to barons, were becoming increasingly aggravated by the situation and were beginning to agitate for the forest areas to be reduced and the punitive laws relaxed.

Devoted as he was to his King, John knew that Richard Coeur-de-Lion was only interested in his French wars, having spent only four months of his reign in England and seeming reluctant ever to return. The monarch was unlikely to agree to any loss of income to his exchequer, which paid for his troops to keep fighting Philip of France. The Royal Forests, which covered almost a third of England, were a lucrative source of income, and the Lionheart needed every penny, as the country was still paying off his huge ransom owed to Henry of Germany. De Wolfe still felt guilty about that, as he had been part of the King's small bodyguard when he was captured in Austria, blaming himself for not being vigilant enough to prevent it.

His ruminations had brought him to the short hill that led up to the drawbridge over the dry moat of the castle. At the top was the tall gatehouse, on the upper floor of which the coroner had his miserable official chamber, grudgingly provided by the sheriff. Grunting at the solitary man-at-arms on sentry duty under the raised portcullis, he turned into the guardroom under the entrance arch and climbed the narrow twisting steps to the second floor.

Pushing through the sacking that hung as a draught-excluder over the open doorway, he entered his office, a dank and cobwebbed chamber under the roof, aired by two open slits that looked down over the city.

On such a long summer evening dusk was still a few hours away, and Gwyn was still here. He lived at St Sidwell's, just outside the walls, and if he wanted to spend the night with his wife and children he would have to leave before the city gates were shut at curfew.

'Where's Thomas?' demanded de Wolfe.

'Probably crossing himself and gabbling his prayers down at the cathedral,' grunted the Cornishman. 'I think he's practising for when he gets restored to Holy Office.'

'I think that'll be a long while yet, in spite of his yearning.'

John gestured at a large jug of cider by Gwyn's stool and his officer poured a generous helping of the turbid fluid into two pottery jars standing on the rough trestle table.

'I thought the bishop and archdeacon had given him some hope, in recompense for him nearly getting hanged by mistake,' said his officer.

The coroner shrugged and took a long swallow of cider.

'There's still plenty of bad feeling against him amongst the other clerics – but at least Thomas is more cheerful these days. We don't want him jumping off more roofs, trying to kill himself again.'

Their clerk, defrocked several years ago in Winchester for allegedly indecently assaulting one of his girl pupils in the cathedral school, was obsessed with regaining his ordination and had become very depressed at the failure to make any progress towards reinstatement.

De Wolfe slumped onto the bench behind his table and they sat in companionable silence for a few minutes, sucking at their mugs of fermented apple juice. Gwyn had been his bodyguard and companion for many years, travelling and fighting with de Wolfe through a dozen countries as far away as Palestine. Always a taciturn pair, they saw no need for idle chatter, but eventually Gwyn asked whether Nicholas de Bosco had thrown any light on the recent murder.

'No, but he gave me the feeling that something is brewing in the forest. I've no idea yet what it could be, but I'll wager there's some politics behind it – which usually means my dear brother-in-law is involved.'

He drained his jar and pushed himself to his feet, leaning with his hands on the table, hunched like a black vulture.

'Talking of that devil, I'd better go across and see

him. I suspect he's already heard of the loss of one of his verderers, but I'll have to make it official.'

Leaving the ever-famished Gwyn to attack a mutton pasty and some bread and cheese that he had bought at a street stall, de Wolfe stumped back down the stairs and turned into the inner ward of the castle. Rougemont had an outer line of defences lower down the hill, where a high earth bank and a ditch marked off a large area in the angle between the north and east city walls. In this outer ward lived many of the garrison and their families, as well as other camp followers. A profusion of huts and shacks, together with stables, forges, armourers and store sheds, turned this outer bailey into a small village. A high, castellated stone wall cut off the upper corner, creating the fortified inner ward, entered only through the gatehouse. Inside was the keep, a three-storeyed building against the far wall, where the sheriff and constable lived. The ward also contained the tiny garrison chapel of St Mary and the bleak stone barn that was the Shire Court. Around the inside of the curtain wall were more lean-to sheds and shacks, some being living quarters, others stables and storerooms. It had been more than half a century since the castle had seen any military action and the place was now hardly a fortress, but more the administrative hub of Devonshire, as well as the home of a few score soldiers and their families.

John de Wolfe strode across the ward, churned by the feet of countless horses, cart-oxen and soldiers into an almost grassless expanse of dried mud. The early evening sun was still warm and outside their huts a few wives were sewing and gossiping, as they watched urchins playing with mongrels or tossing balls of tied rags. Nodding curtly to a few acquaintances as he went, the coroner reached the wooden stairs that led up to the door of the keep, twelve feet above ground. In the unlikely event of besiegers breaking into the inner ward, the stairs could be thrown down and a portcullis dropped over the only entrance to this final refuge. This evening, the only threat to Rougemont's inner sanctum was the grimly resolute look on the coroner's face as he marched in, determined to discover whether the sheriff was involved in any new scheming in the Royal Forest.

On the main floor, above the undercroft that housed the fetid gaol, was the great hall of the castle, behind which were the rooms of the sheriff. The upper floor was occupied by the constable of Rougemont, as well as housing the cramped living quarters of numerous servants and clerks. De Wolfe was making straight for the door of his brother-in-law's quarters, set at the side of the hall, when a voice hailed him from one of the trestle tables that were set out in the large, high chamber.

'He's not there, John. Gone to visit his wife, so he says!'

The coroner turned and saw a large, grey-bearded man wearing a mailed hauberk, sitting with Gabriel, the sergeant-at-arms. He was also in armour, his round metal helmet on the table near by. The senior man was Ralph Morin, the castle constable and a good friend of de Wolfe, who walked across and dropped on to the bench alongside them.

'What's all this chainmail, then? Are we expecting the French to invade us?'

Ralph grinned and waved to a passing servant to bring some ale across to them. He was living proof that the Normans were recent descendants of the Norsemen, as with his fair hair and forked beard he looked as if he had just stepped off a Viking longship.

'Just got back from drilling some idle soldiers on Bull Mead,' he grunted. 'These days, most of the youngsters have never seen a sword lifted in anger – nor even a drop of blood spilt! We need a war to knock them into shape.'

'Too damned hot for running around in a hauberk,' added Gabriel, as a pitcher of ale and some pots were put on the table. The sergeant was a grizzled old warrior, nearing retirement age, who had seen plenty of service in the Irish and French wars. The three professional soldiers spent a few moments bemoaning the soft recruits and easy time that the military had these days, until Ralph Morin returned to the subject of the sheriff. Although de Revelle was nominally the constable's superior, Rougemont was a royal castle, rather than the fief of a baron, so Ralph was responsible directly to the King for its security.

'He went up to Tiverton on Sunday, supposed to return tomorrow. Perhaps his lady feels in need of some service!'

The sheriff's wife, the frigid Lady Eleanor, refused to live with her husband in Exeter in the cold and draughty keep and spent her days either at their manor near Tiverton or at the family home at Revelstoke, near Plymouth. The arrangement seemed to suit Richard, who never lacked for illicit female company in his bedchamber, but every week or two he made short duty visits to his haughty spouse.

'Then he can't yet know that the forest has lost one of its verderers?' observed de Wolfe. He related the story of the curious death of Humphrey le Bonde, and Morin's craggy face showed his surprise.

'I knew le Bonde well – I was at the siege of Le Mans with him. He was a good fellow, a dependable fighter. I'm sorry he's dead.'

'Who the hell would want to plant an arrow in the back of a verderer?' growled Gabriel. 'If it was a forester or even a woodward, I could understand it. Many of those bastards deserve to be slain, but a verderer just holds the forty-day courts.'

'Could it be an aggrieved forest dweller, who was dealt with harshly at one of those courts?' hazarded the constable.

De Wolfe shook his head. 'Those woodmotes can only fine folk a trivial amount for offences against the vert worth less than four pence. Who's going to commit murder in revenge for a few marks?'

Morin gulped some ale and wiped his luxuriant beard with his hand.

'Then you're driven back on outlaws – but if he wasn't robbed, then why should they fire a shaft through his lights? A verderer would have no particular fight with those human wolves in the forest.'

'There's something more sinister going on,' grunted John. 'The Warden's been threatened and someone wants to squeeze him out of his job.'

They kicked the problem back and forth until the ale was finished, then de Wolfe rose from the table. 'If our dear sheriff isn't here, then I'd better get back home and face his sister. She'll be wanting her supper after a hard bout of talking to God at St Olave's!'

He left the two soldiers looking for some food to be washed down with more ale. The sun was now low over the great twin towers of the cathedral, but the streets were still bustling with people. Many citizens were still haggling with traders at booths or at shopfronts, whose hinged shutters were dropped down to make a counter to display their goods. Porters struggled by with great woolpacks on their shoulders or heaving at laden handcarts. Drinkers staggered in and out of the many ale shops on the high street and sumpter horses and pack mules squeezed through the crowds, with their drivers dragging on the bridles, blaspheming every step of the way. The evening air was redolent with the smells of cooking, sewage and horse manure.

Oblivious to the turmoil, the coroner barged his way towards Martin's Lane, a head taller than most of those around him. He turned into the alleyway, shadowed by contrast with the brighter expanse of the cathedral Close at the far end. With a sigh of resignation, he pushed open his front door and turned right to go straight into the hall. His big hound Brutus rose from under the table and came towards him, head down and tail wagging in welcome. A less cordial greeting came from behind the wooden cowl of one of the monk's chairs near the hearth.

'And where have you been gallivanting since just after dawn?'

'Getting my arse sore in the saddle, riding around the county on the duties that you were so keen to shoulder me with last autumn,' he replied sourly, slumping down on to the other settle opposite his wife.

'Your speech is becoming as crude as your habits, John,' snapped Matilda.

'D'you want to hear what I've been doing or not?'

'No doubt you'll tell me only what you want me to know – and leave out the details of your usual drinking and wenching.'

For once, John experienced the indignation of a clear conscience as far as today was concerned, but he checked an angry response, for Matilda usually came off best in a shouting match. He sat glowering at her, bemoaning the day sixteen years ago when his father had arranged his marriage into the wealthy de Revelle family. To be fair, neither had the bride been too keen on the union and had many times since bitterly expressed her preference for the religious life over wedlock.

John looked at her now, as they squared up to each

other across the hearth like a pair of bull terriers. He saw a stocky woman four years older than his forty years, with a square, pugnacious face on a short neck. Her features were regular, and when younger she had been almost handsome in a grim kind of way, but now puffy lids narrowed her blue eyes and her lips were set in a thin, hard line. Her pale hair was confined in a tight coif of cream linen, tied under her aggressive chin, and the rest of her burly body was clothed in a green kirtle which, in spite of the warm weather, was of heavy brocade. John mused that in spite of her devotion to religious observance and her professed yearning to become a nun, she was inordinately fond of fine clothes and had an appetite for food and wine that challenged Gwyn's.

'Well, are you going to tell me or not?' she snapped, interrupting his sullen reverie.

Too weary to argue, he swallowed his exasperation and related the story of the dead verderer.

'Your brother has gone to Tiverton, so I presume that he's not yet aware of the loss of one of his appointees,' he concluded, sensing that she was only mildly interested in his story, as the dead man was merely a minor knight and not one of the county aristocracy. Matilda was an avid follower of the notabilities of Devon and was always angling for ways to ascend the social hierarchy of the county. Being sister to the King's sheriff and wife to the King's coroner was a good start, but she closely followed the activities and intrigues of the barons, richer burgesses and manor-lords, pushing for invitations to feasts and receptions at every opportunity. It was largely at her instigation that her husband had accepted the coroner's post the previous year, with Matilda nagging her reluctant brother to support John's bid. But the violent demise of Humphrey le Bonde struck no chord with her and the only faint interest was that Richard de Revelle would be the one who would recommend his successor for election by the freeholders in his County Court.

Their desultory conversation was interrupted by Mary coming in from the kitchen-shed with their supper. The main meal was dinner in the late morning, but the pangs of night starvation were kept at bay by slices of cold pork on a thick trencher of stale bread, with side dishes of fried onions and boiled cabbage. Fresh bread and hard cheese filled up any remaining empty spaces in their stomachs, washed down with ale and cider.

They moved to the long oak table, where the steady champing of Matilda's jaws removed the strain of devising any further talk, though her husband also acquitted himself well with the food, after a day in the saddle. By the time they had finished and the cook-maid came to take away the remains, it was growing dark in the hall. The one small window-opening, covered in varnished linen, looked out onto the narrow lane lined with high buildings, which was in shadow even when the open cathedral precinct was still well lit. Matilda abruptly pushed back her stool and announced that she was going up to the solar, where her maid Lucille could prepare her for bed.

John, following a well-used pattern, said that he would have some more ale, then take Brutus for a walk. They both knew where the hound was likely to take him, but only a tightening of her lips betrayed her feelings as she stamped off through the outer passage to reach the back yard and the stairs to her upper room.

At about the same time as the coroner of Devon was whistling for his dog, twenty miles farther west in the county, a Cistercian monk was sitting across a table from a horse trader. They were in the large guest house of Buckfast Abbey, in a small room adjacent to the refectory reserved for feeding travellers who sought lodging for the night during the journey from Exeter to Plymouth. Across the large walled courtyard with its two gatehouses was the abbey church with the cloisters and other monastic buildings alongside.

However, Stephen Cruch, the dealer in horses, was no casual visitor to the abbey, as he often spent a night there on business. The austere Cistercians were famed for their prowess in agriculture and animal husbandry. The monks and lay brothers of Buckfast not only kept large flocks of sheep for their wool and meat, but bred both sheep and horses for sale. Richard Cruch had a standing contract as an agent for moving on their horseflesh and frequently came to negotiate with the abbey on behalf of buyers from all over the West Country and beyond.

His contact was Father Edmund Treipas, who conducted most of the trade with the outside world. Though an ordained priest as well as a monk, Father Edmund was a down-to-earth businessman, which was undoubtedly why he was also the abbey's cellarer, responsible for all the provisions needed by the large establishment. In both roles, that of sales manager and storekeeper, he was unique in the enclosed community of Grey Monks, in that he frequently journeyed abroad, visiting Plymouth, Exeter and even Southampton on the abbot's business.

These two unlikely acquaintances now sat head to head across the table, with a flask of mead between them, for Buckfast was famous for its honey. Edmund Treipas held a short roll of parchment, on which were the details of a batch of horses to be taken away the following morning to a buyer in Plymouth, who would ship them across the Channel for resale in Brittany. The priest had been going through the list of thirty beasts, noting whether they were stallions, mares or geldings, ticking off their value on the document with a charcoal stub. Stephen Cruch, who could neither read nor write, was using a tally made of a length of twine with different-sized knots, which he fingered one by one as the priest checked off the animals.

As well as the difference in their stations in life, the two men were markedly unlike each other in appearance. Father Edmund, in his habit of pale grey wool with a black scapula apron, was tall and angular, with a Roman nose and jet-black hair cropped short below his tonsure. He was in his late thirties and had a brisk, businesslike manner, unlike the typical image of a monastic recluse.

The horse-dealer was, by contrast, small and furtive. A dozen years older, he had a leathery, wizened face, darkened by an outdoor life. His mobile features had a sly look, his eyes constantly darting about him. When he spoke, it always seemed to be from one corner of his mouth. He allegedly lived in Totnes, but was always on the move between horse fairs and markets. Some rumours had it that he was an illegally returned abjurer from Wiltshire, but other gossip said that he was an outlaw from Gloucester's Forest of Dean who had slipped back into circulation years before.

When both were satisfied that their lists coincided, Father Treipas rolled up his parchment and slipped it into his sleeve, while Cruch tucked his tally into the pouch he carried on his belt. They raised their pewter cups of mead to seal the bargain and drained them. The priest refilled from the flask.

'My men will rope them up from the top paddock in the morning, Father,' said the dealer. 'We should be in Plymouth well before evening.'

He pushed a heavy leather bag across the table, the

39

neck tied securely with a thong. 'That's the price we agreed. Count it if you wish.'

Edmund Treipas shook his head briskly. 'No need. We've done business too often for you to short-change the abbey.'

He pulled the bag of silver coins nearer, then looked quickly around the room, to check that no one else was within sight. Dipping into a deep pocket in his loose robe, he pulled out a smaller purse and slid it across to Stephen. The bag, clinking a little, vanished as if by magic into some recess in Cruch's brown serge surcoat.

'I don't want to know any details, understand?' said the monk. 'Just don't tell me. It's none of my business how you arrange these affairs.'

He threw down the rest of his drink and stood up, nodding rather curtly at the horse dealer.

'I'll see you off with the beasts in the morning, straight after Prime. And you'll be back here as arranged, in three days' time.'

He strode out without a backward glance.

In the gathering dusk, John de Wolfe made his way across the Close, the large space around the cathedral. It was almost a city within a city, being under canon law, where the jurisdiction of neither the sheriff and burgesses nor himself could run without the consent of Bishop Henry Marshal.

Tonight no offences were being committed there, apart from Brutus's leg-lifting desecration of every tree and occasional grave-mound in the cluttered, rubbish-strewn area. Even the irreligious John thought this place was an eyesore, so close to the magnificent church which had so recently been completed.

However, John's mind was not on the state of ecclesiastical Exeter, but on Nesta, the landlady of the Bush

Inn and his beloved mistress. For the last week or two, he had had the feeling that something was wrong. Nothing that he could put a finger on, but in the back of his mind there was a little flutter of concern. Nesta was as affectionate as ever, as talkative as usual and looked as beautiful as always – but something was amiss. He had caught the odd sideways glance when she thought he was not looking and his ear, attuned by two years of loving her, picked up a change in the timbre of her voice now and then.

Much of the time he berated himself for being an old fool, but the worm of doubt always came back to wriggle in his brain. They had had their bad patches and it was only a couple of months since they had got back together again, following her brief affair with Alan of Lyme, the rogue who had run off with her virtue, a week's takings and her prettiest serving maid.

He could not but help wonder whether some other bastard had taken her fancy, but somehow he thought not. Before the Alan business, he had given her cause for disaffection by neglecting her during a time of particular problems in the coroner's work, but since they had been reconciled he had gone out of his way to be more attentive. He had not seen any of his other women for a long time – one had dropped out of circulation by getting married again and even the glorious Hilda of Dawlish, the blonde he had known from his youth, was unavailable because her seafaring husband was now shore-bound after a shipwreck.

De Wolfe churned all this around in his mind as he loped through the lanes into South Gate Street and across to Priest Street and then down the hill towards Idle Lane and the tavern. His dog zigzagged before him, marking every house-corner with an inexhaustible supply of urine until they reached the inn on its open patch of ground. Its low stone walls supported a huge thatched roof, and over the low front door a bundle of twigs hung from a bracket to mark its name for the illiterate majority.

Inside, the popular alehouse was as full as usual, but at least the normal fug of spilt ale, cooked onions and sweat was free from eye-smarting smoke, as there was no fire in the big hearth on this warm summer evening. Normally, the wood smoke hung about in a haze until it found its way out beneath the eaves, for unlike John's house, most buildings did not have the luxury of a chimney.

From habit, he found his usual seat on a bench near the empty fireplace and Brutus crept into his accustomed place on the earthen floor under the rough table. He nodded to a number of other patrons who were regulars like himself and exchanged a few words with the nearest, who all were well aware of – and applauded – his relations with the Welsh innkeeper.

Usually old Edwin, the one-eyed potman, served him as soon as he arrived, but tonight Nesta herself bustled over with a large quart pottery jar of her best brew.

'And how is the King's crowner tonight?' she asked, as she deposited the ale on the boards before him. In spite of her light tone, John already thought he detected something, maybe a forced gaiety. But he was so glad to see her, to be with her, that he pushed the thought aside in the pleasure of the moment.

'Sit down, my love, and talk to me.' He looked up at her as she leaned against the table, as neat as ever in a gown of yellow linen, tightly laced around her slim waist, emphasising the curve of her breasts above. Her heart-shaped face had a high forehead and snub nose, the full lips made for kissing. Some curls strayed from under her white linen helmet, as russet as Gwyn's beard.

'I can stay only a moment,' she exclaimed, slipping

onto the bench next to him. 'There's a party of wool merchants here tonight and they're clamouring for their supper, so I must chase those idle girls in the back yard.' The kitchen was in a shed behind the inn, the usual arrangement when fire was such a hazard to other buildings. The Bush had a reputation for the best cooking in the city, as well as for being the cleanest place to get a penny bed for the night.

John slipped an arm around her, heedless of the covert grins of some men on the next table. He felt her softness relax against him and somehow he was reassured that she had not found another man. Yet when they started talking about the events of the two days since he had last seen her, John still sensed that there was something she was leaving unsaid. He was reluctant to ask her straight out whether anything was amiss, in case she told him something he wouldn't wish to hear. They talked for a few minutes, Nesta telling him of minor problems of the tavern, which she now ran herself with the help of Edwin, two maids and a cook. Until two years earlier, the innkeeper had been her husband Meredydd, a former Welsh archer in the service of King Richard. John had known him from his campaigning days, and when Meredydd had given up fighting because of a wound, he had taken on the Bush. But within a year he was dead of a fever, and for friendship's sake de Wolfe had loaned his widow enough money to keep the inn going. He had helped her generally to survive, as a young woman trying to run a city tavern was a prime target for the unscrupulous. His protection had turned into affection and then genuine love, but they were sometimes disillusioned, mainly because Nesta fully realised that a Norman knight, married to the sheriff's sister, was a hopeless long-term prospect for a lowly alehouse keeper.

John told her about the murder of the verderer and

she listened carefully, as she always did to his tales of mayhem in Devon. He found it useful to pour out his problems, as it helped clear them in his mind – and her own quick brain not infrequently lighted on some point that he had missed. Sometimes, even more than Mary, she could give him some useful information, as Nesta was a mine of knowledge about what went on in the city and beyond. The Bush was the most popular inn for travellers passing through Exeter and she heard much of the gossip that was bandied about between the customers. This time, though, she had little to contribute.

'I know nothing about these verderers, John, they're just a name to me. Everyone knows of the foresters, though. All the country dwellers hate them for their harshness and corruption, that's common knowledge.'

'You've heard no idle chatter in here, about anything going on in the forests?' he asked hopefully, but Nesta shook her head.

'There was some talk the other day about the outlaws becoming bolder than ever. Some of the carters and drovers from the west were complaining that they sometimes get charged an illegal toll when passing through the more lonely stretches of the high road. They were cursing the sheriff for doing nothing about it.'

'Nothing new about that!' John replied cynically. 'There's no profit for de Revelle in chasing off a few vagabonds from the highway.'

Eventually, he ran out of other news and turned to a more immediate prospect.

'I'm in no rush to get back tonight, madam. Will you be having a quiet hour before midnight?' His eyes strayed to the wide ladder at the back of the inn, which led up to the upper floor. Here Nesta had a small room partitioned off from the rest of the loft, where the straw pallets of the guests were laid. She gave him one of her sidelong glances, then looked away.

'Not tonight, John. It's . . . well, not convenient.'

Gently, she pulled herself away and went off to the kitchen, tapping a shoulder here and giving a greeting there as she weaved through the patrons on her way to the back door. John followed her with his eyes, puzzled and disappointed. Their lovemaking upstairs, in the big French bed that he had bought her, was one of the most satisfactory things in his life. They were both enthusiasts in that direction, which made his devotion to her all the more complete. From her tone, he presumed that the time of the month had conspired against him tonight, but her attitude still made him uneasy. As he sat there despondently, staring down into his ale jug cupped between his hands, he felt the bench creak dangerously. Looking up, he found Gwyn's huge frame alongside him, his eyes twinkling in his rugged face.

'I thought you had gone home to St Sidwell's. It's past curfew now,' grunted de Wolfe, jerking his head at the last of the twilight visible outside the open door. One of the maids was bringing a taper round to light the tallow dips hung in sconces around the walls.

'I was going, but I got into a game of dice with Gabriel and some of the men up at the guardroom. I won three pence from them, so I thought I'd treat myself to one of Nesta's mutton stews and a mattress here for the night.'

'I'm glad someone will be staying up the ladder here tonight,' grunted John sourly. 'But it looks as if it won't be me!'

The Cornishman's straggling red eyebrows rose towards his even wilder hair. 'Problems, Crowner?' he asked solicitously. He had a dog-like fondness for Nesta and had been delighted when she and his master had got back together recently, after their rift a few months

45

earlier. Now the prospect of more trouble genuinely worried him.

'I don't know, Gwyn, something seems to be concerning her. But I've been behaving myself these past weeks, haven't I? There's no reason why she should become cool towards me?'

Gwyn was more than a squire and bodyguard, he was a friend of twenty years' standing, and each had saved the life of the other more than once in battles, ambushes and assaults. John was not the most articulate of men, and Gwyn was the only one to whom he could speak on intimate matters.

His officer scratched his armpit fiercely, annihilating a few fleas.

'Come to think of it, the good woman has been a bit distant lately. Nothing to speak of, but she seems a bit far away sometimes, as if she has something heavy on her mind.'

Their conversation was interrupted by the potman, who stumped up to bring Gwyn a quart of ale.

'You'll be wanting another of the same, Captain?' Edwin asked the coroner. He was an old soldier who had lost one eye and part of a foot in the Irish wars. Both de Wolfe and Gwyn had been in the same campaign and Edwin deferred to them as if he were still one of their men-at-arms.

John shook his head. 'I'd better be getting back home,' he muttered. 'But no doubt my man here will want to be filled up with food.'

Whistling at Brutus to creep out from under the table, where the dog-loving Gwyn had been stroking his head, de Wolfe made for the backyard of the inn, to give Nesta a goodnight squeeze and a kiss, before trudging back to Martin's Lane and his lonely side of an unwelcoming bed.

* * *

An hour after dawn the following morning, a cart drawn by two patient oxen drew up outside the alehouse in the village of Sigford. In the back were two large barrels and as soon as the clumsy vehicle came to a stop the driver and his villainous-looking companion jumped down and removed the tailboard. They propped a couple of planks against the back of the cart and knocked out the wooden wedges that secured the first cask.

As they rolled the heavy barrel to the ground, the door to the tavern flew open and the ale-wife bustled out.

'What do think you're doing?' she screeched. 'I don't need any ale, I brew my own!'

The driver's assistant, a rough fellow dressed in little better than rags, gave her a gap-toothed leer. 'Yes, and it tastes like cow-piss, so I've heard! '

Widow Mody, broad of hip and bosom, advanced furiously on the man and raised her hand to clip his ear, but he gave a her a push that sent her staggering.

'This is some decent stuff, Mother, whether you like it or not.'

Outraged, but now wary after the threat of violence, the woman looked around the threadbare village green for someone to help her. Outside his cottage a hundred paces away, she saw their reeve looking towards the cart and she waved wildly at him.

'Morcar, Morcar, come here!' she yelled, before turning back to the pair, now getting the second cask down to the ground.

'There's some mistake! Where's this come from? I don't want it.'

The carter, a milder-looking man who seemed embarrassed by the proceedings, spoke for the first time.

'It's nothing to do with us, woman. We're just delivering it.'

He started rolling the barrel towards the door of the alehouse, the other fellow grinning as he began to follow him.

'If you've got any questions, ask them!' He jerked a thumb over his shoulder and turning, the widow saw two men on horseback coming into the village. As Morcar arrived, so the riders reined up alongside the cart. By now several other men had been attracted by the shouting and were drifting towards the green, the smith amongst them.

The village reeve scowled up at the first horseman, a thin, erect fellow with grizzled iron-grey hair. He had unusually high cheekbones, over which the skin of his face was stretched like a drum. His chin and hollow cheeks were covered with dark grey stubble, framing a humourless, thin mouth. He wore a green tunic and a short leather cape, the hood hanging down his back. A thick belt carried a short sword and a dagger, and from his saddle hung a long, evil-looking club. On the breast of his tunic was a yellow badge depicting a hunting horn, the insignia of a forester. The other rider stayed a few paces behind in deference to his master, as he was what was euphemistically called the forester's 'page', though he was a rugged bruiser in his late thirties.

Morcar continued to eye the newcomer with distaste. 'What's all this about, William Lupus?'

The forester stared down impassively at the village reeve.

'From today, only this ale will be sold in Sigford. It will save that good-wife from the labour of brewing her own.'

Incredulous, Widow Mody screeched back at the man in green. 'I don't want your bloody ale! Take it away, wherever it came from!'

'Where did it come from, anyway?' asked the smith, truculently.

'From the new brew-house near Chudleigh. From

now on, all the alehouses within a day's cart journey will sell it.'

'Who says so?' yelled the ale-wife, her hands planted belligerently on her hips.

'I say so, woman! On behalf of the King, whose forest this is.'

'And is this ale a present from King Richard?' she snapped sarcastically.

William Lupus looked down at her coldly. 'It will cost you one shilling for a twenty-gallon cask. How much you sell it for is your business.'

For a moment, Widow Mody was speechless at the extortion.

'That's well over a ha'penny a gallon! I can brew it for less than half that price. No one will buy it from me. I'll be ruined and will starve!'

There was a general murmur of horror from the bystanders, who saw their only pleasure being priced beyond their reach, but the forester shrugged indifferently.

'If they don't buy it, then they can go thirsty – or drink water.'

Morcar, though he already had a presentiment that the fight was lost before it had begun, felt that he must make some effort on behalf of his village.

'This is part of the manor of Ilsington, Lupus. I must first hear what our lord William de Pagnell has to say.'

'It matters not what he says, Reeve. He does not sell ale, so mind your own business.'

'I will still have to send word to him and his steward and bailiff, Forester. No doubt he will need to protest this to the verderer.'

William Lupus gave a nasty smile, the thin lips parting over his yellowed teeth. 'The verderer is dead. You all should know that only too well, as his body lay here only yesterday.'

'There will be a new verderer appointed soon,' persisted Morcar doggedly.

The smile cracked even wider. 'There will indeed – and undoubtedly it will be Philip de Strete, who will have little sympathy with your useless complaints.'

There was renewed murmuring amongst the small crowd of villagers who had gathered around the cart. Philip de Strete was about as popular in mid-Devon as Philip of France.

'No doubt our lord will appeal to the Warden, then,' grumbled the reeve obstinately.

'He has no say in the matter – and I doubt he'll be there for much longer,' snapped Lupus. When he saw that the carter and the other man had taken the casks inside, he gave a sign to his thuggish page, who slid from his horse and ambled into the alehouse. The widow took fright and hurried after him, but she was too late. There was a scream of anguish and a splashing of liquid, then the page and the ruffian from the cart reappeared with four large earthenware crocks, each of several gallons' capacity, the dregs of mash and ale still dripping from them. William Lupus nodded at the men, and almost carelessly they tossed them into the air, letting them smash into a thousand pieces on the hard-baked ground.

With a wail and a stream of invective, the ale-wife rushed at the page, but he gave her a resounding smack across the face and a push that sent her to her knees. She began blubbering into her apron, as a woman neighbour ran to comfort her.

There was a general growl of anger from the half-dozen village men and they took a step towards the page. But there was also a rattle of steel as the forester pulled a foot of sword from its scabbard. Wisely, the men subsided into a resentful, sullen silence.

'Let no one get any ideas of brewing their own here, either in the alehouse or your homes. If I get wind of it, the verderer will have you arraigned at the Woodmote faster than you can take a breath.'

He jerked his head at his page to remount, then pulled his own horse around and trotted out of Sigford, leaving the villagers to become more resentful, impoverished and thirsty.

Later that morning, the coroner succeeded in tracking down the sheriff, who often tried to avoid him. As Richard de Revelle was not to be found in his chamber in the keep, he looked in the courthouse, but the dismal hall was empty. Irritated at the waste of time, he went back to the gatehouse and demanded of the solitary guard whether he had seen him. The man pointed his lance towards the tiny building that stood on the far side of the gateway, towards the eastern curtain wall.

'I saw him go in there, Crowner – not long ago, with another man.'

Muttering under his breath, de Wolfe strode across to St Mary's, the little chapel that served the garrison. It was poorly attended except on saints' days and special occasions, so the full series of daily services had been greatly thinned down by the amiable chaplain, Father Roger.

Unlike his sister, Richard was not renowned for his devotion, except when it was politically expedient to appear in church or cathedral, so John wondered why he had shown this sudden urge to go to chapel on a Wednesday morning.

He opened the main door on the side of the building and stepped out of the bright sunlight into the dim interior. As his eyes adjusted, he saw his brother-in-law in the act of closing a smaller door on the other side of the nave, holding up a hand in what seemed to be a farewell gesture.

'Taken to holding your meetings on holy ground now, Richard?' de Wolfe called. The sheriff spun around and peered across the paved floor at him.

'It's you, John! Are you spying on me?'

He walked across the empty chapel towards the coroner. Richard was a head shorter than de Wolfe and lightly built, a dapper man with a taste for expensive and showy clothes. Today he wore a peacock-blue tunic down to his calves, the neck and hem embroidered with a double line of gold stitching. White hose ended in extravagantly pointed shoes in the latest fashion. He had light brown wavy hair curling over his ears and a neat, pointed beard of the same colour. His narrow face wore a permanently petulant expression, especially now, as he seemed annoyed that the coroner had surprised him in some private matter.

'Who was that, then? Your confessor?' snapped John, deliberately provoking his brother-in-law.

'It's no concern of yours. What did you want with me?'

'You must have really pounded the road between Tiverton and here, to arrive by this hour.'

De Revelle shook his head impatiently. 'The dawn comes early in June. I took to the road while you were still snoring, no doubt.'

He came closer and lifted his face to look up at the coroner. 'Were you looking for me for some particular reason?'

Shafts of sunlight poured through the small unglazed windows high in the wall, causing dust motes to dance in the beams. Pools of light fell upon the stone ledges that ran down both walls of the little nave, the only place where the older or more infirm of the congregation could sit. John lowered himself to the cold slabs, but the sheriff remained standing, his gloved hands jabbed impatiently into his waist as John spoke.

'I came to tell you that one of the verderers has been murdered – Humphrey le Bonde. As he was a King's officer like us, I thought you should be told as soon as possible.'

John was puzzled to see a look of relief pass over Richard's face – he seemed to relax suddenly, almost as if the air had escaped from a punctured bladder.

'Thank you, John, but I already knew that. In fact, I have already appointed his successor – that was the fellow who just left through the other door. A messenger came to my manor last night, to tell me of the death.'

The coroner sighed – de Revelle so often seemed one step ahead of him, thanks to the legion of informers that he had scattered around the county.

'You were quick off the mark filling his shoes! Who is it?'

Richard stroked his small beard with his fingertips, a mannerism that annoyed de Wolfe – though almost everything about the sheriff annoyed him.

'Philip de Strete – I offered to nominate him to the County Court just now and he quite naturally accepted,' he said smugly.

John shrugged. 'Never heard of him. Who is he and where's he from?'

'A knight from Plympton, not far from my other manor at Revelstoke – that's how I know him, as a lesser neighbour.'

De Wolfe thought cynically that, like his sister, Richard was ever conscious of his position in the pecking order of the county aristocracy and could not resist emphasising his higher status over this Philip. He wondered why the man so conveniently happened to be in Exeter to be offered the unexpected vacancy, but could not think of any sinister reason for it – though anything involving the sheriff was always liable to be devious.

'Why the rush to appoint someone? The previous incumbent is not even in his grave yet!'

De Revelle began to look impatient, tugging at the cuffs of his gloves and glancing at the door.

'The verderer's work has to go on. The Attachment Court is due next week, over which he must preside.'

'Did you discuss it with Nicholas de Bosco before you offered the job to this man?'

Now the sheriff's impatience turned to annoyance. 'That man is an incompetent old fool. It's none of his business. The appointment is made by the freeholders of the county upon my writ. The Warden of the Forests has no say in the matter.'

He paused, then added angrily, 'Neither is it any of your concern, John. I hear that you went to Sigford yesterday and held an inquest on the dead man. You had no right – forest law prevails there.'

This was too much for de Wolfe. He jumped up to tower over the sheriff, his dark face glowering down at him.

'What arrant nonsense you talk, Richard! I am the King's coroner and it's his rule that runs everywhere in England. The forest laws concern offences against venison and vert, not men being shot in the back!'

Richard's face reddened in anger. 'I dispute that! This coroner nonsense came into being only last year – before that the forest, the stanneries and the Church dealt themselves with matters within their own jurisdiction.'

'Well, they don't now, Sheriff!' bellowed de Wolfe, equally incensed. 'The tinners no longer dispute my right to investigate their dead, even though you, as their Warden, tried to stop me. And the Bishop has agreed that any violence in the cathedral precinct should be handed to the secular powers. So if you wish to question the will of our King Richard, do so and suffer the consequences.'

De Revelle marched towards the door. 'I'll not waste time bandying words with you, John. You'll overstep the mark one of these days and then it will be you that suffers the consequences!'

As the sheriff furiously threw the door open so wide that it banged against the wall, de Wolfe called out a warning.

'Your sudden interest in the forest officers is suspicious, Richard. I trust, if only for your sister's sake, that you're not up to your tricks again – remember that you're still on probation!'

His brother-in-law vanished into the sunlight without deigning to reply and John sank down again onto the stone shelf to ponder the situation. Though he was the King's representative in Devon and the highest law officer in that county, Richard de Revelle had been in trouble ever since he took office as sheriff. Appointed at Christmas '93, he was dismissed by Hubert Walter, the Chief Justiciar, a few months later on suspicion of being a supporter of Prince John's abortive rebellion against the Lionheart, when the King was imprisoned in Germany. De Wolfe well remembered the anguish that his wife showed then, as her brother was her idol. When he was suspected of having feet of clay, Matilda urged her reluctant husband to intercede on de Revelle's behalf with both the Justiciar and William Marshal, the two most powerful men in the land. In the summer, nothing having proved against him, he was reinstated. It was partly out of a begrudging gratitude – and Matilda's insistence – that the sheriff supported John's election to the new post of coroner, offered by Hubert Walter on behalf of the King.

But ever since, apart from the usual embezzlement and corruption that were the hallmark of most sheriffs, de Revelle had begun toying again with a covert allegiance to Prince John. De Wolfe suspected that the Prince had promised the politically ambitious de Revelle advancement at court, should he be successful in unseating his royal brother. Others were of the same mind, including Bishop Henry, brother to William Marshal, several of the senior clergy and some of the Devonshire barons, such as the de Pomeroys. It was only a few months since de Wolfe had caught his brother-in-law in another embryonic plot to foment more rebellion – and again, only Matilda's pleading had stopped him from exposing de Revelle's treachery. Since then, the sheriff had been treading carefully, but John now always kept a sharp lookout for any schemes that Richard might be hatching.

A mellow voice suddenly brought him out of his reverie.

'I'm glad to see you using my humble chapel for meditation, Crowner. Though I didn't take you for someone with strong religious inclinations!'

Standing over him was a cheerful priest with a round face which matched the stomach that pushed out his black Benedictine habit into a comfortable bulge. He dropped down onto the ledge alongside de Wolfe and mopped his brow with a rag drawn from his gown.

'Or maybe it was just cooler in here, Sir John.'

The coroner grinned crookedly at Father Roger, who he found an amiable companion. Only a short time before, the priest's insatiable curiosity had briefly caused him to be suspected of multiple murders in the city, and John was glad that the accusations had soon proved unfounded.

'Not curing souls this morning, Roger?'

'Too hot for such laborious pastimes, Crowner. Thank God I only hold services here in the cool of early morning and towards dusk. Not that many of the heathen soldiery in Rougemont bother to attend, though their womenfolk are more devout.'

The priest had recently come from Bristol to become chaplain of the garrison and was always eager to learn more about Exeter, its people and its intrigues. The coroner told him of the killing of the verderer and the odd meeting in Roger's own church between the sheriff and the new appointee. The chaplain was already well aware of the antagonism between coroner and sheriff and had a shrewd idea of its causes. John went on to recount to him the unrest that seemed to be growing in the Royal Forest and the unexplained antipathy towards the Warden, Nicholas de Bosco. He thought that the ever-curious chaplain might have heard some useful tittle-tattle from the priests in the town or nearby parishes.

'I've heard nothing through the ecclesiastical grapevine,' Roger said thoughtfully. 'But I'll keep my ears open for you. I sometimes meet parish priests from around Dartmoor – they are usually fond of a gossip.'

They chatted for some time, finding that they had many experiences in common. Roger of Bristol had a military past rather like de Wolfe's, having been a chaplain to the King's forces in several campaigns in which both had served, though they had never met before. His loyalty had been rewarded with curacy of the chapel at Bristol castle, until the soldierly Archbishop of Canterbury, the same Hubert Walter who was also Chief Justiciar, posted him to the vacancy at Exeter.

They found that they also had something else in common that morning, as today was a hanging day and it was Roger's turn to shrive the two unfortunates who were to go to the gallows on Magdalen Street outside the city walls. The coroner also had to be present, so that his clerk could record the forfeiture of the felons' property. The two men followed the sad procession as the ox-cart trundled its fatal burden from the castle gaol in the undercroft of the keep. When the condemned men had been dispatched into the next life, John left Thomas in Roger's company and went back home for the midday meal, his appetite none the worse after watching the agonal thrashings of the strangled men dangling on their ropes.

Matilda was away, visiting her cousin in Fore Street, and John ate the boiled pig's knuckle that Mary put before him in peace and quiet. This was shattered just as he was dropping the stripped bone under the table for Brutus.

A hammering on the front door was answered by the maid, as she was bringing a bowl of dried apricots for his dessert. Mary came through the screens into the hall, followed by the thin figure of one of the burgesses' constables, responsible for trying to keep public order on the streets.

'Osric's here, in a lather of excitement,' she said disapprovingly. 'You're wanted urgently, as usual, to the ruination of your digestion!'

The lanky Saxon, who seemed all limbs and Adam's apple, stood awkwardly, twirling his floppy cap in his hands.

'There's been a killing and an assault, Crowner. Not an hour ago, in St Pancras Lane. I went up to Rougemont to report it, but Gwyn said you were at home. He's gone straight to the house.'

At the mention of the address, de Wolfe rose to his feet.

'St Pancras Lane – who's involved?'

'The dead 'un is an old servant. Bottler to the injured party, Sir Nicholas.'

The coroner was already moving towards the door. 'God's toenails, what's going on? I was with both of them only last evening!'

Striding through the streets, with the constable pattering alongside, the coroner looked like a large, avenging bat, his black surcoat flying wide over his long grey tunic. As they thrust aside folk dawdling in the lanes, Osric breathlessly added some details.

'Must have happened earlier this morning . . . only just discovered by the cook who comes to make the dinner. The servant was dead in the vestibule, the master lying out of his wits in his hall.'

There was knot of neighbours clustered outside the door of the Warden's house, kept at bay by the massive form of Gwyn of Polruan, who stood on the step. Grimly, de Wolfe thrust his way through and, with the constable close behind, went into the vestibule with his officer, who slammed the heavy door behind them.

'The cook called an apothecary, who's with him now,' grunted Gwyn. 'The corpse is there, under that table.'

As in John's own house, the vestibule led at one end into the hall and at the other to a passage to the back yard. It was bigger than the one in Martin's Lane and had a bench, a table and a row of pegs for cloaks and sword belts.

The bench was overturned and the table knocked askew. Between the legs was the crumpled body of the old man who had served wine the previous evening.

'Have you looked at him yet?' demanded the coroner.

'Just a quick glance. He's had a beating, poor old devil. Look at his head.'

John motioned for Osric to lift the table away and then crouched down alongside the cadaver, which was on its side, bent so that the knees were almost touching the face. An ominous pool of blood lay under the head, soaking into the earthen floor. When he turned the head, he saw a great tear in the skin of the temple and dark bruising covering most of the cheek.

Something about the ease with which the neck moved gave him further concern.

'I suspect his neck is broken, too. See what you think about it.'

He rocked back on his heels to give Gwyn space to get at the body. His officer was as experienced as the coroner in the various modes of death, learnt in battles, riots and ambushes the length and breadth of Europe and beyond. They sometimes competed with each other over the accuracy of their diagnoses of different types of lethal injury. Gwyn tested the rigidity of the arms first, to compare with the neck.

'Been dead more than a few hours, by the stiffness. I wonder when he was last seen alive?'

As he gripped the bloody head to swing it about, the hovering Osric answered his question. 'Last night, it seems. The cook gave them their supper, then went home. None of the neighbours saw them this morning.'

Gwyn finished his manoeuvres and stood up, wiping his stained hands on his breeches. 'You're right, Crowner. His neck's snapped. Must have been a tidy stroke on his head to do that, though he's a frail old fellow.'

They stood looking down at the pathetic remains of the aged bottler.

'A club or a baulk of timber did that. Nothing sharp edged,' announced de Wolfe, determined to have the last word on fatal injuries. 'Now what about Sir Nicholas?'

He turned to the door into the hall and lifted the crude wooden latch. Inside, he saw the same high, gloomy chamber that he had sat in the previous evening. Now the owner was stretched out on the long table, lying on a sheepskin coverlet fetched from his bed. He was groaning and moving restlessly, with an anxious-looking man standing alongside, a cup of some liquid in his hand. De Wolfe recognised him as Adam Russell, an apothecary from a shop in High Street, a well-known and trusted dispenser of remedies.

'He's getting his senses back, then?'

The apothecary, a small man with a round, owl-like face, nodded thankfully.

'Just these past few minutes, Sir John. He's also had a nasty crack on the skull, though naturally not so heavy as the poor fellow outside. There was nothing I could do for him.'

De Wolfe advanced to the side of the table and looked down anxiously at the Warden of the Forests. Part of his concern was for the victim himself, but part was the fear that de Bosco might not be able to identify his attacker and the possible motive. The man's eyes were open, but rolling about. He was moaning and trying to lift his hands towards his injured head, where a deep cut could be seen through the thin white hair. Blue bruising spread down his forehead and his upper eyelids were black and puffy.

'Can he hear me, I wonder? What potion have you got there?'

Adam allowed himself a slight smile. 'The best medicine for this, Crowner – a little brandy wine.' He bent over the Warden and held the cup to his lips. Nicholas spluttered as the strong spirit burned his mouth, and he struggled to sit up, but fell back with a groan.

'De Bosco, it's John de Wolfe, the coroner. We met only yesterday, in kinder circumstances. Can you understand what I say?'

The victim's eyes stopped swivelling and focused on the speaker's face. His thin lips parted to show his bare gums and a weak voice emerged.

'De Wolfe? Why have they done this to me?'

John bent lower to catch the whispers. 'They? There were more than one?'

The Warden tried to nod, but the movement made him hiss with the pain in his head. 'Two men – burst in here at dawn. I was just out of bed, sitting here drinking ale. I never take food to break my fast.'

De Wolfe had feared that the Warden's mind was wandering, but he seemed to be recovering his wits by the minute.

'Did you recognise them? What did they say?'

The apothecary frowned at the coroner. 'He's not yet in a fit state to talk much.'

John bobbed his head impatiently. 'I know, but just a few words. We need to set up a hue and cry.' He looked down again at Nicholas de Bosco, who returned his gaze through blood-shot eyes, and raised his head a little from the coverlet.

'I recollect very little – not even being struck. But they were rough louts, poorly dressed. They said nothing, not a word.'

He groaned and closed his eyes, his head sinking back again. At the apothecary's disapproving frown, John straightened up and stepped back.

'I'll not bother you more at present. When you are stronger, we'll talk again.'

He looked at Adam Russell. 'Do you want him taken

to the monks at St Nicholas or St John's?' These were
the two priories that had infirmarers with some skill as
physicians.

'There's little they can do that God and time will
not, Crowner. I'll get some men to carry him to his
bed, then I'll send my apprentice around to sit with
him. I'll return myself in a few hours.'

'When can I talk to him again?'

'Try this evening – or better, tomorrow morning.'

With that John had to be content and, leaving the
injured Warden in the care of the apothecary, he took
Gwyn back to their chamber in Rougemont.

Thomas was already there, busy writing up duplicate copies of the rolls, which eventually would have
to be presented to the Commissioners of Gaol
Delivery or the Justices in Eyre when they next came
to Exeter. He sat on his usual milking stool at one
side of the trestle table and pulled his parchments
and inks nearer to give space to de Wolfe, as he
bumped down on to his bench opposite. Gwyn took
up the only other flat surface in the bare room,
perching his broad backside on the stone sill that ran
below the pair of slit windows. The inevitable pitcher
of cider came out for the coroner and his officer,
though the abstemious clerk declined, preferring
water – when he could get any that looked even
halfway clean. He had already heard of the trouble
in St Pancras Lane from one of the guards and started
off the debate about its significance.

'Can this be connected with the killing in Sigford,
Crowner?'

'God knows, Thomas! It could be a chance robbery,
though the cook says that de Bosco never had much
of value in that small town house. He had several
manors out in the country where most of his goods
and his strongbox were kept.'

Gwyn lowered his drinking pot long enough to comment.

'The assailants may not have known that, though. Yet they made no attempt to force either the old bottler nor the Warden to tell them where there might have been valuables.'

John drummed his fingers on the table restlessly. 'To my mind, it's too great a coincidence that a pair of forest officers get attacked within as many days. De Bosco told me that he had had several threats recently, seemingly designed to force him out of office.'

'Three feet of arrow certainly put the verderer out of office!' said Gwyn. 'But I wonder if they intended to kill the Warden – or just beat him up as a warning?'

'Is there no clue as who these villains might be?' piped Thomas.

'No one saw them, except the servant and Nicholas de Bosco,' growled John. 'And one of those is dead and the other has wits back only partly yet. No one saw them in the street, so I suspect they climbed into the garden and came from around the back.'

'Any chance of finding them still in the city?' asked the clerk optimistically.

Gwyn fell back to heckling Thomas, a sign that the clerk's melancholia was improving. 'You're an idiot, little man! Do we go around asking almost four thousand people whether they were nasty enough to batter two old men this morning?'

The clerk stuck his tongue out at Gwyn in a most unpriestly manner, but the officer persisted. 'Even if the sheriff shifted himself to put a watch on the city gates, who would they look for? Two men can walk in and out as they like, especially if they were pushing a barrow or carrying a bale of wool.'

The mention of the sheriff started de Wolfe's fingers drumming again.

'I'll swear he's up to something concerning this affair – but I'm damned if I see what. Why was he in such a hurry to appoint this fellow as a new verderer? Does anyone know anything of this Philip de Strete?'

Gwyn shook his big head, but Thomas de Peyne, whose large ears collected all manner of information, knew a little.

'He's a knight from down the west end of the county, fairly young, I hear. He was in one of the French campaigns and scraped enough loot together to buy out his knight-service and get himself a free-holding.'

The coroner digested this, but was none the wiser.

'Why should he want to burden himself with a thankless, unpaid job like that of a verderer? He'd be better off staying home to look after his flocks and his fields.'

As the words left his mouth, he realised that the same applied to himself and his coroner's appointment – though he had no flocks and fields to labour over. His brother William was quite content to look after the two family manors and John's business partner, city burgess Hugh de Relaga, turned them a nice profit from their wool-exporting enterprise.

But the fact remained that Richard de Revelle had produced this man from nowhere and was going to install him in a dead man's shoes.

'The post may be unpaid, master – but anything to do with the forests is suspect of being involved with extortion and corruption,' Thomas reminded him. They argued the issues back and forth for a time, but with no solid facts to hand it became a futile exercise.

'I'll hold the inquest on the bottler this afternoon in the courthouse – not that it will advance us one inch farther,' grumbled John. 'Gather the neighbours for a jury in a couple of hours, Gwyn. Afterwards, I'll go to see if de Bosco has recovered any more of his memory.'

CHAPTER THREE

*In which Crowner John receives
some momentous news*

Though considerably recovered, de Bosco was of little further help when John went to visit him in the early evening. Adam Russell, the apothecary, was just leaving as the coroner arrived and confirmed that the older man would have a sore head for a week or two, but was in no danger as long as fever did not set in from the gash on his head. When the coroner climbed to the solar where the injured man was in his bed, he found a neighbour's ample wife came to sit with him until nightfall.

Standing alongside the pallet like some great black crow, John looked down at the bandaged head and saw that the eyes were now almost closed from the bruised swelling of the lids. However, what could be seen of them was bright enough and Nicholas spoke quite rationally.

'I suppose you have no hope of catching those murdering bastards?'

He had been told of the death of his bottler and was grieving for the loss of the innocent old man.

'I wish I had better news for you, but there was no chance of finding these men. We had no description whatsoever and they had been gone from your house many hours before you were found. I'm sorry.'

'No matter. When I'm able to move, I'll take myself off to one of my manors, where I can feel safe with my servants around me. For they'll try again, mark my words.'

'So you don't believe they were common robbers?'

De Bosco's toothless mouth made a derisory sound. 'Not at all, Crowner! You can't think that yourself, with the verderer slain not two days before – and me having been threatened to give up my duties.'

'Will this encourage you to do that?' ventured de Wolfe.

'No, be damned to them, whoever it is!' snapped Nicholas. 'I was appointed by my King to do his duty, just as I fought for him in the wars. I'm not going to be frightened off by a bang on the head.'

John forbore to mention that his bottler had suffered more than a bang on the head, as had Humphrey le Bonde. He admired the older man's courage, but hoped that he would do as he promised and retire to the safety of one of his manors to carry out his duties.

'Can you hazard any guess at all as to what's behind this?' he asked, as a last query.

'Someone wants to infiltrate the forest administration, I suspect. But why, God alone knows! There's plenty of graft and dishonesty there, but that's mainly the perquisite of the foresters and woodwards. It would be unusually well-organised corruption if the verderers and the Warden had their fingers in the same pie.'

As John left, he wondered whether de Bosco had struck nearer the truth than he imagined.

In the long summer evenings, they ate supper much later in the house in Martin's Lane, and John found he had a couple of hours to spare before he need sit with Matilda at their silent meal. His feet took him automatically towards Idle Lane, and as he strode through the town his thoughts abandoned dead men and split heads, in favour of his lady love.

He became more uneasy the nearer he came to the Bush. It was over a week now since he had been with Nesta in her room upstairs in the inn. Usually, their lovemaking was carefree and enthusiastic, sometimes even boisterous. Dour as John was to the outside world, alone with the Welsh woman he was a changed man – tender, sensual and happy.

So it was with grave concern that he pondered what had happened over this past week or two. Once again, he tortured himself with thoughts of Nesta being involved with another lover, but somehow the signs of that were lacking. He wondered with dread whether she was ill or sickening for something, though she looked healthy enough. As he stooped to enter the low door of the inn, his resolve hardened to find out what was going on. A coward in the face of embarrassing emotions, he steeled himself to confront Nesta head on tonight. For once, fortune favoured him as he saw her standing at the back of the low room, watching Edwin hammering a wooden spigot into a fresh cask of ale. There were relatively few patrons sitting around and he grabbed his mistress by the hand and pulled her towards the back door.

'We're going for a little walk, madam,' he said firmly, leading her into the yard behind. As she turned a surprised face towards the suddenly masterful coroner, he saw that they were not alone, as one of the cook-maids was coming out of the kitchen shed and a customer was relieving himself against the fence behind the brew-house.

'This way, then,' he snapped, turning sharply to avoid

an audience. He opened the wicket gate that led out on to the waste ground alongside the inn, and with an arm now around her shoulders walked Nesta towards the junction of Idle Lane and Priest Street.

'What are you doing, John? I've got a tavern to run!' she protested.

'The Bush can look after itself for half an hour. I want to talk to you.'

The Welsh woman must have had an inkling of what was to come, for she went along meekly as they walked silently down the steep street towards the city walls near the river. At the south-west corner, a new gate had been cut through in recent years, to reach the quay-side where smaller ships lay beached on the mud outside the warehouses.

John led Nesta over to some casks and crates awaiting shipment, where there was no one within earshot. He sat her on a large bale of wool wrapped in sacking and stood in front of her, his hands on her shoulders.

'Something is concerning you, my love. You may as well tell me what it is, first as last.'

As Nesta looked up at him, her eyes brimmed over with tears. She shook her head and looked away, rubbing her face with the sleeve of her working gown.

'Tell me!' he commanded, his voice almost harsh from fear of what he might be about to hear.

Nesta swung her face back towards him, her eyelids red and glistening. She sniffed back her tears, then leant forwards, her head against his wide sword-belt.

'I think I may be with child, John. I'm so sorry!'

'Sorry? Why should you be sorry, for God's sake?' he bellowed.

After sixteen years of marriage to Matilda, never once had she conceived – though in truth he had been absent for most of that time and for the past few years they had never lain together.

He pushed her gently away so that he could look down at her face, his own expression being a mixture of wonderment and anxiety.

'Are you sure, dear woman?'

She shrugged slightly. 'Not sure, but something tells me that I am. My monthly curse has never been that regular since I miscarried when Meredydd was alive, so it's difficult to tell.'

He pulled her back tightly against him and bent to kiss the top of her head.

'Have you been to see a good-wife who knows about these matters?'

'Not yet – but I will, very soon.'

De Wolfe eased himself away and then sat down alongside her on the bale, slipping an arm around her shoulders.

'This is no reason for tears, Nesta,' he said gently. 'If it really is true, then I will be glad and proud to acknowledge myself as the father.'

Nesta burst into tears, sobs this time, rather than just moist eyes. John jerked her shoulder helplessly, completely adrift with a weeping woman.

'Don't be sad, my love, please! Why are you crying? I said I'll be joyful about becoming a father.'

The Welsh woman shook her head desperately. 'I've brought you nothing but trouble, John. You're a high official, a knight and a Norman gentleman – and what am I? A lowly ale-wife.'

'That be damned. Half the Norman gentleman I know have several families – both sides of the blanket, as they say. Even my poisonous brother-in-law has got two bastards by different mothers. And they are just the ones that we know about!'

Nesta refused to be comforted and continued to sob against his side.

'Matilda . . . she'll make your life a misery if this

comes to light, as it surely must. In this damned city no one can keep a secret longer than a candle burns.'

John gave one of his rumbles, deep in his throat. 'Matilda will be a problem, I'll admit. But she'll just have to accept it and be damned to her.'

They sat quietly for a moment. Realisation began to seep into his mind and for all his bold promises to Nesta he started to see a rough road ahead – mainly because of his wife, who would use this to make his life a torment.

But, pragmatic as always, the coroner decided to face the problem one step at a time – and the first was to make sure that Nesta's suspicions were correct.

'Do you know of a reliable midwife who can confirm what you think?' he asked. 'There is that formidable nun out in Polsloe Priory who seems a fount of knowledge in these matters.'

Sniffing away the remnants of her tears, Nesta sat up straighter on the bale.

'No need to go that far, John. The mother of one of my maids lives in Rack Lane and has a good reputation as a lying-in nurse. I'll see her tomorrow.'

She rose to her feet and looked up at the concerned face of her lover.

'I must go back now, John. Life doesn't stop for things like this.'

She sounded so sad that his heart ached.

'Are you not just a little glad of it?' he asked gently.

She smiled wanly at him. 'Part of me is, John. But I will cause you so much trouble.'

Slowly they walked back towards Idle Lane, as de Wolfe tried to get his mind around the anticipation of this unexpected and profound change in his life – becoming a father.

That evening was to be full of unexpected events for John, as when he arrived back at Martin's Lane he discovered that his brother-in-law had invited himself for supper.

Though usually such a visit would have been received sourly by de Wolfe, he was rather glad of a distraction this particular evening. After having had such potentially momentous news from Nesta, a meal alone with Matilda would have been more of a strain than usual, as her gimlet eyes and shrewd mind may well have suspected that her husband had something new to hide from her. As it was, the patronising comments that were Richard's usual form of conversation could be used as a cover for his own sullen silence, for Matilda was well aware of John's dislike of and contempt for her brother.

'And how are all the corpses today, Crowner?' began de Revelle, in his bantering, sarcastic manner.

'One dead bottler, so far,' muttered de Wolfe, with a scowl that suggested that he would be happy if Richard were to be the next. 'But you must have heard about that, being the guardian of the King's peace in this county!'

He tried to match his brother-in-law's sarcasm, but it washed over their guest like a bucket of water on a goose.

'I heard nothing of it. I leave such minor matters to the constables.'

'Then you'll not have heard that the poor fellow was slain at the same time as they left his master for dead – the Warden of the Forests.'

The sheriff sat up suddenly from the settle in which he had been lounging, almost spilling a cup of wine he was holding.

'Nicholas de Bosco? Holy Mary, I knew nothing of this!'

Rather against his will, John somehow believed him. 'A verderer and the Warden attacked within a few days. What's going on, Richard?'

Matilda had been listening to their exchange, her small eyes flicking from one to the other. 'You told me you had appointed a new verderer already, brother,' she observed.

Richard nodded distractedly. 'Yes, the woodmotes must carry on. This Philip de Strete will be a worthy successor in organising them.'

'What are woodmotes?' she demanded, and her husband answered her.

'Some use that word for the Attachment Courts, others call them forty-day courts. Whatever they're called, the forest folk hate them – they usually mean more fines and punishments.'

'Careful, John, these are the King's forests you're talking about. You don't want to be mouthing treason, do you?'

Both the others knew that de Revelle was sneering at de Wolfe's well-known devotion to Richard Coeur-de-Lion, but his sister was not amused.

'The less you say about that the better,' she growled, and her brother sank back in his settle, suddenly engrossed in the decoration around his pewter cup. This was a sensitive subject and Matilda's warning was the first time she had broached the matter since de Revelle's brush with treachery a few months earlier.

Thankfully, the awkward silence was broken by Mary bustling in with a large bowl of stew, causing them to rise and take their places at the long table. Two fresh loaves cut into quarters and a platter of yellow butter accompanied the mutton-and-onion soup. Mary ladled big portions into wooden bowls and laid deep spoons carved from cow horn before them. Then she came back with ale, cider and more wine, and left them to fill their bellies. This did away with the necessity for much conversation until the second course, a boiled salmon which John dissected with his dagger, placing portions in the empty soup bowls of the other two diners. As they picked out the bones and licked their fingers, the coroner returned to the problems in the forest.

'There is increasing disaffection among some of the barons and manor-lords over this,' he began. 'My brother William down in Stoke-in-Teignhead, who knows more about rural life than I do, told me that in Hampshire and Northampton they are petitioning the King to disafforest some areas. Increasingly they resent not being able to hunt the venison on their own lands.'

De Revelle dug a fish bone from between his teeth before answering.

'They have no chance of that, unless they pay a large fee to the Crown. It was old King Henry who made the largest encroachments into their lands. Why should his sons give any of it up now?'

De Wolfe noticed that he said 'sons', a slip which showed that the sheriff still had John, Count of Mortain, in mind as one of the possible beneficiaries of the fruits of the forest. He thought of making an issue of it, but decided that he was in no mood to reopen the old controversy again and further distress Matilda, as she had been devastated when her brother's active sympathy for the usurper had been discovered by her husband.

She reached across the table to scoop up another segment of pink fish with her spoon. 'Have the Devonshire gentry expressed the same concerns to you, Richard?'

'In passing, yes. Guy Ferrars and Arnulf de Mowbray were moaning to me about having to do all their hunting in their chases and parks, instead of on all the other land they own. But they're always complaining about something – the more they have, the more they want.'

John gave a derisive grunt – that was rich, he thought, coming from de Revelle, who was a champion money-grubber himself.

'Why should anyone want to kill Nicholas de Bosco?' persisted Matilda. 'He seemed a harmless enough fellow. I've often seen him at worship in the cathedral.' Anyone who was a devout attender at Mass was bound to be looked on favourably by her, even if he had horns and a tail.

'Nice he may have been, but I'd prefer to say he was weak,' snapped Richard. 'A new Warden is needed. De Bosco is just an old soldier, given that job as a sinecure for past services.'

He gave a meaningful look across at his brother-in-law as he said this, but John steadfastly ignored the jibe.

'Is it possible that someone tried to remove him from office by an attempt to murder him?' asked Matilda, oblivious of a trickle of salmon fat running down her chin. 'But who would want such a job, so dismal and unpaid?'

John stared pointedly at de Revelle, until the sheriff began to look decidedly uncomfortable. 'Well, Richard, haven't I heard rumours about your ambitions in that direction?'

'If the office happened to fall vacant, then yes, I'd be interested. It would be a challenge, as this de Bosco has let things slip recently. The forests are teeming with outlaws, the discipline of the foresters is all to hell, and I'm sure the royal exchequer is not gaining all the profit it should from the forests.'

De Wolfe leered across the table at his brother-in-law. 'No, I'm sure you would find many ways of increasing the revenue, Richard!'

He avoided saying that much of this extra revenue would never reach the royal treasure chests in

Winchester or Westminster, but the sheriff knew very well what he was implying.

After a bowl of early summer fruits swimming in fresh cream and a glass of sweet dessert wine, Richard left for his apartments in Rougemont and Matilda called for her maid Lucille to prepare her for bed, as the late summer dusk was now upon them.

To give them time for their womanly pursuits in the solar, John took Brutus for a walk around the cathedral Close. Walking amid the graves, the rubbish piles and the rank grass, he pondered the news that Nesta had laid upon him that evening.

Did he really want to be a father? Could he survive the inevitable onslaught from Matilda, who would taunt him for ever with having sired a bastard on a tavern-keeper? Would Nesta survive childbirth, which claimed such a large proportion of new mothers? Why had this come now, when he had been lying with Nesta for two years? And why had none of his other women, going back over many years, ever conceived?

These questions milled about in his mind as he loped around the huge church of St Mary and St Andrew, following his hound, which dashed hither and thither in search of new smells. He passed beggars sleeping alongside new grave-pits, truant urchins playing tag in defiance of their mother's screeching, and lovers walking hand in hand or kissing in dark corners under the cathedral's looming walls. Oblivious to all these familiar sights, he circled the Close and plodded back to his house with none of the questions answered in his turbulent mind.

Hennock lay about two-thirds of the way between Exeter and Sigford and was a larger village than the latter. Early the next morning, three riders came into Hennock and reined up outside the forge. It was a large shack set at the edge of the roadside, its walls of wattle and daub set in a rough timber frame. The sagging roof was covered with faded wooden shingles, which were less inflammable than straw thatch. Behind was a cottage sitting in a patch of garden, with two pigs penned in by a fence and a few chickens scratching in the dust.

The riders sat silently on their mounts for a few moments, listening to the rhythmic clanging of a pair of hammers on the anvil, as the smith and his eldest son rained precise blows on a red-hot length of rod than was destined to be a cart axle. A younger boy, about eight years of age, was in the shadows at the back of the hut, pumping away at a large leather-and-wood bellows to keep the charcoal of the furnace glowing almost white.

Eventually, forester William Lupus gave a curt nod to one of the others and his page slid from his horse and walked towards the forge. Henry Smok was utterly unlike the usual image of a 'page', being a bull-necked man of about forty, with a roll like a sailor and a coarse face surmounted by a tangle of dirty black hair. His breeches were coarse cloth and his brown leather jerkin was tightly belted to carry the weight of a broadsword as well as a dagger.

Smok ambled up to the open double doors of the smithy and stood insolently alongside the anvil, his thumbs hooked into his belt.

'Hey, you! You're wanted outside.'

Eustace Smith jerked his head up to look at the intruder. He was a crop-haired Saxon in middle age, his leathery face pitted with small scars from sparks and hot metal. The alternate clanging of the hammers ceased and the younger Smith stared uneasily at Smok.

'As soon as we finish this piece, before it cools too much,' he grunted.

The page gave the son a shove that sent him staggering. Though both the ironworkers were tough, muscular men, Henry Smok had the physique of a bull and the temperament of a bully.

'Out, I said! Both of you.'

The craftsmen knew very well who Smok was and who would be outside. Like all villagers in the forest, they had suffered the arrogance of the foresters and their creatures for years. Reluctantly dropping their hammers to the floor, they walked out into the morning sunshine and looked up at the other two horsemen. One was the forester, the other Walter Tirel, a woodward employed by the de Pomery estate, but who often acted as an assistant to Lupus.

'Well, William Lupus, what is it now?' asked Eustace wearily. 'Has your mare cast a shoe – or do you just want to increase the private tithes you extort from me?'

His words were bravely defiant, but there was a tremor in his voice.

'Watch that mouth of yours,' growled the forester, looking down at the smith as if he were a heap of manure.

'We've come with some good news for you,' sneered Walter Tirel, who acted as a sycophantic shadow to William Lupus. He was a thin, wiry man with one drooped eyelid that made him look as if he were permanently winking.

'That'll be the day when you bring anything but trouble,' said the smith bitterly.

'The news is that you're going to work for the King,' grated Lupus.

Eustace stood in his scorched and scarred leather apron, looking suspiciously from one man to the other.

'What the hell do you mean?'

'A new forge has been built at Trusham, two miles up the road.'

Eustace scowled at the reminder. 'So I've heard – though why, I can't fathom. There's no need for two so close together.'

Walter Tirel grinned. 'I agree, so now there'll be but the one . . . at Trusham.'

Eustace gaped at the two mounted men, words failing him.

'This forge is closed as from tomorrow,' snapped William Lupus. 'The new rule in the King's forest is that smiths work only for the King. You'll be paid a wage, like any other workman. But you'll labour at Trusham, under a forge-master I've appointed. You'll have company, for Lawrence the smith from Coombe is in the same position as yourself.'

'The Coombe smithy is closed too?' said Eustace's son, aghast.

'It will be from tomorrow, like yours here. Finish what work you've started, then take your tools across to Trusham in the morning.'

The elder blacksmith found his voice again.

'This is madness! I have had this forge for fifteen years. I have a licence from my manor-lord and pay him rent for it.'

'Lucky man! Now you can save yourself the rent,' cackled Henry Smok, swinging himself back into his saddle.

Eustace advanced up to the forester's horse, his fists clenching as incredulity gave way to anger. 'You can't do this! I'm away to see my lord or his steward. He'll soon put a stop to your games.'

'He has no say in the matter. This is forest land, the King does what he wishes here. So keep your tongue quiet and be at Trusham at first light to-morrow.'

'What about the verderer? Does Humphrey le Bonde know of this?'

The smith stopped short, suddenly remembering that le Bonde was dead.

William Lupus leered down at him. 'Yes, he's no longer with us, is he? And the new verderer not only knows of it, he ordered it!'

He pulled his horse's head around, ready to move away. Desperately, Eustace grabbed his saddle-girth.

'What about my sons? Are we all to come to Trusham?'

The forester smacked his hand away with a gloved fist.

'No, we don't want to pay all your damned family. Just you. Be there at dawn, understand – or you'll be in great trouble.'

They cantered away, leaving the smith devastated at the prospect of having his small income halved and his family almost destitute.

Some five miles away, on a densely wooded hillside above the Bovey river, Stephen Cruch was waiting on a sleek palfrey at the foot of some large rocks. Below him was a cataract where the river rushed even faster on its journey down from the moor towards Bovey Tracey and the sea beyond.

Few travellers would risk penetrating the forest alone, especially this far from a main track or a village, but the horse-trader seemed quite at ease as he sat quietly in his saddle. Near by, two sturdy moorland ponies grazed contentedly, secured by their head-ropes to hazel saplings. Stephen looked up at the bright summer sun, occasionally crossed by a few stray clouds, and estimated that it was around the eighth hour. A few minutes more and he started to become a little impatient. Untying a thong on his belt, he raised a cow's horn to his lips, blowing hard through the pewter mouthpiece. The mournful sound echoed through the valley, competing with the rush of water between the granite rocks.

A moment later, there was an answering call from a distance, and with a smile he tied his horn back on his belt and slipped from the saddle. A few minutes later, a handful of men appeared, one on a pony, the other half-dozen on foot. The mounted leader went straight towards the tethered horses and examined them critically, before walking his own across to Cruch.

'Satisfied with them, Robert?' enquired the dealer. 'You said you wanted them small and tough.'

'They look well enough, Stephen,' replied Robert Winter. 'Short legs and good wind is what we need in the woods and on the moor, not some spindly, long-legged racer that would fall at every rabbit-hole and badger sett.'

He threw a leg over the folded blanket that did service as his pony's saddle and came across to Cruch, who turned to his own saddlebag and drew out a leather flask. He held it out to the outlaw who took a long swig of the brandy wine made by the monks of Buckfast Abbey.

'That's something you miss when you live in the forest,' he said appreciatively, drawing a hand across his lips. ''But I hope you've got something even more pleasant for me?'

The horse-trader delved again in his saddlebag and handed over the money pouch that Father Edmund Treipas had given him, though it weighed somewhat less now.

'That's what we agreed – but the price of two good ponies had to come out of it.'

Robert grunted. 'I doubt you've lost on the deal yourself, Stephen. You're a bigger thief than I am!' A grin robbed the words of any offence. The other men, dressed in a motley collection of clothes, stood at a distance and watched the transaction with curiosity. They were a villainous-looking bunch, several of them carrying longbows, the others having pikes.

Robert Winter was a handsome man in his early thirties, with features quite different from those of the other men. Brown, wavy hair and a matching beard and moustache framed a slim face with high cheek-bones. A straight nose, full lips and intelligent hazel eyes might lead an observer to think that he was from an aristocratic family, though Cruch knew that he was from the merchant class. He led a band of several score of ruffianly outlaws that ranged over the south-eastern fringes of Dartmoor, from Moretonhampstead down through Widecombe and across to Ashburton. There were other outlaws scattered throughout the forest, but they had learned not to challenge Winter's supremacy in robbery, theft and extortion.

'Where are you living these days?' asked Cruch casually.

Winter took another drink from the flask and tapped the side of his nose artfully. 'Ask no questions and you'll be told no lies! We keep on the move, that's the secret of survival – not that that bloody sheriff is much concerned with catching us. I'm more wary of that coroner fellow they brought in last autumn. I hear he's a dangerous bastard – and one that's impossible to buy off like most of the other law officers. I'd advise you to keep well out of sight when he's around, Stephen.'

Cruch shrugged – he too had heard about Sir John de Wolfe, but their paths were unlikely to cross unless he did something unwise. As for Winter, after a man was declared outlaw at the County Court he legally ceased to exist and could be legitimately killed by anyone who fancied the attempt. Indeed, an outlaw was declared to be 'as the wolf's head', for if anyone could slay him and take the severed head to the sheriff, he would be awarded a substantial bounty, similar to the persecuted wolf. Stephen Cruch persisted in asking where they lived, and after another swig of brandy wine Robert Winter became more expansive.

'We have a few places deep in the woods, where we keep the ponies – and some caves we keep provisioned in case the going gets too hot. But oftentimes we slink into a village or even a town for a night or two. A fistful of money is marvellous for keeping innkeepers' mouths tightly closed!'

The horse-trader knew that many outlaws crept back to their homes now and then – sometimes permanently. Many moved to another part of England where they were not known and slipped back into the community – some even gaining public office or becoming successful merchants. It was easier in towns, where the population was larger and less incestuous – in villages everyone knew everyone else and the frankpledge system made it difficult for a stranger to become integrated. Cruch often wondered about Robert Winter, as an intelligent man like him was unlikely to spend the rest of his life skulking in the woods. He knew little about his past, except that he was from Exeter and had escaped a hanging there about three years earlier.

The outlaw's voice brought him back to the present.

'Have you any more work like that for me?'

Stephen's monkey-like face wrinkled in thought. 'Not at the moment. But the way I suspect things are moving, you may be needed for some more persuasion very soon. Things are changing fast in this bailiwick, but I can only pass on what others wish to have done.'

Winter rattled the money bag. 'More like this will be welcome any time. Leave a message as usual at the alehouse at Ashburton when you next need to meet.'

Cruch nodded and carefully retrieved his wine flask before mounting up and riding away. Before he reached the track near the river, he turned in his saddle to look back, but men and ponies had already vanished without trace.

By noon, Nesta knew definitely that she was pregnant. She had been taken by one of her maids to a house in Rock Street, where the girl's mother had examined her. She was the self-appointed midwife and herbal healer to the street and the adjacent lanes in that part of the city. A rosy-cheeked widow, fat and amiable, she made Nesta welcome in the pair of small rooms she occupied at the back of the dwelling. After expelling a pair of boisterous children, she asked the innkeeper about her monthly courses and any symptoms that commonly went with being gravid. Then, with the rickety door firmly closed against the urchins, the midwife put Nesta on a low bed against the wall and gently examined her under the cover of her full woollen skirt. After a patient and careful examination with her warm hands, both on her belly and internally, she smiled and invited Nesta to rise, while she wiped her hands on a piece of cloth.

'No doubt about it, my dear. You're going to be a mother, bless you!'

As Nesta shook down her shift and rearranged her skirt, she asked the widow whether she could tell how far gone she was.

'Hard to say, my love. It's early, just enough for me

to be definite about it. But you've plenty of time yet to make swaddling clothes!'

With that Nesta had to be content, and after failing to get the woman to accept any payment she walked silently home with her cook-maid, who solicitously held her arm as if she were likely to go into labour at any moment.

When they arrived at the Bush, Nesta climbed the steps to her room and threw herself on the bed that John had bought her the previous year.

She lay unmoving for a long time, staring up at the dusty rafters and the woven hazel boughs that supported the thatch. It was on this bed, she thought bitterly, that she and John had so often made love – and where she had betrayed him, albeit for such a short time. Nesta was well aware that he had not been faithful to her – but this was the way of men, who could rarely refuse the favours of another woman. Yet she sensed that lately he had not wandered from her, though she was realistic enough to wonder whether this was from choice or lack of opportunity.

But his actions were no excuse for her, though she had been provoked several months ago by his neglect. She had known that it was from force of circumstances, before another coroner was appointed for the north of the county, but she should have been more understanding. As she stared up at the roof, her eyes filled with tears as doubt and indecision clouded her mind. The midwife had confirmed what she knew already, as for several weeks something inside had told her as plain as day that she was with child. She wished that the woman could have been more definite about the duration of her pregnancy, but the widow was no professional and had done her best out of kindness.

Laying a hand on her still-flat stomach, Nesta

wondered whether to love or hate what was growing within her womb. Turning on her side, she wept herself softly to sleep, for once uncaring about her busy taproom down below.

CHAPTER FOUR

In which Crowner John visits a tannery

The next few days passed quickly for the coroner, as there was a Summer Fair in Exeter, including a Horse Fair on Bull-mead outside the South Gate. Hundreds of traders flocked into the city, and stalls and booths sprang up along the main streets, though the focus of activity was in the cathedral Close, the fair being linked to a saint's day. Many fairs in England were franchised by the Church, which made a handsome profit from licences to traders. Unlike some towns, which closed all the regular shops during the fair, the merchants of Exeter joined in the general scramble for custom, and for several days the city was a seething hotbed of buying, selling, trading, entertainment and revelry. Every bed in every inn was taken and the alehouses were over-flowing with drinkers and drunks.

John de Wolfe was kept busy with a number of incidents, most related to the turmoil of the fair. There was a brawl at the Saracen inn on Stepcote Hill, in which a man was killed from being kicked in the head, several others being injured in the drunken mêlée. Then a visiting stall-holder from Dorchester was stabbed in a dark alley behind a brothel in Bretayne, the poorest part of the city. His purse was stolen and he died before he could be carried off to the small infirmary at the nearby St Nicholas Priory.

John managed to get to the Bush for an hour on Saturday evening, and upstairs in her little cubicle a subdued Nesta confirmed to him that she was indeed pregnant. As they both had more or less accepted the fact even before she had visited the midwife, it was no great surprise to him, but Nesta failed to respond to her lover's efforts at reassurance and support. John was puzzled and rather hurt by her lack of reaction to his attempts at being enthusiastic about the future.

'I'll bring the lad up as if he were my legitimate son,' he declared, oblivious to the fact that the child might be a girl. 'If Matilda doesn't like it, then to hell with her. We'll live apart, it will be little different from my present existence.'

Nesta shook her head sadly. 'How can you do that, John? Everyone will know – they'll know even months before the birth, if I judge Exeter gossips correctly.'

'What of it? I've told you before, half the men I know have one or two extra families about the place. Matilda's own brother, for one.'

The auburn-haired innkeeper sat mutely, and John persisted in his uphill attempts to cheer her. 'The name 'Fitzwolfe' sounds impressive, eh? Then later we'll have to decide on his baptismal name.'

At this, Nesta burst into tears and an embarrassed and half-terrified John pulled her jerkily to his chest with spasms of his arm and incoherent mutterings intended to soothe her. He tried to console himself with the assumption that these strange moods were a passing symptom of pregnancy, like the strange appetites that he had vaguely heard about.

Though he hated to admit it even to himself, he was relieved when a tapping on the door heralded the potman. Old Edwin came to tell them that he was needed downstairs, where Gwyn was waiting with an urgent message.

It turned out to be a summons to a house near the East Gate, where a middle-aged cordwainer had returned early from his stall at the fair, to find his young wife in bed with an itinerant haberdasher, who had persuaded her into more than his ribbons and buttons when he called at the door.

When de Wolfe arrived, the haberdasher was lying naked and dead on the floor of the solar and the husband was spread-eagled across him, unconscious and bleeding from a deep gash on his scalp.

'It seems the cuckolded merchant stabbed the fellow in the back while he was lying across his wife,' explained Gwyn. 'Then the woman got up and smashed the water pitcher over her husband's head, in a fury at having been deprived of a far better lover than the shoe-maker!'

The house was in chaos, with Osric the constable trying to restrain the screaming wife. The grandmother and several relatives were all shouting and wailing, and it was midnight before the coroner and his henchman could get away from the turmoil, John deeming it wise to attach the cordwainer for ten marks to appear at the inquest on Monday. There was no way in which the man would ever be convicted of murder, in the circumstances of finding a stranger *in flagrante delicto* with his wife. De Wolfe felt that a low-key handling of the affair was all that was required for the present – let the justices sort the matter out when they next came to Exeter.

The next day was quieter, so John could find no excuse to avoid being hauled off by Matilda to morning Mass at the cathedral, something she succeeded in doing about once a month. Unlike Gwyn, he had no strong objection to going to church, though he was supremely uninterested in both the future of his immortal soul and the boring liturgy purveyed by the clergy. Being dragged to the cathedral was at least preferable to her forcing him to St Olave's, her favourite little church in Fore Street. One of his objections to this place was Julian Fulk, the smug priest who officiated there. During the recent spate of priestly killings in Exeter, Fulk had been a suspect and the collapse of John's suspicions against him gave the podgy priest an extra reason to smirk at the coroner.

After midday dinner, John arranged to met Gwyn and walk down to Bull-mead, just outside the town, where the Horse Fair was still in progress. Like most active men, they were both interested in horses, and this was an opportunity to walk around the field and look at the profusion of animals and gossip about them both with the dealers and many of their local cronies. As the tall, stooping coroner and his massive wild-haired officer paraded along the lines of beasts and watched them being pranced around the display area in the centre, at least one pair of wary eyes followed them. Stephen Cruch, who had a dozen stallions, mares and geldings there for sale, contemplated the former Crusader thoughtfully – and wondered what it was about him that made even the reckless Robert Winter a little uneasy.

It was often mid-morning when new cases were reported to the coroner from outside Exeter. In the summertime, a rider from a town or village in the south or west of the county could leave at dawn and be in Exeter after two or three hours' riding, before the cathedral bells rang for Prime or Terce.

The Monday after the fair was no exception, and before the eighth hour the manor-reeve from the village of Manaton had clattered up to the gatehouse of Rougemont and slid from his horse to enquire for the coroner. Though Gwyn and Thomas were in the

bare chamber above, John de Wolfe had gone across
to the castle keep to view the body of the man kicked
to death in the Saracen inn. Usually, dead bodies were
housed in a ramshackle cart-shed against the wall of
the inner ward, but this had recently been knocked
down for rebuilding. Now any stray corpses awaiting
burial were being taken to an empty cell in the castle
prison, the dismal undercroft beneath the keep, ruled
over by Stigand, the repulsive gaoler. The cadaver had
been carried up to the castle before de Wolfe had
visited the tavern – an offence in itself for which
someone would be amerced – so he was obliged to view
it before the inquest later that morning.

It was here that the gatehouse guard sent Robert
Barat, the reeve of Manaton, a village between
Moretonhampstead and Ashburton, on the south-
western edge of Dartmoor. The reeve, a tall man of
thirty-five, had hair and a flowing moustache of an
almost yellow colour that pointed to Saxon ancestry,
in spite of his Norman name. He was the headman of
the village, responsible for organising the rota of work
in the fields and acting as the link between the lord's
bailiff and steward and the common folk of the hamlet.

Robert cautiously went down the few steps from
ground level into the undercroft, a semi-basement
below the keep which acted as gaol and storehouse.
When his eyes became accustomed to the gloom after
the bright morning sun outside, he saw a low chamber
with stone pillars supporting an arched roof,
discoloured with patches of lichen and slime. The floor
was of damp beaten earth, divided across the centre
by a stone wall containing a rusted iron fence, in the
centre of which was a metal gate leading into a
passageway lined with squalid cells. The only illumi-
nation came from a pair of flickering pitch brands stuck
into iron rings on the wall and a charcoal brazier in

one of the alcoves, where the gaoler slept on a filthy straw mattress. The whole place stank of damp, mould and excrement.

As he went in, ducking his head under the low arch at the entrance, he saw a grossly fat man waddle out of the iron gate, a horn lantern in one hand. He had an almost bald head and rolls of fat hid his neck. Piggy little eyes peered from a pallid, round face, a slack mouth exposing toothless gums.

He wore a shapeless smock of dirty brown wool, which bulged over his globular stomach, covered by a thick leather apron which had many stains that looked ominously like dried blood.

For a moment, Robert Barat feared that this revolting apparition might be the coroner, but thankfully the grotesque figure was followed out of the gate by a tall, dark man dressed entirely in black and grey. The reeve walked towards him and they met halfway from the entrance.

'Are you the crowner, sir?'

De Wolfe stopped and nodded at the man, who seemed to be a respectable peasant, dressed in plain homespun and a good pair of riding boots.

'I am indeed – who are you?'

'Robert Barat, the manor-reeve from Manaton, sir. My lord's bailiff sent me urgently to find you.'

John sighed. How many times had he had a similar visit in the nine months since he had been coroner?

'Tell me the worst, Robert. Is it a beaten wife or a tavern brawl – or has another child fallen under the mill-wheel?'

'None of those things, Crowner. It's a fire in the tannery.'

John's black brows came down in a frown. It was true that fires were within a coroner's remit, but it was rare for him to be told of one in the countryside. In towns or cities it was a different matter, with the ever-present risk of a conflagration sweeping through the closely packed buildings, but out in the villages, fires were less common and certainly less dangerous, so they were rarely reported to him.

'Just a fire, Reeve? Your bailiff must be a very conscientious fellow.'

The tall, fair man shifted uneasily. 'It may be more than that, sir. The tanner is missing, too. We don't know whether he's still in the ashes or whether he has vanished. There's something odd about the fire. I'm sure it was set deliberately.'

John sensed that even this extra explanation was not the whole story, but the reeve was not forthcoming with any more details.

'Who is the lord of Manaton?' he demanded.

'Henry le Denneis, Crowner. Though he holds the manor as a tenant of the Abbot of Tavistock.'

'What makes you think that the place was fired deliberately?'

Robert Barat raised his eyes to look directly at the coroner. 'We have had trouble in the village these last few weeks, Sir John. You'll know we are just within the Royal Forest, more's the pity. Although it has always made things difficult, recently it has got worse.'

John pricked up his ears at this. Almost every day now, it seemed, some problem appeared linked to the forest.

'What sort of trouble?' he asked, as they walked back towards the daylight streaming down the steps.

'I think you had better ask our bailiff or the lord's steward,' the reeve replied cautiously. 'They know more about it, but it all goes back to the new tannery the foresters have set up near Moretonhampstead. They demanded that our small tannery should close down, so that theirs could take its trade.'

Though de Wolfe immediately appreciated this familiar situation, he pressed the other to finish his explanation.

'So what happened?'

'Our tanner, Elias Necke, refused to close down. How could he, for he and his three sons depend on it for their living. He was threatened more than once by that bastard William Lupus. Then, on Saturday night, the place burnt down and Elias went missing.'

Out in the inner ward, de Wolfe stopped and turned to the village reeve.

'I'll come out to Manaton later this morning, with my officer and clerk. I have to attend to an inquest first, but will set off before noon. If you get yourself some food and drink while your horse rests, you can set off ahead of us.'

Robert Barat respectfully touched his forehead and set off for the gatehouse, where his mare was tethered. De Wolfe called after him.

'Tell the bailiff to gather as many villagers as he can for a jury, especially those who may know anything about the fire, even if they only watched it burn.'

The coroner's trio reached the village in mid-afternoon, Manaton being about fifteen miles from the city. It was a hamlet typical of the edge of Dartmoor, nestling on the slope of a valley among wooded countryside. Above it was a hill crowned by jagged rocks, and across the vale was a smoother mound of moorland. In the distance, more granite tors stood on the skyline, like broken teeth against the sky.

The village straddled the crossing of two lanes, and as the three riders came up the eastern track from the Becka waterfalls, they could smell the fire before the remains came into sight.

'What a bloody stench!' grumbled Gwyn. 'Tanneries are bad enough at the best of times, but a burnt one . . . !'

Thomas de Peyne, jogging side-saddle behind them, almost retched as they came up to the still-smoking ruin, which lay a few hundred paces east of the village. A thin haze of blue smoke wavered in the slight breeze and the heat from the ashes caused the distant woods to shimmer in the sun. The tannery had been set in a large plot, giving room for the stone tanks set in the ground, where the skins were soaked and which added their aroma to the acrid stench of scorched leather. Their smell came from dog droppings, as the strong ferments in the excreta were used to strip the soft tissue from the cow hides and sheepskins.

As they halted on the road to look across at the desolation, a group of people came towards them from the wide green in the centre of the village, which consisted of a loose cluster of cottages set around a church and an alehouse. The first to greet them was Robert Barat, who deferentially introduced a fat, self-important man as the manor lord's bailiff, Matthew Juvenis.

'This is a bad business, Crowner. When you have finished here, my master would like to speak with you at the manor house.'

'Has there been any sign of the tanner?' asked John.

The bailiff half turned to wave a hand towards the group of villagers standing a few paces away, most of them gazing at the new arrivals as if they had two heads each. However, three tough-looking young men remained grim faced, the eldest with an arm around an older woman, whose tearful features told de Wolfe that this must be the tanner's wife and the men her sons.

'They're sure he must be in there, sir.' Matthew Juvenis pointed to the blackened ashes. 'He went from their cottage, which is just down the road, soon after midnight to see why his hound was barking – and never came back.'

'Have you looked in the ruins?' demanded Gwyn.

'They were still too hot this morning, but maybe we can probe around now.'

The coroner and his officer slid from their mounts, which were taken off by a couple of villagers to be watered and fed. Thomas let them take his pony, but he kept well back from the smoking ashes. Followed by the tanner's sons, the reeve and the bailiff, they walked to the edge of the scorched patch of grass that surrounded the remains of the tannery.

'There was a two-storeyed building here,' grunted the eldest son, a gruff fellow of about twenty-five. 'And behind it were a couple of sheds, this side of the tanks. All old wood and damned dry in this weather.'

All that remained of the three structures was a tumbled scatter of charred wood, some of the thicker beams still in pieces up to a few feet long, but split and blackened, with smoke still wreathing from the cracks. The rest was grey-black ash and charcoal, with occasional layers of fragile sheets like the leaves of a large book.

'Those are the stacks of cured hides, which were stored upstairs,' explained another of the sons.

John moved nearer, treading among the crumbling ash, which sent up clouds of fine grey dust. 'Did no one try to put the fire out?' he snapped.

'It was impossible,' said Robert Barat. 'I was one of the first here, when the eldest boy raised the alarm. He had gone to see why his father had not returned home. But already the place was like an inferno and the nearest water was the stream down in the valley, apart from a couple of small springs there.' He waved his arm vaguely behind him. 'By the time we had got enough men and buckets, the roofs had fallen in and we couldn't get within thirty paces because of the heat.'

It was still hot, as de Wolfe found as he moved nearer the larger debris in the centre. His feet became warm and, looking down, he saw that the leather of his shoes was starting to blister. He moved back to cooler ground, but a couple of the more enterprising villagers had brought up a few wide, rough planks, pulled from a fence. They laid these end to end into the hot ashes and the coroner walked carefully along them to get much nearer the centre of the fallen building. He peered around him for a few moments, hunched forward with his hands behind his back.

'Pass me a long stick or a pole, Gwyn,' he called. The Cornishman, who was itching to look for himself, relayed the command to the villagers and in a moment one ran back with a long bean-stick, filched from the vegetable plot of the nearest cottage. It was about eight feet long, and with it de Wolfe could prod well into the centre of the fallen beams. They were mostly ash and either crumbled to the touch or rolled over easily. He poked about in various parts of the smoking heap for a few minutes, then walked back and asked the reeve to put the planks on the other side of the cindered plot. This was too much for his officer to endure.

'Let me try this time, Crowner,' he pleaded.' You'll be roasted if you stay there much longer.'

With the hot sun and the radiant heat from the hot ashes, John was sweating like a pig and gladly handed his bean-pole to Gwyn. The big redhead started poking vigorously at a different part of the blackened debris and almost at once let out a cry of triumph. He had rolled over a short, thick length of burnt timber, which had probably supported the upper floor of the main building. 'There's what looks like bone under here!' he yelled over his shoulder.

Using his crooked pole like a lance, he leaned forward to carefully spear something, and a moment later backed down the plank, bearing a bleached white object dangling from the tip.

When he reached the edge of the scorched area, he laid it down gently on the grass and withdrew his bean-stick. The others crowded around, de Wolfe, the reeve and the bailiff in front. However, the sons and their mother were at the other side and a screech went up from the woman. As she burst into a torrent of wailing and weeping, a son and several good-wives clustered around and drew her gently away. What she had seen was the remains of a skull, partly blackened, but the cranium a brittle white from the incandescent heat of the fire.

John dropped to a crouch over it, almost nose to nose with Gwyn.

'Looks like a man to me, by the size and those thick ridges over the eyes,' said the coroner's officer judiciously.

'God's teeth, Gwyn, it's hardly likely to be a woman, in the circumstances,' growled de Wolfe, but his officer just grinned at the sarcasm.

'Talking of teeth, this one's got big gnashers, like a man,' he persisted. The lower jaw had fallen away, but in the upper there were still some teeth, blackened and split at the tips, but still intact.

'What's that big hole in the side?' asked Juvenis.

'Was our father struck on the head by those bastards who set the fire?' shouted the tanner's eldest son, in whom sorrow, revulsion and rage vied for priority.

Gwyn shook his untidy head. 'That's where my stick

went through, I'm afraid. The burnt bone is as soft as dried clay, owing to the heat.'

John de Wolfe stood up and ineffectually brushed the grey dust that had smeared the front of his long black tunic. 'We can never be sure that this is actually your father,' he said gently to the sons. 'Of course, there is every likelihood that it is, I'm afraid – but for all we know, it could just be one of the fire-setters, if that was what happened.'

'So where is my father, if that's not him?' demanded the eldest lad, his attitude belligerent following the tragedy that had befallen their family.

The coroner nodded.

'I agree that there is little doubt that this is your father, and for the purposes of my inquest that is what I will assume. I'm sorry, lad.'

He turned to the bailiff. 'When the ashes are cold, you must make a careful search and retrieve any more bones you can find. What's left of the poor man deserves a decent burial.'

John looked down at the pathetic skull on the grass. 'Be careful with that, it will fall to pieces if it's not handled very gently.'

The bailiff made a gesture to someone on the edge of the crowd and a fat man came forward, dressed like a farm labourer in a rough smock, a shovel in his hand.

'This is Father Amicus, our parish priest. He will take care of any remains and give them a pious send-off in the church.'

The priest looked down rather ruefully at his very secular garb.

'The stipend is poor here, Crowner. I work most of the time in the fields,' he explained. 'But I will do the right thing by poor Elias here.'

John nodded as Gwyn carefully handed the still-warm skull to Father Amicus.

'I will need it to put before the jury when I hold the inquest later this afternoon. After that, see that he is put to rest in a dignified way.'

The priest took it, then hesitated before moving away. 'There is something I should tell you. It may have some bearing on what's happened.'

De Wolfe's dark features stared at him questioningly, especially when the father steered him well away from the crowd and spoke in a low voice, his lips close to John's ear.

'One of the youngsters in the village came to me this morning, in a state of guilt. What he told me was not a confession, in the true religious sense, so I can divulge it.' He suddenly looked rebellious. 'Though maybe I would, even if it had been, given the awful thing that has happened in our village.'

'What is it you have to tell me?' asked John impatiently.

'This lad was out in the fields late last night – with a girl, if you get my meaning.'

John nodded – the meaning was clear and by no means unusual in any place or at any time.

'Just before the fire was seen, these two were lying under a hedge where the strip-fields meet the common land. They saw two men hurrying along the edge of the field from the direction of the tannery, then they went on to the common and vanished into the woods.' He pointed eastwards, where the road ran down towards the deep valley of the Bovey river in the distance.

'Did they see who they were?'

'Not a chance, Crowner. It was a half-moon, but being in an awkward situation so to speak the lad could not move or let himself be seen. And at that moment, of course, he had no reason to think that anything evil was to come to light.'

'Who is this young man?' demanded the coroner.

Father Amicus shifted from foot to foot. 'It's very difficult, sir. If the village get to know about this, there'll be hell to pay, both from his father and the girl's family. You don't need another murder on your hands, do you?'

De Wolfe considered this for a moment. By rights, everyone who had information should speak up at the inquest, but as the boy had no idea who the shadowy figures were – or even if they had anything to do with the fire – it seemed unduly harsh to expose him and the girl to the vendetta that might engulf them and their families in a closed community like Manaton.

He reassured the parish priest that he would keep the information anonymous, then arranged with Gwyn and the manor-reeve to collect as many men as he could for the inquest in a hour or two. This done, he turned to Matthew Juvenis.

'Bailiff, I need to see your lord – and you said he wishes to talk to me.'

The bailiff inclined his head. 'The manor house is just along the track, Crowner, hardly worth getting to horse again.'

They left Gwyn to organise the inquiry, but before they left de Wolfe took Thomas de Peyne aside and gave him some murmured instructions. The little clerk brightened up at being asked to assist his revered master and limped off in the direction of the church. The bailiff walked beside the coroner through the village to the crossroads and turned up the lane that ran northwards past the village green and the church. Most of the dwellings were typical of Devonshire hamlets, small tofts of cob or wattle and daub within rough-hewn wooden frames. They were separated by plots of varying size, crofts now harbouring summer vegetables and grass for goats and the milk cow. At the edge of the green was the alehouse and a small forge, and opposite stood the small stone church which in recent years had replaced an even smaller wooden structure bult in Saxon times. Alongside was a tithe barn and priest's cottage, up the path to which Thomas was pursuing the man with the skull and spade.

The coroner and bailiff continued along the lane out of the village for a few hundred yards past the last of the cottages. Three fields of oats, wheat, rye and beans stretched away from the track in narrow stripes of different greens, then came a patch of common land, beyond which was the old fortified manor, nestling under the slope rising up to Manaton Rocks.

A deep ditch ran around a large square plot, guarded by a high fence of wooden stakes. Double gates stood open to the road, and John's experienced eye told him that the manor had not feared any attack for many years, as the gates were rotten at the bottom, where rank weeds grew up against the planks. He followed the bailiff into the compound and saw in the centre a substantial manor house, built of granite moorstone, with a roof of thick slates. Stables, a byre, kitchen, brew-shed and various huts for servants half filled the rest of the space within the stockade. An older man came out of the main door, which was at the top of the steps over the undercroft.

'That's Austin, the steward,' said the bailiff. 'He'll take you to the master.'

The grey-haired steward, a slow-moving man with a long, mournful face, greeted the coroner civilly and led him inside, the bailiff vanishing somewhere behind the house. The large hall, which had a fireplace and chimney in place of a fire-pit, had doors on either side leading to extra rooms, as there was no upper floor. Knocking at one on the left, the steward stood aside and followed John into a solar, which had glass in its one window, a sign of relative affluence on the part of the owner.

The lord of the manor rose from a window seat, where he had been drinking from a pot of ale and fondling the ears of a large mastiff, which looked suspiciously at the newcomer. Henry le Denneis grasped the coroner's arm in greeting and bade him be seated on a leather-backed folding chair near by. He offered ale or wine, and while Austin brought another tankard filled from a pitcher on the table, de Wolfe took stock of his host.

Le Denneis was a burly man of about his own age, with a rugged, red face pitted with small scars. He was clean shaven and his sandy hair was flecked with grey. A loose house robe of brown wool was draped over his shoulders, revealing a short tan tunic over worsted breeches. He certainly was no dandy like Richard de Revelle, but gave the impression of being more interested in his land and crops, as was John's own elder brother.

Henry le Denneis dispensed with any small talk and came straight to the point.

'Have you found any sign of Elias Necke?' he asked in a deep voice. John told him of the finding of the skull and the assumption that it was that of the tanner. Henry shook his head sadly.

'A sad business. His whole family depended on their labours there.'

John took a deep draught of the ale, thankful to slake a thirst aggravated by the hot weather and the heat of the smouldering building.

'You must already know that the fire was almost certainly started deliberately,' he said. 'His sons told me that he went out because the dog he kept at the tannery began barking late that night. The animal was found wandering later on. And now we have evidence that two men were seen crossing the fields towards the forest at about the same time.'

Manaton's lord stood up and gazed pensively through the narrow window.

'I have been afraid that something like this might happen – but not that a villager would lose his life.'

'What's going on in the forest these days?' demanded de Wolfe harshly. 'A verderer is murdered on the high road, the Warden is attacked in his dwelling – now a man is burned to death in his own tannery, all within a week. Surely this is no coincidence?'

Le Denneis refilled both their ale-pots and sat down with a sigh.

'The tannery did not belong to Elias as a freeholder, he rented it from the Abbot of Tavistock – as indeed, I do this manor. At the Conquest, Baldwin the Sheriff took it from the Saxon Alwi – then it was handed on as a knight's fee of the Abbey to one of my forebears, who came over with William of Falaise and fought at Hastings.' He paused, as if contemplating his ancestors, then, with a jerk, brought himself back to the present tragedy.

'The foresters have always been scheming, grasping swine, as we all well know. But we had learned to live with it over the years – and a few of them, like Michael Crespin, until recently have been reasonable enough in their demands.'

'Who's he?' asked de Wolfe.

'Another of the foresters in this bailiwick. He's been around for many years and though he sees he gets his cut from whatever is going, he's not quite as bad as that arrogant bastard Lupus, who I suspect is behind much of this present trouble.'

'So what's changed recently?' demanded de Wolfe.

'Some weeks ago, they began to put the pressure on, in all sorts of ways. Their extortions became more blatant and penalties against the common folk became harsher and more frequent. Though the Attachment Courts are not supposed to pass judgement on any but minor offences against the vert, they started to mete out severe punishments instead of referring them to the forest Eyre.'

'But that's not legitimate! How can they get away with it?'

Le Denneis sighed. 'Because no one stops them any longer. To be frank, the Warden is a weak man, getting old and largely unaware of what goes on in the forest. De Bosco never comes around to see what's really happening on the ground, he's content to leave it to the verderers.'

'And what about them? Don't the verderers keep a grip on what's happening?'

The manor-lord gave a cynical laugh. 'It's not really their responsibility, they are supposed only to organise the lower courts. The only one to protest to the foresters at some of their excesses was Humphrey le Bonde. And look what happened to him – an arrow in the back!'

John gulped down the last of his ale as he considered what Henry had said.

'So are the foresters responsible for all of this hardening of the regime?' he demanded.

Le Denneis shrugged, his expression despondent.

'They are the instruments of what is happening and they certainly gain personally from the extortions. But somehow I feel there must be others more powerful behind them.'

'Do they actually perpetrate these acts themselves?'

'Some of the time, yes. They – or their thuggish grooms – beat up villeins and free men alike who they consider to have made any infringement of the forest laws or who resist some new piece of extortion. But I doubt they would personally kill a verderer or fire a tannery, even if somehow they are behind it.'

'So who may have done these wicked acts?' persisted de Wolfe.

'There are outlaws galore in these woods and moors. They're not above doing the dirty work for a purse of silver. The main villains in this area are those who follow Robert Winter.'

John nodded. That name was not unfamiliar to him. He stood up ready to leave.

'So where do you stand in all this?' he asked. 'Is there nothing you can do to protect your own villagers?'

Henry le Denneis walked him towards the door of the chamber. 'I have no say in this,' he said sadly.'I run my manor, I have my own moot court to control and discipline my people – but only in matters which are not related to the forest. The mill is mine, but not the tannery. If the foresters set up another in competition over towards Moretonhampstead, it's none of my business.'

After they had said farewell, John walked back to the centre of the village, turning over in his mind what le Denneis had said. Somehow the coroner doubted that the lord of the manor's proclaimed inability to do anything about the tannery was true, and he suspected that he may have had his palm crossed with silver to mind his own business. Yet now he would have the problem of finding other work for the sons of the destitute widow. De Wolfe also wondered what the Abbot of Tavistock would say when he heard that his tannery had been reduced to ashes, its rent so abruptly terminated.

* * *

It was still too soon for the inquest to begin, and when he reached the oblong green in the centre of Manaton de Wolfe looked for his officer and clerk to seek some food in the alehouse. Henry le Denneis had offered him a meal, but he preferred to eat with his own men. Gwyn was already standing at the door of the tavern, a quart pot in his hand.

'Here comes our little spy,' he said affectionately, waving his pot in the direction of the church of St Andrew opposite. Thomas was coming down the path from the priest's house, his limp accentuated by his haste. He crossed the grass towards them, his shapeless cloth pouch of writing materials swinging from his lowered shoulder.

'We can talk over our bread,' snapped John, leading the way into the low, dark room of the alehouse. Most of these primitive hostelries were run by widow women, who had little other means of livelihood and who were often expert brewers. This one was a fat, amiable woman, who in spite of smelling strongly of the privy brought them a couple of tasty mutton pies and a platter carrying a fresh loaf, butter and hard cheese. Thomas, who disliked both ale and cider but was forced to drink one of them by default of anything else, settled for a pint of turbid cider and the two larger men took more ale. They sat at a rough oak trestle, the only table in the room, and as they ate and drank, the clerk told his story.

'This parish priest seems better than many,' he began, his gimlet eyes flicking from one to the other. 'In spite of looking like a serf from the fields, he can read and write and doesn't seem to be a drunk. But he thought I was still an ordained priest myself and I didn't trouble to contradict him, so we got on quite well.'

The coroner had learned that Thomas could be very

useful in ferreting out information from the local clergy by pretending to be in Holy Orders. He was a highly intelligent young man, well educated and with an insatiable curiosity that made him a valuable investigator. On a number of occasions he had been able to tease out local gossip and discover confidential information that the coroner himself would never have obtained.

'It seems that Elias the tanner was a devout man and confided a lot in Father Amicus, especially during his recent troubles.'

'What recent troubles?' demanded de Wolfe.

'Several weeks ago the foresters came and announced that he must close down his tannery, as the King had established a new one near Moretonhampstead.'

'You say 'foresters' – was it more than one?'

Thomas was crestfallen. 'I didn't think to ask that, Crowner. They offered him and his sons jobs in the new place, but Elias told them to go to hell. Apart from wanting to carry on with his own business, he and the lads would have had to travel miles each day and get a pittance in return.'

'So what happened?' asked Gwyn.

'The tanner told them to clear off, but the thug who was one of the forester's henchmen tried to beat him up. The sons dragged him off and gave him a hammering, then the forester and his men rode away, yelling threats of retribution. It looks as if those threats have come home to roost.'

De Wolfe digested this, along with the last of his mutton pie.

'Did the priest tell you anything else of use?'

'He said that the foresters and woodwards have become much more aggressive of late. They used to turn a blind eye to a bit of poaching, if it was only coney or partridge or taking a few fallen branches for firewood, as long as the cottar slipped them a couple of pence now and then. But recently they have come down hard, dragging offenders off to the gaol or hauling them up before the court.'

'It seems the same story all over the forest,' mused John. 'Anything else?'

'Father Amicus reckons the outlaws are becoming more bold around here. One of them, belonging to this gang of Robert Winter, even slips into confession now and then. The priest wouldn't reveal what was said, of course, but he had the feeling that the foresters and the outlaws had agreed not to interfere with each other.'

That was about all that Thomas had to relate before it was time to go outside to hold the inquest on the pathetically scanty remains of the cremated tanner. Most of the village of Manaton was gathered on the green as a jury was assembled and the usual ritual was gone through, with the skull being paraded around carefully by Gwyn of Polruan. The inevitable conclusion was that Elias Necke had been killed unlawfully by unknown persons, but as the coroner was delivering this verdict he was incensed to hear hissing and sullen curses coming from the crowd.

At first he angrily assumed that they were disagreeing with his findings, but then he saw that their eyes were focused on someone behind him. Turning, he saw that a pair of horsemen had come up silently on the turf and were sitting behind the circle of villagers, listening to his final pronouncements.

The growling of the Manaton men increased and a few shaken fists and louder blasphemies showed the depth of feeling against the newcomers.

The leading man was bony faced and grey haired,

sitting stiffly erect on his horse. He wore no mantle over his dark green tunic, on which was the horn badge of a forester. The other man was younger, but coarse featured and unkempt. As the crowd continued to demonstrate their ill feeling, a sneer appeared on the forester's face as he looked down with obvious contempt at those who reviled him.

Father Amicus, perhaps bolder because of the protection of his cloth, pushed forward until he was almost against the stallion's nose. He had donned a rather threadbare cassock for the inquest, in place of his workman's smock. Looking up angrily at the rider, he pointed an accusing finger.

'This is partly your work, William Lupus! I don't know what role you played in the fire that killed this poor man, but Almighty God will know, be assured of that!'

The forester deliberately yanked on a rein, so that the horse's head lunged against the priest and made him stagger backwards.

'You don't know what you're talking about, Father,' he snarled. 'Stick to the cure of souls and keep your nose out of business that doesn't concern you.'

De Wolfe and Gwyn simultaneously moved towards the forester, shoving aside surly villagers to get to the priest's side.

'Are you this William Lupus I keep hearing about?' rasped the coroner.

'I am indeed – and I suppose you're this new crowner I keep hearing about,' replied the forester, with deliberate insolence in his voice.

'Keep a civil tongue in your head!' roared Gwyn. 'Else I'll pull you off that bloody horse and use your face for a door mat!'

Lupus ignored the threat and looked down at de Wolfe.

'You have no authority here, this is the King's forest.'

John looked up at the man with contempt in his dark face.

'Don't talk such arrant nonsense, fellow! I was appointed coroner by the King himself. His writ runs everywhere in England where death, injury or serious crime is suspected. Don't think for a moment that your trivial powers extend to anything other than dealing with the theft of firewood or poaching a buck or boar!'

The taut features of the forester flushed at the insult to his importance.

'You can't speak to me like that, damn you!' he shouted, his normal impassive composure shattered.

Gwyn grabbed his leg and pulled, causing Lupus to sway dangerously in his saddle. Only his feet jammed tightly in the stirrups allowed him to keep his balance.

Immediately, his ugly page Smok spurred his mare alongside Gwyn and aimed a blow at the Cornishman's head with a short staff. Gwyn dodged it easily and with a roar of anger reached up and grabbed Smok around the waist in a bear-like grip. To the cheers of the people crowded around, the ginger-haired giant hauled the page clean out of his saddle and dumped him on the ground, where he aimed a series of kicks at his buttocks and shoulders.

'That's enough for now, Gwyn, let him be,' ordered de Wolfe, after Smok had let out a tirade of yells and curses. Gwyn stepped back and the page scrambled to his feet and backed away, his piggy eyes blazing with hate.

William Lupus sat rigid, tight lipped with anger. It was something new for him to have his authority in the forest challenged so publicly.

'You'll regret this, de Wolfe!' he hissed.

'Sir John de Wolfe to you, fellow,' snapped the

coroner, with deliberate arrogance. 'You'll address a knight who carries the King's commission with proper respect! Remember that you're nothing but a common gamekeeper, even if you wear a fancy badge on your tunic.'

White faced with rage, Lupus pulled his stallion's head around to leave, but John grabbed the bit-ring to stop him.

'Wait, I've not finished with you yet. Get out of that saddle.'

The forester looked about him, ready to break away by force, but he found Gwyn on the other side, grinning up and rattling his sword in its scabbard.

With seething ill grace, he slowly dismounted and handed his reins to Henry Smok, who had got to his feet and was glowering at Gwyn, now his mortal enemy.

'Well, what is it?' he snarled to the coroner.

De Wolfe stood with his hands on his hips, his sword hilt prominently displayed as he glared at the other man.

'I've been hearing bad tidings about you, William Lupus. I don't know what your game is, but believe me, from now on you're a marked man. So tread carefully, forester! Stick to your vert and your venison and don't dare to question the powers of the King's coroner again, d'you hear me?'

In spite of his innate arrogance, Lupus's gaze dropped before the vulture-like figure of de Wolfe. He swung away and muttered threateningly under his breath, 'You've not heard the last of this.'

John caught the words and snapped at the retreating back of the forester.

'Neither has the Warden of the Forests. Nor the Chief Justiciar – nor King Richard himself, if needs be. Watch your step, William Lupus!'

This time the man made no reply, but after an angry gesture at his page he mounted up and the two cantered rapidly away, with the jeers of the villagers of Manaton ringing in their ears.

CHAPTER FIVE

In which Nesta visits Exe Island

While John de Wolfe was riding back from the edge of Dartmoor, his mistress was giving instructions to Edwin and her maids about their tasks while she was away from the inn for an hour or so.

The day was as warm as ever, so Nesta wore no mantle or shawl when she went out into Idle Lane and walked across to the top of Stepcote Hill, the steep lane that led directly down to the West Gate. When she was bustling about the tavern, she always concealed her hair inside a linen helmet, but today she had discarded the coif and allowed her auburn tresses to hang in two plaits over her breast, the ends braided into two green ribbons.

As she passed the Saracen inn, she pointedly ignored the lewd stares and suggestive comments of a pair of foreign seamen who leaned against the wall, quart pots in their fists. The slope steepened and became terraced by shallow steps leading down to the level ground inside the town wall, alongside the appropriately named church of St Mary Steps.

A stream of dirty water washed sewage down the central gutter, much of it contributed by Willem the Fleming, the oafish landlord of the Saracen, who deliberately threw a leather bucket of slops out of the door just after she had passed. Lifting the hem of her woollen kirtle with one hand, she sidestepped the flow and ignored the coarse laughter behind her. Another day she might well have turned and given the offenders a lashing with her tongue, for she could curse with the best of them, both in English and Welsh.

But today Nesta had no inclination for a shouting match. Her spirits were low and her mind troubled. All she could think about was the life that was growing deep in her womb – and the complications that it would inevitably bring. So far, no maternal urges had surfaced; she felt nothing yet for whoever it was that was lodging in her belly. Apart from the loss of her monthly flow – something that happened irregularly from time to time, anyway – she felt no different. It was only the realisation that she was going to have a child, and all the trouble that was to flow from it, which had suddenly turned her world upside down.

As she walked through the West Gate, oblivious of the pushing and jostling of porters with their huge bundles of raw wool and the yelling of drovers bringing in sheep and pigs for slaughter, Nesta thought of John and his avowed determination to stand by her. Was he really happy at her condition? Or was his love for her suppressing his concern for the burdens and aggravation that would descend upon his head once it became common knowledge that he was going to recognise a bastard? And what of the other problem, the one that had kept her awake the whole of the night, giving her pretty face the dark smudges under her eyes and the sad droop of a usually cheerful mouth?

Outside the city walls, she trudged on towards the unfinished bridge across the river, whose many arches curved up over the muddy grass of the tidal valley of the Exe before they came to an abrupt end at the main channel.

Before reaching the ramp to the bridge, Nesta turned

right, down into Frog Lane. This was a track going upstream across Exe Island, worn down by the feet of porters, pack mules and sumpter horses taking wool to the fulling mills at the upper part of the marshy island. There were dwellings dotted along the lane, mostly poor shacks of old timber which housed mill workers and those who could not afford to live within the city walls. Side tracks branched off Frog Lane towards the river, broken by leats that cut through the marsh and which filled up at every tide and when heavy rain fell on faraway Exmoor, the source of the river. Floods often carried away the flimsy huts, and every year lives were lost when spring tides or cloud-bursts deluged the island.

It was on to one of these sodden tracks that Nesta now turned, heading for a solitary shack that looked even more dilapidated than most. Perched on the edge of a deep leat, it was little more than a collection of rotting planks that leaned dangerously to one side. The roof was thatched with reeds, on which ragged grass and weeds were growing. A hurdle that had once acted as a door had crumbled to the ground and the entrance was now covered with dirty hessian from the coverings of a couple of wool bales. The Welsh woman approached hesitantly, thankful that the dry weather had at least turned the usually glutinous mud into damp earth. Having no door to knock on, she stood uncertainly for a moment outside the crude curtain. At her feet, she saw a pile of white chicken feathers, guts and a severed cockerel's head, probably from the vanquished contestant of a cock-fight, given to the old woman who lived here for her dinner.

'Lucy? Lucy, are you there?'

She called several times until a gnarled, filthy hand slowly pulled the sacking aside. A haggard face appeared, and though Nesta had seen this woman many times before her appearance still sent a tremor of fear and distaste down her spine. Bearded Lucy, as she was universally known, had wispy grey hair growing over all her face except for the upper cheeks and forehead. It surrounded her mouth and trailed over her pointed chin. Even the hooked nose was hairy, and a moustache partly concealed the toothless gums when her thin lips parted. Lucy's eyes were milky with cataracts, and with her bent back and trembling claw-like hands Nesta wondered how she had avoided being condemned for a witch.

'Who is it? I can see a woman's shape – do you want what women usually want of me?'

'It's Nesta from the Bush. I need your advice.'

The old crone shuffled farther out of the hut to peer more closely at her visitor. She was draped in shapeless, drab clothes that were little better than rags.

'Ah, the Welsh woman. The crowner's whore.'

Nesta bit her lip to stop an angry retort to the old woman's insolence – she needed Lucy today. 'Can I come in? I'll not keep you long.'

The old crone cackled, but held aside the sacking with a gnarled hand.

'I suppose you want what they all want, my girl.'

With distaste, but driven by necessity, Nesta pulled her skirts closer and edged sideways past the old woman into the dim interior of the shack, which was little bigger than her pigsty back at the Bush. It smelt about the same, too, and she was thankful for the gloom, such that the coarser details of the dwelling were obscured. She skirted a small fire-pit on raised clay in the middle of the floor, filled with dead ashes and reluctantly lowered herself on to a small stool which, apart from a rickety table, seemed to be the only furnishing other than a long box like a coffin against the far wall. Bundles of dried herbs hung from the walls and a perilously slanted shelf held a few pots and pans.

'So tell me about it, Welsh woman,' said Lucy, in her high-pitched, quavering voice. She aimed a blow at a mangy grey cat that sat on the long box, which had a few grubby blankets spread on top and obviously served as the old woman's bed. The cat squealed maliciously and fled through the door, letting Lucy sit down, her joints creaking almost audibly as she lowered herself slowly on to the box.

'I think I am with child,' said Nesta, in a low voice.

'You don't need to come here to discover if you're with child,' said the hag, tartly. 'A score of wives inside the town walls could tell you that. So you must think that I can help you to get rid of it, eh?'

Nesta flushed with sudden shame, but stuck doggedly to her mission.

'That all depends,' she replied in muted tones.

Lucy's sparse eyebrows rose on her lined, dirty forehead.

'That makes a change! On what can such a dangerous matter depend?'

'I wish to know for how long I have been pregnant.'

The crone nodded knowingly. 'Ah, I see! You're not sure who the father might be, is that it?'

Nesta was unable to meet the old woman's clouded eyes, but bobbed her head briefly. Bearded Lucy hauled herself painfully to her feet and held out a shaky hand, the finger joints knobbled like pebbles.

'Let's have a look at you, then, my girl. Open up that kirtle, I need to look at your dugs.'

Reluctantly, Nesta unlaced the front of her bodice and shrugged it off one shoulder. In anticipation of what she would have to endure, she had left off her thin under-chemise, so one of her ample breasts was exposed. The old woman brought her head so close that her hooked nose was almost touching the skin, to give her poor sight the best advantage. With one of her claw-like hands, she grabbed the breast and squeezed, testing the firmness of the gland.

'Is it tender yet, girl?' she demanded. Nesta flinched as the rough massage continued, but murmured, 'A little tense, but not tender.'

Lucy shifted the open bodice to look at the other side, peering closely at the nipple, then pulled the woman's neckline together and stepped back.

'The teats are darkening a little,' she muttered. 'You've not had children before?'

Nesta shook her head and pulled at the lacing to cover up her exposed skin. The hag turned and indicated the grimy blankets covering the box-bed.

'Lay yourself down there and we'll find what's to be found.'

With even greater reluctance, Nesta sat on the bed and swung her legs up on the end. She was already regretting the impulse that had driven her to Exe Island.

'Lie back, this won't take long.'

Lucy hovered over the innkeeper like some huge dishevelled bat, feeling her belly at length through the thin material of her summer kirtle. Then, like the midwife in Priest Street, she examined Nesta internally, a process that the tavern-keeper endured with gritted teeth and screwed-up eyes. In an age when cleanliness and hygiene were usually thought irrelevant, she was unusually fastidious. Nesta washed almost every day and, in the fashion of the Welsh, even cleaned her teeth with the chewed end of a hazel twig dipped in wood ash. It was anathema to have to lie on a flea-infested blanket and have the grimed fingers of an old woman, who had probably not washed since old King Henry was on the throne, pushed into her most private parts.

But she endured it, as she had little choice if she was to learn what she urgently needed to know. Bearded Lucy, still muttering to herself, rummaged about inside her with one hand, the other digging into Nesta's belly just above her crotch. Like all women, the innkeeper wore no underclothing around her hips, so the hag needed only to reach up under her skirt.

After a few moments Lucy grunted and withdrew her hand, wiping it casually on the sleeve of the rags she wore.

'You are with child, girl, no doubt of that.'

Nesta pulled down the hem of her kirtle and swung her legs to the floor, rising thankfully from the grubby bed.

'But for how long?' she persisted.

The old woman rubbed her fingers over her wispy beard, a gesture that irrelevantly reminded Nesta of Gwyn of Polruan.

'About three months, that's as near as I can tell you. These things are never exact.'

A cold hand reached into Nesta's chest and seized her heart. This was the news she dreaded, though it was half expected.

'So it could be before early April?'

Lucy wagged her grotesque head. 'It's now past mid-June, so they tell me – so certainly you conceived not later than the middle or end of March. You may be able to tell that better than me, if you can remember when you rode the tiger around that time!' She cackled crudely.

Nesta ignored her and sank down on to the stool, which at least was wooden and free from obvious filth.

'There can be no mistake?'

'Yes, within a couple of weeks, either way. But if your crowner friend wasn't rogering you for a month or two before mid-April, then he's not the father.' She had astutely guessed Nesta's problem.

The younger woman stared blankly at the floor for a few moments.

'I need to be free of it, God help me,' she said in a hollow voice.

Bearded Lucy stood over her, hands on hips.

'God can't help you, dear – and I'm not sure I can, though so many women think otherwise.'

Nesta raised her head slowly and her eyes roved over the bunches of dried vegetation hanging around the walls. 'Some of them think rightly. Will you try for me? I have money I can give you.'

'I can be hanged for that, Welsh woman. Even for trying.'

'But will you do it? I'm desperate, I cannot have this child. Not for my sake, but for that of a good man.'

The old crone considered for a moment. 'He came here once, that man of yours. He was not unkind, like some who would see me hanged or worse.'

'Then you'll do it?' Nesta's voice carried the eagerness of desperation.

Lucy raised her crippled hand.

'Wait. I'm not doing anything. The days when I could put a sliver of slippery elm into the neck of a womb have long gone. With these poor fingers and my failing sight, I'd as like kill you as cure you.'

Crestfallen, Nesta looked at her pathetically.

'But you can help me some way? Give me some potion or drug?'

Sighing, the old woman shuffled over to her shelf and took down a small earthenware pot.

'You can try these, but never say that I am trying to procure a miscarriage for you. I am only trying to bring back your monthly courses, understand?'

Nesta nodded mutely as Lucy shook out from the pot half a dozen irregular brown lumps, the size of beans.

'What are they? ' she asked in a lacklustre voice.

'A mixture of my own – just to bring on your flow, mind,' she warned again. 'Only herbs – parsley, tansy, pennyroyal, laburnum, rue and hellebore.' She dropped the crude pills into Nesta's hand and closed her fingers over them. 'I make no promise that they will work. You will feel ill after you take them and no doubt spend half the day in the privy. If you begin to bleed, then probably God would have willed it anyway. And if you bleed too much, call an apothecary – but whatever you do, never mention my name. Though my life here is hardly worth living, I prefer not to end it dangling from a gallows!'

In the late afternoon of that day, John de Wolfe was relaxing as best he could before his own cold fireplace. He had not long arrived back from Manaton and, ignoring Matilda's displeasure, was sprawled in one of the monk's chairs with a quart of ale in one hand, the other resting on Brutus's head. His long legs were stretched out in front of him, his feet enjoying their freedom after a day in tight riding boots. His wife's tut-tutting was due to his lounging in his black woollen hose without shoes, especially as one big toe protruded through a hole in the foot.

'You still behave like a rough soldier, John!' she scolded, sitting opposite him in tight-lipped disapproval. 'Why can't you comport yourself like a knight and a gentleman? What would anyone think if they came in now?'

He rolled up his eyes in silent exasperation at her eternal snobbishness.

'I'll do what I like in my own house, wife,' he grunted. 'And who in hell is likely to come calling here on a hot Monday afternoon, eh?'

Promptly, as if the fates were conspiring against him,

there was a loud rapping on the front door. Mary was cleaning his boots in the vestibule and answered straight away, then put her head around the screens to announce visitors.

'It's Lord Guy Ferrars – and some other nobles,' she proclaimed in a somewhat awed voice. Matilda jumped to her feet as if struck by lightning, and hurriedly began to straighten the wimple at her throat and pat down her kirtle.

'Put on your shoes, at once!' she hissed, as John hauled himself from the chair and groped for his house slippers. A moment later, Mary had stood aside for three men to stride past her into the hall.

'De Wolfe, forgive us for intruding unannounced,' boomed the leading man, who sounded as if he was in no way seeking such forgiveness. A powerful, arrogant fellow, some years older than John, Guy Ferrars was one of the major landowners in Devon – and indeed had manors in half a dozen other counties. De Wolfe knew him slightly and disliked him for an overbearing, ruthless baron, whose only saving grace was that he had been a good soldier and a loyal supporter of King Richard.

Behind him was Sir Reginald de Courcy, a lesser light but still an important member of the county elite, with manors at Shillingford and Clyst St George, as well as property outside Devon. The third man was also known to the coroner by sight, being Sir Nicholas de Molis, whose honour included a number of manors along the eastern edge of Dartmoor. Rapidly gathering his wits together after this sudden invasion, John ushered the visitors to the long table, as there were too few chairs at the hearth.

'Mary, wine and some wafers or whatever you have for our guests,' he commanded, pulling out the benches on either side of the table. Matilda, her sallow face flushed with mixed pride, excitement and shame at her husband's dishevelled appearance, stopped bobbing her head and knee and rushed after their cook-maid to accelerate the arrival of refreshments.

John took the chair at the end of the table, with Reginald de Courcy on his left and the other pair to his right. Lord Ferrars began without any preamble, his harsh voice echoing in the bare hall.

'We have just come from the castle, where we attended upon your dear brother-in-law.' The tone was unambiguously sarcastic, and John was glad that Matilda was out of the room. The speaker was a large, florid man with a mop of brown hair and a full moustache, both flecked with grey. He wore a long yellow tunic, slit back and front for riding, with a light surcoat of green linen on top. The last time the coroner had seen him he had had a full beard, but this was now gone. That had been a sad occasion, as the fiancé of Ferrar's son Hugh had been found dead in an Exeter churchyard – and she had been the daughter of Reginald de Courcy.

'Our meeting was less than satisfactory, de Wolfe,' continued Ferrars. 'We went as a deputation of landowners to protest at various happenings in the Royal Forest, but received little satisfaction.'

'None at all, to be frank!' snapped the third man, Nicholas de Molis. 'De Revelle was his usual mealy-mouthed self, full of evasions and excuses.'

Mary bustled back with a tray full of savoury tarts and fresh-baked pastry wafers, together with a large jug of wine. Matilda was close behind and de Molis, a burly man with a face like a bull-dog, snapped his mouth shut on any further condemnation of her brother. She went to a chest against the far wall and took out some goblets of thick Flemish glass, only brought out on special occasions.

When she had poured wine for them all, simpering and nodding at these county luminaries who had graced her house, she retired to one of the fireside chairs. Only the linen cover-chief over her head stopped her ears from flapping, determined as she was to hear every word of their conversation. Guy Ferrars looked across at her in irritation, but he could hardly evict the woman from her own hall. He turned back to the coroner.

'I know you have been involved twice within the past few days on some of these matters, de Wolfe. But our complaints go back much farther.'

'And concern many more than we three,' said de Courcy, speaking for the first time. 'We are but a deputation – the Abbot of Tavistock was to have joined us today, but he is indisposed.'

John knew that Tavistock Abbey was a major land-holder in Devon and anything that interfered with its business would be greatly resented. In fact, he had learned only today that the burned-out tannery in Manaton had belonged to them.

'So what can I do for you in this situation?' he asked cautiously.

De Courcy, a thin, gaunt man with a completely bald head and a thin rim of grey beard running around his jaw, thumped the table with his fist.

'We know you for a man of honour and one totally loyal to the King. There seems to be a campaign afoot to greatly increase the royal revenues from the forest at our expense.'

'Though I wonder how much of this extra profit ever gets to the treasure chest in Winchester,' added Nicholas de Molis, with a look over his shoulder at the woman listening avidly across the room. For once, Matilda took the hint, murmured something about fetching more wine and left the hall. A few moments later, John's keen ears heard the solar door open and close, and guessed that she was listening through the slit high up on one side of the chimney breast.

By now, the three visitors were in full flow, their indignation more potent than the wine in loosening their tongues. 'More and more of the breweries, forges and tanneries in the forest are being taken over by the bloody foresters,' ranted Guy Ferrars. 'I'm losing revenue hand over fist – and when my men protest, they are told that the forest law allows this and there is nothing that we can do to stop it.'

Nicholas de Molis took up the complaint. 'They are enforcing the rules of venison and vert even more strictly than before. I make no complaint about punishing a man who hunts down a stag or wild boar, but for years many a blind eye has been turned to some peasant who traps a coney or puts an arrow in a fox that's been stealing his chickens. Now they treat them as if they are murderers and the families are thrown on the parish for us to support.'

De Wolfe looked from one to the other, as de Courcy completed their protests.

'The Warden seems unwilling or unable to do anything – perhaps we need a different man. Though when I put this to de Bosco, he said that neither he nor any other successor who was appointed could control the foresters.'

Guy Ferrars swallowed some wine, then glared at the coroner.

'What do you read into all this, de Wolfe? The damned sheriff seems indifferent to the problem, but with his history I suspect that he may be involved.'

John, wondering what his wife was making of all this upstairs, gave a guarded reply. 'Something is certainly going on in the forest, but I can't yet make out what it is – or who is behind it. There seems to be a plot to unseat the Warden and I suspect that whoever wants to take his place is fostering trouble to prove that de Bosco is incompetent.'

De Courcy nodded his shiny, hairless head in agreement. 'That crossed my mind, de Wolfe. But who in hell wants a lousy, thankless job like that?'

The four men looked at each other, then Ferrars spoke.

'The same man who hung on to the wardenship of the Stannaries when everyone tried to unseat him . . . Richard de Revelle. But why?'

The other three knew all about the sheriff's dalliance with Prince John's cause and his close brush with accusations of treachery the previous year.

'De Revelle is an expert at embezzlement himself,' said de Wolfe. 'But I fail to see what he could gain from the forests – the foresters have a monopoly on extortion there.'

No one had any better suggestions, but they worried away at the worsening situation for some time, cataloguing the misdeeds of the foresters and their loutish servants.

'This man William Lupus seems to be the most active and obnoxious of them all,' said John, relating the scene at Manaton that very morning.

'Yet I can't see him putting an arrow into the back of a verderer,' objected de Courcy. 'That seems more the style of one of these bands of outlaws. We all know the edge of Dartmoor is infested with them, as well as farther afield in the east of the county.'

'Loyal as I am to our King, I wish he would devote more attention to what goes on in England,' muttered Guy Ferrars, which was the nearest he would ever get to treason, thought de Wolfe.

'Yet Hubert Walter speaks for him in most matters. Is he aware of what is going on?' asked Nicholas de Molis.

'He's in a difficult position,' replied Ferrars, who was nearest to the levers of power in the land and often visited London and Winchester. 'I have spoken to him about this and he says that every penny is needed for Richard's undoubtedly expensive campaigns against the French, so it would be difficult to curb powers in the forest, which means revenue.'

'But that revenue never reaches Winchester,' snapped de Courcy. 'Filling the pockets of foresters is not what we need here.'

Eventually they ran out of new grievances and fell silent. John rounded off the meeting with a question about how to proceed.

'If it gets any worse, then some action must be taken. I have the ear of the Chief Justiciar, as I knew him well in Palestine. If necessary, I will travel to meet him, be it in Canterbury, London or Winchester, and place the case squarely before him. If we can show that these outlaws are colluding with the forest officers, then he must be persuaded to send troops against them.'

'The sheriff will never do that of his own volition,' grumbled Guy Ferrars. 'But I agree that we arouse Hubert Walter's interest if things do not improve.'

The meeting broke up and the three barons left, with John promising to speak sternly to the sheriff about their misgivings. When the heavy oak door had swung shut behind them, John went back to his chair and waited for Matilda to appear. He heard the solar door close and soon she came back into the hall. He wondered whether she would be angered at hearing the remarks about her brother – or chastened by the knowledge that the powerful men she admired were contemptuous of him. For a moment, he was uncertain which it would be, as she walked silently to her chair opposite him and sat down.

'Is he going to be in trouble again, John?' she asked in a low voice.

There had been times when John had relished any opportunity to denigrate his brother-in-law's reputation, but the grief that overcame his wife at the several falls from grace that Richard had suffered had taken away any potential pleasure in repeating the process.

'I don't know, wife,' he replied sadly. 'He seems to have replaced the dead verderer with remarkable haste and his obstinate refusal to take any action against these misdeeds in the forest is suspicious.'

'Is it the John affair all over again?' she asked dully, meaning the Count of Mortain, not her husband.

De Wolfe shrugged, turning up his hands in mystification. 'Again, I don't know. I can't see the connection, so let's hope it's just one of Richard's schemes to fill his purse – and nothing more sinister.'

But privately he doubted it, and as much as living with Matilda irked him he had no wish to make her life more miserable as regarded her brother's transgressions.

After their supper, at which Matilda was markedly subdued, she announced that she was going over to the nearby cathedral. The day's offices were over until midnight matins, so John presumed she was going to spend time on her knees, probably praying that her brother would keep out of further trouble.

After the complaints that the county barons had brought to him, de Wolfe felt that he had better make the effort to get some sense from his brother-in-law, so in the warmth of the evening he strode up to Rougemont. The continued dry weather had turned the mud of the streets into dust, except where the effluent ran down the central gutters – but the downside was the increase in the stink from the ubiquitous refuse. The burgesses had recently invested in an extra soil-cart, which trundled around the city picking up the larger piles of garbage, dead dogs and putrefying offal, but several weeks of heat had so increased the stench of the city that even John's insensitive nose began to notice it.

He wondered whether it might not be a good idea to take himself off out of the city for a few days, down to the healthier air of his family home at Stoke-in-Teignhead near the coast. But Matilda would never come, being flagrantly disdainful of his widowed mother, who was part Welsh, part Cornish. In his wife's eyes, Celts were worse than Saxons, almost on a level with Moors and Barbary apes. John thought that if she had fully realised he had so much native blood, she would never have married him – and now he wished he had impressed this on her before they went to the altar. Ruefully, these thoughts passed through his mind as he climbed the slope to the castle gate – if he had stayed unmarried, this present crisis that loomed over Nesta's pregnancy would never have arisen.

He called in at his room high above the guard chamber, but neither Thomas nor Gwyn was there. The clerk often stayed late, labouring over the rolls needed for inquests or making copies for the King's justices – and Gwyn sometimes slept there when late drinking or gaming prevented him from going home to St Sidwell's after the city gates closed at curfew. Coming down again, John crossed the inner ward, the red stone of the battlements glowing almost gold in the rays of the setting sun. It was quiet there, only a few off-duty soldiers squatting to play dice or sprawled on their backs fast asleep. Some children played outside the huts against the far wall, their mothers gossiping at the doors or preparing food for a late meal.

He loped across to the steps to the keep, his long

grey tunic flapping around his calves and his thick black hair bobbing against the back of his neck. Inside, the main hall was noisy with squires, captains and clerks either finishing their evening meal or lounging at the trestle tables with jars of ale and cider. De Wolfe looked around to see if Ralph Morin, the castle constable, was there, or his sergeant Gabriel, but there was no sign of them. A few other men waved or called out a greeting, some inviting him to join them for a drink, but he made for the side of the hall where a bored man-at-arms lounged at the sheriff's door.

John sometimes wondered why Richard insisted on having a full-time guard deep inside his own castle, but knowing of the multitude of people who had cause to dislike or even detest de Revelle, he admitted that it was probably a wise precaution. The sentinel pulled himself up sharply when he saw the coroner approach and raised a hand to his basin-shaped helmet in salute.

'Sheriff's got a visitor, Crowner,' he advised.

John scowled. He had wanted to get Richard alone, to avoid too much embarrassment about his possible dubious dealings in the forest – though there were other possible reasons for embarrassment when walking in on the sheriff unannounced, as he had discovered several times before.

'Is it a man or a woman?' he demanded, with these last thoughts in mind.

'It's the new verderer, Sir John. Don't recall his name.'

John grunted and turned the heavy iron ring on the door. Inside, his brother-in-law was seated behind his wide work-table, dressed for the warm weather in his usual dandified fashion, with an open surcoat of blue velvet over a long shirt of white linen, cinched at the waist with a wide belt of fine leather. Under the table, John could see fine cream hose ending in shoes with ridiculously curved, pointed toes, a recent fad imported from France, enemies of England though they might be.

A pewter wine cup stood next to his hand and, on the other side of the table, the new verderer sat on a stool with similar refreshment.

Philip de Strete was known only by sight to the coroner, being a rather plump man of average build, nearing thirty years of age. He had ginger hair and a matching moustache of the same colour as Gwyn's, but of much more modest proportions. All that John knew about him was that he had a small manor near Plymouth, had not been to the Crusades, but had fought in some of the French campaigns without any particular distinction.

Richard looked up in annoyance, his usual expression when de Wolfe appeared. De Strete jumped to his feet as the sheriff somewhat reluctantly introduced him and made considerable play of expressing his honour and delight at meeting the coroner. De Wolfe felt that he was insincere and distrusted him from the start, especially as Philip's eyes always seemed to evade direct contact with his.

'De Strete's appointment is to be confirmed at the Shire Court tomorrow,' announced de Revelle.

'How can that be? The time has been far too short to get approval from the King or his Justiciar,' objected John.

The sheriff shrugged impatiently. 'Then it is to be made conditional on that consent being granted. It's a mere formality. Hubert Walter will approve on the King's behalf. I'm sure the Lionheart has not the slightest interest in who is appointed a verderer in a remote county.'

'What's the hurry?' demanded John.

'The next Attachment Court is to be held in a week's

time. There are cases to be heard. We can't wait weeks or months for messengers to go scurrying around the country or even to France.'

De Wolfe sat heavily on the corner of Richard's table, to the owner's annoyance.

'As most of the cases will merely be referred to the Forest Eyre, there can be no urgency. That court sits only every third year!'

Whenever something became awkward, the sheriff managed to change the subject.

'Was there something you wanted, John?' he said pointedly.

'It's about this very matter. You had a deputation today from some of the most influential barons in this area.'

De Revelle's narrow face became wary and his eyes flicked between John and the new verderer. 'How did you know that?'

'Because they came to see me directly afterwards, to express their dissatisfaction. They want some explanations – and some action.'

Richard suddenly stood up to dismiss the new verderer.

'I'll see you at the Shire Hall tomorrow morning, Philip. There are matters I need to discuss with the coroner.'

He almost hustled de Strete from the chamber, thrusting him out into the hall and closing the door behind him.

'That was indiscreet, John, in front of a new forest official,' he snapped.

De Wolfe sat unbidden on the stool that the verderer had so abruptly vacated. He took up the half-full wine cup, threw the dregs into the rushes on the floor and refilled it from the jug that stood on Richard's table.

'Why? Is there something he shouldn't hear about?'

he asked with sarcastic innocence. 'Or might he have said something you didn't wish me to hear?'

'Of course not!' blustered Richard. 'Now, what is you want to say to me?'

'Something's going on in the forest and I want to get to the bottom of it. Guy Ferrars and his friends are becoming restive – they're losing money and they don't like it. And when Lord Ferrars is unhappy, people in his vicinity are apt to become equally miserable. That might include you, brother-in-law.'

'I don't know what you mean,' said de Revelle. 'Why should you think I have any interest in the matter?'

'I know you of old, Richard! You've sailed very near the wind more than once and you can't afford another whiff of scandal. Why are you so insistent that I should not investigate these problems in the Royal Forest?'

'Because you have no authority there, in spite of what you say. The whole point of the forest laws is that they are outwith the common law.'

'Only for misdeeds that affect forest matters, Richard. How often do I need to tell you? You don't seem to want to listen and that makes me suspicious.'

The sheriff's face reddened, whether with anger or guilt John couldn't decide. 'You're a soldier, not a lawyer! Don't take it upon yourself to interpret the law. The forest laws have been in place since Saxon times, whilst your new-fangled coroner's play-acting is not yet a year old.'

John put down his empty cup with a bang.

'Very well, if you want to dispute my authority, I'll ride to Winchester and see the Justiciar. I'll bring back a document confirming my authority to investigate deaths, injury, fires and the rest of it, anywhere I please – or rather where the King pleases.'

He stood up and towered over the seated sheriff like a bird of prey.

'And whilst I'm there, I'll ask him for a Commission to investigate the state of the Royal Forest of Dartmoor. A coroner can be commissioned to undertake any task in the kingdom, if the monarch or his ministers so desire.'

Under direct threat, de Revelle held up a placatory hand.

'Sit down, John, sit down! Let's not fight over this. You're making such an issue of a few coincidences.'

'Coincidences? A verderer shot in the back, the Warden half killed, a tanner burned to death and foresters up to even more of their tricks than usual?'

Richard reached over to pour more wine for the coroner, as if this would solve the problem.

'Calm down, John! These issues amount to very little in the great scheme of things. There are more important problems every day.'

'Tell that to the widow of the dead tanner – or the murdered verderer! Convince me that you have no part in this, Richard. Why have you so rapidly forced this de Strete fellow into the verderer's post – he's a close neighbour of yours at Revelstoke, is he not?'

He threw down his drink and continued his tirade unabated.

'And who is trying to unseat the Warden of the Forests – either by anonymous notes or clubbing him on the head? And why does rumour say that you would like to be the Warden in his stead? You have enough responsibilities now, being sheriff, Warden of the Stannaries and God knows what else. Why seek another unpaid job? It's not like you, is it?'

He thumped the table with his fist. 'There's a common factor in all this and I'm going to find it, Richard. And God help you if I discover that you're involved in some underhand scheming once again. I thought you would have learned your lesson by now!'

He stalked out, leaving his brother-in-law torn between anger and anxiety.

The next morning, John sat glumly in the Shire Hall waiting for the start of the regular County Court, a forum where a mixture of criminal and civil cases were mixed with petitions and a whole range of administrative affairs related to the running of the county of Devon.

Unable to sleep well, he had arrived too early and now sat contemplating the seemingly intractable problems in his personal life. The previous evening, after leaving the sheriff, he had gone down to the Bush, but it was not a successful visit. Nesta had been quiet and withdrawn and all his efforts to cheer her had failed. When he had asked her casually whether she had been out that day, Nesta had suddenly burst into tears and scrambled up to her room in the loft, intriguing many of the patrons, especially when they saw the King's coroner follow her up the ladder. Her door was barred, and, in spite of his hissed demands to be let in, she continued to sob quietly on the other side. Defeated, he went back down, finished his ale and eventually, in gloomy confusion, trudged home, where he found Matilda back from her devotions. She was equally silent, though he sensed that for once her disgruntlement was not directed at him.

He was drawn out of his reverie by the arrival of the participants for the court hearings and tried to raise some interest in the proceedings.

On a low dais in the bare hall the sheriff sat centre-stage in a large chair, flanked by his chaplain, the rotund Brother Rufus on one side and the coroner on the other. They sat on the ends of two benches, which also carried Hugh de Relaga, one of the portreeves representing the burgesses of the city, John de Alençon, the Archdeacon of Exeter, on behalf of the cathedral, and several guildmasters and burgesses from Tavistock, Barnstaple and other towns in the county. Behind them, one man from each Hundred, the smaller divisions of the county, sat as a jury. The cases ranging from applications for fairs and licences for trading to allegations of assault and theft, were dealt with rapidly.

John was always doing his best to divert serious crimes into the royal courts, but many were still dealt with at this ancient county level. Two men were summarily sent to be hanged for confessed robbery with violence, in spite of John's protests that they should be remanded to appear before the next Commissioners of Gaol Delivery, who were due to visit Exeter within a few months. The full majesty of the King's Justices in Eyre had been in the city only a matter of weeks earlier and were unlikely to return for a couple of years, which gave the sheriff and burgesses a good excuse to ignore John's argument that serious cases should only be handled by the royal courts.

As coroner – the 'Keeper of the Pleas of the Crown' – he did his best to implement Hubert Walter's edict of the previous autumn, but it was hard work pushing against the old traditions, especially when the sheriff was violently opposed to anything that reduced his jurisdiction and his opportunity to extract more money from the population.

John had stood to present several cases already, fed to him by his clerk Thomas, who sat among the gaggle of secretaries and scribes on the benches at the back of the platform. When an approver or appealer was called, Thomas appeared behind de Wolfe and thrust a parchment into his hand. As he could not read, the little clerk whispered the content into his ear, a face-saving stratagem that was wasted on the literate sheriff, who watched the charade with a sardonic grin.

The main business of the court lasted two hours and, at the end, Philip de Strete was presented and stood smirking before the dais as the sheriff browbeat the court into unquestioning approval of his appointment as verderer. As John had no official standing in this matter, there was nothing he could say, even if he had had any grounds for objecting to the nomination. When the proceedings broke up for noon-time dinner, de Wolfe walked across the inner ward with his good friend, Archdeacon John de Alençon. The lean, ascetic clergyman, one of the senior canons of the cathedral chapter, asked him about Thomas de Peyne, his own nephew.

'Is he proving satisfactory, John? The poor fellow has had a rough time these past few months.'

De Wolfe gave a rare lopsided grin. 'Being almost hanged for murder after failing to kill himself was certainly a test for his soul! But he is an excellent clerk. His prowess with a quill pen is equalled only by his intelligence.'

The archdeacon nodded in approval . 'He certainly seems more cheerful these days. Though I have little hope to offer him of a return to Holy Office in the near future.'

The coroner grunted his agreement. 'I suspect he would have to move to some place far distant from either Winchester or Exeter. I know an influential churchman in Wales, Gerald de Barri, the Archdeacon of Brecon, who might help him. But to be honest, I am loath to lose Thomas, at least until I know that I could get someone half as reliable to replace him.'

The priest turned to de Wolfe, a smile lighting up his thin, lined face. 'No, John, I don't believe that such selfish motives would ever impede you, if you thought you could help my luckless nephew. Gerald de Barri, you say? Giraldus Cambrensis, a famous man in his own way, though a thorn in the flesh of Canterbury and even the Pope. No wonder you are friends, you are two peas from the same pod!'

They walked on in companionable silence, two figures both dressed sombrely, the one in a black cassock, the other in his grey tunic, until the archdeacon brought up a new subject.

'I hear there is trouble in the forest – that verderer reminded me that one of the parish priests has voiced his concerns to me.'

'Would that happen to be Father Amicus from Manaton?'

'It was indeed – when he brought his tithe money in yesterday, he told me about the dead tanner and of the other problems in the forests.'

De Alencon stopped walking and ran a hand through his crinkled grey hair. He turned a worried face to the coroner.

'I have heard through channels that need not be named that the old trouble may be stirring again, and I cannot but wonder if this unrest in the forest is related.'

De Wolfe rubbed the black stubble on his face.

'You mean the old trouble involving our royal name-sake? How can that be, what could he gain from it?'

They began walking again, down Castle Hill towards the high street.

'More money, more influence, disruption of the existing order,' replied the priest. John did not ask him where he had heard the rumour – it was a poorly kept secret that Bishop Henry Marshal, in common with some other senior churchmen, had been sympathetic to Prince John's abortive rebellion when King Richard was imprisoned in Germany and not expected to survive. They walked on for a few more yards, then the archdeacon spoke again.

'My duties these days are more administrative than pastoral or devotional,' he said rather bitterly. 'I meet many other priests from the diocese and hear many scraps of gossip and chatter.'

De Wolfe waited patiently; he sensed that his friend was gathering himself to tell him something that the secretive ecclesiastical community would rather keep to itself.

'I heard a rumour not only that certain senior colleagues were dabbling again in sedition, but that some particular priest was actively engaged in furthering that ambition.'

They took a few more strides, which brought them into the hubbub of the main street, before the coroner pursued the matter.

'Have you any idea as to his identity? You are not talking about one of the prime movers, I assume?'

He meant the bishop himself, but kept to their coded way of talking.

'No, no, he will keep a low profile until things develop much further, having had his knuckles rapped last time. This priest seems to be some kind of go-between, a buffer to insulate the leading lights from any dirty work that may be needed.'

'And you have no idea who or where he is?'

John de Alençon shook his tonsured head. 'Only that he is not from Exeter, but probably farther west. I have no means of improving on that hint – I had it second hand from someone whose informant unwisely let slip a few words and immediately regretted it.'

As they shouldered their way through the crowded street, with stall-holders and shop men advertising their wares and hawkers shaking trays at them, John once again realised what a dilemma men like himself and the archdeacon faced. They were devoted to the King, both from a sense of loyalty to their monarch and because of his powerful personality and courage. Yet competing reluctantly with these feelings of fidelity was the common-sense realisation that Richard Coeur-de-Lion was not the best head of state as far as England was concerned. In the past six years he had spent a bare four months of his reign in the country; he seemed unwilling ever to return; and he had never even bothered to learn to speak English. His interest in the country seemed confined to how much money he could squeeze from its inhabitants; time and again he had imposed crushing taxes and additional demands on religious houses and nobles alike. He and his Curia Regis strove to raise extra funds for his French wars, on top of the great debt still owing on his ransom to Emperor Henry of Germany. Richard auctioned titles and offices of state to the highest bidder and brazenly sold charters to towns and cities. He was once reputed to have said that he would have sold London itself if he could have found a rich enough buyer!

In contrast to Richard and his careless and profligate manner, his brother appeared to many to be a more practical and prudent caretaker of the island of Britain. Even the rather blinkered John de Wolfe could appreciate that to many the accession of the Count of Mortain, as John was also known, might be advantageous to the country. But never would men like de Wolfe accept this while the Lionheart lived, especially as John's personality was so unattractive. Mean spirited, conceited and arrogant, the younger brother was personally highly unpopular. Having lived for so long in the shadow of his illustrious royal brother, John was disgruntled and jealous.

In his father's time he had almost no territory of his own, being dubbed 'John Lackland', but when sent by Henry II to prove himself by governing the new conquest of Ireland, his rule was such a disaster that he had to be recalled in ignominy. When Richard came to the throne, he was excessively generous to John and gave him six counties for himself, including Devon and Cornwall – and was repaid with treachery when he was imprisoned on the Continent. Even after his release, when he rapidly crushed John's rebellion, Richard was far too forgiving – instead of hanging his brother, he pardoned him and even restored some of his forfeited lands. Now, thought John sourly, the King's compassion was being thrown back in his face, if the prince was once more seeking the throne. But how could this be related to the troubles in the forest?

De Wolfe's cogitations had brought them to Martin's Lane, where the archdeacon left him at his front door.

'I have a suggestion, John,' said the canon, as they parted. 'I know you think highly of my nephew's artfulness. You have told me before that he is adept at worming his way into the confidence of priests, so why not send Thomas out of the city to seek better information?'

He gave the coroner a broad wink with one of his lively blue eyes and strode away, his long cassock swirling as he crossed the cathedral Close.

ChAPTER SIX

*In which both Thomas and Gwyn
leave the city*

The coroner spent the afternoon examining a corpse
discovered in the Shitbrook, a foul stream just outside
the city wall which ran from St Sidwell's down to the
river. It was aptly named, for it served as one of Exeter's
main sewers, the effluent that oozed down many of the
streets eventually seeping to the little valley that carried
the brook. After heavy rain, it tended to cleanse itself,
but most of the time it was a stinking channel infested
with rats. Often a dead dog or cat lay in its ordure, but
today a resident of Magdalene Street, when tipping a
barrow-load of goose droppings into the stream, came
across the corpse of a man. From the state of him he
had been there for some days, and nothing could be
learned of the cause of death. Even de Wolfe and his
officer, hardened as they were to repulsive sights, found
the advanced decay of the body and the putrid waters
of the Shitbrook an unattractive combination in this
hot weather.

The swollen cadaver was totally unrecognisable, and
there was nothing about the nondescript clothing that
helped to identify the man. John was in no mood to
dally with the problem, and after Gwyn had turned the
body over with a stout stick he declared that there no
visible wounds, as far as could be seen. After a few local

men had been herded together as a jury, the coroner held a five-minute inquest on the spot and declared that the unknown man had died from an act of God. He ordered Osric, one of the burgesses's constables, to send for the man who drove the night-soil cart to come and remove the body to the shed behind the cathedral that acted as the public dead-house, until a priest could be persuaded to read a few words over a hastily dug grave in the pauper's corner of the Close.

When they got back to their chamber in the castle, they found Thomas hard at work as usual with quill and ink. After swilling the smell of putrefaction from his throat with some of Gwyn's cider, the coroner gave his two henchmen their orders for the coming few days.

'I have decided to go down to Stoke-in-Teignhead in the morning, to visit my family,' he announced. 'I'll be back in Exeter on Sunday, but I want you two to spend those few days trying to discover more about this unrest in the forest.'

His officer and his clerk looked puzzled, Thomas's concern being mixed with apprehension, as his undoubted intelligence was not matched by his personal courage.

'You want me to venture into the forest, Crowner?' he murmured hesitantly.

John grinned at his clerk's trepidation. 'Don't fret yourself, fellow! I'm not asking you to go charging into the woods waving a broadsword – I'm leaving that to Gwyn. No, I want you to do what you're best at, worming out information from priests.'

He repeated what little he had been told by Thomas's uncle about someone in Holy Orders who might be involved in a conspiracy.

The clerk was anxious to assist his master, but doubtful about his chances of success.

'Where am I to start looking, Crowner, with so little information?'

'These problems seem concentrated around the southern edge of Dartmoor, Thomas. Why not work your wiles on some of the parish priests around there?'

Leaving the little clerk to ponder his instructions, de Wolfe turned to Gwyn, who placidly sat munching bread and swilling cider.

'Go with Thomas as far as Bovey Tracey or Ashburton – make sure he doesn't get lost or fall from his pony! Then while he's wheedling news out of priests, you can tour the alehouses and see what you can pick up. I'm particularly interested in these bands of outlaws. I'm sure they are being used to do some of the dirty work.'

This was a task that suited the Cornishman admirably – sitting in taverns with the blessing of his master was a commission sent from heaven.

'We'll ride out soon after dawn tomorrow,' promised Gwyn. 'And be back here on Sunday, hopefully with some useful news.'

John walked down to the stables opposite his house and arranged with Andrew the farrier for Odin to be groomed and given extra feed, ready for an early start the following morning. Then he went across the lane to confront Matilda, who was sitting up in the solar half-heartedly playing with some embroidery by the light from the only window, an unglazed shuttered aperture looking out on the back yard. She had been unusually withdrawn since the visit of Lord Ferrars and his friends, chastened by the seemingly endless untrustworthiness of her brother. But her husband had to broach a subject that was guaranteed to stir up her emotions – a visit to his relatives in Stoke-in-Teignhead.

'You needn't think I'm coming with you, John,' she snapped, her pug face creased into a scowl. 'I'll not suffer a few hours on the back of a palfrey for the pleasure of enduring a stay in that primitive house with that old Welsh woman and the two yokels you call your brother and sister!'

Her rapid return to her usual rude and abrasive nature caused John to lose any sympathy that might have been lurking over her disillusionment with her brother. Her unreasonable dislike of his family, though nothing new, was no less insulting to him. It was also unfair, for his mother was a sprightly sixty and undeserving of Matilda's epithet 'old Welsh woman'. It was true that she had both Welsh and Cornish ancestry, but she had always tried to be pleasant and kind to Matilda, though her efforts had been in vain. As for the spiteful epithet 'yokel' flung at his brother and sister, William and Evelyn may not have been sophisticated city dwellers, but they were solid, dependable country folk. And to call their manor house at Stoke 'primitive' was nonsense – it had been rebuilt in stone by his father, Simon de Wolfe, when John was a child, and though it may not have boasted flagged floors and a chimney-piece, it was as good as many others in the county – and in his opinion, better than most.

Repressing the urge to say that he had had no intention of asking her to accompany him, he turned on his heel and clumped down the stairs, going out to Mary's cook-shed in the yard for a pint of ale and some soothing conversation, while his temper cooled. The maid easily diagnosed his irritation and turned the subject elsewhere.

'How is Nesta? Is her child-carrying causing her any problems?'

John had confided in Mary soon after he learned that Nesta was pregnant, only narrowly beating the efficient grapevine that spread the news all over the city.

'She has no problems with her body,' he grunted. 'But she is loath to let me acknowledge the child. I can't understand her attitude. I would have thought she would be glad to have me stand by her.'

Mary had her own ideas on the matter, but prudently kept them to herself.

'There'll be several kinds of hell let loose, when she finds out,' she observed, raising her eyes to the solar window at the top of the stairs.

De Wolfe nodded glumly as he drained his quart pot. 'I know, but I've weathered worse before,' he muttered, wiping his mouth with the back of his hand. Rising, he gave Mary a quick affectionate kiss on the top of her glossy brown hair as she bent over a fowl she was gutting for their supper.

'I'll have a quick stroll down to the Bush now, to see how she is. Last night she'd not speak to me – she locked herself in her room to cry.'

He spoke with the wounded bewilderment of a man to whom the moods of women were a total mystery, and Mary gave a secret sigh at the naivety of a man who in all other things was so forceful and dominant. Whistling for Brutus, who was lurking under Mary's table hoping for scraps of offal, he marched away, leaving his maid shaking her head at what was to become of them all.

In the morning, though John left the city at about the same early hour as his assistants, they did not meet, as he went out through the South Gate and they left by the West, crossing the river to reach the main high road that went towards Plymouth.

The coroner's route lay down the other side of the river as far as the port of Topsham, where he led Odin on to the flimsy skiff of the rope-ferry for the short crossing to other bank. In the fine air of early morning, he trotted across the flat, marshy ground of the estuary towards the line of hills that stretched down to the coast. With his sword hanging from his saddle, he had little fear of ambush, even though he rode alone. This well-used coast track was rarely plagued by outlaws, and the sight of the tall, hawkish figure in black on a heavy warhorse was not a tempting prospect for any casual robber.

Little over an hour after leaving the ferry, he found himself approaching the village of Dawlish, on its small creek leading up from the beach. Slowing Odin to a walk, he carefully scanned the few boats pulled up on the muddy bank of the tidal stream. With some disappointment, he saw that one was the larger seagoing vessel that often carried some of the wool sold to Brittany by Hugh de Relaga and himself. It belonged to Thorgils the Boatman, the elderly husband of the beautiful Hilda, who had been John's adolescent sweetheart and occasional mistress ever since. His vessel had been damaged in a storm some time ago, and even now he could see that men were still working on it, replacing ribs and planks along both sides of the hull. Regretfully, he touched his stallion with a spur and moved on – even if Hilda had been available, his sense of loyalty to Nesta in her present condition was too great to allow him to dally in Dawlish, though his recent enforced celibacy, which seemed likely to continue for many months, gave him an uncomfortable ache in his loins. He wondered briefly whether he could last out that long, then chided himself for his selfish lack of honour.

The rest of the journey was pleasant and uneventful, as he gave Odin his head and cantered along the cliff-top track towards Teignmouth.

The sky was deep blue and the heat of the day increased as the morning wore on. The weeks of hot weather were giving manor-reeves and bailiffs concern about a drought, but far out on the western horizon he could see a line of clouds massing, suggesting that another day would see a change. When he reached the Teign, the river was very low and, with the tide out, he could wade his horse across the ford just above the beach, barely wetting his stirrups.

The de Wolfe family had two manors, the main one at Stoke and the other at Holcombe, just off the track between Dawlish and Teignmouth. In fact, the delectable Hilda was the daughter of their bailiff at Holcombe. He often called in passing, both to see her father and to look over the manor, but today he felt a need to see his family without distractions.

His brother William, a few years older and of a quite different temperament, ran their two manors with quiet efficiency. Their father had died fighting in Ireland for old King Henry fifteen years earlier and had left his estate to his eldest son, on condition that he supported his mother and sister and gave a quarter share of the income from the estate to John. This, together with the spoils of war from years of campaigning and the income from his wool partnership, kept John in comfortable security. He got on well with brother William, who, though he looked a lot like John, was of a much milder disposition, concerned only with farming and managing the estate, rather than fighting in foreign lands.

These thoughts usually recurred to John as he was completing the last few miles to Stoke-in-Teignhead, which was in a small valley in the forests on the other side of the river. He came into the vale with his usual feelings of nostalgia, for it was here that he was born and where he spent his childhood and youth. The strip-fields were immaculate and the dwellings of the villeins and free men better built and maintained than in most villages. As he walked Odin down the track towards the manor house, he was met with salutes and beaming smiles from many who had known him all his life. It was a happy place, and he already felt better for the tranquillity that palpably pervaded the whole manor.

His father's house was a square stone edifice behind a palisade of stakes. News of his coming had already been taken inside by an excited urchin running on ahead, and his mother and sister were on the steps of the main entrance to welcome him. A cluster of servants appeared from the cook-house and stables and a groom hurried out to take Odin's bridle as he slid off and bent to kiss his womenfolk. His mother Enyd, a pretty woman still with only a few streaks of grey in her red hair, stood on tiptoe to hug him around the neck, her eyes sparkling with delight at the unexpected arrival of her second son.

'William is off towards the river, where they are cutting assarts. He thinks no one can do anything properly unless he is there to supervise!'

John turned to embrace his sister, more of an armful than his mother. Evelyn was still a spinster, having once wanted to become a nun. She was in her early thirties, a plump, homely girl now satisfied to stay companion to her widowed mother.

The ground floor was occupied by the hall, the solar and several other chambers being upstairs. It was into the hall that John was ushered now, where smiling servants fussed around with food and drink as his mother and Evelyn sat opposite him at a table to make sure that he ate enough after his journey to feed a horse. They pressed him for news, wanting to know all the gossip of the big city, his sister asking unanswerable questions about fashions and the current length of toes on stylish shoes.

'And is that insufferable wife of yours as rude as ever?' asked his mother bluntly. After years of vainly trying to be pleasant to Matilda, she had given up the attempt and now was quite open about her regret at her late husband's insistence on John marrying into the de Revelle family.

'And what about that nice Welsh girl, Nesta?' asked Evelyn. The fact that he had a mistress was no secret, and the practical mother and sister, detesting his wife as they did, were pleased that not only had he found some happiness elsewhere, but also that she was Welsh. As if to underline the point, Evelyn asked the question now in the Celtic language, which they all spoke fluently, as Enyd's father had been Cornish and her mother came from Gwent, as did Nesta.

John smiled wryly at the question. He had not expected the motive for his visit to be arrived at so quickly.

'It's about Nesta that I've come for your advice – not that I wasn't coming to see you anyway,' he added hastily.

His mother gave him a roguish smile and punched him gently on the shoulder.

'Come on, my son, out with it! Are you leaving Matilda and eloping with your inn-keeper?'

'Maybe it will come to that one of these days,' he said wryly. 'Especially after what I've got to tell you now.'

Enyd fixed him with her bright eyes, a knowing smile on her face.

'You've got her with child, haven't you?'

John sighed at his mother's perceptivness. Ever since his childhood he had known that it was useless trying to keep anything from her.

'It's true, Mother. I am to be a father towards the end of the year.'

Evelyn's homely face creased into a smile. She was happy for her brother, who had so far been childless.

Illegitimacy was so common among the ruling class that it was considered normal. Only the poor suffered the stigma of adultery and fornication and had their bastards taken from them to be reared in monastery orphanages.

Her mother turned to a more practical aspect.

'Does your wife know about this?'

'Not yet, though I suspect she will very soon. Exeter is a hotbed of gossip – news travels there faster than forked lightning.'

Enyd de Wolfe dumped another meat pasty on to his pewter platter and gave him a look that defied him to refuse it.

'You'll have a hard time, son, when she does find out.'

John nodded, his mouth full of mutton and pastry. When he had swallowed, he confirmed that he had an unpleasant time ahead.

'She'll go mad, I know. Not because she particularly cares about my sin, but she will be afraid that her grand friends, and all the lesser nobility she cultivates, will think the less of her.'

'Silly cow!' observed Evelyn, with blunt good sense.

'And you, John – are you going to acknowledge the babe?' asked his mother, her voice deadly serious now.

'Of course! What else would I do?' he snapped, rather put out that she needed to even ask such a question. 'But that's the problem, Nesta doesn't want me to suffer in any way because of this and is refusing to let me proclaim the child as mine.'

His mother frowned. 'She is a kind, considerate woman, that much I saw when we met in Exeter that time. But unless she goes away with the infant, perhaps back to her folk in Wales, it's bound to become public knowledge. Do you mind that?'

'Not at all. If people don't like it, be damned to

them. No doubt that swine of a sheriff will make as much capital out of it as he can, especially as his sister will seem to be the aggrieved party, but I don't give a damn. '

'Could it affect your position as coroner?' asked his sister, who was quite proud of her brother's eminence.

'Richard de Revelle will undoubtedly try to stir up trouble – he would dearly like to see me removed as coroner and some pliant nobody elected in my place. I don't need the job, but I've come to enjoy it, I admit. If he tries any tricks, I'll appeal straight away to the Justiciar.'

'Might Matilda leave you?' asked his mother, almost hopefully.

'I doubt it. The house in Martin's Lane is mine – I bought it many years ago with profit from the wars. She has money laid away by her family, I know, but she enjoys good food, clothes and a sound roof over her head too much to desert me. Though God knows, she'll try to make my life hell.'

The two women were agog with excitement and curiosity. John's unexpected visit had been surpassed by this momentous news. Enyd was to be a grandmother and Evelyn an aunt.

'And is Nesta well with her pregnancy?' demanded his mother. 'I remember being so sick when I was carrying William.'

'She is well in body, though it's early days yet. It is only a short time since she suspected that she was with child and had it confirmed by a midwife.'

Enyd immediately picked up on part of his statement. 'What do you mean, John – well in body?' she demanded.

He shifted uneasily on the bench. His mother's interrogations were always searching.

'I told you, she does not wish me to acknowledge

the child, for my sake. But she seems very upset generally, she cries a lot and sometimes refuses to talk to me. The other evening she ran to her chamber and locked herself in. Last night she was better, but seems always so sad and will not talk sensibly to me.'

His mother, wise with her years and from carrying three children, put a hand on his arm affectionately.

'Being gravid affects women in different ways, John. Some say they never felt better in their life, others become weepy and withdrawn. Maybe it will pass soon. You must be patient.'

Privately she could think of several reasons why Nesta was in such a miserable state, but reassurance was what he needed now.

'Why not bring her down here to stay for a time?' she continued. 'Nesta can lodge here for as long as she likes – she could come for childbed when that day comes.'

'Thank you, Mother, you are the kindest person in the world. But she has an inn to run, certainly until near her time.'

'Nonsense, having the baby is far more important. You say she has three servants working there. She could get someone to run the alehouse for a few months.'

With memories of Alan of Lyme in his mind, this idea did not greatly appeal to John, but he agreed to put it to Nesta on his return.

The chatter went on until even the two women had exhausted the subject of childbirth and babies. Almost too full to rise from the table, de Wolfe eventually made the effort and then decided to walk off his full stomach by seeking out his brother in the woods.

While John de Wolfe was riding down the coast, his officer and clerk were making a more leisurely excursion westwards, their speed limited by the shorter legs of Thomas's pony and his awkward posture on its side saddle.

As churches and alehouses were almost invariably twinned in most villages, Gwyn decided to chaperone the little clerk for most of the journey, vanishing into each tavern while Thomas sought out the local healer of souls. The coroner had given them enough silver pennies to provide them with bed and board on a modest scale for four nights, so they looked upon this venture as a rare holiday from their usual routine.

Three hours after leaving Exeter, the pair made their first stop at Bovey Tracey, where Gwyn promptly vanished into one of the two alehouses. Thomas was dressed as usual in his long, threadbare tunic, which looked much like a black clerical cassock, helping to give the impression that he was still in Holy Orders. He made his way to the church and, after much genuflecting and crossing himself, found the parish priest and engaged him in conversation, using the excuse that he had come to see the new stone church built by the lord of the manor, Sir William Tracey. He was one of the four knights who had murdered Archbishop Thomas Becket at King Henry's behest, and the erection of a church was in atonement for his sin. However, the clerk learned nothing useful from the local man, however skilfully he manoeuvred the conversation towards problems in the forest.

The same routine was followed as the coroner's assistants made their way slowly around the villages on the eastern flank of Dartmoor. During the rest of the day, they went from Bovey up to Hennock, then to Lustleigh and finally across to Manaton, where Thomas renewed his acquaintance with Father Amicus and Gwyn drank in the tavern with the reeve, Robert Barat. Here they could make no pretence at being passing travellers, as they were well remembered from the inquest on Elias

Necke, the dead tanner – but after the aggravation with William Lupus, the village men were happy to gossip about the iniquities of the foresters. They had no new information to pass on, but reported that the outlaws seemed to be becoming bolder, often being seen on the roads and lurking in the nearby woods with no concern about being apprehended.

'And who is likely to challenge them?' growled Robert Barat. 'We never see a man-at-arms around here, the sheriff is but a distant figure in Exeter. No local man is going to risk his neck trying to get a wolf's head when the foresters themselves seem to protect the vermin.'

That night Gwyn and Thomas found a free bed in an outhouse behind the reeve's cottage. It was only a pile of straw, but it was clean and the night was warm, though the clouds that their master had seen massing over the sea had rolled in and threatened a change in the weather for the coming days.

Half a penny had bought them a good meal in the alehouse, and in the dusk of a late summer evening they lay sleepily discussing what they had learned that day, which was very little.

'Let's hope we ferret out more than this tomorrow and the next day,' murmured the Cornishman eventually. 'Else the crowner will want his money back!'

The clerk slapped at some ants that were crawling up his face.

'No one has heard of any priest who's in league with either the foresters or the outlaws,' he said. 'I wonder if that's just some idle tale, as no parish priest is able to wander around the countryside as the fancy takes him. Only fairly senior clerics can travel any distance.'

Gwyn rolled over on his heap of straw and pulled up the pointed hood of his leather jerkin to shut out the world.

'Let's worry about that tomorrow, Thomas. I need my sleep now.'

Next morning they worked their way along the very edge of the barren moor, coming down to Widecombe, where the previous year their master had investigated the corpse of a young Crusader found in a stream. From there, they jogged to Dunstone, Buckland and Holne, repeating their routine in church houses and taverns. In the evening, they arrived back on the main Exeter road at Ashburton. This was one of the four Stannary towns involved in the assay of the Dartmoor tin, which along with wool was the major export of the county. Here they had a choice of alehouses, but only one church. Thomas, a poor and reluctant horseman, was saddle sore and weary and could not face replaying his usual confidence game with the local priest that evening. This time they had to pay for a place to stay in one of the inns, and after an indifferent meal of leek stew and a leathery fowl the clerk climbed into the loft to collapse face down on to his hay-filled palliasse, giving his aching backside a chance to recover.

Gwyn, who could spend all day on a horse without a twinge, set off to do a tour of all the other alehouses in the hope of hearing something useful. In the fourth, by which time he had drunk the better part of a gallon of common ale, he fell into conversation with two tinners, who had brought a train of pack ponies down that day from the high moor, laden with crudely smelted tin ready for the next assay. Their talk followed the usual pattern – complaints about the stinginess of their employers, the outrageous taxes on the tin and the corruption of the Warden of the Stannaries, who was none other than Sheriff Richard de Revelle. As the ale flowed and tongues became loosened, Gwyn turned the talk to extortion in the forest and had a useful response from the grousing tinners.

'Thank God we're exempt from the antics of these bloody foresters!' said one. 'The stannary laws and our parliament on the moor make sure that they don't interfere with us. But I pity the folk who live off the land down here, they're getting a harder time than ever.'

Gwyn encouraged them to keep talking by waving down a potboy and getting in more quarts. 'What's going on in the forest, then? I'm from Exeter, we don't hear much about it there,' he added ingenuously.

'More oppression from the foresters. They've become worse lately,' growled the other man, a huge bear of a fellow with a black beard. 'Forcing alehouses to take their brew, setting up forges and tanneries – taking the very bread from people's mouths.'

'Can't they do something about it?' asked Gwyn, his blue eyes radiating innocent curiosity.

'What can they do?' retorted Blackbeard belligerently. 'The manor-lords are either powerless to act against royal custom or their palms are being crossed with silver to persuade them to mind their own business.'

'And the common folk can do nothing,' snarled the other tinner. 'If they complain, they are beaten up by the foresters or their hulking pages. And not only that, but lately they seem to have the damned outlaws on their side. I don't understand it, I tell you.'

He had raised his voice and the other man nudged him forcibly in the side, slopping his ale over the rim of his pot.

'Watch what you say, Tom,' he growled in lower tones. 'That fellow over there, I'm sure he's one of Winter's gang.'

He jerked his head to indicate a young man

slouching on a low window shelf across the room, flirting with one of the slatternly maids who was clearing empty mugs and platters.

'Who's Winter?' asked Gwyn, determined to draw the men out.

'Robert Winter. He runs the main coven of thieving outlaws in these parts,' grunted the smaller man. 'They've become so bold lately they come into town to drink and wench now, for no one seems interested in stopping them. Someone seems to be protecting them.'

'Are there any others in here, d'you reckon?' asked Gwyn, looking around the crowded taproom. Blackbeard cautiously turned his head right and left. Although he was built like a bull, he seemed unwilling to get involved in any trouble.

'No, I can't see anyone else here that I recognise, but I've only seen these villains now and then on the verges or talking to the foresters. Although for all I know, all this damned lot might be wolf's heads.'

The thought seemed to sober the two tinners and they refused to be drawn into any more discussion of the forest troubles. A few moments later they finished up their ale and shambled out, leaving Gwyn with the beginnings of a plan germinating under his ginger thatch.

Within minutes of the tinners leaving, Gwyn quietly rose from his corner bench and made his way to the door. The young man in the window recess was still talking to the ale-maid, trying to pull her to him with an arm around her waist, as she half-heartedly pushed him away with the empty drinking pots she held in her hands.

Gwyn hurried down the main streeet of Ashburton towards the inn where they were staying, stopping only in an alleyway to empty his bladder of some of the vast quantity of drink that he had taken that day. When he arrived at the Crown tavern, distinguished from other houses only by the tarnished gilt sign that was nailed over the door, he pushed his way in through the drinkers and made for the open ladder-like stairs that went up to the floor above. The loft was similar to that in the Bush, though dirtier and more squalid. A row of hessian pallets stuffed with hay lay along one wall, and on the other side a straggle of loose straw offered cheaper accommodation.

The place was almost deserted this early in the evening, but one man lay retching in the straw and, in a corner, another, older man appeared to be shaking with the rigors of some fever, unattended and uncared for. The Cornishman looked along the row of thin mattresses to one with a bulge, where Thomas lay wrapped in his thin mantle in lieu of a blanket. He stumped across the creaking boards and shook the clerk by the shoulder.

'Hey, little man, you're on your own from here. I'm off into the forest to see if I can discover something straight from the horse's mouth.' Rudely awaken and bleary eyed, the ex-priest groggily sat up on his pallet and stared at the tousle-haired giant who had so abruptly disturbed him.

'What do you mean, on my own? Where shall I go, then?'

'Carry on with what you have been doing, man. It's Thursday evening now. I'll meet you back here on Sunday and we can ride back to the city.'

The clerk stared anxiously at his friend in the gloom of the windowless attic. 'I'm unhappy at travelling alone. Must you leave me?'

Gwyn gave him a playful push on the shoulder, which flattened him on to his mattress. 'Come on, have some spirit, Thomas. Who in God's name would bother to rob such a poor-looking waif as you? I reckon a beggar would share his alms with you out of pity!'

'What about your horse?' wailed the clerk.

'I'll give the ostler a couple of pence to feed her until I come back – and put the fear of the crowner's wrath into him not to sell her!'

Agog with consternation, Thomas watched Gwyn stump away to the ladder, then with a muffled wail of anxiety he lay down again and pulled his cloak over his head.

Outside, the coroner's officer made his way back to the other alehouse and slipped back into the taproom, which was even more crowded than before. All the benches were full and men were standing shoulder to shoulder with hardly room to lift their tankards to their lips. There had been a local horse fair that day and some of the patrons were loudly discussing their bargains and their losses.

Gwyn pushed his way to the back of the room and gave a segment of a penny for a quart pottery mug of ale, dipped from an open cask by a slatternly woman with a huge goitrous swelling in her throat.

He turned, his eyes scanning the far corner to see if the young man was still there. The maid with whom he had been flirting was now struggling about the room with new pots of ale, urged on by the landlord, who was yelling at her to keep her mind on her work. Her previous place with the alleged outlaw had been taken by a short, scrawny man with a dark, leathery complexion, who was talking animatedly with the other fellow. Gwyn watched them covertly for a time and tried to edge nearer, though the press of jostling patrons made it difficult. Although the two were talking rapidly to each other, their voices were kept low and Gwyn could not pick up a single word without getting so close as to make them suspicious. Abruptly, the smaller man, after much nodding and gesticulating, turned and forced his way quickly to the door and vanished, leaving the other looking thoughtfully into his empty pot. Fearful that he was about to leave, Gwyn shouldered his way to his side, and with what he hoped was a furtive look behind him, gestured at the ale jar.

'Want another, son?' Gwyn was hardly old enough to be his father, but there was certainly many years between them. The other, a thickset, yellow-haired fellow with disconcertingly pale blue eyes, looked suspiciously at the huge, unkempt figure.

'You buying it?' he asked, in an accent from a long way east of Devonshire.

Gwyn gave another of his exaggeratedly furtive glances over his shoulder, then covertly displayed six whole pennies which he had clutched in his ham-like hand.

'I struck lucky outside the fair today – the other fellow should be back on his feet within the week!' He leered at the blond man, then waved at the chastened potgirl to bring more ale.

'Nobody knows me in Ashburton – yet,' he went on. 'And I'm trying to keep it that way by getting out as soon as I can.'

The quarts arrived and, though the girl risked a simpering smile at the younger man, he ignored her, his attention now on this stranger.

'I thank you for the drink, but what do you want with me?'

Gwyn sensed that here was a man who really did look over his shoulder much of the time. There was an alertness about him that confirmed he was uneasy in crowded places.

'I was told, never mind by whom, that you lived among the wolves,' he said, tapping the side of his nose.

'That's a dangerous thing to suggest, stranger. What if I do?'

Gwyn gulped the better part of a pint before answering.

'I'm by way of seeking a place to lie up for a bit in similar company, if you get my drift. I'm tired of being on the run all the time, sleeping in a pigsty or a ditch and stealing every morsel of food or a few pence for ale – then often being too wary of taverns to spend it.'

The other man relaxed. This scruffy giant, who looked as if he had stolen his clothes from a scarecrow, could easily be another fugitive from justice.

'You look as if you might be handy with a staff or a mace, friend,' he said in a more affable voice. 'How did you come to be on the road?'

Gwyn guffawed and clapped the other on the shoulder.

'Off the road, more like it. I was an abjurer, sent from Bristol to take ship at Southampton, by the evil whim of the bloody coroner. I threw away my cross around the first bend in the road and stole the clothes of the first man who was big enough for them to fit me!'

He laughed uproariously again and poured the rest of his ale down his throat, some of it dribbling down the sides of his long, drooping moustache. 'Now I'm working my way down to my native Cornwall, where I can slip back into my old trade as a tinner.'

The fair-haired man grinned, all suspicion now evaporated. Gwyn's abjurer story was a common one – criminals who sought sanctuary in a church had forty days' grace, during which, if they confessed their crime to the local coroner, they could 'abjure the realm' by promising to leave the shores of England as soon as possible. Dressed in sackcloth and carrying a home-made wooden cross, they would be directed by the coroner to a particular port, where they had to catch the first ship going abroad. If the weather prevented sailing, they had to wade out up to their knees in each tide, to show their willingness to leave England.

From sheer perversity, many coroners would send them to a far-distant port, to worsen their labour of walking and increase the risk of their being killed on the way. If an abjurer so much as strayed a yard off the highway, anyone was entitled to kill him on the spot without penalty. Injured victims or their bereaved relatives were quite likely to do this to the perpetrator of the crime. In fact, few abjurers ever reached their harbour, either being slain on the way or, far more likely, running into the forests to become outlaws, risking the penalty of being beheaded for the bounty.

So Gwyn's story was not only credible but commonplace, and the younger man had no qualms about accepting it. Now it seemed that the hulking Cornishman was looking for a resting place for a time, on his journey home – and from the size of his muscles and his obvious acquaintance with the rougher side of life, he might be a useful addition to Robert Winter's band of desperadoes.

'My name's Martin Angot – buy me another quart with one of those stolen pennies and maybe I'll have some good news for you!'

For John de Wolfe, it was also something of a holiday. For the first time for months – in fact, since he had been laid up with a broken leg – he was experiencing some peace and quiet. The tranquil life of the manor at Stoke calmed his usually restless nature, and the absence of Matilda's carping, surly behaviour felt like a weight lifted from his shoulders. Though he missed Nesta, a small part of his mind experienced relief that he was away from her present unhappy mood and her reluctance to go along with his willing acceptance of her pregnancy. He felt vaguely disloyal about this, but consoled himself that it was only for a couple of days. In the meantime, he luxuriated in the fond attention of his mother and sister, who appeared genuinely delighted to have him home. They fussed over him and over-fed him, as if he was the returned Prodigal Son.

His brother William, a rather reserved and inarticulate man, also seemed pleased to see him, and on this Friday morning they both went hunting together. Being well outside the bounds of the royal lands, there was no hindrance to their foray through the manor woods. John enjoyed a day's carefree riding in the company of pleasant companions, but unusually for a Norman knight he was not a very enthusiastic hunter. Unless an animal was urgently needed for food, as it often was in his former campaigning days, or was a dangerous pest like a boar or fox, he found little joy in killing handsome beasts just for sport.

Today he was on a mare borrowed from William's stables, as Odin was too large and clumsy for hunting. Their steward and two grooms rode with them, as well as a houndsman who handled the four dogs that ran alongside.

The Stoke lands stretched down towards the river, where thick woods lined the tidal mud banks. For a couple of hours they traversed commons and clearings, as well as the forest, without raising a single beast apart from a fox, who outpaced the hounds and vanished down a deep hole under an oak tree. Eventually they halted and let their mounts graze in a clearing while they took refreshment.

The steward had a bag of bread, meat and cheese on his saddle, and one of the grooms had a stone flagon of cider. William, though always treated with the greatest respect by his servants, had an egalitarian streak that was hardly typical of most manor-lords, and the other hunters sat with the brothers and shared the food, passing the crock of cider around from mouth to mouth.

Though the sky was half filled with cloud today, it was still fine, and in the warmth of early summer, with the birds bursting themselves with song in the surrounding trees, John lay back against a trunk and felt at ease with the world. The conversation drifted from topic to topic and came back to the lack of any success in the hunt that morning.

'Do you not keep a woodward these days?' he asked his brother.

William shook his head. 'I've neither the time nor the inclination to spend half my life chasing around after buck and hind,' he replied. 'There's no Royal Forest within five miles of here, so why go to the trouble and expense of a woodward?'

A woodward was to a private estate what a forester was to the royal lands. Hunting grounds of large estates, especially those running adjacent to royal demesnes, were called 'chases' – or, if walled or fenced, 'parks' – and the landowners were obliged to employ woodwards to police them and preserve the wildlife. These men had divided loyalties, for although employed at the landowner's expense, they had to abide by the same code as the royal foresters and to swear fealty to the verderers, Warden and the King, reporting any breach of forest law that affected the royal interests. Most of the problems arose where a chase abutted against the King's forest, and complicated rules existed to prevent beasts from the royal land from escaping – or being driven – into private ground.

William explained all this to his brother, heartily glad that these problems did not afflict his manor.

'The barons and lords who have bigger fiefs up against the King's forest are having increasing problems,' he explained. 'They can no longer trust their own woodwards, who are often under the thumb of the foresters. I hear there are new tricks that are being played, like driving deer from the chases and parks into the King's land – the very opposite of what traditionally used to happen.'

The conversation brought John's mind back to the duties he had waiting in Exeter, and he wondered how Thomas and Gwyn were faring on the expedition he had commanded them to undertake. He knew his officer could look after himself, but he worried slightly about the timid Thomas, who openly admitted to his own cowardice. Still, he thought, talking to a string of priests could not present much danger, and he dismissed his concerns as the hunting party gathered themselves to resume their search for the elusive animals.

In the next two hours they found nothing, but then the hounds caught the trail of a roe deer. Before long they had brought it down and the huntsmen dispatched it cleanly within seconds. They decided to call it a day and wended their way back to the manor house, with the fresh carcass slung across the houndmaster's mare.

'We've brought you tonight's supper, Mother,' announced William, with some satisfaction, as the women came out on the house steps to greet them. The steward and other servants went off to deliver the venison to the kitchens, and the brothers flopped on to benches in the hall. A jar of wine appeared between them as they regaled Enyd and her daughter with exaggerated tales of their prowess in the hunt. This was a fairly short story and the conversation soon came around to John's domestic problems.

'How will you deal with this matter of the baby, my son?' asked his mother, concern in her voice. She offered no censure to John over the affair, accepting that this was what men did, marriage or not. She knew that even her own late husband, Simon, had a bastard somewhere in the north, a product of a long sojourn away during one of King Henry's campaigns. Her worry was over the practicalities of the child's upbringing, especially knowing of Matilda's vindictive nature.

Her younger son scratched his head through his black thatch.

'I've not given it that much thought yet, Mother,' he admitted. 'He'll not want for anything, I assure you – including my love and affection.'

'You seem very sure it's going to be a boy, John,' said Evelyn.

His sister's prim nature made her slightly more uneasy with the situation than her mother. She had wanted to become a nun years before, until, on the death of her father, his widow had vetoed the ambition and made her stay at home to help with the household duties.

Her brother grinned sheepishly. 'Of course it'll be a boy! How could I ever sire a daughter? I need to teach him to swing a sword and hold a lance!'

'Will the babe live in the inn? Is it a suitable place?' asked Enyd, still worrying away at the problem.

John considered this. 'I think it will serve. There's plenty of room upstairs. I can get another room built alongside Nesta's chamber, then hire a good woman to look after the child while Nesta runs the inn.' He grinned. 'At least she'll not need a wet-nurse, as nature provided well for her in that regard!'

Evelyn pursed her lips primly. 'You shouldn't jest about such things, John, it's not decent.'

His mother laughed at her daughter's prudishness, and even William's long face cracked into a smile. 'The babe will certainly be well fed, as far as I remember from my one meeting with the young woman.'

'This will be my first – and probably only – grand-child, John, so look after it well,' commanded Enyd. 'You should get her seen by that woman in Polsloe Priory that you told us about. She seems wise in the ways of women and childbirth.'

'You mean Dame Madge, the nun?' responded John. 'Yes, that's a good notion, Mother. She helped me several times when women's problems were an issue.'

Dame Madge was a gaunt sister at the Benedictine priory just outside Exeter, a woman well versed in diseases of women and the problems of childbirth. When John had had cases of rape and death from miscarriage to deal with, she had proved of consider-able help, in spite of her forbidding appearance and manner.

'And don't forget, my son, you tell Nesta that this house is always open to her at any time. She can come down here when she is heavy with child and go to childbed here, if needs be. She can scream out her labour pains in Welsh, for we'll understand her well enough!'

CHAPTER SEVEN

*In which Gwyn takes to the forest and
Thomas to an abbey*

Gwyn woke up at dawn to find himself staring at a rocky ceiling. He was used to curling up in a wide variety of places and could sleep soundly anywhere, from the heaving deck of a fishing boat to the open deserts of Outremer. However, since settling down a couple of years ago, he now usually awoke either in his family hut in St Sidwell's – or somewhere in Exeter, if he had been out drinking after the city gates closed at curfew.

He stared at the damp rock for a moment, gathering his sleep-fuddled senses, before recollecting that he was in an outlaw's cave about five miles north of Ashburton. After leaving the alehouse the previous evening, Martin Angot had walked with him out of the little town for about a mile up the road towards Haytor. It was almost dark by then, though a pink summer glow in the west gave enough light for them to see their way. At a bend in the lane, Martin suddenly plunged off the road and, a few hundred paces through the trees, came upon a sturdy pony on a long head-rope, contentedly cropping the grass in a clearing.

'You'll have to walk behind, it's a couple more miles at least,' he said rather thickly, as the outlaw did not have the iron head that Gwyn possessed when it came to drinking ale.

They plodded for an hour along an ill-defined track through the woods alongside a valley, then came out on moorland and began to climb towards the rocks of a jagged tor silhouetted against the sky.

A full moon now rose above the eastern horizon, and for another mile the coroner's officer, who had given his name as Jess, followed the rump of the pony up towards the high moor.

There was a hoot ahead which was a fair imitation of an owl, though Gwyn was well aware that it came from a human throat. Martin Angot called a soft reply and a moment later the figure of a sentinel loomed up from behind a rock, a lance in his hands.

'Who's this, Martin?' he demanded.

'A new recruit – an abjurer who lost his way,' jested the blond man.

The guard waved them on, and in a few minutes they came upon a deep dell set into the edge of the escarpment. Behind a barrier of piled moor-stones the glowing ashes of a fire remained, one fed only with dry wood to avoid smoke. A few crude shelters made of stones and wood, with turf roofs supported on branches, were propped against the rocky faces of the dell, and at its apex was a wide, shallow cave. Snores from the shelters and the cave drew Gwyn's gaze to about a score of sleeping men, wrapped in cloaks and rough blankets. Martin slid from his pony and pulled off the oat sack he used for a saddle. Giving the beast a slap on the rump to send it out of the dell for the night, he muttered, 'It'll not go far, there are others tethered around the corner. Find a space in the cavern – at least it's better than a ditch or pigsty,' he grunted, making for one of the turfed shelters. 'I'll take you to the chief in the morning – he'll either accept you or slit your throat.'

Now, at dawn, Gwyn lay wondering what he had let

himself in for, penetrating this den of thieves. If any of them recognised him as the coroner's henchman, he was in big trouble, but he felt it worth the risk if he could learn something useful for his master.

The danger was that, though probably none of the gang of outcasts would have seen him before, the description of a huge, ginger-haired Cornishman acting as the crowner's officer might be common enough currency in the countryside to give him away. It would surely happen sooner or later, but as he intended only to spend a day or so as an outlaw, he gambled on it being later.

As the dawn strengthened, men began to move, stretching and cursing as they pulled on their boots. They drifted to the fire, which someone had blown into life, piling on fresh wood, so that a cauldron of yesterday's stew could be heated for breakfast. Some stale bread, stolen at knife-point from some village bake-house days before, was the only accompaniment, washed down by a sour ale.

The other men, who varied from hideous ruffians to weak-looking runts who must have been clerks escaping from embezzlement charges, seemed incurious about him, and Gwyn assumed that the membership of the gang was a fluid affair, with much coming and going. During the desultory converation around the cauldron, he stuck to his story about being 'Jess', an absconding abjurer, and no one seemed interested enough to question him in any detail about his orginal crimes. Thankfully, no one leapt to his feet and pointed a quivering finger at him, accusing him of being the Exeter coroner's officer.

After they had finished picking out shreds of fatty meat and gristle from the pot with their knives and drinking the thin soup dipped out with their empty ale-mugs, a dozen of the outlaws trooped off on foot, one of them telling Gwyn that they were going up to the high moor to steal some sheep belonging to Buckfast Abbey. For some reason, the mention of this religious house seemed to cause some amusement, and Gwyn heard one man cackling about 'Biting the hand that feeds you!'.

As they left, Martin Angot came across from one of the shelters, walking with a tall, slim man with brown hair and beard. He was better dressed than the others, with a green tunic circled with a belt and baldric from which hung a heavy sword. Ankle-length boots were worn over cross-gartered breeches, and his head was partly covered by a pointed woollen cap that flopped over to one side.

'Is this the man, Martin?' he asked his lieutenant. Gwyn recognised that his voice was more cultured than the other men's, though he spoke English with a Devon accent.

Gwyn lumbered to his feet and nodded to the newcomer, who he assumed was Robert Winter. 'Jess is my name. I seek somewhere to stay in peace for a time, until I can carry on with my journey.'

The outlaw grinned, his face lighting up pleasantly, his intelligent eyes scanning Gwyn's huge frame and his dishevelled clothing.

'Martin tells me you've walked from Bristol? You look as if it was from York, by the state of you.'

Now it was Gwyn's bulbous features which cracked into a smile. 'Almost as far, for I walked from Anglesey in Wales to Bristol, having taken ship from Ireland.'

He knew Ireland and Wales well and felt easier talking about somewhere that was not pure invention.

'What were you doing in Ireland?' asked Martin.

'Selling my sword-arm as usual. But they've run out of wars there at the moment, so I was making for home. Then, being without money after a gaming match, I relieved a Bristol merchant of his purse, but the damned man had two servants following behind. I laid them out, but then had to run for sanctuary.'

It was a simple enough story to be credible, and neither of the outlaws seemed suspicious.

'D'you mind risking your head as an outlaw?'

Gwyn grinned at the question.

'It makes no odds to me whether my neck is severed or stretched on the gallows tree, which is what would happen if Bristol caught up with me!'

Winter looked keenly at the big man, sizing up his huge muscles before his eyes settled on the broadsword hanging from his baldric.

'Are you any good with that thing, Jess?'

Gwyn rattled the battered blade in its scabbard of scuffed leather.

'It's kept me alive these past twenty years, so I reckon on being able to use it well enough – though I'll admit I'm no bowman.'

Both Robert Winter and his deputy Martin Angot asked some more questions, mainly about his origins and where he had served as a mercenary soldier. Once again, Gwyn stuck as near to the truth as possible, which he could do without difficulty. His accent confirmed him as a Cornishman and he correctly claimed to be the son of a tin miner who had given up the trade to become a fisherman at Polruan, where Gwyn had spent the first sixteen years of his life. As to campaigning, he stuck to his actual escapades in France, Ireland and Wales, leaving out any mention of the Holy Land or Austria, which might have brought him uncomfortably near John de Wolfe.

After a few minutes, the other men appeared satisfied that this dishevelled giant was what he claimed to be.

'You're welcome to stay with us, Jess, until you want

to move on. But you'll have to earn your keep and our protection,' said Winter.

'Anything you say, Chief,' rumbled Gwyn. 'What happens today?'

The outlaw leader looked at Angot, who jerked a thumb towards the men sitting around the fire.

'A few of them are doing a little task for a forester today. Go with them, Jess – there's hardly likely to be much rough stuff, but someone your size might be useful if any persuasion is needed.'

Apparently satisfied, the two outlaws sauntered back towards the bigger shelter, leaving Gwyn to his own devices. He wandered over to the rest of the men and squatted down with them.

'I'm to go with you on some persuading expedition,' he announced. 'What's it all about?'

Like their leaders, the men seemed to have accepted Gwyn without query. He suspected that there was a high turnover of similar recruits and deserters in the gang. One of them spat into the fire before answering him.

'We're going to shake up some freeholder who refused to honour his obligations to William Lupus,' explained the man, a tough-looking fellow of about twenty. He had a fringe of dark beard and a jagged scar on his right cheek. The name Lupus rang an alarm bell in Gwyn's mind.

'Who's he?' he asked gruffly, not wishing to show that he already knew.

'One of the foresters around here. This bloody pig-keeper refused to feed the horses belonging to him and his page, so we're to teach him some manners.'

Gwyn leaned forward to push a log farther into the fire.

'Why are we doing such a favour for a forester? Where I come from, we prefer to cut their throats!'

One of the other men answered this time, a young weasely fellow with a bad squint.

'It pays not to ask too many questions around here,' he advised.

Gwyn shrugged indifferently.'I don't give a damn. When are we going?'

For an answer, three of the men, including the one with the scar, clambered to their feet. One ambled across to a pile of weapons and brought over four heavy cudgels, one of which he handed to Gwyn.

'Here you are, Jess. You won't need your sword today – this isn't the Battle of Wexford!' said the bearded youth.

There was no way that Gwyn was going to be parted from his blade, but no further jest was made when he left it hanging at his side. The four men set off down the steep heathland, leaving a few outlaws back in the camp. A few hundred yards below the rocky outcrop, the bare ground gave way to trees, and soon the single file of marauders was winding its way along an ill-defined path through dense woodland down into the valley. Gwyn was in the rear, the leader being Simon, a swarthy ruffian of about thirty who reminded Gwyn of a wild boar, as his dark hairy face and boasted a mouth that had a pair of large yellowed eye-teeth projecting like tusks from his lower jaw. He loped through the fallen leaves and wild garlic with the assurance of one who knew every step of the way, swinging his ugly-looking club in one hand. The other two, Scarface and the one with the squint, were dressed in little better than rags, and Gwyn wondered what sins had driven them from home to eke out this miserable existence in the forest.

After the better part of an hour's silent tramping, they skirted some cultivated fields where the valley began to widen out and reached a narrow track, rutted by cartwheels. After following this for half a mile, they crossed a wider road which Gwyn recognised as the highway from Ashburton to Moretonhampstead. He could see a small hamlet in the distance, but after furtive glances up and down the road, Simon marched them straight across and took a path that led into the trees on the other side. This wound along for a while until it debouched into a large clearing in which there was a fair-sized cottage built of whitewashed cob, a mixture of mud, horsehair and dung, plastered on to a lattice of hazel withies.

A couple of sheds stood behind it, alongside a wattle fence enclosing a large patch of stinking mud in which more than two score pigs snuffled and grunted. In front of the dwelling was another fenced area, planted with orderly rows of beans, cabbage, onions, lettuce and herbs. Simon came to halt facing the cottage and pointed towards it with his club.

'Right, boys, we're to beat him up a little, but not enough to croak him – understand?'

Gwyn became very uneasy – as the dilemma had presented itself so abruptly. Simon stood at the fence around the plot and stared at the silent cottage, the others gathering behind him.

'What are we here for?' grunted Gwyn.

The leader turned his ugly head. 'To teach this fellow a lesson – and to oblige William Lupus.'

'Can't a forester settle his own problems? What's this cottar done to offend him?'

'You ask a lot of questions, for a newcomer,' snapped Simon.

'It's because I'm a newcomer. I don't know what's going on,' Gwyn replied reasonably. One of the younger men explained.

'He wouldn't give Lupus everything he wanted. Under forest law, everyone dwelling in a royal forest must give the putre on demand to any forest officer and his groom, as well as fodder for his horse and food for his hound.'

'What the hell's "putre"?'

'The forest fee – bed and board, oats for the horse, two tallow candles a night and black bread for the forester's dog.'

'So why's bed and board a problem?' muttered Gwyn.

'Edwin, the freeholder here, refused to give Lupus everything else he wanted, including a couple of pigs and some fowls – in fact, he and his two sons threatened to give him a beating if he didn't go away.'

'So why didn't this Edwin give the forester what he was entitled to?'

The cross-eyed outlaw sniggered. 'Because Lupus had been back three times inside two weeks, demanding his dues. He'd cleaned the old man out of the last of his fodder, I heard. The final straw was him wanting three of his best breeding sows.'

Simon smacked the lad around the head with a heavy hand. 'For Mary's sake, give over gossiping! There's work to be done. Go and chase those bloody pigs into the forest. That'll get him into trouble for unlawful agisting, especially this time of year, in the fence month.'

Rubbing his sore head, the youth loped away towards the back of the cottage, while the leading outlaw gave the other youngster a push on the shoulder. 'You, get in that garden and wreck those plants of Edwin's. Let him go hungry, after he's recovered from his thrashing.'

He motioned to Gwyn to follow him and made for the front of the cottage.

The coroner's officer was feeling increasingly uneasy at what was happening, especially when he saw the carefully tended vegetables being either uprooted or trodden underfoot by the ruffian in the garden plot. But for the moment he could hardly afford to abandon his deception, just when he might be able to learn something. Reluctantly, he tramped after Simon, the cudgel he had been given dangling from his hand. As they neared the heavy sheet of thick leather that hung over the door of the window-less dwelling, he heard the squeal of pigs as they were chased off into the woods behind, from where it would be a marathon task to gather them together again.

As they stood near the rough timber frame of the door, there was still no sound from within. The youth was still crashing about in the vegetable plot, but there was no reaction from inside the cottage.

'Maybe he's not here,' said Gwyn, trying to keep the relief from his voice. There was no way in which he could stand by and let these thugs assault an innocent man, even if it did expose him as a spy.

Simon looked disgruntled at the prospect of a wasted journey. 'It's a market day in Moretonhampstead. Maybe the bastard has gone there to sell some of his hogs.'

He pushed aside the leather with the point of his cudgel and peered into the single room. 'No one here, blast it!' he snarled.

Gwyn decided to use the anticlimax to try to wheedle out some more information.

'I still don't see why we're doing the forester's dirty work.'

Simon turned impatiently from the door. 'Because Winter gets paid to do it, that's why. And the rest of us get a share-out now and then. Where else d'you think we get money for ale and wenching when we slide into the town?'

'Who pays him, then?' asked Gwyn, boldly.

The outlaw glared suspiciously at him. 'You're a big fellow, but you've got an even bigger mouth! Why d'you want to know? It's none of your business.'

Gwyn held up his hands apologetically. 'I've just got a curious nature – I'm no sheriff's man, for God's sake!'

This seemed to amuse Simon.

'Sheriff's man – that's a laugh, that is! Now shut up and get in there and smash everything within sight. If we can't break Edwin's head, we'll just have break up his homestead.' To demonstrate what he meant, Simon pulled violently at the leather door flap, ripping it from its fastenings.

As if this was a signal, all hell was let loose.

There was a warning scream from the lad in the garden and a pounding of feet from the direction of a small shed at the side of the house. Two men came flying around the corner, one hefting a three-foot piece of branch, the other waving a small but wicked-looking firewood axe. With yells of defiance, they fell upon the two men at their door, the younger fellow catching Simon a heavy blow with the branch, which he fended off with his left arm. The older man, obviously his father, took a swing at Gwyn with his axe, but the experienced fighter easily parried it with his cudgel, the blade becoming deeply embedded in the wood.

Edwin and his teenaged son were courageous enough, fighting desperately for their home, if not their lives. But once the element of surprise was lost, they were no match for the outlaws, especially when the two others came running, one from the garden and the other attracted by the noise on his way back from chasing the pigs. As Edwin, a grizzled, toothless man of about fifty, struggled to pull his axe from Gwyn's club, the Cornishman put a massive arm around his shoulders and pulled him close.

'Stop struggling and you won't be hurt,' he whispered into his ear. The older man looked at him in surprise, then went limp. At the same time, Simon, rubbing his bruised arm, was dodging another blow from the son, a burly youth who was red in the face with mixed anger and fear. The outlaw, no stranger to vicious infighting, rapidly rallied against the unexpected attack and swung his own club, striking the son hard on the shoulder, making him howl. By now, the two other ruffians had arrived and grabbed the son by the arms. He managed to pull his right one free long enough to deliver a swinging blow with his branch to the temple of the youth who had trampled his garden, sending the fellow to the ground as if poleaxed. Gwyn had to hang on to the father as he struggled and swore when Simon drove his fist into the son's belly, causing him to double up. The lad sagged in the grip of the other outlaw, as he vomited his breakfast on to the ground.

The younger outlaw gave him a cruel kick in the ribs as he dropped him to the floor and turned to see what Simon was going to do to the father.

'Well done, Cornishman! Now we'll punish the silly old fool for daring to attack us.' As he spoke, Simon drew back his arm and punched Edwin in the face, splitting his lip and making his nose bleed.

'That's just a start – you can let him go now, Gwyn. I want to kick him around the garden for a bit.'

Gwyn reluctantly decided that this was the moment of truth.

'Leave him alone, Simon. And the boy.'

The outlaw stopped with his fist already raised for another blow, a puzzled expression on his face. His two yellowed fangs stuck out as his mouth stayed open in surprise.

'What the devil are you playing at, man? Get out of the way!'

By way of reply, Gwyn gave him a push in the chest that sent him staggering back into the younger outlaw. The cottar's son was recovering by now and was leaning against the whitewashed wall, wiping vomit from his chin with the back of his hand. His father wriggled from Gwyn's loosening grasp and went to the aid of his boy.

'Look, we've done them enough harm already,' barked Gwyn hurriedly, in an attempt to preserve his cover. 'Wrecked their garden, driven off their pigs – why not call it a day and let the bloody foresters do their own dirty work?'

Simon stared at the big redhead in amazement. 'What are you saying, you damned fool? Even if we weren't being paid for this, I'd half kill these swine for this – look what they did to Ralph there!'

In a fury, he pointed to the other outlaw, who was groaning as he slowly pulled himself to a crouch, blood oozing from between the fingers he held to the side of his head.

Simon advanced on Edwin and his son, his cudgel raised, but Gwyn swiftly stepped between them, his own club held out as a protective barrier against the angry outlaw. 'I said leave them alone!' he boomed, resigned now to abandoning any hope of further deception.

The thug's ugly face creased into a sneer and Gwyn recognised that here was a man who revelled in inflicting pain, suffering and humiliation on others.

'Right, you've had your chance, you big Cornish bastard!' he snarled. Pulling a long dagger from a sheath on the back of his belt, he came at Gwyn, club raised in one hand, the knife in the other. The bearded ruffian was close behind him, as the other young outlaw struggled to his feet a few yards away.

Gwyn smiled beatifically at the prospect of a good

fight. Though he had had a few skirmishes since becoming coroner's officer, they were few and far between compared to his old warrior days, and he missed the rough-and-tumble of confrontation. As Simon lunged at him with the blade and swung at his head with the club, he dodged and used his own club to give the attacker a crack on the wrist that made him howl, the dagger flying off into the dirt.

'Watch the other one!' yelled the cottar, as the other outlaw dived at Gwyn, his heavy stick raised. The defender parried the blow, the crack of wood on wood echoing from the cottage wall as he brought up his foot and kicked the youth hard between the legs. With a scream, he backed away, clutching his groin, but he stayed on his feet. By now, Ralph had recovered enough to stagger upright and was fumbling to draw his own knife. Simon, his left hand numb from the blow he had taken, had dropped his bludgeon and groped for his fallen dagger. A moment later, Gwyn faced two very angry men clutching long-bladed knives and another with a large club and a score to pay for his bruised testicles.

The coroner's henchman quickly decided that, in spite of his greater size and fighting experience, it would be politic to draw his sword. With a metallic rattle, he removed the tempered steel from its scabbard and waved it in an arc before the advancing outlaws.

'That's enough, boys!' he snapped. 'You've done enough here for one day. Now just go home, there's good fellows.'

He was wasting his breath, however, as the men, livid with excitement and fury, came on to crouch in a semicircle just beyond the reach of Gwyn's weaving broadsword. Edwin, a few feet away to the left, now drew his own knife, and his son had recovered enough breath to grope for his fallen stave of timber.

'Keep out of it. These bastards are killers!' boomed Gwyn, seeing the movement out of the corner of his eye. With Simon feinting with his dagger right in front of the Cornishman, the two younger outlaws rushed in from either side, creating a situation that even the battle-hardened Gwyn found disconcerting. He slashed his sword forward to keep Simon at bay, and simultaneously swung a massive arm towards Ralph, an arm that had an oaken cudgel on the end. It connected with the youth's already battered face, and for the second time in a few minutes, Ralph staggered back to collapse on the ground.

However, Gwyn had but two arms, and without the intervention of Edwin and his son he would have been in serious trouble, as the other ruffian was coming at his side with a very sharp knife. The cottar dived at the youth's dagger-arm just as the tip stuck into Gwyn's thick jerkin of boiled leather. He stopped the momentum of the thrust and his muscular son followed up by jumping on the man's back and getting his neck in an arm-lock. Between them they wrestled him to the ground, but not before Edwin suffered a long slash across the back of his forearm.

With both young villains out of the fray, Gwyn turned his full attention to Simon. The long reach of his sword completely outclassed the other man's dagger. The outlaw now bitterly regretted having left his own at the camp, as he had expected today's activity only to be an easy roughing-up of a simple freeholder.

'Drop it, Simon, or I'll have your head off your shoulders!' bellowed Gwyn.

The man with the boar's teeth stared at him for second, as if debating whether to chance an attack, then his knife-arm drooped towards the ground. 'You'll answer for this, Jess. What in hell's name has got into you?' he snarled.

'Let's just say that I've got a particular hate for bloody foresters. This poor fellow here should get a bounty for telling one to go to hell, not get roughed up.'

Gwyn began to wonder whether he could yet retrieve something from this fiasco, but Simon was not forgiving.

'You're dabbling in affairs you know nothing about. This is more than just stirring up some petty free-holder.'

Gwyn lowered the point of his sword. 'Drop that knife, then we can talk about it.'

'Don't trust the swine!' yelled Edwin, looking up from where he was kneeling on the young outlaw's legs. His son had dragged the boy to the ground and was holding him there with the branch pressed across his throat, half strangling him. The other youth, having had his head cracked twice within three minutes, was crawling away across the garden on his hands and knees. These events distracted Gwyn's attention for a brief moment, which was almost his undoing. Simon's knife shot up again and he lunged at Gwyn with a fero-cious cry.

Caught unawares, Gwyn was unable to step back as he was against the wall of the house, but his fast reflexes allowed him to twist sufficiently for the dagger to snag in the diagonal shoulder band of his baldric, which was hard leather a quarter of an inch thick. The keen blade sliced across the wide strap and embedded its point in his jerkin, but the force was lost and Gwyn suffered only a shallow cut on the skin of his midriff.

Though the Cornishman's body was hardly injured, his pride at being caught off guard suffered greatly. With a roar of anger, he whistled his sword in half a circle above his head and brought it down on the outlaw, catching him between the base of his neck and his shoulder.

As the man crumpled in a welter of blood, Gwyn prodded him in the breast-bone with the point of the sword, so that he fell away on to the grass, twitching his last agonies at the edge of the garden that he had so successfully ordered ruined.

'Are you hurt, man?' gasped Edwin, his eyes like saucers as he watched the rapid dispatch of the evil Simon. Gwyn put a hand into his jerkin and looked ruefully at his severed baldric and bloodstained fingers. 'Nothing a jug of good ale couldn't put right. What about you and your son?'

Edwin rubbed a hand across the drying blood on his face and the slash on his forearm. 'We'll survive – until those bastards come again.'

Gwyn took a couple of steps towards Simon, who had stopped jerking and was lying in a widening pool of blood that was soaking into the dry soil. 'He'll give you no more trouble – what about that one?'

He moved to stand over the younger outlaw and rested the tip of his sword gently on his belly. 'You can let him go now, son. Pity to choke him to death with a stick, when hanging's so much easier!'

As the two cottars released the lad and stood up, there was a scuffling noise behind them as the third ruffian managed to get to his feet and tottered rapidly towards the ring of trees around the homestead.

'He's getting away! After him, Garth,' shouted Edwin. Gwyn put out a hand to restrain the son from pursuing the terrified fugitive, who had just seen the summary dispatch of his leader.

'Don't bother with him. Let's see what this one has to tell us.' He grinned down at the youth under his sword-point, who stared back fearfully.

'Who are you?' he croaked. 'Why have you turned against us?'

'I'm the officer of the King's coroner for this county,

that's who I am. And you are in big trouble, my lad. A fatal kind of trouble!'

Edwin looked at Gwyn, then at his son. 'The crowner? That's the Sir John de Wolfe that we heard looked into that death of the tanner in Manaton last week.'

Gwyn nodded. 'The very same – and foresters were mixed up in that affair, too.'

The cottar's face darkened. 'Those swine – they're the cause of all this.' His arm swept around to encompass his ruined vegetable plot and the corpse still oozing blood into his soil. He gave the prostrate outlaw a hefty kick in the ribs to relieve his feelings.

'What are you going to do with this piece of filth?' he demanded.

Gwyn looked down and grinned again. 'I could cut off his head and give it to you. With the other one there, you could claim four shillings bounty, if you took them to the sheriff.'

The young outlaw, having seen what this hairy giant had done to Simon, was in no doubt that Gwyn was quite capable of carrying out his promise. He began squirming under the sword and babbling pleas for his life.

'Let's see if you can change my mind, lad,' offered the coroner's henchman. 'Tell me what you know about this campaign to terrorise law-abiding dwellers in the forest – and what the foresters have to do with it.'

The boy protested that he knew next to nothing and in spite of a few small pricks with Gwyn's sword-tip all he could say was that he had once seen William Lupus talking amicably with Robert Winter on the roadside near Ashburton – and that occasionally a man who was said to be a horse-trader came to meet Winter and money was handed over.

In spite of futher threats, which reduced the youth

to a state of abject terror, it became obvious that he was such a minor part of the outlaw gang that he had no significant knowledge to disclose. Against the inclinations of the cottar and his son, Gwyn decided to send him on his way, rather than be saddled with a pathetic and useless prisoner who would inevitably end up on the gallows. He dragged him to his feet and gave him a push to help him on his way. As he tottered across the garden in the wake of his fellow villain, both Edwin and his son gave him a series of buffets across the head as parting gifts. The last they saw of him was a ragged figure stumbling into the shelter of the trees.

The freeholder stooped to pick up the torn door-leather and stood looking sadly at the ruin of his vegetable plot.

'There goes much of our food for the winter. And what's to become of us now? Those bastards will be back as soon as they hear what happened here.'

Gwyn slid his sword back into the scabbard, after wiping it on the grass.

'I've a feeling that all this trouble will be settled before long. The coroner will have to get help from outside if the sheriff won't act. Have you nowhere you can go for a few weeks?'

'There is my brother near Moretonhampstead. We can round up most of our pigs and drive them over there. My wife died last year and there is little else of value here now, only the land itself.'

Garth went off with a dog that had been locked in one of the sheds, to see if he could gather the hogs together, while Gwyn helped Edwin to load some of his meagre household goods on to a small handcart.

As they worked, the coroner's officer learned more details of the brush with the foresters.

'These past months it has become much worse,' said

the old man, repeating the same litany that had been told elswhere in the forest. 'They always had the right to demand a night's lodging and food from any forest dwelling, together with feeding their horse and hound. But lately they have been grossly abusing the right, coming every week, bringing their pages as well – and claiming extra fodder for their mounts, which they take away across their pages' saddles. They have been deliberately provoking us – for other cottars in the area have been treated likewise.'

He threw a couple of coarse blankets on to the cart as he spoke.

'The last straw was William Lupus claiming three of my best sows last week. That's well outside the law, but he threatened us when I told him to clear off. My other son was here that day, the one who works with my brother, so we were enough to turn him away. No doubt he's behind what's happened here today.'

'Is it always this Lupus fellow who causes such trouble?'

'Most of the time, though Michael Crespin, the other forester in this bailiwick, sometimes gets up to the same tricks.'

'Why do you think all this has blown up only in the past months?' asked Gwyn, as he helped Edwin throw a securing rope over the pile of belongings on the cart.

'It seems that they are doing this as part of some plan to create chaos and dissatisfaction in the forest. The death of the verderer, who was a decent man, all seems part of something – though God knows what!'

There was little more to be learned, and while the father went off to help his son find their missing pigs, Gwyn dragged Simon's body into the woods and buried him in a shallow depression, covering the corpse with armfuls of last autumn's leaves, though no doubt foxes and badgers would soon unearth him. Coming back, he covered the bloodstains with soil, using a wooden shovel he found in a shed.

By now, Garth and his father had returned with all but two of their pigs, and soon set out with the little cart and their dog, driving the grunting flock ahead of them the few miles up the road to Moretonhamstead and relative safety.

With a sigh at the sad sight of a dispossessed family, Gwyn left them at the junction of their lane with the high road and set off briskly for Ashburton to reclaim his horse.

John de Wolfe's holiday passed quickly and pleasantly in the company of his family. Though he had the worry about Nesta niggling at the back of his mind the whole time, he still managed to enjoy the copious food and drink and the obvious delight of his mother and sister at the chance to coddle him for three whole days. His brother's welcome showed a more masculine restraint, but was none the less warm and genuine, so the days passed very pleasantly indeed.

He went out hunting again for one morning and spent a considerable time walking or riding with William around the manor. His brother showed him all the agricultural activites with obvious pride – and as part of John's income came from the products of William's enterprise, his interest was unfeigned. On the Friday evening, as he relaxed in the solar after a good meal, his mind strayed again to his two trusted servants, Gwyn of Polruan and Thomas de Peyne. He wondered how they had fared and looked forward to seeing them safely returned to Exeter when he got back on Sunday.

* * *

At the moment that de Wolfe was thinking about his clerk, Thomas was in his element in the new church at Buckfast Abbey. Secure in his masquerade as a priest, for no one here knew him, he was standing in the quire of the lofty building. Squeezed on to the end of a row of monks, he was chanting his heart out in the responses that were bringing the office of Compline to a close. He had arrived that afternoon, following a fruitless day jogging from one parish church to another, and went to enrol for the night at the large guest hall across the abbey compound from the imposing church, using his story of being a parish priest on his way to a living in Cornwall. The lay brother who administered the hall looked at this travel-weary little man and took in his worn clerical gown and his ragged tonsure.

'You are a clerk, sir? Perhaps you would be better lodged in the dorter in the abbey over the way, rather than here among the common travellers.'

Thomas felt a pang of guilt in keeping up the deception that he was still in holy Orders, but a combination of intense longing, together with the knowledge that he was on the business of the King's coroner, managed to dampen his misgivings. He mumbled something that sounded vaguely confirmatory and the custodian took him by the arm and walked him across to the main abbey buildings. They entered through a small door between the church and the imposing abbot's lodging and passed through to the cloisters, a pillared arcade around four sides of a grassy square. In his seventh heaven, Thomas lingered behind his guide, basking in the serene peace of the monastic surroundings. Several monks passed, treading softly in their white robes, covered at the front by a brown scapular apron. They nodded at Thomas, but the strict Cistercian vow of silence forbade them from offering any other greeting. The lay brother, uninhibited by any such restraint, urged Thomas along and pointed out some of the main features of interest in the relatively new building, which before the Cistercians had been a Savignac house, and before that a Benedictine abbey founded in Saxon times.

They walked around the cloisters and then up some stairs to reach the long dorter, where the monks slept in spartan conditions, their hard pallets devoid of bedspreads and their clothing and meagre belongings conforming to the harsh edicts of the Rule of St Benedict, which the Cistercians had reintroduced earlier in the century. The lay brother stood with Thomas, looking down the long bare dormitory.

'You may have been more comfortable in the guest hall, brother,' he admitted rather sheepishly, but the coroner's clerk was only too delighted to share the rigours of these men of God. An aged monk appeared from a small anteroom and introduced himself as Brother Howell, the curator of the dorter. He was allowed to talk when business demanded, especially to those not of his order, and soon settled Thomas on a spare mattress in a corner of the long, high-roofed sleeping hall.

'We have no separate hospitium for accommodating visiting priests, but these pallets are reserved for them.'

'You can eat in the refectory with the rest of the brethren,' advised the lay brother as he left. 'Though if you want anything other than vegetarian fare, you'll have to come across to the guest house.'

Just as John de Wolfe was enjoying his visit to his old home, Thomas de Peyne was also relishing these two nights and a day in this beloved environment of a religious establishment. He went to every one of the six daily services, took the sacrament twice and was over-joyed on the second occasion to be asked to assist near the altar, attired in a borrowed surplice over his grubby robe.

So elated was he by his good fortune, Thomas almost forgot why he was there, and certainly, during his almost trance-like state during the offices, he had no thoughts to spare for the coroner's problems. In the refectory, where he shared the extremely simple fare, eaten in silence whilst extracts from the Gospels and from the Rule of St Benedict were intoned by a brother standing at a lectern, there was nothing to be learned about the politics of Buckfast. However, during the brief periods after meals when conversa-tion was allowed, he remembered his role as a spy and did his best to pick up any useful information. In truth, there was very little that the monks them-selves could tell him as they led a very introverted existence and knew little of what went on outside the abbey.

What meagre information he did manage to pick up came not from them, but from the lay brothers, who were local men who worked for the abbey for their bed and board plus a small wage. This was the workforce of the Cistercians, labourers who worked the huge estate, herded the sheep and cattle, ploughed the land, harvested the crops and did all the construction and maintenance work on the buildings. In his walks around the abbey compound and short forays out into the gardens, where huge vegetable plots and numerous beehives provided the sustenance for the community, he spoke to many of the workers, the majority of whom were happy to lean on their shovels or brooms for a moment to gossip.

In the stables, where his pony was also enjoying a well-fed respite, Thomas talked to the grooms and the farrier, storing up a picture of the abbey's lifestyle and governance in his clever little head. Out of all this, Thomas gained very little of use to his master in Exeter, but one item of intelligence intrigued him, though he had no real reason to think that it had any bearing on his mission. On Saturday afternoon, he was exchanging small talk with the loquacious custodian of the guest hall, both of them standing outside the door in the sunshine, as the threatened bad weather had cleared after a mild thunderstorm the previous night. They were idly watching the comings and goings of people in the wide courtyard, which was bounded by a wall joining the abbey buildings, the large guest house opposite and the north and south gateways. A man came striding towards them, his clothes streaked with road grime, a saddlebag slung over his shoulder. A short fellow with a tanned, leathery face, the traveller gave a friendly nod to the lay brother and walked straight through the door with an assurance that indicated his familiarity with the place.

'One of our regulars,' commented the custodian, as if sensing Thomas's thoughts. 'Stays here every few weeks – more often that that, sometimes.'

'Does he work for the abbey?' asked the ever-curious clerk.

'No, he's a horse and stock dealer, but he does a lot of trade with us. He's forever closeted with Father Edmund, bargaining over sales of our sheep, cattle and horses, especially breeding stock, for which Buckfast is famous.'

Thomas's interest waned a little – he was not interested in the sale of beasts. However, a priest had been mentioned, one that he had never heard of before.

'So who's Father Edmund? One of the monks?'

'Yes, he's a senior man in the chapter is Father

Edmund Treipas. A Cistercian, but also an ordained priest, like you. He came here from Exeter a couple of years ago to be the cellarer, though now he's far more than that.'

'How do you mean, more than that?'

'Well, he's more like the abbey's ambassador, always travelling to buy and sell in the world outside. A big place like this is an industry in itself – and the abbot and the brothers don't like going outside much, with their vows of silence and suchlike, so he does all that business side. We needed a clever mind, after that demand from the King in '93, when were almost ruined over the wool crop.'

Thomas had the sense not to draw too much attention to himself with more enquiries, but the presence of a much-travelled senior ecclesiastic caused him to make a special foray early on Sunday morning, between services in the church. After taking directions from a porter in the courtyard, he made his way into the cloisters and sought out a small door off the southern arcade. Tapping gently on the heavy panels, he did not wait for a response, but pushed it open and peered around the edge. He saw an untidy room, looking quite unlike any other part of the well-ordered abbey. A wide table was covered with open rolls of parchment and a long rack on a side wall was filled with dozens of rolls sticking out of pigeon-holes. The floor was cluttered with crates and boxes, even a full bale of raw wool, some sticking out of the hessian covering as if having been sampled.

Behind the table was a monk in a Cistercian habit, but with a wide leather belt around his waist, which carried a large document scrip.

The cellarer was standing up, sorting parchment lists with an air of grim determination, his strong features set in concentration. He looked up at the sound of the door opening, irritation on his face at the interruption.

'What is it? Who are you?'

As Thomas's objective was merely to get a look at the man, he took the quickest means of escape. Fumbling in his scrip for some coins, he made the excuse that as a passing priest grateful for accommodation for a couple of nights, he thought he should give his widow's mite to the abbey – and having heard that Father Treipas was the focal point of the management, he had come to offer a few pence, which was all he had.

The burly priest waved him away impatiently.

'There's an offertory in the church, brother – and another in the guest hall. Put it in there, don't bother me with such trifles. I've two hundred bales to be carted to Plymouth tomorrow.'

Thomas bobbed his head apologetically and withdrew rapidly, but not before impressing the father's face on his mind, in case he needed to recognise him again. Content that he had done all he could for the coroner, Thomas made his way reluctantly to the stables to collect his pony. As he rode out of the abbey compound under the south gatehouse towards the high road, he looked back longingly at the place where, for a few short hours, he had been a priest again, among his own kind and the prayers, chants and ceremonies that were so dear to him. He had given up all thoughts of trying to end his miserable life, as God had given him a sign when he had failed in his solitary attempt – now perhaps this was another sign, for if his uncle's attempts to have him reinstated in Holy Orders failed, then perhaps he could seek solace by spending the rest of his life as an unordained monk.

As he turned his pony's head towards the Exeter road

and his rendezvous with Gwyn at Ashburton, he clung on to his side saddle in a better frame of mind than he had experienced for many months.

ChAPTER EIGHT

In which Matilda goes to Polsloe

It was early evening before all three of the coroner's team got together at Rougemont. De Wolfe had arrived back from Stoke-in-Teignhead late in the afternoon, to find no sign of Matilda at home. Thankful for a postponement of her inevitable sniping at his visit to his family, he assumed she had gone either to St Olave's or to her long-suffering cousin in Fore Street. Neither Mary nor Lucille was at the house in Martin's Lane, but as it was Sunday they were entitled to a few hours' freedom.

He promised himself a visit to the Bush as soon as possible, but before that he wanted to make sure that his two assistants had returned safely and to hear what they had learned, if anything. When he climbed the stairs to his chamber above the gatehouse, he was relieved to find that they were both there. Thomas had met Gwyn as arranged at the inn in Ashburton, and together they had travelled back to Exeter. John lowered himself to his stool behind the table and glared at his two henchmen, his habitual fierce expression disguising the fact that he was relieved to see them safe and sound.

'Why the new baldric strap?' he asked, looking at the band of new leather running diagonally across Gwyn's huge chest. His officer's red moustache lifted as he grinned.

'A long story, Crowner, but some bastard outlaw sliced through the other one. I must be getting old, it took me several seconds to kill him!'

Their more timorous clerk blanched at this casual talk of slaying, even though he had already heard the story. Now he heard it all again, as Gwyn related his brief penetration of the outlaw gang and then summed up his conclusions.

'It's clear that they are being paid by someone to aggravate whatever's going on in the forest. As well as their usual tricks of thieving and robbery with violence, Robert Winter and his mob are doing dirty work for the foresters – or at least for two of them, William Lupus and Michael Crespin.'

De Wolfe considered this for a moment, brooding over his table like a great black crow. 'Why are they doing it – and who's paying them?' he ruminated, half to himself.

'It can hardly be for personal gain,' piped Thomas. 'To pay men to beat up some cottar just because he refused to give them a bit of fodder and a couple of pigs seems ridiculous. I think it more likely that there's a campaign to make the forest administration look unmanageable – closing forges and burning tanneries, penalising alehouses. Surely that must be to make the forest dwellers so outraged that they demand change.'

'Who the hell cares about how the forest is run?' objected Gwyn, who usually appeared to ridicule anything the clerk said, though in reality, he had a deep regard for the little man's intelligence.

John rasped his fingers thoughtfully over his black stubble – he had forgotten his Saturday shave the day before, being in Stoke.

'Yes, who could possibly gain by it?' he pondered. 'But what if someone wanted to replace the existing senior forest officers by making it obvious that the present regime had lost its grip?'

Gwyn nodded his shaggy head. 'We've had a verderer murdered and the Warden attacked and half killed. That's a good start towards getting new officers.'

'And our sheriff appointed a new verderer almost before the slain one was cold!' added Thomas.

'One of the outlaws sniggered when I suggested that their behaviour would have the sheriff down upon them,' Gwyn recollected.

De Wolfe beat an agitated tattoo on the table with his dirty fingernails.

'Yes, the bloody sheriff! He hinted to me that he would like to be Warden of the Forest himself. Though God knows why, there can't be much money in it. There's no salary and I can't see the foresters sharing the loot from their extortions with him.'

There was a silence as John worked things over in his mind. Gwyn took the opportunity to lug out his pitcher of cider and get three pottery cups from a niche in the stony wall. Shaking out woodlice and spiders, he filled the mugs and handed them around.

'Did you learn anything else in your brief sojourn as an outlaw, Gwyn?' grunted the coroner.

'Not much – only confirmation that the foresters have stepped up their oppression in the last few months. But we knew that already. The odd thing is that this Robert Winter – who seems quite a smart fellow –is getting paid for helping the foresters create their disturbances. I'll wager that it was one of their gang who put an arrow in the verderer's back, probably for money.'

'So who the hell is paying them?' mused de Wolfe, sipping his cider.

'They seem to be quite bold in their dealings with townsfolk. I saw this Martin Angot deep in conversation with someone in the tavern in Ashburton,' said Gwyn. 'Someone like that could easily be passing on orders and payment.'

'Did you recognise him?'

'No, but I've got a feeling I've seen him here in Exeter at some time. He was a little, dark-featured fellow with a face like a dried fig.'

At this, Thomas sat up and took notice.

'I saw a man in Buckfast yesterday who looked like that,' he squeaked. 'A lined, leathery face and no taller than me.'

The coroner looked dubious. 'Plenty of men look like that.'

Thomas was not to be put off. 'This one was a horse-trader, they told me. I don't know his name, but he did a lot of business with the abbey, through Father Edmund, the cellarer.'

Now it was Gwyn who looked interested. 'A horse-trader? One of those outlaws said that a horse-trader came in to see Robert Winter now and then. Could be the same man.'

'Who's this Father Edmund you speak of?' demanded John.

'He's a priest-monk, but seems to conduct all the business for Buckfast. Came from Exeter a couple of years ago, but by his accent he's from up north somewhere. I went to take a look at him, but I've never seen him before.'

De Wolfe rasped his chin again as an aid to thought.

'He's a senior priest from west of Exeter, which fits with the vague hint I had from your uncle. Though there's plenty of them about.'

'But worth looking into, if he has dealings with this horse-dealer, given it's the same fellow as the one in the alehouse,' recommended Gwyn.

'I'll ask about him, too,' ruminated the coroner. 'Ralph Morin is the one to talk to about horses. He has to buy them for the garrison.'

They chewed over the scanty information for a few

more minutes, but failed to distil anything further from it. When the cider was finished, for which Thomas's more fastidious palate was thankful, they went their various ways and John returned to his house in Martin's Lane.

There was no one in the hall when he put his head around the screens, and when he climbed the stairs to the solar John found that empty as well. When Matilda went to her cousin's house, she occasionally stayed until late – and sometimes, when she was particularly annoyed with him, she stayed the night without bothering to let him know. He was therefore not much concerned at her absence and decided to go straight down to the Bush to see Nesta and have something to eat.

As he clattered down the steep steps into the yard, Mary came out of her kitchen shed a few yards away and stood waiting with her arms folded in what struck John as a rather belligerent attitude.

'She's gone, you know!' she said challengingly.

John stopped on the last step and stared at his maid.

'I know that! Is she at church or at her cousin's?'

'Neither – I told you, she's gone. This time for good,' she said!'

He took Mary by the arm and led her back into her hut, pushing her gently down on to a stool, while he stood towering over her.

'What's all this about? How can she have gone – and where?'

The dark-haired maid, usually on his side against his abrasive wife, looked up accusingly. John had the feeling that she was siding with all the women.

'You've really done it this time, Sir Crowner!' Mary only used that half-cynical title when she was annoyed with him. 'Your lady wife has discovered that you've got Nesta with child – and she's up and left you.'

De Wolfe groaned. It had to happen sooner or later, but he had hoped to put off the evil hour a little longer. Nesta was not even showing her pregnancy yet.

'She'll be back,' he said half-heartedly. 'She's taken umbrage many times before and gone to her cousin for a few days or so.'

Mary shook her head with disconcerting assurance. 'Not this time! She's taken herself to Polsloe and says she's going to stay there for the rest of her life.'

John's heart leapt in his chest. 'The priory? I can't believe it!'

There was mixed doubt and elation in his voice. This was something he had hoped for and even fantasised about for ages. He had been intending to ask his archdeacon friend whether Matilda taking the veil was equivalent to an annulment of his marriage, as this was the only way he could see himself ever being free of her, short of her death, for which he had never wished.

Mary was still glaring at him, from solidarity with all wronged women, but he pressed on with eager questions.

'How did she find out? No one knows except a few at the Bush – and you. When did all this happen?'

Rapidly, he drew the story from his cook-maid, and once again it transpired that he had his brother-in-law to thank for stabbing him in the back. Richard de Revelle had turned up at the house the previous morning, and within a minute of being closeted with his sister in the hall there had been an outburst of yelling from Matilda. This was soon followed by a slamming of doors as she swept up to the solar, the sheriff letting himself out of the house with a satisfied smirk on his face.

'I can't think how he found out, damn him!' muttered John, but Mary, familiar with the gossip network that connected every alehouse, shop and doorstep in the city, was in no doubt.

'The sheriff has informants everywhere – and it was not that much of a secret, anyway. I heard of it from the pastry-shop man who drinks in the Bush, even before you told me.'

She continued her tale of Matilda's departure. It seemed that his wife had screamed at her maid Lucille to pack some clothes into a bag and then go to the high street to order a two-horse litter. Within an hour, Matilda appeared, still in a towering rage and dressed in her best black kirtle with a white wimple and gorget. With a weeping Lucille trailing behind, lugging a large bag, she proceeded up to the corner of the lane, where a litter was waiting. They vanished, and Mary had heard nothing of them since.

John listened in silence. Once the first surge of hope had passed, he became more realistic and had grave doubts about Matilda really having left for good. After her occasional flounces to stay with her cousin – and once even six weeks away at her distant de Revelle relatives in Normandy – she always came home when her temper cooled. He supposed he had better take himself to Polsloe to see what the true situation was and bring her back, if the worst of her passion had subsided. But first he was going down to see Nesta and talk it over with her.

'What about me, how do I fare in this?' demanded Mary, as he started to leave. De Wolfe stared at her, then slid an arm reassuringly around her shoulders.

'You stay right where you are, good girl! You're almost a wife to me yourself. You feed me, clothe me, clean my house and tell me when to wash and shave. How could I ever do without you?'

She looked up at him with the suspicion of a tear in her eye. This was the only home she had, with her mother dead and her father an unknown soldier who had only stayed for her conception, not her birth.

'What will happen to Lucille?' she sniffed. 'A nun can hardly keep a personal maid with her in the priory.'

De Wolfe shrugged. 'This won't last, mark my words. If Lucille comes back, tell her she can keep her room under the stairs and I'll still give her twopence a day until the situation gets settled.'

His conscience assuaged, de Wolfe whistled for Brutus, who was lurking in the back of the kitchen, aware that something unusual was going on. Together they set out for the Bush, John's head spinning with a mixture of hope and guilt, as well as recognition that this situation was too good to last.

In Idle Lane, he pushed through the tavern door impatiently, all his reluctance of past weeks vanished. The taproom was crowded, with a clamour of noise and a fug of the usual spilt ale and sweat. He saw Nesta at the back of the room, haranguing one of her serving wenches. Brutus, used to the ways of the Bush, sloped off to the back door, where he knew he could cadge some old trenchers and other scraps from the outside kitchen, leaving John free to march across and take Nesta by the arm.

'Upstairs. We can't talk in this hubbub!' he growled. Something about his manner stopped her from making her usual protests about how busy she was, and she climbed ahead of him up the wide ladder in the corner.

In her room, he dropped the latch inside the door and sat on the bed, motioning her to come alongside him.

'Matilda has left me,' he said without any preamble. 'She's gone to be a nun at Polsloe, though whether it will last I fear to hope.'

Nesta stared at him wide eyed, then began to cry,

turning John's insides to water. He slid an arm around her shoulders as she leaned into him.

'It's my fault – everything is my fault. I wish I was dead!' she sobbed.

Desperately, he murmured useless soothing noises.

'She's discovered I'm with child, hasn't she?' moaned Nesta.

John was unable to deny it. 'It seems so, my love – though it would have happened sooner or later. It alters nothing. In fact, if she's gone for good, we are freer than ever!' He tried to sound cheerful in the face of his mistress's obvious distress. 'That bastard brother of hers told her, I don't know how he found out,' he concluded.

Nesta sat up, sniffing loudly and wiping her eyes with the hem of her apron.

'Everyone else seems to know already – either my maid or her mother, the midwife, must have let it out,' she moaned.

John tugged her towards him. 'It doesn't matter how it came out. I've told you, I'll openly acknowledge the babe and cherish him as much as I cherish you. There's no problem, my love, really.'

This only provoked another flood of tears from Nesta, leaving John even more discomfited and mystified at the ways of women. They sat in mutual misery for a few more minutes, his mistress rubbing her reddened eyes against the shoulder of his tunic, until she pulled herself together a little and sat up straight.

'What are you going to do about your wife?' she demanded.

De Wolfe looked down at the upturned face with puzzlement.

'What am I going to do? I wasn't going to do anything,' he said. 'Matilda's a free woman, she has money of her own from her family. She's got this mania for religion, so it's up to her what she wants to do with her life. Though I suspect that the food and raiment of a nunnery won't be to her liking for very long. This is just a petulant gesture born of her anger. It won't last once she gets a taste of monastic life.'

He sighed and hugged her to him again. 'I've dreamt of something like this ever since I met you, Nesta. But it's just a dream. I'll never get free of her, will I? But at least it gives us a short time when I don't have to creep back into her solar and get an earful of abuse every time I've been down to see you.'

The Welsh woman was putting herself back into order, sniffing back the last of her tears, while tucking her unruly red curls back under her cap.

'You must go to see her, John, straight away,' she said in a voice filled with new determination.

'And say what?' he asked in some surprise.

'Beg her to come home, John. It's ridiculous that the crowner's wife should take off to a nunnery. You'll be the laughing stock of the county. Get her back – and quickly, John.'

He shrugged, bemused by her reaction. 'If you say so, my love. It makes no difference to us, everything I said about the child stands. It would be easier if Matilda was out of the way, but that's too much to hope for.' He looked wistfully at her. 'I was even going down to talk to John de Alencon, to see if her taking vows would be equivalent to a divorce.'

At other times this might have squeezed a smile from Nesta, but she remained blank faced, a kind of miserable determination etched on her features.

'We'd better go down. I've work to do,' she murmured.

He kissed her tenderly and handed her up from the bed, now totally confused as to her mood. As they left the little room, she spoke again.

'Promise me that you'll go to see your wife – this very night.'

He nodded, almost afraid to argue with her, and they went back down to the taproom. The level of noise dropped as they descended the steps and a number of curious faces turned up to watch them, then hurriedly dropped away and pointedly ignored them.

As John squeezed her hand for the last time and turned to the door, he saw two familiar figures standing inside. Gwyn and Thomas had turned up, and their first words told him that they had heard the news about Matilda's departure.

'Bloody hell, this city is beyond belief!' he snapped. 'You can't fart here without everyone knowing about it within the space of a dozen heartbeats!'

'We wondered if you were all right?' said Gwyn solicitously. 'And if we could do anything to help you both?'

Gwyn was very fond of Nesta in an avuncular fashion and had been delighted when the recent rift between his master and the innkeeper had been healed. Thomas too, was devoted to Nesta, who treated him like a lost dog, sympathetically feeding and petting him. It was not long ago that she had given him free bed and board, when he had been evicted from his meagre lodgings in the cathedral precinct.

'That's kind of you both,' muttered John, embarrassed by even a hint of solicitude from a rough diamond like his officer. 'But I must go up to Polsloe now and see what the hell this woman is thinking of!'

Gwyn offered to ride with him and, glad of the company, de Wolfe arranged to meet him at the East Gate after he had got his horse from Andrew's stable. Gwyn went off to fetch his own mare from the garrison stables in the other ward of Rougemont, leaving John standing with Thomas de Peyne.

'There are worse things than taking vows, Crowner,'

209

said the little clerk tentatively.'Since staying in Buckfast, it occurred to me that if I cannot regain my place in holy orders, maybe I will enter some monastery.'

John looked down with half-concealed affection at Thomas, who was trying to console him, unnecessarily as it happened.

'She'll not stay there long, Thomas. My wife is too fond of the good things in life to put up with austerity and hardship. She's tough and will do exactly what she feels is in her best interests. It's Nesta that concerns me. She seems so unhappy, though there's no need for it.'

It was unheard of for the coroner to unbend his habitual stern manner enough to say these things to his servant, but today was fraught with unusual emotions.

'You go off to see your wife, master,' replied his clerk. 'I'll see if I can comfort the lady here. When I was a priest, I had some pastoral skills and maybe some still remain,' he ended, rather wistfully.

John patted Thomas awkwardly on the shoulder and went to the door, Brutus abandoning a sheep's bone to lope after him.

It was less than a mile and a half from the East Gate of the city to Polsloe, the track curving through some dense woodland after leaving the village of St Sidwell's, where Gwyn lived. The two horsemen reached the priory of St Katherine well within half an hour and sat in their saddles for a few moments outside the encircling wall. De Wolfe seemed reluctant to go in to face his wife, and Gwyn asked whether he wanted him to accompany him. The last time they had been to the priory they had been chasing a murderer, and it felt odd to be here now on a more delicate mission.

'No, you stay out here, unless you want to wheedle

a jug of ale from someone. I'm not sure how welcome men are in this nest of women.'

The thought of a drink overcame any concerns the Cornishman may have had about nuns, so they approached the low arched entrance together. An aged porter opened the wooden door when they banged on it and, after lashing their horses to a hitching rail, directed them across the wide compound to the West Range. This was a two-storey building, behind which were the small cloisters, all built of timber. The priory had been endowed over thirty years ago by Sir William de Brewer and, like Bovey Tracey, its church of Thoverton stone was dedicated to St Thomas the Martyr, another building funded by William de Tracy, in penitence for killing Becket. There were fourteen nuns here, and John wondered whether there would soon be fifteen.

Gwyn sloped off to the kitchens attached to the end of the West Range, marked by a basket of vegetable scraps outside the door, in the hope of scrounging something from one of the lay sisters. John climbed a step to an entrance he remembered from his last visit and knocked firmly on an open door to attract attention. In a moment a woman appeared from a side chamber, dressed in the dark habit of a Benedictine. Her hair was hidden under a flowing head-veil, her throat swathed up over the chin in a linen gorget. A wooden crucifix swung from her braided belt, as her moon-like face stared at him suspiciously.

'I am Sir John de Wolfe, the King's coroner,' he began, thinking it as well to pull rank from the start.

The nun did not ask his business, but stood aside and motioned him to enter. She led the way to the room from which she had emerged, a small chamber with nothing inside but a small table, a stool and a large, rather crude cross nailed to the wall.

'Please wait here in the outer parlour. The prioress will be here in a moment,' were her first and last words, as she glided out and vanished.

John, somewhat bemused by his reception, stood looking around at the bare cell. If this was what a nunnery had to offer, he thought glumly, Matilda would be back home within hours. A few moments later, another lady appeared, with another nun hovering behind as a chaperone.

De Wolfe recognised the prioress from his previous escapade here and gave her a stiff bow of respect.

'I believe that my wife may have arrived here yesterday, Dame Margaret. I wondered if I might speak to her,' he said humbly.

The prioress was usually an amiable-looking woman, but now her expression was forbidding. 'I am well aware of the situation, Sir John. But Matilda has said – in the strongest possible terms – that she does not wish to see you.'

John stared at her. He was not used to being thwarted, especially by a woman. 'But she is my wife!' he snapped. 'I have the right to speak to her – and to take her home, if it pleases me.'

He immediately wondered why he had said that, as the last thing he wanted was to have Matilda back in his house, where she would give him hell, then continue to ruin his life. But his father's legacy of Norman blood had broken through to assert his dominance as a husband – and an arrogant dismissal of anyone who denied it.

However, he seemed to have met his match in Polsloe. The prioress looked at him calmly and explained as if she were talking to a child.

'Once inside the walls of a monastery, sir, the laws of the outside world no longer apply. Indeed, in some orders, entrance equates with death. The person no longer exists in the secular sense.'

'My wife is not a member of your order, lady! She is presently not in a rational state of mind and unable to make reasoned decisions about her future.'

Dame Margaret smiled sadly. 'That is for her to decide, Crowner. She needs some time to reflect on her position. Until then, she wishes to stay here – and we are happy to shelter her.'

John's instinct was to argue, but he managed to stifle his annoyance, deciding that it was against his own interests to demand her 'release'.

'What's to be done, then? Do you need my support for her sustenance here? I am willing to pay.'

The prioress shook her head. 'She came well provided, Sir John. There will be time to deliberate about any endowment if and when Matilda decides to enter upon her vows. At the moment she is but a candidate, not even a novice.'

John silently hoped that the process would last indefinitely, but said nothing. It seemed obvious that Matilda had brought a dowry with her – he knew that she kept some treasure in a locked trunk in her solar, money that was hers alone, derived from an annuity from the de Revelle estates. He had never queried nor coveted anything of hers – he was comfortably provided from the income from his wool partnership with Hugh de Relaga and his share of the manorial profits from Stoke-in-Teignhead.

There seemed little more to be said, as the prioress stood placidly but still quite adamant that he was not going to be allowed to speak to his wife. He cut short the impasse by nodding respectfully to her again and turning to the door.

'Please tell Matilda that I was here and was concerned for her. If there is anything she requires, please let me know.'

The prioress bowed her head graciously.

'If there is any change in the situation, I will make sure that you are informed. I am still indebted to you for the help you provided when we had that unpleasantness some months ago, so I am distressed at this problem in your personal affairs.'

With that, she swept away, her chaperone hurrying after her, leaving John to find his way to the outer door. He collected Gwyn from the kitchen, where he had charmed a buxom lay sister into giving him a pasty and a quart of ale, then they made their way back to their horses and began plodding back to Exeter, the coroner in a silent, pensive mood.

Thomas found Nesta in the brew-shed, one of the outhouses of the tavern which shared the backyard with the kitchen, privy and pigsty.

After the coroner and his officer had left for Polsloe, Nesta had gone about her usual business in the inn, but listlessly, with none of her normal bustling efficiency. When she disappeared through the back door, Thomas followed her, glad to get out of the taproom. He disliked alehouses, he drank reluctantly and sparingly, and usually only entered inns when he had to accompany either Gwyn or John de Wolfe.

Padding up the yard in the approaching dusk, he stopped outside the brew-house door and heard the sound of soft sobbing from inside. Tapping gently, he put his head around the door and saw Nesta sitting on a milking stool, a long paddle, used for stirring the ale mash which was stewing in several large wooden tubs, in her hands.

Her head jerked up at the intrusion, but her face softened when she saw it was the little clerk.

'Thomas, what is it?' she asked.

'I'm the one who is supposed to say that!' he replied

with a wry smile. 'Is there anything I can do for you – or anything you want to talk about, dear Nesta?'

She shook her head mutely, her eyes again moist with tears. He went over to her and knelt on the dusty earth floor at her feet.

'Even if I am no longer a priest, able to take confession, I am still your good friend, Nesta. Can't you tell me what's wrong? I have seen both you and my master becoming more unhappy as the days go by. It grieves me sorely and I know Gwyn feels the same.'

Nesta put a hand on his thin shoulder and shook her head silently.

'Everyone knows the babe is at the root of this matter,' he said softly. 'Yet John de Wolfe has acknowledged it and even seems glad about being its father. This nonsense concerning his wife will pass, I know. As little as I know about family affairs, it is common for a man to have children outside marriage – and he has none of his own.'

Through her tears, she smiled sadly at his innocence.

'Dear Thomas, it is far more complicated than you imagine. I have sinned, I have attempted greater sins, and now contemplate an even greater sin.'

The clerk looked up at her, his brown eyes wide with apprehension.

'What are you saying, woman? You are goodness itself. What's this talk of sin?'

She gave a great sigh, then put both her hands on his shoulders, feeling the bones through his threadbare tunic. Face to face now, she told him of her despair.

'Thomas, you just said that John is glad to be a father – but he is not a father, though he doesn't yet know it.'

As the clerk gaped at her, she went on, the words spilling out now that she had taken the plunge. 'The father is Alan of Lyme, that viper I took to my bosom some months ago, when your master and I had fallen out. I had hoped against hope that it was not so, but when I visited Bearded Lucy down on Exe Island, she found that the time I have been with child makes it impossible for it to have been John's.'

Thomas's head sagged so that his forehead rested on her knees for a moment. Then he looked up, his face filled with compassion.

'That was your first sin – so what are these others?'

Nesta's hands left his shoulders to drop into her lap and screw up the folds of her thin leather brewing apron into a creased bundle.

'I have tried to rid myself of this traitor in my womb. I have taken every herb and potion I could obtain. All they have done is make me sick, but not shifted this legacy of my infidelity!'

Thomas rocked back on his heels in the dirt, staring up at her.

'That is indeed a sin, Nesta. Understandable in your distress, but a sin nevertheless. You call the child a traitor, but he knows nothing of his creation, he can have no fault – at least until he is born, when he will have the same original sin as the rest of us.'

Her hands left the torturing of her apron to rub her filling eyes again.

'You are right, Thomas, the babe is not the one at fault, he is but the instrument of my own misdeeds. Anyway, these pills and potions failed, so the matter is of no consequence. I have ruined John's life, his marriage, perhaps his standing as a high official.'

The clerk made twittering denials at this.

'Come, Nesta, be realistic! Every Norman knight has by-blows, some by many different women. It's not something that is even worthy of mention in their company. Matilda's own brother has several, that everyone knows

216

about. And as for the crowner's marriage, you know as well as any of us that it is an unhappy sham. If only this child were his, then it would have been one of the best things to happen to him.'

'That's the very point, can't you see!' she wailed. 'It's not his and when he discovers that, as he is bound to before long, then I will have destroyed him. He will hate me, reject me and that I cannot bear! There is only one course left.'

He gaped at her, uncomprehending at first.

'You should know, Thomas, you have been down that same road yourself, not long ago.'

'No, Nesta, not that! Never that, you must never even think of that.'

The clerk was aghast at what finally he understood her to be contemplating.

'It is the only way, Thomas. He would be rid of the fruit of my wickedness and rid of me at the same time – me, who stands between him and fulfilment in his life.'

De Peyne jumped to his feet, agitated and desperate. This time it was he who seized her by the shoulders and virtually shook her.

'No, Nesta, no! You must never even think of it again! Yes, you said I had been down that road – but I turned off that road and now I know that madness had enveloped me at that time. My desperation was different from yours, but none the less awful!'

He stopped for breath and shook her gently again.

'Yet when I tried, God showed me I was wrong. He stopped me and now I would never, never contemplate that again! In fact, only yesterday I found another answer, if the need arises – to enter the peace of monastic life, like Matilda. There are always answers, Nesta – always!'

He stood now with his arm around her as she sat on

the stool, her head sinking against his waist. They were both shivering with emotion, as he crooned further encouragement to her.

'If you harmed yourself, you would also wound John de Wolfe for life. I know he loves you, in spite of his gruff ways. And what of Gwyn and myself? We cherish you too. Think how we would be devastated if you were no longer with us.'

They talked in low tones for a long time, Thomas gradually winning from her a solemn promise not to harm herself or the child. Though a former priest, he made no threats of eternal hellfire or the damnation of the Church. Rather, he played on the desolation that would fall upon de Wolfe and the sadness and grief that would be inflicted upon her friends.

'But what's to be done, Thomas?' she whispered, when her tears had almost dried and she was rational again. 'Am I to tell him the babe's not his?'

This was where the clerk's exhortations, fluent where mortal sin was concerned, became rather thin when applied to earthly practicalities.

'Is he bound to find out, if we say nothing?' he asked.

Nesta turned up her hands helplessly. 'It's a great risk, especially if some busybody puts it about – and there are plenty of those in Exeter, God knows! Look how soon his wife was told of my condition.'

Thomas nodded sadly. He was well aware of the gossip machine that operated so efficiently in the city.

'Then you must tell him yourself. It would be far better coming from you than for him to be shocked by hearing it from some common chatter.'

Nesta considered this, the worried look on her face deepening.

'How could I screw up enough courage to break that news to him?'

'Better from your lips than from anyone else,' advised the clerk.

She sighed and stood up to lean against one of the mash tuns.

'You must be right, good Thomas. I must pick the right moment and pray to God that he does not spurn me for ever.'

'Amen to that!' he replied fervently.

Back in his own house, de Wolfe sat by his hearth, the unlit wood behind the iron fire-dogs emphasising the coldness of the lofty hall. Strangely, he already felt lonely, in the knowledge that the solar above his head was empty. Even the presence of his surly and unpleasant wife made the house more than just a pile of timber and stone, which was what he felt it to be at that moment. Brutus had slunk away to the back yard to seek the company of Mary in the cook-shed, instinctively aware of some sea change in the household that day.

John rarely drank wine except at meals or in the company of others, but today he went to a chest against the wall and took out a pottery flask of his best Loire red. He broke the wax seal and twisted out the wooden bung, pouring a liberal measure into one of the glass cups that he had looted in a distant campaign in Brittany.

Sitting back in one of the hooded chairs, John drank and brooded on the day's events. There was nothing more he could do about Matilda. He had made his best attempt to see her and persuade her to come home, so his conscience was clear on that score, if not on the cause of her leaving in the first place. She had long known of his affair with Nesta, as she was aware of his occasional fling with Hilda of Dawlish.

It was his imminent fatherhood which seemed to

have pushed her over the limit of her tolerance. John, in some ways a simple man, failed to see why having a mistress or two was at least grudgingly accepted, yet paternity was beyond the pale, even when it was the natural sequel to adultery. He reasoned that most men of his acquaintance had at least one bastard lurking somewhere – some of them even had a whole brood!

Dimly, he comprehended that a difference might be that Matilda and he had never had children of their own – though the opportunities for conception had been very limited during their married life, as he had been absent for most of it and, since he had returned from the Crusades, their marital relations had rapidly dwindled to nothing. John's insensitive nature failed to appreciate that even if the most unmotherly Matilda had never desired the burden of maternity herself, she might be flagrantly opposed to her husband providing it to any other woman.

He growled under his breath at this attack of introspection, so foreign to a man of action like himself. Pouring another cup of wine, he tried to divert his mind back to coroner's business as a welcome relief from the worries forced on him by the machinations of women.

Going over the meagre reports that Gwyn and Thomas had brought back from their expedition to the fringes of Dartmoor, he began arranging the intelligence alongside what they already knew.

There was a concerted plan to cause trouble throughout that part of the Royal Forest, in which the foresters and probably the new verderer was involved. There was a plot to remove the Warden of the Forests, by violence if required, and to replace him with someone else. It seemed likely that this someone was Richard de Revelle, but de Wolfe could not decide whether this was mere opportunism or whether the sheriff was an integral part of the plot. Against the latter, he failed to see what even the avaricious sheriff could hope to gain.

In any event, he thought as he gulped some more of the rather sour wine, the outlaws under Robert Winter were deeply involved. They were acting as mercenaries in assisting the foresters to cause disaffection amongst the forest dwellers, being paid for their efforts through some intermediaries. This horse-dealer was a possible candidate for that, if the man Gwyn had seen in the Ashburton tavern was the same as that seen by Thomas at Buckfast – though both incidents may have been quite innocent, unless there was some proof to the contrary. Against that was the tenuous rumour about the involvement of a 'priest from the west'. The frequent dalliance of the horse-dealer with this Cistercian from Buckfast was probably sheer coincidence, but it was worth looking into.

Here John's deliberate diversion from his marital problems dried up, just as the last of the wine drained from his flask. With a sigh, he hauled himself up and went down the alleyway to the back yard to find Mary.

She had softened her attitude since his visit to Polsloe and listened quietly as he brought her up to date with the situation.

'So the mistress will not be home yet awhile, until she works off her disaffection with me, Mary,' he concluded. 'But no doubt when the novelty of pretending to be a nun wears off, she'll return to make my life even more miserable than before. I'll never hear the end of this.'

His maid looked doubtful. 'If you say so, Sir Crowner – but I'll believe it when I see it. I've never seen her in such a state before, not in all the other times you've fallen out with the mistress.'

He shrugged helplessly. 'We'll just have to see, good girl. What about Lucille, has she shown up yet?'

Mary nodded and pointed to the box-like structure beneath the high supports of the solar steps. 'She came back an hour ago, full of weeping, and shut herself in. I told her what you said about keeping her on and she seemed a little easier then.'

Matilda's maid was a refugee from the Vexin, the part of France north of the Seine which was fought over continually by Richard the Lionheart and Philip of France. Lucille had no surviving family, though John suspected that Matilda had taken her on at the suggestion of her Normandy relatives, more from the social clout of having a French maid than from any feelings of compassion.

'Did my wife take all her finery with her?' he asked, knowing of Matilda's attachment to her wardrobe. He knew that Mary could not have resisted a quick foray into the solar, once she knew his wife had left.

'Hardly anything, apart from a couple of shifts and chemises. That's why I think she's really serious this time.'

John responded with his habitual growling in his throat, which could mean anything. 'I think I'll take a walk into the Close to see the archdeacon,' he announced. 'Then I'm to bed. It's been a hard day!'

Though the longest day of the year was fast approaching, it was almost dark when de Wolfe called upon John de Alençon at his house in Canon's Row. There was still an hour to go before the archdeacon had to leave for matins in the cathedral, and John joined him in his bare study for a cup of wine and a talk. The coroner first related the story of Matilda's departure and the reason for it. De Alençon listened gravely to his friend's admission of Nesta's pregnancy, a rather shamefaced account of the fruits of his adultery, in that he was making it to a senior man of God. In fact, the canon was already well aware of the matter, as was most of the city, but he listened with a grave face as if it were news to him.

'It seems typical of our sheriff that he should delight in distressing his sister with the revelation,' he commented. 'But again, it is another manifestation of his desire to do you as much harm as possible.'

John steered the conversation on to the matter of his marital status.

'If my wife really has left me for good and intends taking her vows as a nun, does this annul our marriage?'

The archdeacon steepled his hands as if praying for guidance.

'My friend, the honest answer is that I do not know, but I doubt it very much. This situation is outside my experience, for almost invariably, most mature women who take the veil are widows. The majority of nuns are younger girls who enter as virgins, but married women with living husbands must be exceptionally rare candidates.'

De Wolfe's spirits sank. 'But surely I have heard that in some of the most strict monastic orders entry is equated with death and all civil rights of that person are extinguished?'

'That is so for men, John. But we know that in our Norman and Saxon society, there is no equality for women – they are but chattels of men, unlike in the Celtic lands of Ireland and Wales, where women stand on the same level as men in almost all things.'

De Alençon saw the disappointment on the coroner's face and sought to ease his gloom.

'In any case, I think you are crossing your bridges before you come to them,' he said gently. 'Like me, you must surely doubt that the good Matilda will persist with this intention. You have wounded her more than usual and, in her typical fashion, she has flared up into a passion of outrage. But how long will it last?'

His thin face, under its shock of wiry grey hair, fixed seriously on John's more saturnine features.

'You know as well as I, John, that though she is a devout Christian and a constant attendant at her devotions, she is also fond of her earthly pleasures of food and fine clothing. Before you make great plans for the future, I advise you to wait a few days, weeks or even months before counting your unhatched chickens!'

With this wise if discouraging advice, de Wolfe had to be content, so he moved to the other matter that had brought him to the cathedral Close.

'You mentioned some rumour to me the other day about a senior priest outside the city, maybe somewhere to the west, who may have an involvement with these problems in the forest.'

De Alençon looked warily at the coroner, perhaps now regretting even this most ephemeral of revelations. 'It was perhaps unwise of me to mention that. I have heard no more about it, John.'

De Wolfe shook his head, his black locks bouncing over the collar of his tunic. 'I ask for no more confidences, only information on a name which has turned up in my enquiries. Do you know anything of the monks of Buckfast?'

The ascetic face of the archdeacon expressed surprise, his bright blue eyes opening wide.

'Buckfast? Our diocese has no jurisdiction over them. They look only to their mother house of the Cistercians, at Cîteaux in France.'

'Yes, but I wondered if you had any knowledge of individuals there.'

'I have met Abbot William several times, a good and holy man.' De Alençon smiled rather roguishly. 'That institution is not only a great religious house, it is one of Devon's biggest traders. They probably produce more wool that anyone else here in the west.'

De Wolfe rasped his fingers over his stubble, now a full week's growth.

'That may be connected, in fact. Do you know of the man who seems to conduct the fiscal affairs of the abbey, one Father Edmund?'

John saw a fleeting look of understanding pass over the archdeacon's face, before it settled into its usual serenity.

'Ah, Edmund Treipas! Yes, I know of him. He spent a few weeks here several years ago, but in some personal attachment to Our Grace the Bishop.'

'What can you tell me about him, John?' asked his namesake.

'I knew him only slightly, but gossip is as rife in these cloisters as in any marketplace. He came here from Coventry, where I seem to recollect that he was a chaplain to the bishop there. As you know, our Henry Marshal was a close associate of the former Bishop of Coventry.'

He said this with a hint of sarcasm, the gist of which was not lost on de Wolfe. During the abortive rebellion of Prince John a few years back, that bishop had been one of the ringleaders – and Henry Marshal, Bishop of Exeter, supported him, though far back enough in the column to avoid any direct repercussions later.

'So how did this Edmund end up in Buckfast?'

'When he was here, he was just an ordained priest, not in any monastic order,' replied de Alençon. 'He became a Cistercian only on moving to Buckfast, where I understand he is now the linchpin of their economic success. In fact, I am sure that is why he was sent there, because in his early career, before entering the Church, he was a merchant in Coventry, well used to the ways of the world and its commerce.'

He glanced up at the open shutters over his small window and saw the darkened sky. 'I must prepare for Matins soon, John. But why are you interested in Edmund Treipas?'

The coroner shrugged as he rose to leave. 'His name has come up in passing, though I have no real reason to think anything sinister about it. It is is just that he might be in frequent contact with someone involved in this trouble in the forest.'

The archdeacon gave his friend a quizzical look, but held his peace.

CHAPTER NINE

In which Crowner John attends a woodmote

The next day began a new week, and it started relatively quietly for the King's coroner. After he had woken at dawn in an empty bed, Mary brought his solitary breakfast to the gloomy hall. Boiled oatmeal with honey and salt bacon and eggs fortified him enough to go and find Thomas in the nearby Close, where he had a free mattress in the servants' quarters of a canon's residence.

Together they walked to the dismal dungeon beneath the keep of Rougemont, which acted as the prison for those awaiting trial either at the Sheriff's Court or the infrequent King's Courts. This morning John had to take confessions and depositions from several 'approvers', robbers who were attempting to avoid a hanging by incriminating their accomplices. To achieve that, they would later have to fight these others in legal combat to the death, any vanquished survivors being hanged.

After he had finished, he came out of the rusted gate leading to the cells to find Osric, one of the city's two constables, waiting to lead him down to deal with a rape in the mean lanes of Bretayne. By the time they arrived, the culprit had been beaten almost to death by the girl's outraged relatives and neighbours. It only remained for the coroner to take statements from those who were capable of giving a coherent story and to examine the girl to confirm the 'issue of blood' that was necessary to establish a charge of ravishment. Then Osric arranged for the battered perpetrator to be carried to the fetid town gaol in one of the towers of the South Gate. Here, if he failed to die of his injuries, he would probably succumb to the overcrowding and insanitary conditions long before he could be brought to trial.

Following these diversions, John retreated to his chamber in the gatehouse of Rougemont, to take his usual morning ale, bread and cheese with his assistants. He wanted to know from Thomas how he had found Nesta when he had spoken to her the previous day.

'She was in low spirits, master,' Thomas said guardedly. 'She needs constant reassurance and comfort, else I fear she will slip into a decline.'

Still a priest at heart, Thomas felt that what she had revealed to him about the true father of the child, as well as her thoughts of self-destruction, was as sacrosanct as the confessional, and it was not his place to tell the coroner. However, he wanted to ensure that de Wolfe was aware of her present vulnerable state, as Thomas knew that his master was not the most perceptive of souls when it came to personal relationships.

John rumbled and nodded and huffed his agreement, promising to go down to the Bush as frequently as possible to bring comfort and cheer to his mistress, but Thomas was not convinced that he was aware of the seriousness of the situation. Later in the day, John walked down to Idle Lane to spend the evening with Nesta – with the expectation of extending his stay overnight. He sat at his favourite table behind a wattled hurdle next to the fireplace and had a hearty meal of spit-roasted duck, onions, turnip and beans, served on a thick trencher of two-day-old bread, with extra crusts to dam in the gravy on the scrubbed boards of the table.

Nesta came to sit with him as he ate, bobbing up and down to attend to the various crises that frequently occurred between the potman, her two maids and the customers. Each time she came back to de Wolfe, she screwed up her courage to tell him the dread news about the true paternity of her baby, but each time her tongue cleaved to her palate and she was unable to get the words out. To John she appeared quiet and distant all evening, as he had no inkling of her inability to bring down the heavens upon him with her terrible confession.

After finishing his food, he sat with a quart of her best ale and tried his utmost to be loving and cheerful to his mistress, but had little response.

Time and again, he reassured her to the point of monotony that he was delighted at her being with child and that he would be the most devoted father. She smiled wanly and nodded and rested her head against his shoulder, but she lacked conviction, and even the insensitive John felt uneasy at her lack of encouraging response to his blandishments. Her strongest reaction was when he talked about Matilda and the impasse at Polsloe.

'It doesn't seem right, John, a wife hiding away from her husband like that. And it's all my fault.' Once again, her eyes became moist.

'She'll not stay there long, *cariad*,' he said, lapsing into the common Celtic speech that they habitually used together.

'I'm not sure of that, John. This is a different situation to any we've suffered from her in the past. She always had this leaning to religion. Look how much time she spends in St Olave's or the cathedral.'

He squeezed her shoulder.

'Yes, but have you seen her eat and drink? She's in the same league as Gwyn when it comes to victuals. And she spends a fortune at the cloth dealers and the seamstress. I can't see her giving all that up for a black habit and the dismal refectory at St Katherine's.'

Nesta refused to be convinced. 'You must go back and talk to her, John. Over and over again, if needs be. It's all my fault!'

She became damp eyed again, burying her face in his sleeve. Though he knew all the patrons of the Bush were well aware of the situation, he was glad that they were shielded by the hurdle from their curious gaze.

As the evening light faded, he thought of his empty house and his barren bed.

'Shall I sleep with you tonight, Nesta?'

She shook her head. 'Best not to, John. Now that I am gravid, we should not endanger the babe.' This was a secret lie, given that she had done everything so far to rid herself of it. But John would have none of her excuse.

'I said sleep and I mean sleep, my love, if that's what you desire. I've seen enough rapine in Bretayne today, anyway. I just want to hold you close and comfort you, rather than stew alone in that empty house.'

Nesta melted immediately. He sounded like a young boy asking for sweetmeats.

'Very well, John – but only slumber, understand?'

Later, as they curled in each other's arms in the big French bed, she lay awake while he snored, still having been unable to say the devastating words that she had promised Thomas that she would utter.

Tuesday was a hanging day, when John had to go out of the city to the gallows tree along Magdalene Street, to record the executions and tally up the possessions of the felons, which were forfeit to the Crown.

But before this regular chore, de Wolfe decided to cross the inner ward and have a few strong words with his brother-in-law over recent events. He found him in his chamber, surrounded as usual by rolls of parchment and two agitated clerks.

Richard de Revelle preferred to administer his county from behind a table, rather than by riding around the broad expanses of the countryside for which he was responsible to his king. In this, he was the complete opposite of the coroner, who wanted always to be out and about, meeting people and getting on top of any problem in the most direct fashion. Their meeting followed the usual pattern of mutual dislike and antagonism, fuelled by Richard's jealousy of his brother-in-law's stronger personality and his resentment of the hold John had over him because of his past personal and political misbehaviour. The inevitable quarrel was started off provocatively by the sheriff.

'So now you've driven my poor sister to seek refuge in Polsloe!' he brayed, waving a rolled parchment at him. 'You've betrayed her many times before, but fathering a bastard on a tavern-keeper is the last straw.'

De Wolfe glared at him, but kept himself under control for his riposte.

'I hope your family is well, Richard,' he said sarcastically. 'And I mean all of them, including your son in Okehampton and the other one in Crediton.'

The sheriff's face flushed above his neatly trimmed beard, as his clerks gaped at the confrontation. They all knew that de Revelle's legitimate children lived in Tiverton and Revelstoke.

'That's none of your business, John.'

'Neither is it your business to go creeping behind my back with gossip,' retorted de Wolfe, resting his large fists upon the table to glare straight into Richard's face.

'It most certainly is my business!' retorted the sheriff. 'Matilda is my only sister. You have wronged her often enough with your fornicating and adultery, which the whole county knows about. It was my brotherly duty to let her know about your begetting a bastard upon a Welsh alehouse whore!'

Enraged, John drew back his arm to knock his brother-in-law clean off his chair, but he managed to restrain himself and stepped back to be out of temptation.

'Then perhaps I should fulfil *my* duty by telling your Lady Eleanor about the harlots you entertain in there,' he snapped, pointing to the adjoining chamber, which was the sheriff's bedroom. 'And report to her the fact that not many weeks ago I rescued you from a burning brothel in Waterbeer Street.'

The two clerks were now standing slack jawed at these revelations, until, with a squeal of dismay, their red-faced master sent them hurrying out of the room. John came back to lean on the table and the sheriff flinched back, but relaxed a little when he found that his brother-in-law's attack was to be verbal rather than physical.

'So just keep your long nose out of my personal affairs, Richard! Matilda has gone off in a fit of pique, but no doubt she'll soon be back, when she gets tired of a hard bed and miserable food in Polsloe.'

He slammed a hand on the edge of the table.

'But enough of this! There are other matters between us – this scandal in the Royal Forest.'

Relieved at any change of subject, but uneasy at the current topic, de Revelle pulled at his beard.

'Are you still interfering in that?'

'It's long past the time when someone should – and

you show mighty little interest in keeping the King's peace in your own county!' retorted John.

The sheriff sighed, rapidly reverting to his favourite pose as a long-suffering adult humouring a naughty child. 'How often must I tell you that the forest has its own laws – the King's laws – which are outwith the common law, John,' he said patronisingly. 'They go back to Saxon times, though they've been improved by us Normans. Let well alone, man.'

'You're not only a knave, you're a fool, Richard!' bellowed de Wolfe. 'How can I get it through your thick head that the forest laws have jurisdiction only over the venison and the vert, not other crimes. The Manor Courts, the Hundred Courts, your own Shire Court and the Commissioners and Justices of the King's Courts must deal with everything else. You just don't want to listen, do you? It suits some hidden purpose of your own to keep up this charade.'

The sheriff rolled his eyes to the ceiling and pretended to be a martyr.

'What's brought all this on again?' he asked testily.

'You know damn well what's happening,' retorted the coroner. 'If your spies are able to report my family affairs to you, they can also tell you that matters are going from bad to worse in the forest, especially in the eastern bailiwick.'

'Such as what?' asked Richard, with feigned boredom.

'There is a group of outlaws under this damned Robert Winter who are being paid by some outside party to help the foresters foment trouble. I know now where one of their camps is situated – and I know through whom and by what route their payment and instructions enter the forest.'

This was something of an exaggeration, but de Wolfe wanted to provoke the sheriff. This he did, for De

Revelle sat up and took more notice.

'How do you know that? Who pays them and by what means?'

Given the possibility of de Revelle's own involvement, John was not prepared to divulge this and possibly ruin his chances of entrapping the couriers, so he hedged the question.

'Never mind that now. What are you going to do about it? You're the King's representative in Devon, yet you're allowing anarchy to reign in his own forests. There's a small army of rogues out there, wolf's heads every one, doing the dirty work for corrupt forest officials – yet here you sit on your backside in Exeter, not raising a finger to exterminate them.'

The wily sheriff seized on one of John's words as an excuse.

'What would you have me do, John? You say there is an army of these ruffians, spread out over a hundred square miles of forest. I have no similar army to do battle with them, even if they could be found in that wilderness. All I have is a small garrison, intended to defend Rougemont and the city – though God knows if they could do even that, as most are young yokels who have never seen a fight. All they can do is march up and down the bailey, waving pikes about.'

Although this last was partly true, to the exasperation of Ralph Morin and Sergeant Gabriel, John was well aware that it was an excuse to do nothing. As he moved towards the door, he threw a last shaft at de Revelle.

'I tell you, the barons are becoming increasingly angry about their estates losing revenue and their tenants being harassed. Unless you want men like Guy Ferrars and de Courcy chasing you again, you should take some action. They have powerful voices in the

Curia, so your shrievalty might be in jeopardy if you fall foul of them.'

As he went out, he called over his shoulder.

'And keep your nose out of my personal business in future!'

Slamming the door, he glared at the two smirking clerks who had been exiled from the chamber, and stalked off.

The next morning, John went back to Martin's Lane, where Mary insisted on him having his overdue weekly wash and shave in a bucket of warm water in the back yard. He hacked at his black stubble with a knife kept specially honed for the purpose, rasping it over his skin, through a weak lather of soap made from sheep tallow boiled with powdered beech ash. She took his shirt, hose and tunic for the wash and made him delve in his chest in the deserted solar for clean clothes. Mary was busy at being indispensable, in case the mistress did decide to stay away for ever.

'Any news from Polsloe, Sir Coroner?' she asked, trying to conceal her anxiety.

He shook his head. 'She won't talk to me, though I'll try again later today. Perhaps she'd speak to someone else?'

Mary shrugged. 'It's no good me going up there. She can't stand the sight of me.' She glared in mock anger at her employer. 'And that's your fault! She suspected us from the start. You're a devil, John de Wolfe, you need to keep your breeches laced up more firmly!'

De Wolfe grinned and planted an affectionate kiss on the woman's cheek.

'What about Lucille?' suggested Mary. 'Would she talk to her? I wonder.'

'There's no hurry, good girl. It would be nice to have

some peace for a few days or weeks. Matilda will be home soon enough, without forcing the pace, though I'd better go to Polsloe later on, to show willing.'

This was what he did, a few hours later. After five pathetic felons had been turned off the carts below the long beam of the gallows tree, all for thefts to the value of more than twelve pence, John turned Odin's great head towards Polsloe. When he arrived at the priory, he was received politely by Dame Margaret, but once again told firmly that his wife did not wish to speak to him – either then or evermore. He remonstrated, albeit rather mildly, but the prioress was adamant. There was nothing more to be said, and after wishing her a good day and receiving God's blessing in return, he left and made for his horse, tethered inside the outer gate.

As he walked across the peaceful compound, he heard footsteps behind him. Turning, he found the figure of a tall, gaunt nun following him. It was Dame Madge, the expert in midwifery and women's ailments, who was the hospitaller in charge of the small infirmary at St Katherine's. John had the greatest respect for both her expertise and her strong but ever helpful character. She had been of great assistance to him in several cases involving ravishment and miscarriage.

They greeted each other civilly – any observer might have been reminded of two large rooks in a field, both being tall, bony, slightly hunched and dressed in black.

'I have met your wife here, Sir John. I am sorry for the discord that has arisen between you.'

'And I, Sister!' he admitted ruefully. 'I fear all the fault is on my side.'

'It was ever thus in the world, Crowner. Men are at the root of most evils – but God made them that way, so who are we to dispute it?'

'Matilda stoutly refuses to see me or speak to me. I have no idea how this will resolve itself.'

Dame Madge tut-tutted under her breath. 'You have wounded her deeply, sir. She is a devout woman and may well decide she has found peace here. But I will talk to her again and see if she will at least speak to you, even if it is only to recriminate with you for the last time.'

She raised her hand and made the sign of the Cross.

'May God be with you, Sir John.'

Turning, she glided away across the compound like a ship under sail.

Later that afternoon, the parish priest of Manaton was ambling along on his pony back towards the village, on the track that came from Bovey Tracey. He had been to visit the sick wife of an agister, a minor forest officer who regulated the pasture in the forest, collecting the dues from those who sent their pigs to feed on acorns and beech nuts and their sheep and cattle to the lush grass of the large clearings. His wife was in the last stages of phthisis, emaciated and coughing blood, though she was barely twenty-five years of age. The priest knew that the next time he visited it would be to administer the last rites if he arrived in time – or to shrive her corpse if he did not. The husband, a good man who loved his wife, sat with her day and night – it was as well that he had little work for the coming month, as for two weeks each side of Midsummer Day, called the 'fence month', agistment was forbidden by forest law, as it was the time for the hinds to give birth and no disturbances were allowed.

Father Amicus was reflecting on the mysteries of birth and death, wondering what the young wife would find on the other side, when the last breaths of her diseased lungs finally ceased. His pony lumbered slowly along, needing no directions to take it to the sweet summer grass in the vicar's meadow behind the churchyard. Suddenly, the beast stopped dead and tossed its head with a worried neigh, agitated by something at the side of the road. Woken from his sleepy reverie, the father looked down and saw a very real manifestation of the death he had been contemplating. In the long grass and flowery weeds at the side of the dusty track, face up, lay a man, one whom the priest recognised at first glance. He saw that it was Edward, a villein who lived in a mean hut at the extreme eastern end of the straggling village – in fact, little more than a few hundred paces away.

Clambering from his pony, Father Amicus hurried across to the verge, but he could have taken his time, as the man was undoubtedly dead. He wore a short tunic of worn brown wool, darned in several places and ominously stained with blood in both armpits. His legs were bare and crude home-made sandals covered his calloused feet. Cropped yellow hair marked him as a Saxon, and the priest knew him as an unfree man of about thirty-five who worked in the fields five days a week for the manor-lord. His lips were turned back in a rictus of agony, revealing a few blackened teeth, and his open blue eyes were already clouding over with the veil of death.

Murmuring some words in Latin as a makeshift requiem, Father Amicus pulled at a stiff arm to look under the body. A dead coney, as stiff as the man himself, hung by a string from his belt, but, far more ominous, the bent shaft of an arrow was embedded in his back, blood soaking all the surrounding area of clothing.

Gently letting the body sink back to the ground, the priest looked behind it and saw a track of flattened vegetation running back into the trees, only a few yards away. It looked as if the victim had staggered or crawled out of the forest to the road's edge, before finally collapsing.

Father Amicus wiped his bloody hand on the long grass and stood up, staring down at the corpse, undecided as to what he should do next.

He could hoist it on to the saddle of his pony and take it back to the village, but after his recent experiences with the coroner he knew that it should be left where it was. In addition, his experiences with the foresters strongly suggested that John de Wolfe should be involved from the start, if justice was to be done.

But how could he leave Edward's body lying at the edge of the forest, prey to stray dogs, rats and even the few wolves that were still hereabouts? It was not seemly, with the man's cot only just along the track. As he stood there worrying, it seemed as if Providence was for once on his side, for coming towards him from the direction of Manaton was a flock of sheep, being driven by a man with a dog – and behind them was a figure on a horse. The shepherd was Joel, one of his parishioners, moving part of the manor flock to a new pasture half a mile down the road. As they came nearer, he saw with relief that the rider was Matthew Juvenis, the manor bailiff. A moment later, bleating sheep were swirling around him, but after one look at the cadaver Joel sent the dog on ahead, the intelligent animal being quite capable of driving the flock to its destination without human help.

Dismounting, the bailiff hurried to join the shepherd and the priest, who told them in a short sentence what he had found. Matthew also pulled the corpse on to its side and they looked at the missile lodged in the back. The head was deep in the flesh, but the shaft was still complete. The green wood had snapped when the victim fell on it, but not parted completely, and bedraggled feathers still formed the flight.

'Poor fellow. His wife will be greatly anguished,'

commiserated the shepherd. 'They have four children to feed.'

'He was well known for poaching,' said the bailiff. 'But he didn't deserve this, just for a rabbit.' He pointed to the smaller corpse.

'Who could have done this?' asked the priest, sadly.

'Either those bloody outlaws – or the foresters,' declared Joel.

Matthew Juvenis shook his head. 'I doubt it's Winter's gang – or even any stray wolf's head. This was one of the poorest men in the village, with hardly a penny to his name. He had to take a few coney and the odd partridge to keep his family from starving. What robber is going to waste an arrow on him?'

The shepherd agreed. 'Now I come to look at it, that's too good an arrow for an outlaw. That's a real fletcher's shaft – the sort a forester would have!'

The bailiff let the corpse drop back to the now bloody ground.

'What are we coming to, Father?' he asked bitterly. 'We've all lived here the whole of our lives, yet never known a time like this. Is there no end to it?'

No one had an answer for him, and with a sigh Matthew turned to more practical matters. 'We must tell the crowner about this. He's the only one we can trust to do right by poor Edward,' he said, echoing the priest's thoughts. 'I was riding to Lustleigh, but now I must go straight on to Exeter and fetch John de Wolfe.'

'He'll not be able to get back here until morning,' said Father Amicus, looking up at the position of the afternoon sun. 'What are we to do with the corpse until then?'

Joel took the initiative. 'I'll check that damned dog has put the sheep in the right place, then I'll get back to the village and have men bring four hurdles down here. We can set them around the body to keep off any beasts during the night.'

The bailiff mounted up and prepared to spur his mare towards the city, some fifteen miles away. 'Get word to my Lord Henry what's happened – and tell my wife I'll not be home tonight.'

As he left at a trot, the priest and the shepherd also parted.

'I'll have to call at his croft and give the sad tidings to his wife,' said Father Amicus. 'A task I'm not relishing, telling the poor woman she's destitute.'

Despondently, he clambered on to his pony and set off up the road.

The now familiar pattern of a coroner's investigation was repeated yet again. The bailiff of Manaton arrived at Rougement after almost a three-hour ride and sought out Gwyn, whom he remembered from the recent inquest on the tanner – who could forget Gwyn?

In turn, the coroner's officer arranged for Matthew to sleep in the garrison's quarters overnight, then went to find de Wolfe.

It was not hard to guess where he was that evening, and soon the Cornishman was sharing his table at the Bush, his big nose buried in a quart pot. Though John was supposed to be keeping his mistress company in a lover's tête-à-tête, he was secretly glad to be interrupted by his henchman. Try as he would, he seemed unable to shake off Nesta's apathy, which was just as bad as it had been the previous evening. She had given up weeping, but sat with eyes downcast, answering when spoken to, but otherwise in the lowest of spirits. Her face was pale and drawn and the tendrils of hair that escaped from her cap seemed limp and lustreless, compared with their usual red glory. She frequently had to visit the privy in the yard, John putting it down to the effects of her pregnancy. It was in a sense, as the substances Bearded Lucy had given her were still upsetting her bowels, without any other effect.

For her part, Nesta's desperate resolution to pluck up courage to tell him of Alan's fathering had evaporated, and she knew now that, in spite of her promise to Thomas, she would be quite unable to get the words out. The realisation of her cowardice added to her general despair, plunging her into the depths of a depression from which she could see no escape. Even the running of the inn, which she prided herself was the best in the city, no longer seemed important, and she let Edwin and the girls carry on without her usual constant chivvying.

She was also relieved to see Gwyn appear, trusting him to lighten the atmosphere, as his nature was even less sensitive than John's. It was only the timid, gentle Thomas who sensed people's inmost feelings and responded to them in a like manner.

Now Gwyn was telling his master about the summons to Manaton.

'Another corpse at the roadside with an arrow in his back!' he boomed in western Welsh, the language of his youth. 'But at least it's some wretched serf this time, not a verderer.'

De Wolfe shook his head in baffled astonishment. 'This situation is getting out of hand. There'll be another fight over jurisdiction, I can see it coming. Forest law against the common law – and, damn it, they're both the King's law, that's the rub!'

'So are we off at dawn, Crowner?'

'Yes, back in the saddle at first light. At least I've not got my wife to nag at me for being away most of the time.'

To their mutual but unspoken relief, John told Nesta that he would sleep in Martin's Lane that night, to be able to get Odin from the farrier's before dawn and be on their way as soon as the city gates opened.

By the eighth hour next morning, they were trotting up the slope above the deep wooded ravine which hid the Becky waterfalls. They had made good time from Exeter, in spite of Thomas's usual slower progress. De Wolfe had recently offered to buy him a woman's palfrey, a larger mount than the pony he had, but the clerk resisted the exhortation to give up his side saddle and ride like a man.

Gwyn was the first to see the spot they were seeking. Ahead, on a straight part of the track, a group of people were waiting for them alongside a box-like erection of wattle panels. As they approached, they recognised Robert Barat, the village reeve, and Father Amicus. Hovering behind were a couple of villagers, including the shepherd, who had had the foresight to bring a handcart to take the body away.

'Nothing personal, Crowner, but we're seeing too much of you lately,' said the priest, motioning to the reeve to pull down the hurdles.

De Wolfe and the bailiff stood contemplating the corpse, around which flies and bluebottles were already congregating, while Father Amicus enlarged on the story already related to John by the bailiff.

'I found him just as he is, yesterday afternoon. He's not been moved, except to lift him to see where that blood was coming from.'

The coroner and his officer knelt on the grass and began to examine it as the priest went on with his tale.

'I went to his cot up the road and broke the sad news to his wife. They are a poor couple, finding it hard to make ends meet. And she'll find it harder still, though the village will rally round as best it can.'

As John felt the rock-hard stiffness in the arms and legs, Father Amicus continued.

'We all knew he took a coney or a bird from the forest now and then – and he's not the only one in the

243

vill who does that. Until recently the foresters turned
a blind eye, as long as deer or boar were not the targets.
His wife said that latterly the coneys had been playing
havoc with his young vegetables behind the cottage –
they depend on them for much of their food. So
yesterday, he went out at dawn to see to the traps he
had laid the previous night.'

'Where were they laid?' asked Gwyn.

'There's a small warren in a clearing a few hundred
paces into the forest behind their dwelling, riddled
with burrows. These rabbits are becoming a pest. A pity
our Norman grandfathers ever brought them into the
country!' The priest's annoyance suggested that his
own garden plot had suffered as well.

Gwyn hauled the cadaver over on to its face and the
two men sat back on their haunches to look at the broken
arrow mutely protruding from the back, as the priest
continued his tale.

'But he never came back – he should have gone to
his work in the strip-fields soon after daylight, but they
saw no sign of him. The wife sent the son out to search
for him, but he found nothing, except that his traps
around the warren had been pulled out and thrown
aside.'

That was the whole story, and there was silence as
the onlookers watched the coroner working out the
arrowhead, just as he done with the verderer before.
Owing to the long shaft, the tunic could not be taken
off over it, so John pulled the arrow out first and laid
it on the grass near by.

'Different from the verderer's,' grunted Gwyn.
'Better made than that one.'

'That's what I said yesterday,' chipped in the shepherd. 'It's the sort the foresters buy from the fletcher
in Moretonhampstead,' he added with deliberate
emphasis.

The coroner and his henchman went through their usual routine of raising the dead man's tunic, examining the wound and the rest of the body. Then de Wolfe stood up and motioned to the shepherd and another villager that they could load the corpse on to the cart and trundle it off to the village.

'We'd better have a look in the forest, now we're here', grunted de Wolfe. He led the way along the trampled grass and weeds into the tree line, followed by Gwyn and Matthew Juvenis.

'A few spots of blood here and there, nothing else.'

After a few yards the trail almost petered out, as the grass finished under the shade of the tree canopy. Some broken wild garlic and scuffed leaves could be seen for a short distance, then there was nothing that could be distinguished from the tracks of deer, badgers and foxes.

'Where's this warren they spoke of?' demanded John.

Matthew led them away to the left for a while, swishing through the dead leaves in the silence of the deep woods, broken only by birdsong high above and the sough of the wind in the tree tops. They came out in a clearing around a huge fallen beech, which was rotting and half covered in moss. Around the exposed root was a patch of soft earth covered in grass and riddled with rabbit holes.

'Here's one of his snares,' said Gwyn, picking something from a bramble bush, where it had snagged on a brier. A sliding noose of thin wire was attached to the top end of a stout wooden peg. The snare would have been hammered into the ground alongside a run leading from a burrow, the loop arranged so that the head of a running beast would be trapped, strangling the animal.

'They've been pulled out – there's another one over there,' said the bailiff.

'Not much doubt who did that – and to be fair, it's their job,' grunted de Wolfe. 'But putting an arrow into a poor coney-trapper's back is hardly justified.'

'But what about this?' called Gwyn, who had wandered across to the fallen tree. He bent and held something up. The others hurried across to him as he straightened up and held out a short, curved bow.

De Wolfe took it from him and studied it closely. 'Home made – you couldn't do much damage with this. Not even strung – and where are the arrows?'

'Was he hoping to drop a buck or a doe with this?' asked Gwyn.

'He had been poaching for years, so he knew what he was up to,' observed Matthew Juvenis.

'Much more likely he used it for partridge or pheasant,' said John.

Gwyn suddenly crashed away, vaulting over the old tree trunk.

'Here are some arrows! Short ones, all snapped in half.'

He came back with some rather crude arrows in his hand, all three broken in mid-shaft. There was nothing else to be found, and they made their way back to the road, where Father Amicus was waiting with the horses. They walked towards the village, leading their mounts by the bridles. When they reached the village green, John gave his orders for the inquest.

'Two hours after noon, Gwyn. Get as many men as you can from the village. We have no chance of collecting them from farther afield in time. But everything points to those bloody foresters being involved, so do your best to get them here.'

Gwyn looked dubious. 'Where shall I look for them?'

'You've four hours yet. Send a few men to the next villages to seek them.' He turned to the bailiff. 'Have Lupus and Crespin been seen here recently?'

Matthew turned questioningly to the villagers who had gravitated around them since they got back to the green.

'They rode through yesterday,' offered one man. 'Didn't stop here, just carried on towards Bovey.'

De Wolfe grunted. 'So they were in the vicinity when he died. We need to get their side of the story.'

'If they deign to come, the bastards!' complained Gwyn.

Gwyn's pessimism was justified, for when the hour came for the open-air inquest on Manaton's village green there was no sign of any of the forest officers. Two villagers, who had joined the bailiff and reeve in riding to nearby villages, returned to say there was no sign of them, but the reeve reported that he had come across both William Lupus and Michael Crespin in an alehouse in Lustleigh. Not only had they refused in the strongest possible language to attend the inquest, but they had threatened the reeve with immediate violence if he didn't clear off that instant. The aggressive page Henry Smok had grabbed the reeve by the neck of his tunic and dragged him out of the tavern, throwing him to the ground outside.

'Tell that damned crowner that he has no right to interfere in the affairs of the forest!' Lupus had yelled as a parting shot from inside the taproom. The reeve was still seething with anger when he reported this to de Wolfe, and the coroner added a few more black marks to the reckoning that he intended to have with the foresters.

Without the most obvious witnesses, the inquest was a waste of time.

John went through the usual formalities quickly, mindful of the distress of the family. The wife, a sickly-looking woman, bare footed and wearing a patched kirtle, stood with her arms around two small, thin girls, a boy of about fourteen standing protectively at her side. They were Saxons, and the Presentment of Englishry, which at least avoided any question of a murdrum fine, was made by two villagers who said they were cousins of the dead man.

The jury consisted of almost all the male inhabitants of Manaton, who filed past the handcart and were shown the wound and the broken arrow. Father Amicus was the First Finder, and John accepted that his calling the bailiff, reeve and shepherd was enough to constitute raising the hue and cry. Though technically the coroner could have amerced the village for not sticking rigidly to the legal requirements of knocking up the four nearest dwellings, his anger at the forest officers outweighed any thought of adding to the burden of the villagers.

He called the villagers, bailiff and reeve to state for the record, which Thomas was busily writing on his roll, that William Lupus and Michael Crespin had been summoned but had not appeared.

'I therefore attach them in the sum of five marks each to appear before the next County Court to answer for their failure.'

He was not sure whether he had the power to do this, especially as the sheriff, who ran the County Court, would do all he could to frustrate him. Theoretically, if they failed four times to answer a summons to the County Court, they could be declared outlaw, but with de Revelle's present attitude, this seemed impossible. The coroner could attach them to appear before the King's Justices at the next General Eyre, but as the last one had been held in Exeter only recently, it was unlikely to return for several years. The Commissioners of Gaol Delivery were due in a few months to try those languishing in prison awaiting trial, but he was not sure whether non-appearance at an inquest was enough to imprison the foresters, unless he brought in a verdict of murder against them. And even if he did, who was going to arrest them? Given the strange situation in the forest, the usual officers of law enforcement, such as the manor bailiffs and the Hundred sergeants, would be likely to be either unwilling or incapable of arresting officials who seemed to have the backing of the sheriff, the new verderer and even a gang of outlaws.

Still, John was damned if he was going to let them get away with either murder or flouting the King's coroner, so he rounded off the short inquest with his directions to the circle of jurors.

'My inquest is to determine who, where, when and by what means this body came to his death. His identity is well known to you all and his Englishry confirmed. You have seen the wound, a cowardly shot in the back, so the means of death is clear and the day it was inflicted, namely yesterday, equally certain. The foresters William Lupus and Michael Crespin were known to have passed through here then. The arrow is of a type used by them and the deceased was admittedly a well-known poacher.'

He paused to glare around the assembly from beneath his beetling black brows.

'Take all together and it is obvious that we needed to hear from these forest officers. But they have not deigned to attend and have ill used your reeve, who was sent to summon them. In their absence, I cannot hear any explanation from them and the evidence is so scanty that no verdict can be reached today. I therefore must adjourn this inquest to another time determined by circumstances.'

He nodded dismissal at the throng and then walked across to offer his awkward, but none the less sincere, sympathy to the widow. The parish priest was now at her side and John turned to him.

'I trust there are some means of giving support to this unfortunate woman, Father,' he growled. 'She seems to have had little before and now has less.'

Father Amicus nodded. 'We will do our best, Crowner. Her husband was a villein of our manor-lord. I am sure he will feel some responsibility for her sustenance. Maybe he can employ her in the kitchen at the manor house.'

This reminded de Wolfe of Henry le Denneis' absence.

'I presume your lord knew of this matter? Was he told?'

The bailiff nodded. 'I went to give him a full report this morning. He was unable to attend the inquest as he had a flux of the bowels.'

That sounded too convenient to be true, thought the coroner. He guessed that the lord of Manaton was afraid of offending either the forest regime or the King's coroner and had decided to keep clear of them both. As the handcart was pushed into the churchyard opposite for a night in front of the altar before burial, John had a final word with the bailiff.

'I need to confront these two foresters as soon as I can. Are they still likely to be found in Lustleigh?'

'I doubt it, Crowner. Robert Barat says they were merely eating and drinking there, so God knows where they are by now. But I know where they must be tomorrow, for there's a Woodmote to be held, and they must appear before the verderer to present their cases.'

This was another name for the lower court of the forest, officially called the Attachment Court, held every forty days, which gave it yet another title.

'And where will that be held?' demanded de Wolfe.

'In this bailiwick, always in Moretonhampstead, in the market hall. You'll undoubtedly find Lupus and Crespin there.'

John looked at Gwyn and Thomas de Peyne, who had just gathered up his parchments and writing materials and stuffed them into his sagging shoulder pouch. 'Right, you two, we're having another night away from home. It's not worth riding back to Exeter and returning in the morning, so we'll take ourselves to Moreton and find a bellyful of food and a penny bed.'

Moretonhampstead, known locally as Moorton, was a large village part-way between Ashburton and Chagford, two of the stannary towns of Devon where crude tin was assayed. Moorton, though there was much tin-streaming near by to the west, was primarily an agricultural centre and boasted a covered market-place at its central crossroads.

Though only an open structure of wooden posts supporting a steep thatched roof, it was a prestigious symbol to the inhabitants and brought in many traders, itinerant chapmen and their customers to spend their pennies in the alehouses, tannery and forges. Tuesday was their big market day, when in addition to the crowded stalls and floor displays in the market hall there were sheep, pigs and cattle for sale and barter in two open spaces a few yards up the road.

However, even on other days the market was still in use, with regular booths for butchers and pastry-cooks. Country men and women sat on the earthen floor, offering a chicken, a duck or a kid – or vegetables from their tofts. But every forty days the traders knew that there was no space for them in the market hall, as the woodmote required it for its proceedings. This was where all offences against the forest law were first prosecuted, though only transgressions against the 'vert', the greenery of the forest, could be judged, and then only if the worth of the offence did not exceed four pence. All other matters, especially those against the 'venison', the beasts of the forest, could only be recorded and sent on for trial to the Forest Eyre, the great Assize of the Forest that met no more often than every three years. Those unfortunate enough to be imprisoned to await trial, rather than be bailed by attachments, often died in the squalid gaols, like the miscreants imprisoned in the city.

An hour after the early dawn, the coroner's trio rolled off their straw pallets in the loft of one of the three inns. They had eaten well enough the previous evening and John and Gwyn had drunk and yarned in the taproom until late, while Thomas had wandered to the church to pray, meditate and indulge in his favourite pastime of misleading the parish priest into believing that he was still in Holy Orders. By dusk, they had rolled themselves in their cloaks in lieu of blankets and slept soundly, in spite of the ever-present fleas – though both John and his clerk had a few minutes unease over Nesta, before slumber overcame them.

That morning in the inn they ate bread and cheese and drank sour cider, a pale shadow of the food on offer at The Bush. Gwyn felt obliged to supplement this meagre breakfast with a mutton pie from a stall, as, although the market was closed, the wooden houses on the corners of the crossroads opposite had shops at ground level, their goods displayed on the lowered shutters. Booths, stalls and pedlars' trays offered plenty of sustenance, so even on a Woodmote day no one with a few coins need go hungry.

The three sat on a big log placed outside the alehouse as a seat and watched the participants gather for the court. A chair, a trestle table and a few stools had been set up inside one end of the market hall, the only gesture to formality. Gradually, people began filling the space, mostly men, but some with a woman clinging to their arm, wondering what further burdens would be added to their lot before the end of the day.

Soon a large cart trundled down towards the cross-roads, drawn by a pair of ponderous oxen, and Gwyn pointed at it with the remnants of his pie. A mangy, emaciated bitch had slunk up to him and, being an inveterate dog-lover, he was sharing the last crusts with her.

'Here come some of the worst customers,' he observed.

About half a score tattered and dirty men were crowded into the cart, and when they were prodded out by the ruffianly driver and his mate, John saw that they were roped together by their manacled wrists. They were led into the market and made to sit in a row across the floor.

'I heard the foresters have got a gaol over at North Bovey – they say it's as bad as the tinners' prison at Lydford.' As Gwyn had been incarcerated in Lydford not long before, he said this with some feeling.

A group of riders now appeared in the distance, and John soon recognised the foresters and their pages, as well as the new verderer.

A couple of clerks jogged behind on their ponies, and the whole entourage dismounted alongside the market. The two pages led the horses off to graze in a field up the road, while the others went into the hall.

'Are we going to beard them in their den straight away, Crowner?' growled Gwyn, already spoiling for a fight.

'Leave it a while. Let's see what they do in this damned court.'

There were many people milling about the cross-roads now, some of them traders, pedlars and beggars taking advantage of the influx of people for the

Woodmote. Some were pushing into the market itself, either to be involved in the proceedings or merely to be entertained, so in spite of their size, de Wolfe and Gwyn were able to lean half concealed behind one of the stout pillars at the back of the hall. The much smaller Thomas slipped unobtrusively into the throng.

The verderer had taken the only chair and the clerks were squatting on the stools, their writing materials on the trestle. People were jostling about the rest of the floor behind the prisoners until William Lupus banged on the table with the hilt of his dagger and yelled for order.

John watched with interest as the proceedings got under way. The two foresters and their so-called pages strutted about with arrogant efficiency, hauling the offenders up before the new verderer with deliberate brutality, as they called their names and recited their offences. The prisoners from the cart were dealt with first, the long rope being untied from their wrists so that, still manacled, they could be dragged and kicked to stand before the judgement table.

Most of these were the more serious offenders against the venison, to be remanded to the distant Forest Eyre. The majority of their sins seemed quite minor to de Wolfe, mainly poaching of coneys, squirrels and various birds. One had shot a fox that had harried his chickens and another was alleged to have killed a boar, though the body of the beast was never found and the man hotly denied the charge. Only one fellow was charged with hunting down a roe deer, as the skin and bones were found buried behind his cottage. All he had to look forward to was either mutilation, castration, blinding or hanging, so the more sensitive Thomas covertly crossed himself and prayed that he would perish in jail.

Two men were accused of failing to 'law' their dogs,

which meant cutting off three claws from each forepaw to prevent them running after game. The only way to avoid this was to pay a heavy exemption fee, called 'hound-geld'.

'Bloody barbarians, all of them,' snarled the dog-loving Gwyn under his breath, as Michael Crespin, a thickset middle-aged man with cropped blond hair and watery blue eyes, intoned the requirements for this mutilation, even down to the size of the block of wood, the two-inch chisel and the mallet. One of the accused pleaded that his dog was small enough to be exempt from lawing, and an argument developed between the foresters, the verderer and the man as to the criteria for exemption.

'If a hound can crawl through a stirrup, it need not be lawed!' claimed the man, indignant at being locked in a filthy gaol for three weeks on such an accusation.

Crespin gave the man a gratuitous blow on the shoulder. 'You're a liar, man. That bitch could not be passed through the five and three-quarter inches of a Malvern chase strap, which is the legal measure.'

'Did you actually try the dog against that measure?' asked Philip de Strete.

'I had no need, sir. I could tell from experience that it would not pass.'

Gwyn again rumbled his resentment as this distortion of justice, but de Wolfe laid a restraining hand on his arm. The accused man was trying another stratagem.

'If you will not believe that, then let me pay the hound-geld now. That dog is too small to hunt anything bigger than a rat, but I am willing to pay, rather than perish in that foul prison!'

The mention of money sent the foresters to the table to murmur with the verderer and, after some nodding of heads, de Strete scowled at the prisoner and gave him an option. 'Five marks hound-geld or take your chance at the Eyre.'

The man winced and looked desperately into the crowd, where his wife, brothers and father were listening anxiously. After some worried consultation, they nodded and, without further ado, Crespin pushed the man towards the driver of the ox-cart, for him to release the irons on his wrists. Five marks was a fortune to a peasant, who would have to borrow hundreds of pennies from his relatives and probably go hungry for many months to come.

The coroner and his officer waited while the rest of the venison cases were dealt with by the arrogant forest officers, who took every chance to commute crimes for cash. One man was accused of 'stable-stand', being seen on a horse carrying a bow. Another was committed for a 'bloody-hand' offence, being found with bloodstaining on his breeches, though he loudly proclaimed that he had merely been killing one of his own geese, but had no witness to prove it. A similar situation involved a free man who was accused of both 'back-bear' and 'dog-draw', being seen carrying the carcass of a fox while walking in the forest with his dog. He insisted that he had found the fox dead with injuries inflicted from a wolf's fangs and that, as his dog was properly lawed, it was quite legal. No notice was taken of his protestations, but he was allowed to be mainprised, a form of bail, on the payment of two pledges from his family, each of four marks.

As soon as these cases were finished, the Woodmote moved on to the larger number of offences against the vert. These were dealt with rapidly, and again it seemed to John that financial extortion was the main object. In many cases, guilt was declared with almost no evidence and with no chance for the accused to utter a word in his defence. The choice was usually offered of paying a fine or being committed to the Forest Eyre, even when the value of the transgression was patently over the threshold of four pence. When someone declined to pay the amercement, he was bound over with a much greater attachment fee, to ensure his appearance at the distant court, so in either event he was financially crippled either personally or after having to borrow from his family.

Though the system was no different in principle to that of the other courts, it was being applied with a ruthless and avaricious disregard for natural justice. Philip de Strete seemed only to be a figurehead in the proceedings, and appeared to accede to all the murmured advice from the two foresters.

'This is a damned disgrace!' rumbled Gwyn. 'I wonder how faithfully those clerks are allowed to record all these payments. I'll wager the biggest portion goes into the officers' purses every forty days.'

They waited a while longer, listening to a series of cases concerning the illegal cutting of branches of more than an inch thick, of the offence of 'purpestre', which was the building of a hut on the owner's land without a fee; causing 'waste' by cutting down bushes; and illegal 'assart', the removal of stumps and roots to enlarge cultivated ground. A few were fined for wrongful 'agistment' – letting their livestock feed in the forest either without sufficient fee or during the current 'fence month', fifteen days either side of the feast of St John the Baptist, when the hinds were calving. John was interested to hear all these archaic regulations, some going back to the Saxon kings. He knew of some of them and decided not to mention to Gwyn that it was Edward the Confessor who had brought in the mutilation of forest dogs – not by lawing the claws, but by 'hombling and hoxing', cutting the sinews of the back legs so that they could hardly walk, let alone run.

As the cases were completed and the remaining prisoners were herded back to their cart and the rest of the crowd began to thin out, de Wolfe decided it was time for him to have words with the foresters.

With Gwyn close behind, he pushed himself from his pillar and thrust his way through the spectators to reach the front of the court.

Philip de Strete gaped up at them in surprise, then rose in reluctant greeting to a more senior law officer. The two foresters and their thuggish pages made no effort to be civil, but stood to one side, scowling at the coroner and his massive henchman.

'What brings you here today, Sir John?' asked the new verderer, anxiously. The sheriff's description to him of the coroner's personality suggested that his presence would not bring him joy.

'I have some serious questions for these officers of yours, de Strete. And I think this is one case that has not been brought to your attention during today's proceedings.'

Lupus and Crespin glowered at the coroner, well aware of what he meant.

'Murder was done in the forest two days ago. Has your court no interest at all in recording that?' he boomed. 'Do you all still deny that such a major breach of the King's peace does not come under the common law? And if you do, why have you not dealt with it yourself, as by default it must lie within *someone's* jurisdiction?'

It was a neat trap, and the inexperienced, rather stupid verderer could only gape ineffectually at the coroner. 'What murder is this?' he managed to croak, after a moment.

'Edward of Manaton – shot in the back with an arrow. An arrow that strongly resembles those used by your foresters – the same foresters who were seen passing through Manaton at about the time of the murder.'

De Strete jerked his head around to stare at his men. 'Why wasn't I told of this?'

William Lupus ignored him and spoke directly to de Wolfe.

'It was no murder, Crowner, ' he said contemptuously. 'It was a justifiable killing under forest law.' His skull-like face was impassive as he tried to stare down the coroner.

'But I should have been informed, William!' bleated de Strete.

Lupus turned to him slowly and spoke with naked insolence in his voice.

'You are new to the task, Verderer. Your court deals only with offences against venison and vert. We are not concerned with deaths.'

John de Wolfe exploded at this. 'Ha! For once your corrupt tongue speaks some truth! Any sudden death is within the purview of the coroner – so don't ever try to contradict me again.'

The forester flushed at de Wolfe's scathing tone.

'Not in the forest, Crowner, when the death is within our laws.'

Gwyn took a pace forward and thrust his big, red face towards Lupus.

'Don't talk such bloody nonsense, man! You can't have it both ways.'

De Wolfe beckoned Thomas out of the small crowd of people who were now gathered around, their ears almost flapping at this diverting quarrel involving the officers they hated most.

'Take note of what is said, clerk, and write it on your rolls when we are finished,' he snapped.

William's oafish page, Henry Smok, stepped to the side of his master.

'You're finished now, Crowner! Clear off, back to your city. You'll never understand the ways of the forest.'

The pugnacious Gwyn moved to flatten the man, but John halted him with a gesture.

'If by that you are suggesting that the King's writ runs in Exeter but not here, then you could be arraigned for treason. Even your thick neck would stretch nicely at the end of a rope.'

Both Smok and Philip de Strete paled at the pure menace in the coroner's words, for it was obvious that he meant what he said. But now he reverted to the original business.

'You admit then, William Lupus, that you killed Edward of Manaton?'

The forester's impassive face moved to look briefly at Crespin.

'I admit nothing. It matters not who actually put the arrow into the poacher. It's a forester's duty, whoever bent the bow.'

The audience was hushed as de Wolfe faced Crespin.

'Then it was you who murdered the man?'

'Murdered be damned!' blustered the other forester. 'I'll not say who shot this poacher. But the law allows us to stop any fugitive offending against the venison by whatever force is necessary. During the hue and cry, or if the offender will not stop when escaping, we are at liberty to kill.'

Philip de Strete nodded vigorously in his officer's defence. 'That's quite right, Crowner. As a new officer, I have been studying the forest laws most assiduously and what Michael Crespin says is correct.'

William Lupus brought his harsh voice back into the argument.

'This miserable thief had set traps all around the clearing. We had known him as a poacher for years, but this time we caught him in the act, with a coney on his belt and a bow in his hand. I called on him to stop, but he ran, so an arrow was quite properly put into him.'

De Wolfe noted that they had carefully avoided naming the person who shot the fatal shaft. Crespin had regained his confidence after the support from the verderer and Lupus. 'Yes, though I thought he was only winged. He gave a great yell and ran on into the trees. It was not worth us chasing him, so we pulled out his traps and left.'

'Not worth your chasing him?' snarled the coroner. 'You had no concern that he might be wounded or dying – as indeed he was?'

Lupus shrugged. 'Why should we care?' he answered callously. 'If we had caught him, we would either have cut his throat as the *coup de grâce*, or if we brought him out he would have hanged for carrying a bow.'

John, in spite of the endless atrocities he had seen – and even been part of – during his years of campaigning, was angry at this cold-blooded contempt for life shown in what should have been the peaceful English countryside.

'Whether your casual killing was justified is not for you to decide,' he snapped. 'I have already attached you to attend the next Shire Court in Exeter to have your actions examined.'

Lupus sneered, and even the two pages grinned at this threat.

'The Sheriff's Court? He won't want me there, that I can tell you now, Crowner. You're wasting your time, for we're not coming.'

'Then I'm also attaching you to attend the next visit of the King's judges as Commissioners, in a month or two. You'll not get out of this, for if you fail to appear you'll be declared outlaw and can go to join your friend Robert Winter and his gang.'

Even this threat failed to make any impression on the forest officers, for they continued to smirk complacently at de Wolfe. 'And who is going to get us to the court, Crowner? We deny your powers in this. The forest laws were set in place long before your recent office was even thought of!'

'You'll attend or suffer the consequences!' snarled de Wolfe, now becoming increasingly outraged by the contempt with which these men viewed the King's Court.

'Are you coming to take us to Exeter yourself?' gibed Crespin. 'Or will you send the sheriff to arrest us?' All four men, the foresters and their pages, guffawed as if this was the best joke they'd heard that month.

'Or maybe the Lionheart will come back from France with his army to take us!' cackled Henry Smok, emboldened by his masters' attitude.

De Wolfe smothered his rage as best he could and glared at the grinning faces.

'For once in your life, Smok, you may have got near the truth,' he snapped. 'I doubt your sovereign lord will come in person, but after this I'll see to it that Winchester and London attend to this problem. Not all of Richard's army is in France, remember!'

He turned on his heel and, motioning his officer and clerk to follow him, he stormed out of the market, coldly determined to find a radical solution to the fear in the forests.

In the city that evening, John decided that it was pointless going to Polsloe again, merely to be turned away once more. He reasoned that if and when Matilda wanted to speak to him he would soon know about it. Instead he decided to go to the Bush some hours after returning from Moretonhampstead, spending the time until then with his friend Ralph Morin, the constable of Rougemont. De Wolfe wanted to sound him out about the possibility of taking some of the garrison's men-at-arms to arrest the foresters and clean out Robert Winter's outlaw camp.

Sympathetic though he was, Ralph could see no way in which he could help in this.

'Without the sheriff's agreement – which he'll never give me – I can't take troops out of here, except in a dire emergency. Though we've had no trouble for fifty years, I'm sure it's a hanging offence leaving a royal castle undefended.'

John reluctantly agreed with his point of view, but tried a compromise.

'Just a few men, together with Gwyn and myself, could surely take those forester bastards and their pages?'

'I've no doubt we could, John – but without Richard de Revelle's consent, think what the consequences would be! One set of king's men arresting or even slaying another set of royal officials. No, I'm sorry, I can't risk either my job or my neck, even for you.'

The coroner sighed. 'You're right, Ralph. The only way is for me to get Hubert Walter to authorise a foray against all this unrest. Even then, he'll take some persuading, as it looks as if a couple of bishops and their Prince John allies have a finger in this pie.'

The castellan nodded. 'Finding the Justiciar is the problem. He's so often away from Winchester or Westminster. I heard that he was visiting the King in Normandy some weeks ago, but whether he's back or not, I can't tell.'

'It's a long ride to Winchester, if it's for nothing,' agreed John glumly. 'But I'll have to do it soon, after I've spoken again to some of the barons like Ferrars and de Courcy.'

He had hoped that the atmosphere might have

improved down at Idle Lane, but when he arrived at the inn he found Nesta still in the same apathetic state. As always, she got her maids to provide him with a good meal and sat quietly with him as he ate, but she was downcast and had little to say for herself. He gave her a detailed account of his visit to Manaton and the Woodmote, partly in an attempt to fill in as much of the silence as possible. Then he launched into his intention to ride to the seat of England's government, wherever he could find it, to seek out his old commander in Palestine, the Chief Justiciar.

Nesta responded with little more than monosyllables and sighs, until John pulled her to him on the bench behind the screen and tried to get at the root of the trouble. He had little success, however, as she dissolved into quiet weeping again, which both embarrassed and terrified him. Peering over the top of the hurdle, he looked to see if the patrons were eavesdropping, but the relatively few drinkers were either unaware or were studiously pretending not to notice. John wished that they were upstairs in the privacy of her room, but for her to stumble across the taproom, red eyed and sniffling, would be worse than sitting tight. He wondered whether he really wanted to ask her whether he should stay the night – and immediately felt disloyal for preferring even his empty house to the prospect of endlessly trying to break through the barrier that had sprung up between them.

For her part, Nesta knew that nothing had changed, but that some kind of nemesis was fast approaching. Try as she would, she could not bring her to tell him that he was not the father of this creature in her womb, as she had begun to think of it. She knew well enough that this big, awkward, craggy man was doing his utmost to be kind and gentle to her, but the great lie that she was living prevented her from responding.

Eventually, as the evening wore on, she did invite him to stay, managing to reason that she might as well lie passively in his arms all night as suffer alone. John took this as Fate's rebuff to his previous reluctance to share her bed and, as the daylight faded, the sad pair climbed the ladder to her tiny chamber.

CHAPTER TEN

In which Crowner John follows a horse-trader

The following day, John was called to the port of Topsham, some four miles downriver, to deal with two deaths on a trading ship. The vessel had been beached on the mud alongside the wharf for unloading, but when the tide came back in the hull suddenly tilted over, as the uneven removal of a few tons of cargo had made her unstable. One stevedore was crushed between the ship's side and the wharf, while a sailor who had been mending rigging was tossed into the swirling flood tide, his drowned body being recovered a quarter of a mile upstream.

The examination of the scene and witnesses, followed by an acrimonious inquest, in which de Wolfe accused the ship-master and the wharf-owner of negligence in discharging the cargo, lasted much of the day, and it was early evening when he returned to Exeter.

He went straight to Martin's Lane and sat quietly in his echoing hall with his dog and a quart of cider for an hour, trying to deny to himself that he was reluctant to go to the Bush and face his mistress's misery. Mary came to refill his pot and then stood looking down at him sternly, one fist on her hip, her handsome face creased in a frown.

'What's to become of me, Crowner?' she demanded. 'I've not cooked a meal for days, I've hardly seen you and you've slept here one night since your wife left. Should I look around for another master? – though God knows where I'll find one.'

'Mary! Don't talk like that. I've told you everything will go on as before,' he said placatingly. 'Whether Matilda comes home or stays away, I have to live somewhere, break my fast, have my shirts and tunics washed and my fire made up in winter.'

'And what if your Welsh lady decides to do all that, where will I be then?'

'That seems very unlikely, good Mary. I just don't know what's going to happen between us.'

He looked so crestfallen that she softened immediately, as she had done so often in the past. Crouching down beside him, she listened while he poured out his tale of woe concerning Nesta.

'She's lonely and frightened, John. Afraid of losing you and of a hopeless future for herself.'

He waved his hands in desperation. 'I've told her over and over, I'm glad about the child and will stand by her. Why won't she listen?'

Mary stood up, shaking her head helplessly. 'You men will never understand, will you? A pregnant woman, especially one in her position, is uncertain, bewildered, vulnerable – not that I've been like that myself, but I've seen it in a few.'

Unable to help him any more, she took herself off to her kitchen to make him some supper, for he guiltily decided to delay going down to the Bush until later. As fate decided, he was destined not to visit the inn that evening, for a couple of hours later, as the sun was setting, Gwyn turned up at his front door. Usually, his blustery arrival was a summons to some new death, assault or rape, but this evening he had more interesting news.

'I've been having a few jugs in the White Hart,' he

267

announced, mentioning an alehouse in Southgate Street. 'There's been a horse market on Bull Mead today and some of the buyers and dealers were in the tavern. I saw that little fellow again, the one the outlaw was talking to in the alehouse at Ashburton.'

De Wolfe waved him to a chair and filled a pot for him from his ale-jug. Normally Gwyn would never come into the hall if he could help it, in case Matilda was there, as she thought him a Celtic barbarian and made her feelings painfully clear.

'You mean the man who seemed to have some dealings with … what was his name, Martin Angot?'

'That's him! Now tonight I did some eavesdropping and found that this fellow's a horse-trader,' explained Gwyn, pleased with his spying activities. 'I even got his name, listening to people who were either contented or complaining about what they had bought or sold. They'd all been drinking a fair amount, so they weren't speaking in whispers, by any means.'

John was used to his officer's long-windedness. 'So what was his name?' he asked patiently.

'They called him 'Stephen' and 'Cruch', so I reckon he's Stephen Cruch,' he grinned, wiping ale from his huge moustache. 'I gathered from the potman that he was sleeping tonight in the loft of the White Hart – but I also heard him tell some fellow that he was leaving early in the morning for Ashburton.'

'Our Thomas said that he had come across a horse-dealer in Buckfast who had dealings with this priest, Edmund Treipas. What shall we do about this, Gwyn?' pondered de Wolfe.

'We could jump him and beat some truth from the fellow. I could take him blindfold, with one hand in my pouch!'

John grinned at his henchman's enthusiasm. 'Would he recognise you, if he saw you?' he asked.

Gwyn shook his shaggy head. 'I very much doubt it. I kept well back in the tavern in Ashburton and didn't approach Martin Angot until this Cruch fellow left. There's no reason for him to have remembered me from a crowded taproom. And he certainly wouldn't have seen me tonight. I kept well down on a stool among the throng that was there.'

De Wolfe thought about this for a moment.

'He's never seen me, to my knowledge. Tomorrow, could we not follow him discreetly to see if he gets up to anything near Ashburton?'

The Cornishman readily agreed. 'Surely, if we keep well back, he'll not notice us on the main west road. There are always travellers going back and forth.'

The coroner hawked and spat into his empty fire-place. 'It would be good to catch him meeting up with an outlaw again. Then we could seize the pair of them and make them talk.'

It was agreed that they should ride out of the West Gate as soon as it opened in the morning, keeping a sharp eye open for the horse-dealer. They would ride a few miles along the Plymouth road and hide in the trees to await his passing, then follow him at a distance.

John suggested that, as they would both be up before dawn, they had better get a good night's sleep, a rather shamefaced excuse not to go down to the Bush that evening.

'We're not taking the little fellow with us, I hope?' grunted Gwyn.

'No damned fear. He'd stand out like a sore thumb, sitting sideways on that old nag! If there were a chase, he couldn't keep up.'

'And if there were a fight, he'd wet himself and run!' chortled Gwyn, not without some affection for the timid clerk.

In the early light the following day, they sat waiting

for the city gate to open, lurking up the street towards the little church of All Hallows-on-the-Wall, whose priest had come to a nasty end a few weeks earlier.

De Wolfe watched the crowd clustered inside the gate, in case Stephen Cruch had also risen early, but there was no sign of him as the stout iron-bound gates swung apart. They waited for the confused thrusting and shoving to abate, as the people going out pushed past the traders and herdsmen coming in to market, driving sheep, calves and pigs before them, followed by a cavalcade of country folk carrying baskets of vegetables, poultry, eggs and everything else to satisfy the hunger of the citizens of Exeter.

Once the road was clear, they trotted out and forded the river, de Wolfe's legs getting wetter than usual as he had borrowed a smaller mare from Andrew the farrier, the huge destrier Odin being too conspicuous for a surveillance exploit. As they clipped down the road that led to Cornwall, John decided to increase the distance before they turned aside to wait for the horse-dealer.

'If he's going to meet anyone, I doubt it'll be much before Ashburton, as it's too far away from your outlaw's hideout. So we'll put a good ten miles between us to avoid having to follow him too far.'

He silently hoped that Cruch was going to ride out that day and not decide to sleep off his drinking on his mattress in the city. It was pure speculation that he might be meeting anyone, other than in the course of his legitimate business.

An hour and a half later, John decided that they had gone far enough and turned off on a stretch of track where the trees came close to the edge of the dusty, rutted road. They found a place where some blackthorn bushes gave cover, then put their mounts on head-ropes farther back in the trees, where a small clearing offered them some grass to crop.

From where they sat on the ground behind the bushes, they could just glimpse the road, enough to see who was passing. Gwyn had taken the inevitable bread and hard cheese from his saddle pouch, along with a flask of cider, and they waited in comfort for over half an hour.

As Gwyn had prophesied, there was a constant trickle of traffic along what was the busiest road in this most western part of England. Ox-carts laden with goods, bands of pilgrims on their long journey to Canterbury, drovers with cattle and sheep, merchants on horseback and lesser folk on foot – all passed the gap in the black-thorn bushes. Only priests and the poorest folk trav-elled alone, having nothing worth stealing, the rest being in groups for mutual protection. A couple of clumsy horse-drawn carriages bore manor-lords or their wives and had an armed escort of a few men with pikes and swords against possible attack by footpads and outlaws.

After three-quarters of an hour, when all the cider had gone, Gwyn began to get restive. 'D'you think the bloody man isn't coming? Maybe I misheard what was said. I couldn't get too near.'

'Have patience!' muttered De Wolfe. 'Though if he's a horse-dealer, he should have a good mount, which should have got here quicker than we did.'

Another ten minutes went by until Gwyn hissed in his ear.

'That's him, the fellow on the white stallion!'

John peered through another gap in the bushes and saw a rider trotting past on a big, good-looking horse. He was a small man in a brown tunic and breeches, with a floppy woollen cap on his head. As soon as he had passed, Gwyn jumped up and collected their own mounts, coiling the head-ropes on to his saddle bow.

The coroner climbed on to his chestnut mare.

'There's no great hurry. We don't want to get too near. That big white steed's all too conspicuous.'

They waited until a pair of merchants with two well-armed servants passed, then swung behind them and tried to keep Stephen Cruch in view. All was well for a mile or two, but the horse-trader was riding slightly more quickly than the merchants and was pulling ahead, so eventually the coroner and his officer had to risk overtaking.

Thankfully, a few minutes later two other riders came out of a sidetrack just behind Cruch and gave cover for another couple of miles until once again John and Gwyn were obliged to pass them.

'This is getting difficult,' growled John. 'Try to make yourself look smaller!' he added facetiously to the great red-haired lump.

'Can't be that far to Ashburton now. Perhaps the bastard is just going about his normal business,' offered Gwyn.

They slowed up as much as they could, the merchants almost on their heels. Then the difficult situation was avoided as they rounded a slight bend and saw a tiny hamlet ahead. It was little more than a few cottages, one of which had a bush hanging over its door to signify an alehouse. The place was an outlier of a larger village half a mile off the road, the additional strip-fields here having being assarted by the manor-lord, being just outside the boundary of the Royal Forest.

'He's stopping there, Crowner,' hissed Gwyn. 'We'd better pull up.'

They reined in and let the merchants pass, getting curious looks at their riding antics. Their quarry had pulled over to the hitching rail of the tavern, where several other horses were tethered, then dismounted and gone inside. The merchants and their escort also stopped and entered the low building, while the coroner and his officer eased their horses on to the verge, partly sheltered by a scraggy elder tree.

'Now what do we do?' demanded Gwyn. 'I could do with a quart myself, but we can't go near that place in case there's someone in there who would recognise one of us.'

De Wolfe pondered the situation, indulging in his habit of rasping his fingers over his stubble, which was again, almost due for its weekly mowing. 'Depends on who might be in there with him – though he might just have fancied a drink. You can't go, for if it's one of Winter's band, he'll know you, like as not.'

Gwyn reluctantly agreed. 'But you're too well known as the coroner throughout the whole county, so you can't risk it. We're stuck here, then!'

They waited behind the stunted tree for what seemed an age. Gwyn dismounted and squatted on a dry-stone wall at the edge of the field, which contained serried rows of crops slanting up the hillside. De Wolfe lay on his side in the weeds, chewing a stem of long grass while he kept an eye on the alehouse, a few hundred yards away. After years of campaigning, he was well accustomed to waiting, as most soldiering consisted of weeks of inaction before a few hours of bloody battle. Almost an hour went by and the midsummer sun rose higher in a pale blue sky, making the morning hotter and hotter. Gwyn's dust-laden throat was crying out for a jug of ale, but his saddle flask was empty.

Suddenly, John sat up on the grass. 'There's a priest just come out of the door,' he whispered. 'Get a good look at him and fix his face in your mind.'

They saw a fairly tall man in a dark clerical tunic go to the hitching rail and untie a handsome russet mare. Even at that distance they could see his bald scalp where his tonsure had been shaved, below which was a ring of dark hair above a shaven neck. Tucking his gown up between his legs, he swung himself expertly into the saddle and trotted off westwards, away from them. They had time to see that he had a strong, fine-featured face. His black hair had been shaved high on his neck, so that it looked almost as if a band of fur was wrapped around his head below the baldness of his tonsure.

'Who the hell is he?' growled Gwyn. 'It can't be Thomas's monk from Buckfast – he was a Cistercian.'

His master was not listening. His eyes had swivelled back to the door of the alehouse. 'Look who's here! Our horse-trader! And staring after the priest. Maybe he's his confessor!'

Stephen Cruch had indeed emerged and, after standing a moment to gaze after the diminishing figure of the cleric, went to his own horse and led him over to a water trough against the inn wall, placed out there as an encouragement for travellers to stop to relieve their own thirst. When his stallion had satisfied itself, he climbed into the saddle and walked his horse away, following the priest.

'Now what? Do we carry on after him?' queried Gwyn.

'We've no choice or we've wasted a day,' growled de Wolfe. 'But wait until he's far enough away before we follow.'

Cruch seemed in no hurry; his pace was much slower than when approaching the ale-house.

'If he's going to Ashburton or Buckfast, why didn't he meet this fellow there, instead of making him ride up this far?' grumbled the Cornishman. A few moments later, the horse-dealer answered him by wheeling his horse to the right and vanishing into the trees.

'Now where the hell's he gone?' snapped de Wolfe, as they cautiously followed to the spot where Cruch had turned. 'I trust he's not spotted us and is about to disappear.'

However, when they came level they saw that a narrow

track led off the main road, leading north towards the distant high moors that could be seen through gaps in the trees.

'How can we follow him along there without being seen? It's little better than a footpath.' Both Gwyn and de Wolfe were about eight feet above the ground on their mounts, hardly inconspicuous in a forest lane.

They waited uncertainly at the entrance to the trail. 'We've got to do something, or we'll lose him altogether,' snapped the coroner. 'As far as I remember, Owlacombe is on the other side of this bit of forest, then far beyond is Widecombe, where we had that Crusader's body in the stream last autumn. It's nowhere near where you found your outlaw's camp.'

'Only a few miles as the crow flies,' objected Gwyn. 'Winter has far more men than I saw there. He must have several camps dotted around the forest. Maybe there's another near here.'

De Wolfe threw his leg over his saddle and dropped to the ground.

'We daren't take the horses, so we can't both go. You stay here on the road – or better still, go back to the alehouse to wait for me.'

Much as the prospect of a tavern appealed to him, his officer was reluctant to let his master go. 'I'm coming with you! I'll hobble them, they'll be safe enough.'

De Wolfe waved him away imperiously. 'No, Gwyn, not this time. He can only be tracked on foot and I'll not leave the horses. If I don't go now, I may lose him.'

He allowed no further argument and Gwyn watched anxiously as he loped away up the track, keeping to the edge where fallen leaves deadened his footfalls. His henchman waited until he had vanished around a bend, then slowly and unhappily rode back down the main road, leading the hired horse alongside him.

* * *

When Thomas de Peyne went as usual to the chamber in the gatehouse, he found it deserted, and it remained so for the rest of that morning, there being no sign of his master or Gwyn appearing for their usual food and drink. This was not all that unusual, as sometimes they were called out overnight and left the city without him. The clerk had plenty of work to get on with, copying duplicate rolls of inquests, confessions, depositions and other parchments that must eventually be presented to the Commissioners or the royal justices.

Eventually, he decided to walk down to the Bush inn. This was partly because he thought he should have some food, though poverty had trained him to be a frugal eater. After his disgrace in Winchester, he had been virtually a beggar until he walked to Exeter, where his archdeacon uncle had prevailed upon the coroner to employ him. However, a stronger reason for his going to Idle Lane was concern over Nesta, who had been so kind to him a couple of months ago, when he had been evicted from his lodgings on the false suspicion of being a murderer. Her present troubles preyed on the mind of the compassionate clerk, especially since she had revealed the identity of her child's father and her thoughts of doing away with herself.

He walked down from Rougemont and through the crowded High Street to reach the lower town, his lame leg aching a little today, accentuating his slight limp. At the inn, one of Nesta's maids, who both treated Thomas like a stray kitten, brought him a cup of watered wine and a bowl of stew with a small loaf of coarse barley bread. There was no sign of Nesta, and after the clerk had finished his simple meal he signalled to Edwin, the one-eyed potman.

'Where's the mistress? Is she brewing or baking?'

The old soldier looked uneasy. 'She went out an hour ago, without a word to anyone. Mind you, she's said very few words this past week. The girls and I are getting worried about her, poor soul.'

'Any idea where she's gone?'

'No. She's taken to walking by herself lately. I saw her going down towards the Water Gate on Thursday evening.' He hesitated, his whitened eye rolling horribly in its scarred socket. 'It didn't help that the crowner failed to turn up last evening. She said nothing to us, but we could see she was on the lookout for him until dark.'

'I think I'll take a walk and see if I can find her, give her a little company,' murmured Thomas. He hauled himself to his feet and put a quarter segment of one of his precious pennies on the table for his meal.

Edwin pushed it back to him and shook his head. 'We've got strict orders from the mistress not to take anything from you, Thomas. Go you now and talk softly to her.'

Outside, the clerk surveyed the rough weed-covered ground either side of the tavern and the built-up lanes that led from it. On his right Smythen Street led down past the Saracen to Stepcote Hill and the West Gate. In the other direction, Priest Street crossed the end of Idle Lane, dropping down towards the Water Gate.

Remembering what Edwin had said, he decided to take the latter route, walking down past the lodgings of vicars and secondaries, with mild envy at their secure position in the ecclesiastical life that he longed for.

At the bottom, he turned left towards the Water Gate, which only in recent years had been knocked through the southern corner of the ancient city walls to give easier access to the quayside. Outside, the steep slope gave way to a level platform along the muddy river, part of the length being built up into a stone quay. The tide was in and several vessels floated against the wall: more were moored out in mid-stream.

Thomas stood amid the bales of wool heaped on the quay, waiting to be loaded. A procession of labourers were coming down two gang-planks from the nearest vessel, jog-trotting like a line of ants, each with a heavy sack on his shoulders. The rest of the wharf was cluttered with boxes and casks and heaps of rope, chain and bits of maritime equipment, between which sailors, labourers and merchants went about their business. The clerk searched the whole panorama for any sign of Nesta, but the only women in sight were two girls with reddened cheeks and lips who were eyeing the passing seamen with a view to doing business, even at that time of day.

Having no better plan, Thomas began walking downstream, as behind him was nothing but the unfinished bridge, the ford and the footbridge on Exe Island. He passed through the bustling activity on the stone quay and kept on along the natural bank of the river, which had a grassy rim below which was thick mud. At low tide this mud stretched halfway across the channel, on which vessels would heel over until the water flooded back again. To his left, past the wooden warehouses, the ground rose to the Topsham Road, where there were a few new dwellings and many more mean huts, the overspill of the thriving city. Thomas kept going until there were only trees and bushes on the bank, with a dusty path along the edge of the river. A growing stench told him he was nearing the Shitbrook, at the point where it vomited its sewage into the river. An old tree trunk had been rolled across it to act as a footbridge and, holding his breath against the smell and hoping that he could keep his footing on the mossy bark, he gained the other side. He walked on for a short distance until he decided he was foolish to keep going along a deserted path for no real reason.

Then, just as he was about to turn back, he glimpsed a flash of white some yards ahead. Staring, he made out the top of a linen coif, on the head of someone who was just below the lip of the river-bank. Hurrying as fast as his infirm leg would allow, he came up to the woman and saw that it was indeed Nesta, crouching in the long grass and cow parsley, within arm's length of the turbid brown waters of the Exe. She appeared oblivious of his approach and was rocking herself dangerously back and forth on her heels, soft keening coming from her throat.

Afraid to surprise her too abruptly, lest she fell forward into the swirling flood tide, Thomas squatted on the path and whispered her name, repeating it until she stopped whimpering and slowly looked around.

'Thomas? What are you doing here?'

'Looking for you, dear woman. Come here, take my hand.'

Gently, he coaxed her away from the bank and they stood on the path, arms around each other. She was an inch taller than the clerk, but they leaned together with chins on each other's shoulders, Thomas patting her gently on the back.

'They are worried about you at the Bush, Nesta,' he said after a moment. 'I came to look for you. What are you doing down here?'

She pushed back from him and dropped her eyes.

'I came to think, Thomas. To think about ending it all.'

He knew better than to scold or plead with her at this stage.

'Then like me, when I fell from the cathedral roof, the good God has sent you a sign, Nesta. I never expected to be worthy enough to be the Almighty's messenger, but so it seems to have turned out!'

'I'm not sure if I believe in God any longer, Thomas.

He took my husband from me, then he taunted me by giving me John, only to make me drive him away.'

The little-ex-priest took her hands in his and gazed earnestly into her eyes. 'That cannot be true, good woman! Yes, many lose good husbands, just as so many women lose their newborn and husbands lose their wives in childbed. That is the way of the world, and always has been. But to say that you have driven John de Wolfe away is just not true.'

Tears welled up in her eyes, dry until now.

'But it is only his honour that forces him to say that he welcomes the child . . . and that in ignorance of knowing who the real father must be.' She moved forward again and pressed her face into his faded tunic. 'I tried to do what you advised, Thomas, truly I did! But the words would not pass my lips, for I knew they would finish everything between us.'

The clerk slid his arm around her and gently eased her along the path, a step at a time. 'Jumping in the Exe will not benefit the crowner, my dear. It would destroy him with guilt. He would never be the same man again.'

She gripped his arm so tightly that he winced.

'So what shall I do, Thomas? Life is too difficult.'

'Your life belongs to God, Nesta. He gave it to you and he will take it away in his own good time. As he showed me, poor sinner that I am, it's not for us to decide when it shall end.'

He grinned wryly, in an attempt to lighten the mood.

'And certainly not in the river, just downstream of the Shitbrook!'

De Wolfe cautiously followed Stephen Cruch for a mile up the track, which became narrower and more over-grown as he went. In some places the passage of the stallion had broken off thin branches which overhung the path. He kept well back for fear of being detected, but could hear the rider ahead by the occasional crack of a stick under the horse's hoofs. The coroner wondered why this track existed, as they were now well away from the patch of cultivation near the alehouse and were in deep forest. Whatever it had been, it was clear it was a long time since it had been in use.

Eventually, John realised that he had heard nothing from up ahead for several minutes and stopped in case he overran his quarry. Leaving the path, he slid between the trees to one side, then struck off diagonally again. Soon the gloom of the oak-and-beech canopy seemed to lighten ahead and, as he crept forward, he saw a large clearing where trees had been felled in the past. Concealed behind a trunk, he realised that this was an abandoned settlement, possibly an illegal assart from many years earlier. Though there were no large trees, bushy saplings were springing up among the thick undergrowth and in a few years' time this scar in the forest would have healed itself. Among the profusion of weeds and bushes he saw the remains of a burned cottage, the surviving timbers wreathed in ivy.

What was more interesting was the sight of the horse-dealer sitting in his saddle, in the act of raising a cow horn to his lips. Three mournful hoots echoed through the woods, then Cruch sat immobile, intently watching and listening. Nothing happened and, a few minutes later, three more blasts were given on the horn. Then, distantly, came an answering blast, repeated four times, on a horn with a higher pitch.

Soon, two riders came into the clearing from the opposite side and met Stephen Cruch in the centre, alongside the ruined hut. They were astride moorland ponies and wore swords, with maces hanging behind their saddles. John recognised neither man, but

suspected from Gwyn's description that these were
Robert Winter and Martin Angot.

They remained on their horses and began an
animated conversation, but from a hundred paces away
John had no hope of catching any words.

A leather bag was passed over to the bearded man
that he assumed was Winter, but again he had no way
of knowing whether it contained money.

The meeting was very short, for as soon as the bag
was stowed away in his saddlebag the leader raised his
hand in salute and the pair pulled their short-legged
ponies around and walked out of the clearing the way
they had come. Stephen Cruch also turned and
departed much faster than he had arrived.

De Wolfe was in a quandary as to what he should
do. He doubted both the wisdom of following the
presumed outlaws and his ability to do so, as only God
knew how far they intended riding, and even in the
woods he could never keep up on foot for any great
distance. And what could he do, if he ended up at an
outlaw camp with twenty or thirty desperate villains
against him? Discretion seemed not only the better part
of valour, but eminently more sensible, so he decided
to retrace his steps and get back to Gwyn. He was eager
to get a better description of the two outlaws, now that
he had seen them with his own eyes.

No doubt Thomas would have advised him that 'man
proposes, but God disposes', for as he left the shelter
of his tree trunk to find his way back to the path, there
was a bull-like roar from his right and a yell from his
left. Two ragged men hurtled towards him through the
trees, kicking up showers of dried leaves as they came.
Shocked for an instant, as he had thought himself
alone, he barely had time to draw his sword before the
first was upon him. Thankfully – for it probably saved
John's life – the other caught his foot in a trailing brier

and fell heavily on his face, delaying him for almost a minute.

During that time, the first man skidded to a halt before the tip of the coroner's weapon, his expression suggesting that he had not expected to be confronted by a fighting man wielding a Crusader's broadsword – and one who appeared to be well accustomed to using it.

'I'll get you, you bastard!' he yelled, lifting a ball-mace in one hand, the other brandishing a dagger. He was not a big man, being a fellow of about twenty years, dressed in a tattered tunic which was pulled up in front between his legs, the hem tucked into his belt. His head was covered in unkempt brown hair which merged with a wispy beard of the same colour.

John took in all this in the instant the man came to a stop in front of him, which was his undoing. With a quick prod, almost a reflex, the coroner jabbed the sharpened point of his blade into the fellow's left forearm and the dagger went spinning away as the man howled in pain. Clutching the bleeding arm against his chest, he made a vicious swing with the mace, a studded metal ball on a chain attached to a short rod. If the chain had wrapped itself around John's sword, it would have snatched it from his grip, but wise to the ways of infighting he dropped the point and stepped back, letting the ball whistle past his nose. The momentum of the heavy weight turned the assailant's shoulder towards de Wolfe and, without hesitation, he slid his sword into the armpit, deep into the man's chest. It was killed or be killed, and after twenty years of prac-tising survival, the coroner gave not a second thought to inflicting a fatal wound.

But his minute was up, and as the first man stag-gered away to die the other, now recovered, was upon him. Seeing what had happened to his mate, he was more cautious and stopped when de Wolfe swung round to menace him with his sword, held two-handed before him.

'Clear off, or I'll kill you as well!' snarled the coroner. The outlaw's eyes flicked briefly to where his partner was oozing his lifeblood into the leaf mould.

'You'll not be so lucky this time, whoever you are!' snarled the lout.

Even in such a perilous situation, John realised that the attackers had no idea who he was. Cruch must have sensed that he was being followed up the track and had told the two outlaws. They had presumably left a couple of sentries outside the clearing and had now told them to circle around and get rid of whoever had been spying on them. John fervently hoped that there were no more of them around, as without Gwyn odds of two to one were the most he wanted to cope with.

This man was older and more heavily built, bare footed and wearing a torn leather jerkin over brown serge breeches. A florid, dirty face was cracked in a ferocious grimace, exposing crooked, yellow teeth. He gripped a heavy pike, a dual-purpose weapon which was both a staff and a lance, having a sharp spearhead on one end. For a moment, they faced each other without twitching a muscle, each waiting for the other to make the first move. John knew that the pike had a much longer reach than his own sword – it could not slash sideways, but as a stabbing weapon it easily surpassed his own in range.

Suddenly, the outlaw lunged, and though John hacked at the pike shaft to divert it, the edge of the iron tip scored through his tunic over the left side of his hip bone. A searing pain swept up from his loin, but he sensed that the wound had not gone deep. His adversary was still out of range and drew back for another lunge, grinning evilly at having made the first strike. They feinted again and John saw that his hacking blow with the sword had cut through half the thickness of the pike, just below the head. Another swipe might sever it completely, and he deliberately left himself open for a split second to tempt the outlaw. But the man was too canny a fighter to be tricked and backed off, giving John time to wonder whether he was facing another old campaigner.

'You're bleeding, Big Nose!' taunted the ruffian. 'In a minute, I'll have you gutted like a goose!'

John could feel the warmth of blood seeping into his clothing, but he had no time to look down at the damage. The other fellow made another sudden charge, aiming for de Wolfe's heart, but this time the coroner was ready for him. As he twisted away, he snatched his left hand from his sword hilt and grabbed the spear just below the head, throwing his weight sideways, so that it fell full on the weakened shaft. With an audible crack, the wood split and the wicked iron point fell uselessly to the ground. Off balance, John had no chance to land a precise blow with his sword, but he swung it wildly and was rewarded with a bellow as the heavy cutting edge sliced into the thigh of his opponent.

Then things happened with lightning speed, as the enraged man used the shaft of his broken pike to deliver a smashing blow to de Wolfe's left shoulder, numbing his arm completely. A fraction of a second later, John, though reeling from the pain, lunged forward and jabbed his sword into the lower belly of his antagonist, feeling the point go in until it crunched against bone. As he pulled it out, the sharp edge was dragged across the man's groin and a fountain of blood spurted from the severed main artery. With a scream of mortal agony, the outlaw used the last of his strength to swing his pike handle again. This time it caught John cleanly across the temple and he collapsed unconscious on to the forest floor.

With no clock nearer than Germany, Gwyn had no way of knowing how long he sat outside the alehouse on the Plymouth road, but judging by the height of the sun it was noon by the time his patience ran out. He had seen the horse-dealer trot past the inn in the direction of Exeter about an hour after leaving his master, showing no signs of having been in a fight. Unsure of what to do next, Gwyn spent the next couple of hours drinking several quarts of ale, eating a loaf and cheese and, not long since, a sheep's knuckle with fried onions. He had also questioned the crippled man who ran the tavern about the priest and his acquaintance – and discovered that the smaller, wizened fellow was indeed a well-known horse-dealer by the name of Stephen Cruch. The landlord had no idea who the cleric was; he had never seen him before.

In between these activities, Gwyn had paced up and down outside with increasing concern, looking a hundred times back down the road to where the entrance of the track lay. He blamed himself for letting the coroner go into the forest alone, though he knew that de Wolfe's stubborn streak could not have been overcome. The road continued to be fairly busy, with travellers within sight every few minutes, but there was no sign of the coroner emerging from the lane.

Eventually, Gwyn could stand it no longer. He went around to the side of the crude wattle-and-daub building to check on the horses, which he had tied up in the shade, with two leather buckets of water dipped from the ditch behind and a ha'p'orth of hay bought from the inn. Satisfied that they were safe to leave, he tightened up his sword belt and stalked off down the road, with a foreboding that all was not well with John de Wolfe.

Reaching the old track in a couple of minutes, he turned into the cool green of the trees. Going as cautiously and quietly as his large body would allow, he followed the path into the forest, noting the few recently broken twigs and branches that told of the recent passage of a rider. He stopped every few minutes and listened, his hand on the hilt of his big sword, but there was nothing except the twitter of birds and the occasional rustle of some small woodland animal.

Obliviously, he passed the spot where the coroner had cut off left from the path, as there was nothing to show for it. Like John, he now saw the brightening ahead where the clearing lay, and even more cautiously he walked to the edge of the trees and looked around. All was quiet and, after a moment, he advanced to the charred timbers of the old cottage and saw the crushed vegetation in the centre of the clearing. A pile of fresh, still-moist horse droppings lay there and, looking beyond them, Gwyn saw that more disturbed grass and bracken indicated that at least one rider had gone off through the far side of the clearing. He stopped to consider what he should do. For all he knew, Stephen Cruch, as he now knew him to be, had himself ridden straight across, but the width of the flattened under-growth suggested that several horses had turned around here. He walked to the opposite trees and went into the wood again for a few hundred yards, finding nothing. Returning, he stood again in the clearing and risked giving a few piercing whistles, ones that he knew the coroner would recognise from their old campaigning days. There was no response and he circled the perimeter of the clearing, whistling again, then finally calling 'Crowner!' at the top of his voice a few times.

Only the birds replied.

Worried and frustrated, he began a more systematic search of the edges of the clearing, reasoning that if there had been some meeting there his master would have been spying on it. Of course, there was always the possibility that he had followed the other party, presumably outlaws, in which case he could be miles away by now.

The Cornishman decided on one more circuit, this time a few trees back from the edge, where John may have been hiding to be within sight of the conspirators. Halfway around, he stopped, fear suddenly gripping him. On the waxy green leaves of some wild garlic, he saw a spatter of blood. A few feet away there was more, and scuff marks through the fallen leaves were deep enough to expose the almost black leaf mould beneath. With his heart in his mouth – and his sword in his hand – he followed the intermittent trail for a dozen yards, to the lip of a depression which looked like an old badger sett, drifted over with leaves. Three or four feet lower, he saw the inert body of a man, which instinct told him was a corpse. After the first lurch of fear, he saw straight away that it could not be the coroner, though the head was buried in leaves where he had pitched face down. The clothing was brown and the fellow was bare footed.

Sheathing his sword, Gwyn tipped the dead body over and saw a total stranger, but enough of a ruffian to qualify as one of the outlaw band. The cadaver was still warm and the limbs and jaw were slack, so he had been dead less than a few hours. The eyes were wide open and the mouth gaping. His jerkin and tattered tunic were saturated with blood from the waist down and, on probing, Gwyn saw a gaping slash in his upper thigh and gouts of blood clot oozing from a wound in his lower belly.

'This is John de Wolfe's work, I'll wager!' he muttered to himself, letting the corpse fall back again. 'But where in the Virgin's name is he?'

He began yelling again, uncaring about concealing his presence, then began following the blood trail back in the opposite direction. Unfortunately, it virtually petered out just at the point where he had first seen it. A close search revealed a few spots ten yards away, but there were no visible tracks in the forest floor. Two deer trails crossed near by, which confused the issue, and in spite of many minutes casting about, he failed to find anything to help him locate the coroner.

He leaned against a big oak, to recover his wits. There was a dead outlaw back there and it was highly likely that John de Wolfe was responsible. But that by no means meant that the coroner was still around here – or that he was dead or injured. Had he taken off after the other outlaws?

Gwyn sighed and scratched his tangled hair in indecision. There was no way in which he could search the forest – it went for miles in various directions. For all he knew, de Wolfe might emerge somewhere else and either walk or borrow a horse to come back to the alehouse. But some sixth sense niggled at him to say that the situation was not that simple – so he must have help to look for his friend and master.

Having made a decision, he now hurried to carry it out. Still yelling John's name at intervals, he strode back to the track and jogged down it to the main road. At the inn, he slapped a couple of pennies down before the cripple, telling him what had happened and to care for the hired horse until it was collected the next day. With a last admonition to keep a sharp lookout for the coroner, he spurred his big mare towards Exeter to get help.

* * *

Even pushing his strong mount as hard as he could, it took Gwyn almost three hours to reach Rougemont. The first person he saw when he clattered his steaming mare under the gatehouse arch was his drinking and gambling friend, the garrison sergeant.

'Gabriel, the coroner's gone missing!'

He poured the whole story into the sympathetic ear of the old soldier, who was another who thought highly of Black John.

'But we don't know for certain he's in trouble, just because he saw off some bloody outlaw!' Gabriel tried to be reassuring.

The coroner's officer shook his head. 'I've got a bad feeling about this, friend. He wouldn't have gone off for hours, leaving me and the horses without any word.'

'So what do you think may have happened to him?'

'With a dead man there, there's no doubt he's been in a fight. We must go to look for him. He may be lying wounded. It needs more than a few men to search that area. I couldn't do it alone.'

Gabriel worriedly chewed his lip. 'The bloody sheriff won't be too keen on sending men-at-arms to look for John de Wolfe. He'd be glad to see the back of him.'

'Surely his sister would give him hell if he refused!' bellowed Gwyn.

'Let's find Ralph Morin. We can get some sense out of him.'

They found the castellan in the lower ward, inspecting some repairs to the palisade that topped the high earth bank of the outer defences.

He listened gravely to Gwyn's urgent news and without hesitation agreed that a search party must be mustered without delay. To their great relief, Morin also said that Richard de Revelle had just gone on one of his duty trips to his manor at Tiverton, to spend Sunday with his wife.

'So I'll take it upon myself to assume that he would have been anxious to safeguard the well-being of his dear brother-in-law!' he said sarcastically, a broad grin splitting his bearded face. 'So let's get a posse together, right now!'

Gabriel looked up at the sky which, though still blue, showed a sun leaning well over to the west. 'By the time we get men mounted up and ride almost to Ashburton, there'll be precious little daylight left.'

Gwyn, though he had already sat six hours in the saddle that day, was in no mood for delay. 'Can't be helped. The crowner may be bleeding to death somewhere. Let's go!'

Such was their devotion to de Wolfe that the three men almost ran back to the inner bailey, where their horses were stabled. As they went, Gabriel and Ralph Morin yelled orders at some of the men-at-arms standing about, who in turn began running to knock up their fellows in the huts and lean-to buildings within the castle precinct. Before the three leaders returned on horseback, the outer ward was buzzing with activity, as a dozen soldiers took their mounts from the main stables and saddled up with the help of the ostlers and farriers.

A crowd of wives, children and off-duty members of the garrison came to gawk at the urgent preparations and cheered as the troop trotted briskly through the outer gate. As they hurried through the city, scattering the crowds in the High Street and Fore Street, the Exeter rumour mill started in full swing. In these peaceful times in the West of England, the sight of what looked like a war party of soldiers racing out of the city gave rise to all manner of speculation, from a French invasion to a new rebellion by Prince John! It was only when a couple of pedlars, who had been selling trinkets to wives in Rougemont, came out of the castle with the news that the King's coroner was missing, probably wounded and quite possibly killed, that the rumour took on a new twist, spreading like wildfire throughout the city.

With the sense of urgency that Gwyn had engendered, the posse made good time to the alehouse on the Ashburton road. In the cooler part of the day, they trotted and occasionally cantered the fifteen miles from the city and arrived there when there was still some of the evening left, it being now early July. They stopped at the tavern for the troop to water their horses, while Gwyn went with the constable and sergeant to see whether the landlord had any news of de Wolfe.

The twisted man leaned on his stick and shook his head. 'Not a sign of anyone asking for you, sirs.'

'Where does that track lead to, the one just down the road?' demanded Gwyn.

'Nowhere now. It used to go to a woodward's dwelling, but it caught fire and he died in the flames, some ten years ago.'

'What's beyond it, in the other direction?' asked Ralph Morin.

'Just trees, your honour. Miles of them, till you come out towards Halshanger Common, up on the moor. Not that anyone would want to go through there, unless you had armed men like your party. Riddled with outlaws it is, these days.'

The horses attended to, they rode on quickly to the lane and turned in off the road. Gwyn had considered dismounting and walking up, but thinking that even minutes might be precious he led the posse along the mile of track on horseback, now careless of any noise. The troops were told to keep their eyes open for anything to be seen on either side, though the low sun and dense bushes along the path made this difficult.

The men were not in full battle array and wore only round helmets and leather jerkins, rather than their mail hauberks. Some wore swords, others had pikes and there were two bowmen, though this was meant to be a rescue mission rather than a fighting force.

Soon the clearing was visible ahead and Gwyn reined in his mare to point off to the left. 'That's where the dead man is, a couple of hundred paces away and just in from the edge of the trees.'

Everyone dismounted and lashed their reins to the nearest sapling, then Gabriel took three men and fanned out in the direction that the coroner's officer had indicated. Morin led the way into the clearing and headed for the other side with three of his soldiers, while Gwyn struck off with the rest on the other side of the path, a direction in which he had not searched earlier. For a few minutes there was a general rustling of leaves and snapping of twigs as fifteen men searched the forest. Then a loud shout came from the left, which Gwyn recognised as Gabriel's voice. He was calling the Cornishman's name, so he went back to the path and dived into the darkening wood on the other side.

'I'm coming! Have you found him?' He was almost afraid to ask, in case the sergeant had stumbled upon John de Wolfe's body.

Gabriel directed him by shouting and, as he approached, he called a question. 'I thought you said this corpse had been stabbed through the belly and groin?'

As Gwyn stumbled up to Gabriel and another man-at-arms, the sergeant said, 'This fellow's had a sword stuck into the side of his chest, man.'

As he looked down, Gwyn's bushy eyebrows rose an inch up his forehead.

'That's not him! That's another one!'

This was a much smaller, younger fellow, with brown

hair and a thin beard. His hessian tunic was saturated with blood all down his right side, clotting into the leaves beneath him.

'The coroner's been having a field day, if he saw this one off as well!' observed Gabriel. A yell from another soldier announced that the first outlaw that Gwyn had come across had also been found, a hundred yards away.

'To hell with these two,' growled Gwyn. 'Where's the coroner, that's all that concerns me.'

The search went on as the light began to fade. Ralph and his men tramped about the far side of the clearing and worked their way around to where the corpses lay, meeting up with Gabriel's party, without finding anything. Constantly, the men called de Wolfe's name without success. Gwyn went back to the other side of the path and combed the area with his soldiers. Eventually, as dusk fell, they all gravitated despondently to where the horses were tethered, tired and anxious.

'God knows where he is!' exploded Morin, his forked beard jutting like the prow of a ship. 'We must have covered almost a square mile all around that clearing – but he could be five miles away.'

'It'll be pitch dark in half an hour. There's little more we can do until morning,' said Gabriel, mournfully. He was almost as devoted to de Wolfe as was Gwyn and the thought of him dying alone in some deserted forest was hard to bear.

Slowly and uneasily, the party went back along the track. This time they walked in single file, leading their steeds by the reins. In the near twilight, they still peered hopefully to either side and continued to call the coroner through cupped hands. Now even the birds were silent and only the rustle of the wind in the tree-tops answered them.

When they reached the road, a gloom deeper than

the dusk settled upon them as they were forced to acknowledge their failure.

'At least we didn't find him dead or wounded.' Ralph Morin tried to lift the mood, which was affecting even the youngest of the garrison guard, as all of them knew something of John de Wolfe's past military reputation. As they walked up the road towards the inn, intent on some getting some food and ale inside them, Sergeant Gabriel voiced their concerns. 'Now what do we do?'

Gwyn looked at the castle constable. 'I don't know what you intend, but I'm going back in there at first light – and I'm not leaving until I've found him, dead or alive!'

Morin grunted his agreement. 'We'll stay with you for most of the day, but I'll have to take the men back before de Revelle returns. He'll go crazy if he discovers that I've been away that long with some of the best of the garrison – especially if it was because of John de Wolfe!'

In an oppressive silence of defeat, they trudged up the road towards the alehouse.

CHAPTER ELEVEN

In which Crowner John glimpses his wife

In Exeter, the Saturday evening drinkers wandered from one tavern to another, the rumour about the coroner being embellished every time it was repeated. The same was happening around the market stalls and the trinket booths along the main street, where good-wives and their sisters gossiped incessantly about everything under the summer sun.

The tale grew from Sir John being lost in the forest to his having been abducted by Barbary pirates – and from his being kidnapped by Prince John to his having been beheaded by outlaws. Whatever version was related, the basic truth undoubtedly seemed to be that something very serious had happened to Black John. He was well known to virtually every one of the few thousand citizens of Exeter, and even if many were somewhat wary of the stern-visaged law officer, they all respected his reputation for even-handed honesty, uncommon amongst officials in authority. It did not take long for the rumours to reach Idle Lane.

A somewhat inebriated butcher, who had been thrown out of the White Hart for trying to pass a clipped coin, rolled into the Bush as the cathedral bell was tolling for Compline. He slumped down at a table and waved at Edwin for some ale. Across the room he noticed three acquaintances drinking near the window opening.

'Heard the news, boys?' he called across, his voice slightly slurred, but still piercing. 'Our crowner's been killed. The whole garrison rode in full armour this afternoon, to avenge him!'

There was a sudden silence in the taproom, immediately shattered by a crash as a pair of quart jugs full of cider exploded on the floor at the back of the room. Pandemonium broke out as Nesta slumped to the floor amongst half a gallon of drink and shattered pottery. As one of her maids, Edwin and a couple of customers rushed to her aid, another drinker cuffed the butcher's ears for his insensitivity.

Another unlikely patron also hurried to Nesta's side, as Thomas had just entered the inn. He had been worried about the Welsh woman all afternoon, since he had brought her back from her sorrowful escapade on the river-bank. As there had been no sign of Gwyn or de Wolfe for many hours, he had moped about the coroner's chamber, too distracted to do much writing. Eventually he had gone to his lodging and then to a service in the cathedral, missing the dramatic return of Gwyn and the hurried departure of the posse from Rougemont. Not until a few minutes earlier had he heard the rumours about the coroner that were flashing about the city, which sent him hurrying down to the inn, fearful of the effect of the news upon Nesta in her present vulnerable state.

He was too late by a minute, but joined the throng clustered solicitously around the fallen landlady. One of them happened to be Adam Russell, the apothecary, who pushed his way through to where one of the serving maids was pillowing Nesta's head on her apron.

'She's fainted, but she looks terrible,' said the girl.

The apothecary dropped to his knees alongside the Welsh woman and felt her pulse and lifted an eyelid. 'Get her to her bed, that's all we can do.'

Edwin looked dubious. 'That's up the bloody ladder, Adam! Hard to do until she comes to her senses.'

'Put her on my pallet in the cook-house,' suggested the maid. 'That's good enough until she can climb to her own bed.'

With much fussing and concern, willing hands lifted Nesta and carried her through the back door to the large hut in the yard, where the two maids lived and where they also prepared food. Thomas insisted on accompanying them, and as he was virtually accepted as a priest by the staff of the Bush, he was as welcome as the apothecary.

As they laid her on the long hay-filled sack that was the maid's bed, and covered her with a coarse woollen blanket, Nesta began to stir and moan. Her eyelids fluttered and a moment later she was staring blankly at Thomas.

'What's happening?' she began, then gave a weak cry as memory flooded back. 'He's dead! My John, he's gone!'

'Hush, girl, it's just a rumour,' crooned Thomas. 'We don't know what's happened yet.'

Edwin chased everyone out of the hut except the apothecary, Thomas and the maid and stood guard outside the door, leaving them to comfort his mistress. Nesta tried to struggle upright, but Adam gently pushed her back on the pallet. 'Stay quiet for a time, keep your head low until you feel stronger,' he advised.

As Thomas held her hand and spoke softly and reassuringly in her ear, the apothecary felt the pulse in the other wrist, a worried expression stealing over his face.

'Get her some wine with hot water in it,' he murmured to the maid. 'I'll go back to my shop and get something to soothe and strengthen her – some valerian and other herbs might help.' He rose and left, while the girl went out to the brew-house to find a flask of wine. Thomas was left with Nesta, who was gripping his hand tightly.

'Tell me again it's not true, Thomas,' she whispered.

'It's certainly not true, good lady,' he said with a confidence he did not really share. 'I don't know the truth of everything, but it seems he's got lost in the forest. Knowing the crowner, that's no great hazard, after all the wars he's fought in his lifetime.'

She made no reply, but two tears appeared from under her closed eyelids and trickled down her cheeks, which were so pale as to look faintly green in the evening light from the unshuttered window.

The maid came back with a cup of hot, watered wine and managed to coax her mistress to take a few sips. Thomas sat for a long time holding her hand, gazing anxiously at her pale face. Nesta appeared to be sleeping, but when he tried to gently slide his hand from hers, her fingers gripped his to restrain them.

Eventually, Adam Russell came back with some potions in two small flasks and tried to persuade the landlady to drink the bitter fluids. As Thomas and the girl attempted to lift her up a little, Nesta groaned and her free hand slid to her belly. 'It hurts me!' she muttered.

With a look of concern, the maid lifted the blanket and looked underneath. Dropping it, she looked at the apothecary.

'She's losing blood down below. Her gown is soaking!'

Propriety prevented him from looking for himself, but he readily accepted her word. 'Her pulse told me something was not right,' he murmured, looking anxiously at the increasing pallor of Nesta's face.

'What can you do?' demanded Thomas desperately.

Adam shook his head. 'This is beyond my skill. I'm an apothecary, not a physician or midwife. Everyone knows she is with child. This is clearly some problem with that condition.'

There were no physicians in Exeter, all medical care apart from apothecaries' drugs being provided by the infirmarians in the five priories in and around the city. Thomas thought rapidly, drawing on his experience with the coroner and his officer.

'Then she must be taken to St Katherine's in Polsloe. There Dame Madge is an expert on these matters.'

Adam readily agreed, not wanting to take any responsibility for a worsening condition. He jumped up and went back into the inn, returning a few moments later with the news that one of the local carters would willingly take her to the priory in his wagon.

As the man went off to harness up his ox, Thomas remained with Nesta, while the two maids scurried around fetching more blankets and some clothing for their mistress to take to Posloe.

'We must take you to be cared for by the nuns, Nesta,' said the clerk gently. He had to lean close to her as she lay pale and motionless on the mattress, but her lips moved in reply.

'Then both John's women will be in Polsloe,' she murmured.

'It's the best place for you to recover, Nesta,' advised Thomas. 'You remember Dame Madge, who helped us some months ago? She will soon get you well again.'

'Am I losing the child, Thomas?' she whispered.

He was unable to lie to her, though he had no real knowledge.

'I don't know, my girl. I just don't know. It's in God's hands.'

He crossed himself surreptitiously.

'It's God's judgement, Thomas. As with you and the cathedral roof – he refused to let us take our own lives, but now he's taking the babe's instead.'

'You don't know that, Nesta. I know nothing of women's ailments, but at Polsloe they may make everything well again.'

She shook her head weakly.

'No, dear Thomas. This is God's retribution upon me … maybe it's just as well, for now there'll be no child to be born in sin. And I'll not have to tell John the truth after all.'

The tears forced their way from under her lids again as she sank her head wearily back on to the rough hessian of her maid's bed.

Gwyn slept fitfully on the floor of the alehouse, getting up just as a trace of dawn had lightened the eastern sky. All around were the men-at-arms, snoring as they lay rolled in their riding cloaks. Ralph Morin and Gabriel had opted for a penny bed in the loft, but Gwyn had been too restless to bother with a mattress. He wandered outside and, to clear his senses, doused his head in cold water from the horse trough. Three of the soldiers were sleeping on the ground near the animals, with another acting as sentry trying to keep awake. Gwyn grunted at him, then wandered around the inn, willing the dawn to strengthen, so that he could begin the search again.

He had had a fantasy the previous evening, while walking from the lane back to the alehouse, that maybe he would walk into the taproom and find Crowner John sitting on a bench waiting for their return. Unfortunately it remained a fantasy, and he faced the day with foreboding. Ralph and the garrison men might leave later, but Gwyn was determined to stay and search these woods until he discovered what had happened to his master. They had not been together across most of the known world for almost twenty years for him to abandon him now, within a few miles of home.

To kill time until it was fully light, he wandered around the back of the small, low building, where there was a ramshackle privy alongside a stinking midden. Needing to rid himself of the last of the previous night's ale, he loosened his belt and pulled down the front of his breeches to relieve himself into the ditch that ran behind the tavern, only a few yards from the first of the forest trees. The trunks were just visible in the growing light, and as he stood there he tried to throw his mind into the darkness to seek out John de Wolfe by sheer will-power.

Nothing happened, but from the other side of the privy came a low-throated growl. Tying up the thongs of his breeks, he wandered towards the noise, always unable to resist looking at a new dog.

The rattle of a chain drew his eyes down, and he could just see the outline of a large hound, straining at its leash, which must have been secured to the wall. He gave it some friendly words, but the animal took no notice of him. There was enough light now to see the silhouette of sharp-upstanding ears as the dog stood quivering, intent on something out in the forest.

Intrigued, Gwyn felt for the chain, risking a sudden bite from an unknown guard dog. He felt the last link, which had been dropped over an iron pin hammered into one of the frames for the wattle panels. Using the tension of the straining beast to pull it off, he urged it onwards, and without hesitation the hound scrambled down into the ditch and leapt up the other side, with Gwyn dragging along behind.

The dog panted and pulled, its ears now flattened, and made for the first line of trees. Once the were inside the wood, even the faint daybreak was extinguished. Gwyn stumbled along in the darkness, his feet catching in roots and brambles, until they reached the barer ground deeper under the trees, where leaf mould was the only hazard, apart from fallen branches.

The hound aimed off slightly to the left and, straining its powerful shoulders, took the coroner's officer at an uncomfortably fast pace several hundred yards into the forest. Gwyn began to wonder whether the damned beast was merely after a badger or a hind, though it should have been well used to those where it lived, but a moment later his affection for dogs was given a massive boost. The tension in the chain suddenly slackened and the dog started to whine and pant.

'Stop licking me, you bastard!' came a wonderfully well-recognised voice from the gloom.

'Crowner! Is that you?' shouted Gwyn, almost overcome with joy.

'Gwyn? What in hell are you doing here at this time of night?'

The harsh voice was weak, but grated beautifully on Gwyn's ears.

He bent down and, pushing the clever hound aside, found the coroner stretched out, his shoulders against the bole of a tree. The light had increased marginally and Gwyn could just make out de Wolfe's long body.

'Are you injured, Crowner? Where in blazes have you been?'

'I took a blade across my side, but it's nothing, though I've shed some blood. It was a bad knock on my head that did for me, though I can't remember much about it.'

Gwyn told his master to lie still, then stumbled partway back towards the distant alehouse, yelling for help in a voice that could surely be heard in Ashburton itself. Some men came running with a couple of pitch flares and before long Ralph Morin, Gabriel and the rest of the soldiers were clustered around the fallen coroner.

The lights now showed that he had a huge blue bruise across his left temple, spreading on to his ear, which was torn at the edge. Of more concern to Gwyn was the ominous dried blood that stained his tunic over his left side, but when they looked underneath, the slash, though four inches long, had been stopped by his hip bone and would not be dangerous, as long as it did not suppurate.

'Can you get up – or shall we make a stretcher for you?' asked Morin.

'Get me up and on to my horse!' snarled John, struggling to rise. He promptly fell down again and Gwyn and the castle constable, both huge men themselves, stood either side of de Wolfe and locked an arm around his, lifting him to his feet. With the flares guttering before them, they slowly walked him back to the edge of the forest, the hound prancing about delightedly in front of them.

In the alehouse, Gwyn bound up John's wound with a length of clean linen provided by the landlord, whose stock of bread, cheese and ale was rapidly exhausted by the posse and the rescued victim, whose appetite seemed to have easily survived his ordeal. As they ate and drank, the story came out, as far as the coroner could recollect. He remembered felling the first outlaw and being threatened by the second, but from there his memory was a blank until he recovered consciousness. Gwyn explained that the corpse of the first man was near the scene of the fight, but not that of the second, who must have staggered off until he collapsed and died where they found him.

With a terrible pain in his head and a bleeding wound in his side, de Wolfe had stumbled as best he could towards what he thought was the direction of the path. Then he must have collapsed again, for he remembered nothing but jumbled memories of weaving through the trees and repeatedly falling down in a stupor – due either to blood loss or the effects of the blow on the head. Eventually his head had partially cleared, but it was now dark and he groggily gave up until dawn, slumped at the foot of the tree where the dog had discovered him.

When all the excitement had died down, the coroner told Morin of the assignation they had witnessed between Stephen Cruch and the outlaw chief, as well as the mysterious priest that they assumed had met the horse-dealer in that very room.

'What's to be done about these foresters and outlaws, John?' asked Ralph Morin, as they finished the rest of the landlord's meagre food supply.

'Depends on Richard de Revelle,' growled the coroner. 'So far, he's done everything he can to be obstructive over this, which makes me suspect that he's got an interest in the matter.'

'Even if he allowed the garrison to be used for a sweep against the outlaws, I doubt if we'd have enough men. I couldn't take all of them away from Exeter at once. We've got only sixty all told.'

'And many of those are little better than raw youths,' added Gabriel glumly. 'These men here are some of the best, for I picked them myself.'

De Wolfe, whose tough body was rapidly recovering, swallowed the last of his ale. 'Then I'll have to go to Winchester and see if Hubert Walter is willing to act. It's his bloody country, after all, for as long as the King is absent.'

'And this horse-dealer and the priest? What about them?' persisted the constable.

John gingerly felt his bruised head before he spoke. 'We can't prove that anything illegal passed between them, though the landlord here confirms that they met and spoke together here. But Stephen Cruch is guilty of consorting with outlaws, for I saw him with my own eyes.'

'Seize the fellow and ask him a few questions in the undercroft in Rougemont,' suggested Gwyn grimly. 'That fat bastard Stigand will soon get some answers from him.'

'Maybe, but I must think about it first. Perhaps soon we should take a ride to Buckfast and see what this priest has to say for himself, if it's the same one that Thomas met.'

An hour later, John pronouced himself fit to ride and was helped up into the saddle of his borrowed horse by solicitous hands. Slowly, they made their way up the high road at a walking pace, Gwyn and Ralph riding closely on either side of the coroner, in case he was taken dizzy again. However, his iron constitution and his determination to see this crisis though kept him in the saddle for the next four hours. He had a sore scalp and a throbbing headache, as well as a burning pain in his hip wound, but he had suffered worse many times before.

When they reached the city, the constable and his men hurried back to the castle, trusting that the sheriff had not yet returned from his conjugal duties in Tiverton. Gwyn went with his master back to Martin's Lane, insisting that he took to his bed for the rest of the day

For once, De Wolfe seemed amenable to the idea, feeling even more exhausted after the long ride, but once again fate had other ideas.

After leaving the hired mount at the stables opposite, John preceded his officer into the house and made for the stairs to his bed in the solar. But as they came into the yard from the passage, Thomas de Peyne almost hopped out of the kitchen hut, Mary close behind him.

The clerk's face lit up when he saw his master alive

and relatively intact, but Thomas's expression told John straight away that something was wrong.

'Thank Almighty God that you're safe, Crowner!' gabbled the clerk, crossing himself furiously.

'What's wrong, Thomas?'

The little ex-priest came close and put a skinny hand on his master's arm, a thing he would never have done in less fraught circumstances.

'It's Nesta. She's with the nuns in Polsloe.'

For a moment, de Wolfe's bruised brain thought that, like his wife, his mistress had also taken the veil, until the memory of Dame Madge and her special art came to him. Now the words were tumbling out of Thomas, as he explained what had happened, carefully leaving out any hint of the fatherhood of the child.

'Some fool came into the Bush blathering a rumour that you were dead – that's what did the damage, in the fragile state that she was in,' he concluded.

John felt as if the whole of this day was a bad dream – or a nightmare.

His head ached, he had flashing lights in his left eye and he could feel blood still oozing out through the rough bandages on his side. To be faced now with the news that his mistress had narrowly been saved from throwing herself into the river, before possibly miscarrying his child, was almost too much to be taken in. He stood in the yard, dazed by the overload of events. Gwyn, himself shaken by this news of a woman for whom he had such affection, rested a fatherly hand on John's shoulder.

'I'll ride to Polsloe this minute, to see how matters stand. You must get some rest – and have that wound attended to.'

John abruptly threw off his confusion. 'We'll go together, Gwyn. And thank you, Thomas, for your aid to the poor woman. You're a good man and I'll not forget it!' The clerk gaped at these unheard-of words of thanks from his dour master, but was warmed inside by their sincerity.

With Mary and Thomas staring anxiously after them, the two men left to reclaim their horses from across the lane, John having Odin saddled up this time. Half an hour later, they were at the door of the little priory outside the city. Someone must have seen them walking across from the gate, for by the time they reached the door in the West Range, Dame Madge herself was waiting there to greet them. Her tall, hunched frame was draped in her usual black habit, but over it she wore a white linen apron, which ominously had a few spots of blood upon it.

The nun's gaunt face displayed the suspicion of a smile as she noticed John's eyes stray to the apron. 'No, that's from another woman in childbed, Sir John. Come with me.'

She stepped outside and walked along a gravel path to the left, aiming for the kitchen and the South Range beyond. 'This is where we have our infirmary now. Your friend is there.' She used the word carefully, with no hint in her voice of disapproval.

'So what happened? And how is she faring?' queried John, almost afraid to ask, in case the answer was devastating.

'She has lost the babe, may God bless it. I fear she is not at all well, both in body and mind. There was a great issue of blood when she miscarried, which has weakened her.'

'But she will recover?' demanded John, his legs feeling weak as he anticipated the answer.

The dame pursed her lips. 'As long as no puerperal fever or white-leg sets in, she should survive. The loss of blood is the main problem. But I am concerned for her state of mind. She seems to have little will to improve herself.' She looked askance at the coroner. 'All she does is ask for you!'

They had reached the door into the infirmary and entered a short corridor off which were several small cells. Farther along, the corridor opened into a larger room from which came the murmur of a number of voices.

'She's in here – you can see her only for a brief moment,' commanded the formidable nun, standing at the door of the first little cubicle. Stepping inside, John saw that the only furnishings were a low bed, a stool and a large crucifix on the wall. Beneath that was the heart-shaped face of Nesta, deathly pale against the red hair that flowed over the pillow.

Her eyes were closed, but when he spoke her name they opened and the most radiant smile he had ever seen in his life spread across her face, like the sun rising on a clear morning.

'John! You are alive – or are we both in heaven?'

'If heaven be Polsloe, then yes, we are both dead – but together!'

John bent to smooth a hand over her high forehead and gently kiss her cheek. Even the nun, aware of his wife somewhere under the same roof, could not resist a benign smile – and Gwyn was unashamedly delighted.

'The babe has gone, John. It must have been God's will,' murmured Nesta. Privately, Dame Madge was not so sure. She saw too many infants failing to survive to believe that the Almighty wished to lose any more. After a few short minutes, she firmly expelled John and his henchman from the room.

'The girl is very weak. She needs quiet and sustenance to build back the blood she lost,' she said as John reluctantly left, with a promise to visit as often as he could. As the door closed, the nun looked down at the large stain that darkened his tunic.

'Speaking of lost blood, what have you done to yourself, Crowner?'

Though John falsely protested the wound's triviality, Gwyn joined her in pushing the reluctant warrior across the corridor into another small chamber, where basins of water, cloths and shelves of salves proclaimed its function. In minutes he was placed on a stool, his tunic stripped off and the top of his breeches turned down to expose the blood-soaked dressing that had been put on earlier that morning.

With much tut-tutting, the dame called down the corridor for another elderly nun and between them they uncovered his wound and cleaned it up. Then, with a needle and thread, she pulled the edges of the slash together with three neat stitches, John gritting his teeth as the bodkin pushed through his tender flesh. Covered with salve and neatly bandaged with a long strip of linen wound around his waist, he felt infinitely more comfortable.

'In more ways than one, I owe this priory a great deal for the help I have received,' he said gratefully to the infirmarian.

'It is our duty to use what gifts God gave us for the good of all,' replied Dame Madge.

'You will find me not ungenerous after all this,' murmured de Wolfe, but the indefatigable nun had an answer for everything.

'You are a good man, as men go, Sir John. But your best gift to God would be to conduct your personal affairs as honourably as you do your public duties!'

With Gwyn trying to suppress a grin behind him, the chastened coroner left the treatment chamber. As he stepped into the passageway, he saw a figure at the far end and stopped dead. For a long moment he locked eyes with his wife, her square face holding an inscrutable expression. She wore a plain black robe and a white head-rail, almost identical with that of the nuns, and was carrying a tray.

John started towards her, but Dame Madge's strong hand restrained him. A second later, Matilda swiftly turned her back on him and vanished into the larger room.

'Does she still refuse to see me?' he demanded, almost plaintively.

The tall nun steered him towards the outside door.

'In the circumstances, could you think otherwise?' she asked reasonably.

De Wolfe rode back to the city in a chastened mood. His wife still refused to acknowledge him, his mistress was desperately sick in both body and mind, and he had just lost his child. He had a sore head, a stinging wound in his side and a problem in the forest that seemed elusive and insoluble. Life was none too great today, and Gwyn, sensing his black mood, wisely kept silent during the short journey.

Passing through East Gate, they turned up Castle Hill at the top of which John glowered at the sentry as he entered Rougemont. Throwing Odin's reins at the man, he slid from the saddle with a grimace of pain from the pull of his new stitches and loped off across the inner ward towards the keep. As he had half expected, the sheriff had not yet returned from his manor in Tiverton, and John returned to the gate-house, where Gwyn was sitting in the guard room with a jar of ale.

'Go home to St Sidwell's and see your wife, she'll have forgotten what you look like,' John said gruffly. 'And I thank you once more for your faithful service. I just might not have got from against that tree if you'd not persisted in looking for me!' Like Thomas, Gwyn was unused to any thanks from de Wolfe and scratched his crotch vigorously to cover his embarrassment.

'You look after that wound, Crowner,' he grunted. 'You'll be at Polsloe often enough now, so get them to put a clean bandage on it.'

John nodded and ended their brief intimacy by stalking out to his stallion. In the absence of his brother-in-law, he decided to talk again to the Warden of the Forest, so walked Odin through the narrow streets to the house in St Pancras Lane.

There was a new, middle-aged retainer there in place of the murdered steward, and the man showed him into the gloomy hall, where Nicholas de Bosco sat by the empty fireplace, a blanket thrown over his shoulders. He seemed ten years older than on the coroner's last visit; the attack he had suffered had suddenly aged him. John accepted a cup of wine and, sitting on a stool opposite the older man, brought him up to date with the latest events in the forest.

'I should already have known about all these matters,' de Bosco said sadly. 'Here I am, the King's warden, and none of my own officers tells me anything! They ignore me and treat me with contempt.'

'It's all part of the plan,' said de Wolfe, trying to reassure him and restore some of his injured feelings. 'But have you heard nothing of the new verderer, this Philip de Strete?'

'Not a word! The damned fellow hasn't been near me. Not that he needs to legally, as the Forest Eyre is not due until next year at the earliest. But as a matter of courtesy, you'd think the devil would come to pass the time of day, as the verderers from the other bailiwicks do occasionally.'

He pulled his blanket closer around him, though the day was warm.

'And I've had several more demands to resign – a

letter from the sheriff, damn his impudent eyes, saying that he had reports of continual unrest in the forest and holds me responsible!'

'You said several?' said John.

'The other from Henry Marshal – or at least from his chaplain on his behalf. I suppose the bishop is too grand to write to me direct. Almost word for word what the sheriff claimed. It's a damned conspiracy!'

De Wolfe felt sorry for the old warrior. He had been given this sinecure as a reward for his long and faithful service to the King – and now treacherous elements were trying to take it from him.

'It's just as well that we have Hubert Walter behind us. Neither a sheriff nor a bishop can prevail against his will. I'm going to see him very soon. I'll make sure he keeps confirming you in office – if that's what you really want.'

He added the last in case Nicholas decided that a quiet retirement was preferable to constantly looking over his shoulder for more assassins.

'I no longer relish the damned job, but I'm not going to be frightened out of it by the Count of Mortain and his scheming curs!' snapped the Warden, defiantly.

The coroner stayed a while to talk with him, though there was nothing useful de Bosco could tell him, as he had been ignored since the attempt on his life. When he climbed stiffly back on to Odin's back, John almost fell off with a sudden attack of dizziness, and with a throbbing head and an aching side, he slowly let the beast take him home to Martin's Lane.

Andrew helped him down and took him across to his house, sitting him down on the bench in the vestibule. The farrier called Mary from the back yard and the pair half dragged him up to his bed in the solar, where the maid clucked over him like a hen with a sick chick. John had intended going back to

Rougement to confront Richard de Revelle when he returned, and then returning again to Polsloe, but the strong-willed Mary kept him in bed.

She undressed him to change his bandage, which was still weeping thin blood. The maid had seen him naked at close quarters many times before, though this time he was in no condition to take advantage of her – not that Mary would have objected too much, with both his wife and mistress well out of the way. She forced him to take some hot broth and a herbal remedy, which cured his headache by driving him into a deep sleep.

The next thing he knew, it was morning. Feeling stiff and haggard, he dragged himself from his bed, but found that he could deal adequately with Mary's robust breakfast of oat gruel, salt bacon, eggs and fresh bread. His wound seemed to have dried up and the dressing was clean, so they decided to let well alone. His forehead bruise looked worse than ever, a purple stain creeping from beneath his thick hair to spread down to his eyebrow and back to his left ear, but it was less painful to the touch and his headache had dulled down.

He had missed his Saturday shave, but no way was he going to attack his stubble with a knife until his facial injuries had abated, so Black John looked blacker than ever.

'All the better to confront the bloody sheriff!' he growled to Mary, before he left the house. 'Maybe I can frighten the swine into submission.'

On his slow walk to the castle, he received many congratulations and genuinely thankful greetings from passers-by, some of whom he did not even recognise. They seemed truly glad that the rumours of the previous couple of days had proved to be false, and although he acknowledged them all only with a stern jerk of his head, he felt an inner glow of satisfaction that so many people seemed to approve of him.

At Rougemont, de Wolfe went straight to the keep, without going up to his garret in the gatehouse. He marched straight into de Revelle's chamber, intending to launch a blistering attack on his brother-in-law about the problems in the county.

Somewhat to his surprise, but soon to his gratification, he found two other men there on much the same mission. Once more, Guy Ferrars and Reginald de Courcy had come to protest to the sheriff about the situation, and this time they were in no mood to be fobbed off.

Ferrars was in full flow as John entered, leaning over Richard's table and haranguing him at close quarters, while de Courcy sat grimly upright on a chair alongside him, nodding agreement to every point that Sir Guy was making. When they heard de Wolfe enter, all three pairs of eyes swivelled to the door and Guy Ferrars paused in his lecture to the sheriff.

'God's knuckles, de Wolfe, yesterday we heard that you were dead!' bellowed Ferrars. 'Then today that you were half dead – now you walk in on us, quite alive!'

'That's a powerful bruise you have on your head,' commented de Courcy. 'And why are you limping?'

John dropped the buttock on his uninjured side on to the corner of the table.

'You may well ask, de Courcy! Two bastards attacked me in the forest and I suffered from both ends of a pike. Still, their bodies are rotting under the trees now.'

Guy Ferrars, his red face almost pulsating with indignation, turned back to the sheriff, who sat there bemused by what was turning into a three-pronged assault.

'There, de Revelle! More evidence of what we were

telling you! This forest situation is out of control, and if you'll not do anything about it then we'll go elsewhere for relief!'

Richard opened his mouth to protest again, but the choleric baron gave him no chance. 'I've been telling this man of the latest outrages, de Wolfe. I'll repeat it for your benefit, as will de Courcy here – but first, what's been happening to you?'

John told his story with some relish, even pulling up his tunic to show them his bandage, through which a slight stain of blood had again appeared to give credence to his tale. He omitted the fact that Ralph Morin had taken men-at-arms from the castle to search for him, as he wanted to avoid giving Richard grounds for complaint. Something also made him hold back any mention of the mysterious priest, as if the sheriff was involved he might put out a warning. But he was quite happy to tell them about the horse-trader.

'This Stephen Cruch is involved, beyond any doubt,' he said. 'My officer saw him with one of Robert Winter's outlaws – and then with my own eyes I saw the same man at a rendezvous with Winter in the forest, just before some of his men attacked me. There's little doubt he's acting as a go-between for someone outside and the rogues who are doing the dirty work for the foresters.'

Richard de Revelle looked desperately uneasy at this revelation, but Guy Ferrars was exultant. 'It all fits together, Crowner. I know this man Cruch, my steward has had dealings with him over horses. A sly, crafty devil – there are rumours that he was outlawed himself, years ago.'

'That's just gossip,' blustered Richard. 'We know nothing of this man.'

'Are you defending him?' shouted Ferrars. 'Do you

doubt that de Wolfe's telling the truth?' He turned to Reginald de Courcy. 'Repeat for his benefit what you told de Revelle here.'

The other landowner was less fiery than his companion, but his voice was bitter as he related his most recent complaints.

'The fees for agistment in four of my manors have been doubled! Right up to the start of the fence month, it was half a penny a beast per year – then my villeins come and tell me the agisters are going to claim a full penny after the glades are open again next month. When they complained, the blasted foresters threatened to give them a beating.'

'And that mealy-mouth new verderer, Philip de Strete, confirmed it when I challenged him,' cut in Ferrars, unwilling to be left out of the drama.

'It's more than the damned pigs are worth, for the sake of them grubbing at some beech mast and a few acorns!' went on de Courcy. 'And to add insult to injury, they've set up two new forges on my land, which will take half the business away from the ones I've had there for twenty years and more.'

He glared at the sheriff. 'And you seem quite content to let this go on unabated. I tell you, whatever money I lose over this is going be taken from what you screw from me for the county farm. How are you going to explain to the Chancellor why you're short, when you next take your loot to Winchester, eh?'

De Revelle, whose face under this barrage of complaints had gone as pale as the others were suffused, turned up his hands in a Gallic gesture of helplessness.

'You are talking of the Royal Forests, sirs, the domain of the King himself! I have no power there, all this is due to the incompetence of the Warden. I have done my best to help by installing a younger, more active verderer in at least one of the bailiwicks.'

'Yes, a bloody idiot! The Warden says he has no power to intervene, so where are we?' rasped de Courcy in his steely voice.

'There are three other verderers in the Devon forest – are they also to be shot in the back so that new ones can be installed?' asked Guy Ferrars, with heavy sarcasm.

John followed all this with satisfaction, relishing the evasive cringing of his brother-in-law in the face of these two powerful men. He almost forgot his aches and pains as they continued to hammer de Revelle.

'Tell them of your problems, Ferrars,' said Reginald icily.' Some that should concern him, as a coroner.'

'Ha, yes! A dead body is involved, if only we could find it.'

Guy Ferrars dropped heavily on to the chair behind him and leaned forward towards de Wolfe, ignoring the sheriff altogether.

'On one of my manors near Lustleigh I have a chase which abuts on to the edge of the Royal Forest – even though all the bloody land belongs to me on both sides of the boundary. There is a small valley leading from my chase into the King's ground – and a week ago those damned foresters built a saltatorium just a few yards on their side.'

John, though not a keen huntsman, knew that a saltatorium was a 'deer leap', a deep ditch with one vertical wall, the opposite one being sloping. The agile beasts could easily leap down the steep face and run up the other side, but could not return. The device was used to trap wild deer to increase the stock in a private chase or park, but was illegal on private ground within two miles of a Royal Forest, for obvious reasons.

'Now these cunning swine have reversed the rules!'

fumed Guy Ferrars. 'They deliberately sited the leap inside their territory, so that beasts from my chase will run into their forest and not be able to return down the valley, which is one of the main deer tracks.'

Richard de Revelle listened in silence, but de Courcy egged his friend on. 'But that's not the half of it. Tell the crowner the rest.'

Guy Ferrars banged the desk with his fist.

'When my bailiff took a pair of my woodwards to break down the illegal leap, a pair of foresters appeared with their ruffianly pages and threatened to thrash them all if they persisted. On my own land, was this! The two woodwards refused to fight, saying they had sworn the forest oath and had to do what the foresters told them, even though I'm the one who pays the bastards!'

From his recent research, John knew that woodwards, though employed by the landowners of chases and parks, were in a difficult position, as they had a divided loyalty to both their employers and the Royal Forest.

'So what of this dead man you mentioned?' he queried, puzzled as to where this was leading.

'You may well ask, de Wolfe!' trumpeted Guy Ferrars. 'When my bailiff returned with the news, my temper knew no bounds. I sent my steward and three bailiffs, together with six men-at-arms from my own retinue, back to destroy the saltatorium. They had been there less than an hour when they were ambushed by a rabble hiding in the trees. Almost twice our number, they were undoubtedly part of this band of outlaws you describe, run by the man Winter. But one of my bailiffs said that he clearly saw a forester lurking among them at the rear.'

'So what happened?'

'There was a short, sharp fight and several of my men were wounded by arrows. We killed two of their ruffians and eventually drove them back, but one of my guard vanished. Another man said that he saw him fall during the fight, but as they were still being plagued by arrows from behind the trees, my men failed to find him or his body. Next day, I sent a party to search, but they found nothing except the two dead outlaws, which we left there.'

Still the sheriff kept silent, but John pressed Ferrars for more details.

'So the dead man is still there somewhere? This is another murder – I should have been informed.'

'We had no body to show you, Crowner,' snapped the baron. 'I have no doubt he is dead, but as yet there is no actual proof, though the fellow has certainly disappeared.'

Reginald de Courcy was becoming impatient. 'What's to be done about all this? De Revelle here seems remarkably loath to take any action.'

He turned to glare at the sheriff. 'It is no secret that you have ambitions to become Warden of the Forest, though God knows why. It makes your motives in refusing to act all the more suspicious – and with your history over the past year or two, you can ill afford for that to happen.'

Richard glowered back at the rich landowner. ' There are those who think otherwise, sir – and many are barons with considerable influence. I am a servant of the King, but no king reigns for ever!'

Guy Ferrars, a staunch supporter of the Lionheart, turned almost purple.

'Have a care, de Revelle!' he yelled. 'Your neck will stretch the same as any other man's who contemplates disloyalty!'

'This is getting us nowhere,' complained de Courcy testily. 'Crowner, you have had evidence of deaths and crimes aplenty in the forest, against the King's peace. What do you suggest?'

'It's not his place to suggest anything,' yelped de Revelle. 'I am the sheriff in this county, and I say that the forest laws look after themselves. De Wolfe has no jurisdiction there.'

'Nonsense, de Revelle! What do you say, Crowner?' snapped Ferrars.

John hesitated for a moment while he found the right words.

'I need to resume several inquests, as no satisfactory evidence was offered. I have to enforce the attendance of two foresters, who refused to come to a King's Court – and a greater force of arms is needed to rout out these outlaws who seem to be mercenaries for the forest administration.'

'And how are we going to achieve that?' grunted Ferrars. ' I've only a few men left in my retinue, the rest have gone to fight in France. And de Courcy here has none at all.'

'Then we must petition the Curia, through the Chief Justiciar. I'll have to ride to find him, wherever he is, though I cannot leave for some days, owing to personal circumstances.'

'Ha, we all know what they are!' sneered Richard, spitefully, but the others ignored him.

'I'll do that towards the end of the week, but first I need to ride down to Buckfast to satisfy myself about a certain priest.'

He caught his brother-in-law's eye and held it until Richard's gaze dropped.

Other duties kept him occupied for the rest of the day, including riding just outside the city to the village of Clyst St Mary to see to a thief who had taken sanctuary in the church. The man refused to confess his crime, which was stealing a silver candlestick from the house of the parish priest. As the object was a personal belonging of the incumbent, rather than in the possession of the church, the offence of sacrilege could not be brought. If it had, then sanctuary would have been forfeited and the miscreant could have been dragged out of the church. The manor of Clyst St Mary belonged to the Bishop of Exeter, which explained why the priest was affluent enough to possess such a valuable object.

John failed to persuade the miserable thief, who cowered near the altar, to confess his sins and abjure the realm, which would at least have saved his neck. As it was the coroner ordered the villagers to guard the church for the next forty days, unless the culprit had a change of heart. If, at the end of that time, he still refused to confess and abjure, the coroner would order that he be deprived of food and drink until he died.

In fact, a large proportion of sanctuary-seekers were allowed to escape, as the villagers begrudged the expense and effort of feeding and guarding the criminal for almost six weeks, even at the cost of being fined by the coroner. In this case, however, the irate priest was likely to exact his revenge on the man and force his parishioners to do their legal duty.

In the early evening, de Wolfe went again to Polsloe Priory to see Nesta. She was much as before, very weak and as pale as skimmed milk.

The Welsh woman was ineffably sad and spoke very little, but lay quietly, with her hand in John's as he sat alongside her low truckle bed in the bare cell. He talked soothingly to her and gave her news of how Edwin and the girls were faring well in running the Bush in her absence. They hardly spoke about the loss of her child; John was too timid to risk provoking a flow of tears. Instead, he sat talking of other things, like his problems in the forest and his trip to Clyst St Mary. Between these tales, he awkwardly murmured repetitively that all would well between them and that she must get well and come home to the Bush, whereupon things would be just as before. Matilda was not mentioned between them and, when he left, there was no sign of her in the infirmary corridor.

As he went to the door, Dame Madge appeared and brusquely ordered him into the treatment room to have his wound inspected and a new dressing applied.

'It looks healthy. You are a tough man,' she proclaimed, tugging at the linen stitches, which made him wince. 'The edges of the wound are a little red, but there's no pus at all.'

As she skilfully wound a new strip of linen around his waist, she told him that Nesta was still quite ill, having lost a great deal of blood after her miscarriage, though this flow had now abated. When he hesitantly asked about his wife, she shook her head sternly and said that there had been no change in 'Sister' Matilda's attitude towards him.

When he returned to Exeter, he could not face the Bush without Nesta there, so went with Gwyn to the New Inn in the high street and sat there drinking until dusk, when his officer left to go home to St Sidwell's before the curfew. John told Gwyn about the increasing impatience of the barons to have some action over the worsening situation in the forest.

'We'll have to go to Winchester soon, though I want to make sure that Nesta is out of any danger before I leave, as we'll be away for at least a week.'

'You also said you want to see about this priest that Thomas suspects,' grunted Gwyn.

'Yes, we must ride to Buckfast before Winchester. Will there be time after the hangings tomorrow, I wonder?'

'There's no one to be turned off today,' said Gwyn. 'We're right out of felons this week!'

So it was that the next day saw another early start as the trio set out along the Cornwall road for the three-hour ride to Buckfast Abbey. Thomas was more cheerful than usual when on a horse, as any opportunity to visit a religious house was a treat for him, especially Buckfast, which had treated him as a genuine priest when he was last there. He was a little anxious about their reaction if they recognised him as one of the coroner's team, but Gwyn magnanimously suggested that he could pretend to be the coroner's chaplain!

However, when they arrived at the abbey Thomas slipped away into the church and stood praying and crossing himself in the quiet gloom, to avoid drawing attention to himself outside.

Gwyn and his master left the horses at the stables and went to the guest house as travellers to claim a meal, for which they donated a penny to the abbey funds. As they sat at the long tables in the large refectory, John looked around at the dozen other people eating there.

'No sign of that bloody horse-dealer,' he growled. 'I wonder where we can lay hands on him?'

'If Winter's men have told him that he's been seen with them, he'll be keeping his head well down. Though if he's to continue making a living, he'll have to keep appearing at horse fairs and the like.'

As they left the hall, John questioned the lay brother in charge, who was not aware of their identity, believing them to be a passing knight and his squire.

'I thought I might have chanced upon my old friend Stephen Cruch, the horse-dealer,' John said. 'He calls here from time to time, I know.'

The amiable brother, always ready for a gossip, shook his head.

'Haven't laid eyes on him for almost a fortnight. He comes now and then to deal with Father Edmund, but there's no knowing when we'll see him. Depends on what animals the abbey's got to sell, I suppose.'

They left him to walk across the wide outer court between the abbey itself and the various buildings opposite, which comprised the large guest hall, the manorial court, the stables and the smithy, as well as the two gatehouses. The court was clean and tidy, unlike most public places in the towns and cities, and beyond it were orderly gardens and orchards, dotted with the beehives for which Buckfast was famous.

'Do you want me to collect the little turd from his devotions?' asked Gwyn, as they approached the door to the abbey cloisters.

'No, let him be for now. I know he's afraid of being recognised if he's with us. Give him an hour of make-believe, poor sod.'

They went into the passage and reached the arched cloister, Gwyn scowling at the sight of silent Cistercians perambulating the paved arcades.

'How they can think that keeping their gobs shut for years on end makes them holy, I just can't see!' he muttered under his breath.

John grinned at his officer's determined antipathy to religion, a most unusual phenomenon and one for which he had never discovered the cause. He asked a passing lay brother, who was lugging a leather bucket of hot water, where he might find Father Edmund Treipas.

'He's not here, sir,' said the old man. 'He went off to Plymouth yesterday to arrange a shipment of the abbey's wool to Barfleur.'

De Wolfe cursed under his breath at the prospect of a wasted journey from Exeter. 'Well, is the abbot in residence?'

'I'll take you to his secretary, sir, if you'll follow me.'

He dumped his bucket in the cloister and shuffled ahead of them to another door which led to the abbot's house, on the south-west corner of the cloister. Inside the abbot's lodgings, they were led up a staircase to a room where a young, rather supercilious monk sat behind a table covered with scrolls and writing materials. The Cistercian rule of silence was hardly compatible with the administration of a large organisation like Buckfast and, having enquired as to their identity, the secretary's aloof manner moderated in the presence of the King's coroner. He went to an adjacent door, tapped and went in. A moment later he returned and ushered them into the abbot's parlour, a large, plainly furnished room with a glazed window that overlooked the outer court.

Abbot William was an austere man, with a shock of white hair surrounding his shaven crown. He reminded de Wolfe of his friend John de Alençon, with his narrow face and clear blue eyes. William was an eminent personage, having acted as a Papal Legate five years earlier. He graciously waved them to chairs on the other side of his plain table and John sat down, but Gwyn stood stiffly behind his master. The abbot enquired politely as to the nature of their business with him.

'It's a delicate matter, sir,' began de Wolfe, rather unsure of his ground here. 'I am investigating a series of crimes and disturbances in the Royal Forest, especially in this bailiwick. We have problems with a band of outlaws who appear to be getting support from outside for their nefarious actions.'

Abbot William looked mildly surprised.

'The abbey is outwith the Royal Forest, though some of our more distant land and pastures lie within its bounds. What is this to do with us?'

John made one of his gargling noises to cover his indecision about suggesting that one of the senior monks was involved in treason.

'It has been noted that a certain trader has been involved as a go-between with this band of outlaws,' he said, in as neutral terms as possible. 'This trader is also a frequent visitor to the abbey and seems to have close ties with one of your brethren.'

The abbot's brows came together in a frown. 'We have many traders coming to us. We are one of the largest landowners in the area and produce a great deal of wool, beasts, honey and other provender. It is inevitable that such dealers frequent the place.' Of a sudden, the atmosphere in the chamber seemed to have become chilly.

'This priest has also met with our suspect dealer well away from the abbey, such as at an alehouse near Ashburton.'

William became impatient. 'Let us not beat about the bush, Sir John. Why not name names? You are no doubt referring to Father Edmund, as you said 'priest', not 'monk'?'

John inclined his dark head. 'Indeed, that is so. And the dealer was Stephen Cruch, a fellow of dubious reputation from the company he keeps.'

The abbot waved a hand as if brushing away a fly. 'I know nothing of the tradesmen who deal with the abbey,' he said sharply. 'In fact, that is why Edmund came to us, as he had a reputation for worldly expertise and seemed capable of managing the outside affairs of the abbey.'

'How was it that he did come to Buckfast?'

'My friend in God, Bishop Henry, arranged it. I understand that Father Edmund was beneficial in restoring the fortunes of the See of Coventry and had in fact been a merchant in that city before he gave up the worship of Mammon for the cloth and later the cloister.'

He fixed de Wolfe with a steely eye. 'I fail to see what

gain you expected by coming to Buckfast, Crowner. I can assure you that this abbey has no interest whatsoever in fomenting trouble in the Royal Forest. What exactly is it you think has been going on?'

John decided that it would be best to be quite frank with this perceptive old man.

'There are coincidences that need explanation. Undoubtedly forces are at work stirring up trouble in the forest, the object of which is not clear at the moment. But money is changing hands towards that end and this horse-dealer seems to be one of the channels through which it passes. Your cellarer, Edmund Treipas, is in regular contact with the man – and that good father came via Bishop Henry Marshal from his previous master, the Bishop of Coventry. It is common knowledge where their sympathies lie.'

Abbot William stared at de Wolfe for a long moment.

'Ah, I see how your mind is working, Sir John! You suspect the common factor is the Count of Mortain, don't you?'

His voice was level and controlled, but John sensed the anger beneath.

'You are well known as a staunch King's man and I applaud you for that. And I am no traitor either, though my allegiance must be to God first and to men second.'

He paused to choose his words carefully. 'Yet you must understand that many people, especially in this abbey, have mixed feelings about who would make the best king. We can hardly feel unstinting devotion to Richard Coeur-de-Lion, who openly expresses his dislike of the Cistercians.'

William slapped his hands on the edge of his table.

'And what of his actions two years ago, when he stripped us of every penny of our wool revenues for a whole year, to help pay for his ransom? We almost fell into financial ruin through that punitive act – our brethren ate poorly that winter, I can assure you! And before that, we had to forfeit some of our treasured silver chalices from the very altar itself, to fund his wars!'

De Wolfe always took poorly to any criticism of his monarch.

'Buckfast was not alone in that, Abbot. The whole country had to make sacrifices at the times of the wars, the Crusade and the King's capture.'

'But why should we? We have a king who thinks of nothing but fighting abroad. He spends no time in England, he bleeds the country dry and yet expects unswerving allegiance! Is it any surprise that some wonder if his brother John might make a better sovereign? He certainly has promised we monastic orders some preferment when he comes to the throne, as come he must before long. It's only a matter of time before our foolhardy Richard gets himself killed in some rash combat.'

John testily thought that anyone other than a senior cleric could be arraigned for sedition for uttering such sentiments, yet an abbot could get away with it.

'Are you saying that you condone any activities such as I suspect your cellarer might be engaged in?'

'Of course not!' snapped William. 'And I am confident that Edmund is not involved in anything illegal or unchristian. Frankly, I think your suspicions are based on nothing but rumour and supposition.'

He stood up abruptly and, picking a small handbell from his table, rang it for his secretary. The young monk appeared with such alacrity that de Wolfe suspected that he had been listening with his ear to the door.

'The coroner is leaving now. See them to the court and ensure they have refreshment in the guest hall before they ride back to Exeter,' he commanded. He offered them a courteous but cold farewell, and soon de Wolfe and his officer were outside, feeling somewhat chastened by the peremptory manner of the elderly monk.

'We'll learn nothing more here today,' grumbled Gwyn. 'Our only chance would be to catch this Edmund red handed, passing a purse of silver to Stephen Cruch.'

'Little chance of that now. They'll have been warned both by the knowledge of someone stalking their meeting in the forest – and now by us coming here.'

There was nothing for it but to collect Thomas from the church and set off for home. When they reached Rougemont, it was still only early afternoon, as their seven-hour expedition to Buckfast had begun soon after dawn and these midsummer days were long. A messenger was waiting for John, a man in the service of Guy Ferrars, who requested his presence at his son's town house in Goldsmith Street. The baron himself lived at several of his manors, as the fancy took him, often at Tiverton, where he had an estate which dwarfed that of his neighbour, Richard de Revelle.

His son Hugh was a rather stupid young man, fond of hunting, gaming and drinking. The previous autumn, the coroner had been involved in investigating the death of Hugh's fiancée, a tragedy that had led to murder. Since then, the son had added wenching to his list of pastimes, much to his father's displeasure, and it was rumoured that Lord Ferrars was now actively involved in finding a wife for his son, in an attempt to bring him to heel.

John mulled over these memories as he walked behind the servant the short distance to Goldsmith Street, which was off High Street behind the Guildhall. The house belonged to a friend of Reginald de Courcy, and the Ferrars rented the two rooms on the ground floor, where Hugh lived with a squire when he was in the city. Today, his father was there in his stead, sitting in the small hall adjacent to the street door, with a flask of best Loire wine by his side.

His servant poured one for John, who sat on a bench facing the baron.

'De Wolfe, since we last spoke I've been thinking about this servant of mine who vanished in that ambush. You're right – if he's dead, he should be found and the villain who killed him brought to justice.'

John nodded gravely. 'I agree wholeheartedly, my lord. If he is dead, then it is my duty as a law officer to hold an inquest. But I thought you had failed to find any trace of him?'

The florid-faced baron, a large, beefy man with a permanently pugnacious expression, glowered at his wine cup.

'So my men told me. But I have had a thought that we could return to the scene and use some hounds to track him. His wife can provide some remnant of his clothing that will have his scent, so surely a good dog could find him?'

John knew that there were three types of dog used in hunting: the big liam hound for starting the quarry from its lair, then the 'leparii', the lean greyhounds which hunted by sight, but mainly the ordinary hound, the 'brachetti', which hunted by scent. It seemed a good idea of Ferrars', if the brachetti would accept the human smell from clothing.

'I'm damned if I'm going to let these forest bastards get away with this,' snarled Guy. 'Trying to steal game from my chase is bad enough, but then to kill one of my own men is beyond reason.'

John told him of his visit earlier that day to Buckfast and the abbot's admission that many favoured Prince

John, especially those to whom he had promised favours, such as the monasteries.

'The King is the King!' roared Ferrars, spilling some of his wine in his passion. 'If Richard was to die, which God forbid, then I would be equally loyal to the next monarch – though I view the prospect of John Lackland on the throne with dismay and contempt.'

Though Ferrars was an overbearing bigot and a harsh, unforgiving landlord and master to his subjects, he was totally devoted to Richard the Lionheart, having fought alongside him many times. De Wolfe could forgive him his rough nature because of his loyalty, even though he could never generate any affection for the man.

'So what's to be done about the matter?' he asked, partly to cool the baron's rising temperature, already fuelled by too much wine.

'Can you join us tomorrow morning, Crowner, if I get a search party and some hounds? I'd give much to find this corpse, for my own satisfaction, though no doubt his family would like to see him given a Christian burial.'

They arranged to meet at one of his manors near Lustleigh the following morning, John groaning inwardly at the thought of yet another two-hour ride soon after dawn. As he was leaving, Guy Ferrars followed him to the door.

'I'll bring that bumpkin of a son of mine, too. He's not the brightest of men, but he's big and fit and can wield a sword after a fashion.'

John went from Goldsmith Street to his house, where he collapsed into his fireside chair to rest his aching limbs. Though he was well used to spending much of his time in the saddle, these past few days had put a strain on him, having to ride long distances following his head injury and the still-painful slash across his hip.

The thought came to him as Mary bustled about getting him a meal that he was getting old. He was now forty-one, and though he knew of men eighty years of age, relatively few survived past fifty or sixty. True, the upper classes fared better, though being killed in battle was an ever-present hazard. The villeins and serfs had a far lower life expectancy, threatened by pestilence, starvation and accidents, many being fortunate to reach thirty.

As he sat in his gloomy hall, hung with faded tapestries to hide the timber walls, he thought about death and how it would come. He hoped it would be sudden, unexpected and bloody, rather than a slow wasting from a seizure or a long fever or some variety of pox. If it were not for Gwyn and the tavern hound, he could have died this week, slumped bemused in that forest, fading in and out of consciousness and with a bleeding wound.

He shook himself free of these morbid thoughts as Mary brought in his dinner. At the table he found that she had fried him three trout, which rested invitingly on a large trencher of barley bread, with turnips and leeks on a side platter. Wild berries, white bread and cheese followed, with a quart of best ale to wash it down.

'I went down to the Bush for a gallon, just to cheer you up, Sir Crowner!' she announced, in her part-mocking, part-affectionate way.

'I thought you might have forgotten the place, now that your lady friend is no longer in residence.'

Then, becoming serious, she enquired after Nesta's health. 'I heard that she is still very weak, poor girl. Maybe I can walk up to Polsloe some time to see her and take her a decent morsel of food. I doubt they get anything very tasty in that place.'

John slipped an arm around her waist as she stood near him at the table.

'Your heart is in the right place, Mary, apart from being in a very shapely chest!' he said. 'Soon I will have to be away for at least a week, travelling to Winchester, so it would be good if you could visit her when I'm gone.'

His meal finished, he crawled to his bed for a few hours' rest to ease his aching side, but in the evening he borrowed a mare from the farrier and rode gently up to Polsloe. Nesta was much the same, though perhaps even more pale and wan. Her face was so white that her cheeks seemed almost green below the eyes. When she rested her hand in his as he sat at the bedside, he saw that her nail-beds were the colour of milk, without a vestige of pink. She spoke little, as if the effort of talking was too much, but seemed somehow more content, even in her exhausted state.

John attempted to make largely one-sided conversation, no mean feat for such a taciturn man. Nesta lay listening, savouring the thought that she would no longer have to screw up the courage to respond to Thomas's plea to tell John that the child was not his. Her feelings about losing the babe were strange, and she was almost frightened by her own lack of emotion about the miscarriage. There was a natural element of deep shock and sorrow that was inevitable in any woman, but overlying this was the feeling of relief that she had escaped from an intolerable situation – one that had almost driven her to take the life of both herself and the baby she carried.

As John faltered to the end of his stock of small talk, which mainly concerned his problems in the forest and the day's excursion to Buckfast, she lay sleepily under the influence of Dame Madge's infusion of gentian. As he fell silent, she squeezed his hand and remembered something to tell him.

'Dear Thomas came to visit me this afternoon, while

you were snoring in your bed,' she said softly. 'He is a good little man – he has been kinder to me than you would ever imagine.'

'Is he another fellow for me to be jealous of, a rival for your affections, madam?' he said jocularly. 'Will I have to fight him with broadswords for your favours?'

'I can't see little Thomas fighting anyone. He is a true man of peace – and one who has the greatest devotion and affection for you, too. He has promised to teach me to read and write when I am recovered, so that I can keep accounts in the inn.'

'Then you can write me love letters – and I will speed up my own learning so that I can read them!'

Their tender flirting was interrupted by the forbidding figure of Dame Madge coming into the room. She looked impassively at the sight of the county coroner holding hands with an innkeeper, while his noble wife was hardly a dozen yards away under the same roof.

The angular nun advanced on the bed with some brown potion for Nesta. 'She needs to build back the blood she lost, Sir John. There's no more I can do for her, except keep watch against a fever and give her the best nourishment.'

John expressed his deep appreciation of the treatment she was receiving. 'I have to go to Winchester in a few days and will be away a week or more. Can she stay here until I return? Her maids at the inn are diligent, but I would be more content if she was cared for here.'

'She'll not be fit to return for some time yet. Be assured that we will look after her here.' She looked sternly at the coroner's own battered face, where the bruises on his temple were beginning to turn yellow at the edges. 'I want to see that wound in your loin before you leave, Crowner. It's time the dressing was changed again.'

Even Nesta managed a smile as the coroner meekly trailed out to the treatment room after the nun, the pair looking like two skinny rooks in their black plumage.

CHAPTER TWELVE

In which Crowner John follows a dog

Guy Ferrars had gone to Lustleigh the previous evening and billeted himself, his son and servants on his tenant there, Roger Cotterel. The manor was not an ancient one, being ignored in William the Bastard's great survey over a century earlier. It had been hewn from some of Baldwin the Sheriff's lands many years before, and Ferrars' father had purchased it as an addition to his extensive estates in the county.

The manor house was small, but built of stone with a slate roof, and when John de Wolfe and Gwyn arrived the next morning, the bailey within the surrounding fence was humming with activity. Guy Ferrars had brought eight of his private soldiers from Tiverton, together with his hound-master, steward and bailiff. Half a dozen lean brown hounds yapped excitedly in an empty pigsty, where they had been confined for the night.

Ferrars invited the coroner and his officer into the hall, which occupied the whole ground floor, Cotterel's living quarters being on the upper floor. The reluctant host was a tall, thin man with sandy hair, who was trying his best to look as if he enjoyed having his landlord and his retinue foisted upon him for a day and a night. Food and drink were plentiful on the trestles, and they all filled themselves ready for the search in the adjacent forest.

Together with Cotterel, his manor-reeve and a dozen villagers, the party moved out on foot, as the edge of the woods was barely a quarter of a mile to the west, beyond which the land dropped down into the valley of the Bovey river, with Trendlebere Down on the other side. As they walked ahead of the motley crowd, the dogs now following slavishly behind the whip-carrying hound-master, Ferrars explained the lie of the land.

'I own everything as far as you can see,' he bellowed, waving his arm expansively at the tree-covered horizon. 'I use the land beyond the village fields as part of my chase, which extends for four miles north of here. But farther up, the bloody Royal Forest comes right across the river.'

They walked on for half an hour, diving into the trees and turning right within sound of the Bovey in its deep valley. John and Gwyn, who had their own swords buckled on, saw that every man was armed in some way, two of the retainers being bowmen. They seemed a large enough party to repulse anything other than a major force of outlaws, but John felt vulnerable after his recent experiences and kept a wary eye open for any sign of opposition. Hugh Ferrars walked with them in the vanguard. He was a younger version of his father in build and colouring, but had barely half his father's personality and energy. John assumed that the tragic Adele de Courcy had been given little choice in her betrothal to this boorish young man. The manor-lord, Roger Cotterel, was the first to spot the demolished deer-leap that had caused this trouble. He pointed ahead to a tumble of earth and turf among the trees.

'There's the saltatorium, so we're in royal territory now, by a few hundred paces.'

The leap had been built across a narrow defile which carried a well-trodden deer path down the centre. Though it had been partly destroyed by the efforts of

Ferrar men, John could see that an eight-foot bank had been thrown up from a deep ditch, which sloped gently up on the far side. The agile deer could easily spring down the sheer face and scamper up the slope, but the return journey was blocked as they could not get enough of a run in the ditch to scale the vertical wall.

The party scrambled down the tumbled earth and stood in the partly filled trench to await orders from the baron. He called over his steward, a venerable-looking elder with snowy hair.

'Have you got that clothing from the widow?'

The steward unslung a leather shoulder bag and produced a ragged pair of woollen breeches. 'These had been discarded but not washed, my lord. They will have his scent upon them.'

Guy Ferrars put his nose to the rags and grimaced. He held them out to John, who even at arm's length could savour the mixture of stale sweat and urine.

'Don't need a bloody dog. I could follow that myself!' said Gwyn, when he had also sampled the odour.

Ferrars threw the garment at the hound-master, a wizened fellow dressed all in green, with a horn hanging around his neck on a leather thong. He caught it and looked dubiously at the hounds.

'I've never tried this before, sir. They'll follow a fox or a stag to the ends of the earth, but I don't know if they understand about humans.'

He called his beasts to him and, as they clustered excitedly around his feet, held the breeches to their snouts. The hounds looked puzzled but willing, and seemed to understand when he waved them away and gave a blast on his horn as encouragement. He started running away from the deer-leap farther into the King's forest, the dogs running yelping before him. They began spreading out and putting their noses to the ground and to bushes and tree trunks. In a moment they all seemed to converge on to a side track and went racing away, barking excitedly.

'Looks as if they've got the idea!' said Gwyn, to whom dogs were preferable to most men. They all hurried after the hound-master, who was trying to keep up with his charges. The party swished through the sparse undergrowth beneath the tall trees, the stench from crushed garlic strong on the still air. After some four hundred yards, labouring up a slope from the defile, they saw the green tunic of the hound-master in a small hollow at the base of a huge oak. As they panted up, the man looked crestfallen.

'I think they've been misled by the scent of a fox, my lord.'

The six dogs were milling around a wide hole between the roots of the great tree, which was poised on the edge of a dip in the ground. Red Devon earth was exposed, and fresh soil was scattered downhill from the tunnel mouth. The hounds were milling about in circles, yapping and barking, and one had his head in the hole, trying to worm his way inside.

Gwyn bent to look closely at the ground around the hole.

'This doesn't look right for a foxhole or a badger sett,' he grunted. 'The earth has been thrown up against the bottom, not dug out from it.'

The hound-master looked and agreed with him. 'There was a sett here – a big one, but it's been partly refilled.'

The two men, watched by the rest of the party, seized a couple of fallen branches and broke off four-foot lengths to use as crude spades. They attacked the soft, crumbly soil, pulling it back to slide down the slope below the hole, which now appeared as a much larger aperture. The dogs, which had been hovering excitedly around them, whimpered even louder, and one, more daring animal again dived head first into the hole. The houndsman yelled at it and gave it a smack across the bottom to get it out. Gwyn took its place, dropping to his knees to peer down the shaft, which went obliquely down between the tree roots.

'See anything?' snapped the impatient coroner.

Instead of answering, his officer dropped on to his side, careless of the damp rusty earth soiling his clothing, and stuck his right arm up to the shoulder into the hole. The onlookers watched his face change to an expression of disgust as he pulled his arm out of the tunnel and looked at his hand.

'No wonder the hounds were so excited,' he said with his usual infuriating slowness in imparting information. 'How long has this man been missing?'

A jabber of consternation broke out among the watchers as Gwyn held up his hand to show a piece of greenish skin stuck to his palm.

'Is that human?' demanded Guy Ferrars.

'It slid off something with five fingers and a thumb!' answered the Cornishman with black humour. 'I think he's in head first, with the legs under this earth.' He clambered to his feet and pointed to the soil that was still piled below the hole. Now the baron snapped into activity, shouting orders at his retainers, while de Wolfe and his henchman stood and watched. The dogs were called off and three Lustleigh men energetically began scraping away the earth with pieces of wood. Within a couple of minutes one of them gave a yell and bent to brush away loose soil with his hand, exposing a bare foot. It was white and wrinkled but not decomposed, and very soon both legs were uncovered.

'Can you drag it out now?' demanded the manor-reeve, who was hovering over the three villagers. They dropped their branches and heaved on the ankles of the corpse. After a momentary hesitation, there was a

341

minor avalanche of powdery earth and the body slid out of the hole, into which it had been pushed up to the knees, then covered with loose soil. One arm below the elbow had been exposed within the tunnel, and it was this that Gwyn had felt. The diggers brushed off most of the earth from the body and stood back to allow everyone to see the dead man.

'There's no doubt it's William Gurnon,' said the reeve. 'He's not too mortified, considering it's a week since he died.'

'The earth helps preserve them,' said John de Wolfe, an expert on corpses. 'Only that hand is green and slimy, because it was out in the air.'

'Some animal, rats or a fox, must have unearthed it,' added Gwyn, not to be outdone in matters of death. 'All the tendons on the back have been laid bare where it's been nibbled.'

Guy Ferrars was more interested in what had killed his servant, rather than the effects of death. 'Have a look at him, de Wolfe. He's a coroner's responsibility now.'

John and his officer went into their familiar routine of examining the cadaver. As he squatted by the body, de Wolfe observed aloud that someone had already committed several offences, by failing to report a sudden death to him and by concealing the corpse from his view. A week's hot weather had begun to affect the body, though as John had already pointed out, being buried in a cool wood had markedly slowed down putrefaction. The dead man wore a short tunic and knee-length breeches, his feet being bare. The upper garment had ridden up over his worn leather belt and the exposed belly was greenish and slightly swollen. His face was somewhat flattened from the weight of soil on it and the eyes were collapsed and opaque, but the features were still recognisable to the other men from Lustleigh.

'Here's the trouble, Crowner!' said Gwyn, pointing

to ominous brown staining on the neutral-coloured wool of the tunic. On both sides, coming around under the armpits, the staining was partly obscured by adherent loose soil, but when Gwyn rolled the corpse over, the whole of the back of the clothing, from shoulder blades down to waist, was stiff with dried blood. When the belt was removed and the tunic pulled right up, the cause was obvious.

'Stabbed in the back – twice!' barked Ferrars, who was peering over John's shoulder.

'Bloody cowards! Two with arrows in their backs, and now a knife in the same place,' added his son belligerently.

The coroner traced out the two wounds with his finger. One was a few inches from the centre of the back on the right side, where the lower ribs began. It was two finger-breadths wide and shaped like a teardrop, with a sharply pointed lower end and a rounded top.

'A single-edged knife, that!' said Gwyn. 'Quite a wide blade, too.'

'Probably the same weapon did this other one,' observed de Wolfe. He rested his forefinger alongside the second stab wound, which was slightly higher and in the exact centre of the back, over the knobs of the spine. It was half the length of the other, but had the same shape.

'A tapered blade couldn't go in so deeply, because of the bone underneath,' he muttered, half to himself. He poked his finger into the hole to measure the depth and gave a short exclamation as he jerked his digit out again and examined the tip, which now had a small cut on it.

With a curse, he wiped it on the dead man's coarse tunic, then sucked it vigorously, spitting repeatedly on to the ground.

'Careful with that, Crowner!' growled Gwyn. 'Corpse juice can give you a nasty septic wound. Was it a spike of bone that you hit?'

'Didn't feel like it. Let's have a better look.'

He pulled out his own dagger from the back of his belt and enlarged the stab wound over the spine with a slash a few inches long. Taking the free edge of the dead man's tunic, he carefully mopped up the blood and tissue fluid from the wound, revealing a metallic glint inside. Using the point of his dagger, he levered out a piece of steel, which he displayed on his palm.

'Whoever did this snapped off the tip of his knife in the bone,' he announced to the heads craning over him to see what he was doing. 'The other wound was the one that killed him. It's gone deep into his chest and belly.'

He displayed the small triangle of sharp metal, which had an irregular edge where it had been snapped off. As he wrapped it in a dock leaf and put it away carefully in his belt-pouch, he turned to Guy Ferrars.

'At least we've found your man and you can take him back to his family for a decent burial.'

The baron glowered at the corpse. 'I want the swine who killed him. Was it these outlaws or the foresters? Whoever it is will be sorry when I catch up with them.'

'The King's law will deal with them. But we have to find them first.'

Ferrars ordered his men to make a rough bier of branches to carry the body home and they then set out on the tramp back to Lustleigh.

'De Wolfe, I've been thinking about your journey to Winchester. In the circumstances, I've decided to come with you. I need to go there soon on other business, but you may need a little extra persuasion to get the Curia to send a force down here. To them, Devon is a distant country full of yokels and savages, good only for producing tin and wool for their benefit.'

Privately, John felt that his personal connections, especially with his old crusading commander, Hubert Walter, would be sufficient, but he was in no position to contradict Lord Ferrars. He accepted with good grace, and on reflection thought that however proficient he and Gwyn were with swords, a larger party would be that much safer on the long road to Hampshire.

When they arrived back in Lustleigh, they delivered the dead man to his wailing wife and grieving family. For formality's sake, to fulfil the legal requirements, John held a five-minute inquest using the members of the search party as jurors, to deliver a verdict of murder by persons as yet unknown. Thomas was not there to record the very abbreviated proceedings, but de Wolfe could dictate the essentials when he returned to Exeter.

Ferrars and his son and steward were going back to Tiverton, so John bade them farewell at Lustleigh, arranging to meet them at Honiton, on the road to the east, at noon in two days' time, all prepared for the journey to England's royal capital.

John debated whether or not to take Thomas de Peyne with them to Winchester. He doubted whether such a poor horseman could keep up with the party, especially as Ferrars was such a short-tempered, intolerant man. However, on Gwyn's suggestion, they hired a better horse from the farrier's stables for the clerk, a sturdy but docile palfrey, meant for a lady's mount. In the one day they had before leaving, Gwyn insisted that Thomas give up his side saddle and 'sit on a horse like a man', as he put it. Ignoring Thomas's protests, he made him practise up and down Canon's Row for an hour until the little fellow learned not to fall off. On

Friday morning, the three of them set of for Honiton, which was a convenient meeting point for riders from both Exeter and Tiverton. Guy and Hugh Ferrars arrived with half a dozen men-at-arms in leather cuirasses. These were covered with tabards bearing Ferrars' armorial emblem, in the new fashion for displaying the family crest – in this case a golden arm grasping a hammer, on a field of crimson. De Wolfe suspected that Ferrars was developing political ambitions to match his increasing lands and wealth and wanted to make an impression on the established grandees who ran England in the continued absence of the King. It was probably this motive, as much as concern about the forest problem, which was taking him to Winchester.

The journey was long but uneventful, apart from Thomas slipping from his saddle near Wimbourne Minster, to the great amusement of Ferrars' soldiers. The distance from Exeter was over a hundred miles, and at a steady pace the journey took them three days.

They stopped overnight at Dorchester and Ringwood, where Ferrars claimed hospitality from manorial lords that he knew – in one case, he actually owned the manor himself. He, together with his son, steward and John de Wolfe, fed and slept in the manor houses, while Gwyn, Thomas and the men-at-arms found a heap of straw in the outhouses and barns and ate well in the kitchens, to the delight and amusement of the maids.

During the many hours of riding through the long summer days, John had plenty of time to mull over his personal affairs back in Exeter, not that such prolonged meditation brought him any nearer a solution. What did he really feel about the women in his life? Similar to his devotion to King Richard, his ingrained sense of honour tilted him towards his duty to Matilda, much as she exasperated and annoyed him for most of his waking hours. It had been a marriage of convenience, and though John had had virtually no say in the decision, the bond had been made under the judicial and spiritual laws and was almost impossible to put asunder. His hopes that Matilda's entry into a nunnery would annul the marriage contract seemed doomed, as John de Alençon, who should be best informed, seemed to be pessimistic about his chances.

In any case, would Matilda stay in Polsloe? After more than sixteen years of wedded purgatory, he knew his wife's character very well indeed, and was all too aware of her fondness for good food and fine clothes. Though he did not doubt her genuine regard for the Church and all its appurtenances, as well as her faith in God and all his saints, he also well knew that there was a large social element in her endless attendances at St Olave's and the cathedral. They were the places to be seen with the wives of burgesses, knights and guild-masters – venues for showing off her newest kirtles and mantles and currying invitations to feasts in the Guildhall.

As they trotted along through endless lines of trees and past a legion of strip-fields around the villages on the Winchester road, his thoughts turned to Nesta, whom he had left still pale and fragile in a priory cell.

She had changed somehow, he reflected. In the weeks since she had announced her pregnancy, she seemed to have shrunk away from him, though since her miscarriage her attitude had slanted a different way, one that his blunt masculine sensibility could not fathom. He felt recently that even Thomas now had more of a rapport with Nesta that he did himself. Though it would be ludicrous to feel any jealousy for the little clerk, he had the impression that there was some secret between them to which he was not privy.

He loved Nesta, he decided with some trepidation – and having got used to the idea of becoming father to her child, the sudden ending of that prospect seemed to have left him adrift.

Was he being punished for his sins? he wondered. Like everyone – with the possible exception of Gwyn – he believed in the Almighty. He had never even contemplated not believing, as faith was an ingrained part of life, like sleeping, eating and making love. It was dinned into everyone from the moment they could crawl – mothers, fathers and the priests built up a solidly tangible milieu of God, Jesus Christ, the Virgin Mary, the saints and angels, as well as heaven, hell and the Devil. Sin was inescapable: the clerics thundered that every child was born with original sin and you should spend the rest of your life trying to diminish its burden before you died. Most people lost no sleep over this, and though they never dreamt of questioning it most never gave it a thought, except perhaps during the hour spent standing in a cold church being harangued by the parish priest.

But maybe he had done something so wrong that his burden of sin had increased almost beyond redemption, and now he was being warned to be vigilant before it was too late. As he rode along, he went over all his potential mortal sins during the past forty-one years. He had killed plenty of men, God knew – and, of course, God did know. But they were all slain in battle or self-defence, so surely that was no sin? He had dispatched two in the forest only a few days ago, but it was him or them. He had killed dozens in Palestine, but surely ridding the Holy Land of Mohammedans was the whole point of the Crusades! Did not the Church actively canvas for recruits to liberate Jerusalem? John himself had accompanied Archbishop Baldwin around Wales in '88 in an intensive recruiting campaign for the Third Crusade. In the Irish and French campaigns, again he had slain countless men, but that was for his King, the anointed of God. No, a soldier's duty could be no sin.

He had never raped a woman, though he had had plenty of willing ones. He had never robbed anyone, for looting in war was legitimate. What other transgressions could have been responsible for his present state? Yes, he had been jealous on occasions and covetous of other men's wives – who hadn't? If avarice, extortion and embezzlement were heinous sins, then why was his brother-in-law apparently so comfortable with himself? He should be frying in hell by now.

At the end of it all, John was driven back on his love life to explain his present unease. He had been constantly unfaithful to Matilda all his married life, but he would be hard pressed to think of a man of his acquaintance who was different. In his many years away at the wars, he had lechered and whored like anyone else – and since he had been home, he had dallied with the delicious Hilda of Dawlish whenever he had the chance, as well as their maid Mary and a certain widow in Sidmouth – and a few more he could hardly recall. And, of course, Nesta, sweet Nesta, was the culmination of them all. So that must be the answer, he concluded gloomily – his infidelity had been punished by taking away his first son before it was even born, leaving him in limbo between an absent wife and a mistress whose attitude towards him seemed to have become strange.

Thankfully, these dismal thoughts were brought to an end by Guy Ferrars yelling up ahead and waving his arm at the village of Ringwood to indicate that this was where they would spend their last night before Winchester.

With a sigh, he switched his mind from women to the prospect of a good meal, a few quarts of ale and a palliasse in the hall of the manor house.

Early the next evening they entered the bustling city through the West Gate and the two Ferrars and their steward made their way to an inn which they habitually used on their visits to Winchester. Their men-at-arms were given a few pence and told to fend for themselves until the morning. John de Wolfe and his companions found another tavern which provided straw-filled mattresses in a barn behind the main building, and after a meal in the taproom below, John sat with his officer having a few jars of ale and gossiping with other patrons.

Thomas had wandered off on a nostalgic tour of the city he knew so well and which had been the scene of his downfall. In truth, he was somewhat apprehensive of being recognised and perhaps reviled by old acquaintances, so he slunk along in the shadows of the approaching dusk, his eyes wary for any familiar face. He went cautiously into the cathedral and knelt in a dark corner, crossing himself and praying. The little clerk's eyes were full of tears for what might have been, if he could have stayed long enough to gain a prized prebend. He might have become a canon in the place where he had studied, been ordained and taught, until the wiles of women and his own misguided foolishness had brought about the catastrophe that had all but ended his life.

As the twilight deepened, Thomas made his way back to the inn at the bottom of High Street, and wearily laid himself down on his bag of straw, pulling his thin cloak over him. He was still awake when the other two came to their own pallets, aching after a long day in the saddle, but the old campaigners were snoring within minutes of lying down fully clothed on their thin mattresses.

The morning came all too quickly for the tired travellers, but an hour after dawn saw them eating thin oatmeal gruel and coarse barley bread in the alehouse. Gwyn grumbled about the quality of the food, but as the price of their penny bed included the morning meal, they ate it on principle, though the Cornishman vowed that he would visit the first pie stall they saw when they went out. He did this on the way up the hill to the castle, where they had arranged to meet the Ferrars in the hall of the keep.

Winchester Castle was larger than Rougemont and far busier, so they had to push their way through the throngs of people in the vaulted chamber to reach the baron. He was standing with his son and steward, talking to a sombrely-dressed cleric who was one of the Justiciar's chamberlains.

'We're fortunate, de Wolfe,' Ferrars said as they approached. 'Hubert Walter is here today, but leaves for London in the morning and then goes on to York.' The itinerant Chief Justiciar combined running the political machinery of England with heading its Church as Archbishop of Canterbury. Hubert was an elusive figure, as he liked to inspect the kingdom at first hand as much as possible and was always on the move.

The chamberlain promised to expedite their audience with him, but they still had to cool their heels in the great hall for another two hours before they were taken to a chamber on an upper floor to meet the most powerful man in the country. The Justiciar was a down-to-earth man and rarely indulged in the pomp and ceremony that his rank allowed. He rose from his table to greet them, dressed in a plain brown tunic that displayed neither his political eminence nor his supreme ecclesiastical rank. The only token of his religious status was a small silver cross hanging on a chain around his neck.

He greeted Guy Ferrars first, as befitted his barony, but his arm clasp for John carried an extra warmth for an old friend and battle comrade. Hubert was a tall, strong man with a lean, leathery face tanned by his past campaigns and his constant travelling. He looked far more the soldier-statesman than Prelate of Canterbury. His businesslike manner marked him out as the genius behind England's survival after the crippling financial crisis that the more feckless of King Richard's wars and ransom had caused.

Gwyn and Thomas, together with Ferrars' steward, retired to the back of the room to stand inconspicuously with several clerks, who hovered anxiously with parchment rolls for the Justiciar's attention, while John, Guy Ferrars and his son were ushered to chairs in front of Hubert's table. The chamberlain's snapping fingers brought wine from a side table and then the Justiciar got down to business.

He listened intently as Ferrars bluntly outlined the problem in the Royal Forest of Devon and the coroner supplied more details of the transgressions of the foresters and the increasing boldness of the outlaws.

'So Richard de Revelle may be up to his old tricks again?' observed Hubert when they had finished. 'I thought he might have learned his lesson after that trouble when I was in Exeter last.'

The archbishop had visited the city the previous autumn, when the coroner and the sheriff were locked in a dispute over jurisdiction and the courts. Both then and a few months later, de Revelle had sailed very close to the wind of treason, and only John's reluctance to fully expose him – mainly because of Matilda's pleas for her brother – had saved his shrievalty and possibly his neck. But Hubert Walter was well aware of the doubtful loyalty of the Sheriff of Devonshire.

'Perhaps we should have got rid of him then,' he observed. 'Or even earlier, by refusing to confirm him as sheriff last year, when his original appointment was suspended for three months.'

'The man's been a bloody liability all along!' rasped Guy Ferrars. 'Can't you just dismiss him? Surely you can persuade the Curia to throw him out.'

The Justiciar steepled his hands to his chin. 'It's not so easy. He has influential friends in Prince John's camp. The Bishop down there supports him, as do some of your fellow barons, like the de Pomeroys.'

Ferrars made a rude noise, to indicate what he thought of the Pomeroys of Berry Castle. 'They're all part of this conspiracy to bring back John,' he snarled. 'Even the ringleader, Hugh of Nonant, is still plotting away, even though his fellow bishops dismissed him from Coventry. Now he skulks in Normandy, waiting his chance.'

'So what can be done about this immediate problem in the forest?' asked de Wolfe, afraid Ferrars would divert the discussion into broader issues.

Hubert pondered for a moment. 'The Council wouldn't back me in removing de Revelle as sheriff without clear proof of his involvement, but I can certainly block any ambitions he might have of becoming Warden of the Forests. In fact, plans are under way to hold a Commission on the Stannaries to unseat him from his position there as Lord Warden.'

He looked across at the coroner. 'What about the present Warden, Nicholas de Bosco? We gave him that post almost as a sinecure, a reward for his long service. But is he up to it, in the present unrest?'

'He has little real power, so I think he should stay,' replied John. 'It would help if some strong endorsement of his position came from you or the Curia, just to warn off de Revelle. It's these outlaws that concern us.'

'We don't have enough men to make a determined sweep of the forest to get rid of them,' snapped Ferrars. 'Many of my tenant knights and their men-at-arms have been taken to France to fight with the King.'

De Wolfe explained how he was sure that they were being financed by Prince John, through a devious route, probably involving the Church.

'It's a hell of a coincidence that this Father Treipas, who is in a Cistercian house that strongly favours the Prince, came from Coventry, where he was an acolyte of Hugh of Nonant. And then he moved to Devon, via a close connection with our own Bishop Marshal!'

Guy Ferrars snorted. 'It's clearly a conspiracy. Without the help of these bandits, the foresters and verderer could not stir up so much trouble. The object seems to be to dislodge the Warden, as well as increase the forest revenues for John's benefit, when he attempts another rebellion through the south-west.'

The Justiciar drummed his fingers restlessly on the edge of the table

'It's not only the south-west, in fact. Similar things are happening in other forests, like Essex and Savernake, though so far there's been no outlaw involvement there.'

He thought again for a moment, staring blankly at a sliver of sky visible through a slit window on the opposite wall.

'This is what I'll do, de Wolfe. When I established the coroner system last September, the main object was to raise revenue in the royal courts as well as keeping a check on all these rapacious sheriffs. But I also made provision for coroners to be given roving commissions on an ad hoc basis, when some particular problem arose.'

John waited tensely. This sounded very interesting.

'So I'll draft you a King's Commission this very day, which should solve most of the problems. I have every faith in you, John, to carry it out, just as you did your duty in the Holy Land and when you did your best to safeguard the Lionheart in Austria. I know I can depend on you.'

For an instant de Wolfe felt tears of pride prickling his eyes at this endorsement of his loyalty, and even the self-centred Lord Ferrars looked at him with new respect – this was fulsome praise from a man who was the virtual Regent of England.

They both leaned forward expectantly, as the Justiciar outlined his proposals.

CHAPTER THIRTEEN

*In which Crowner John goes
campaigning once again*

It was Thursday evening before John returned to
Exeter, but before entering the city he called at Polsloe,
leaving Gwyn to escort the timid clerk the last
remaining mile or two. He found Nesta even less well
than when he had left. Though she was still deathly
pale, there was a flush on her forehead and her eyes
appeared slightly suffused.

'She has a slight fever, which gives us some concern,'
said Dame Madge, when she took John aside and
insisted on inspecting the healing wound on his hip.

'Is she in any danger?' asked John anxiously.

The cadaverous nun shrugged. 'Not at present,
though everything is in the hands of God. Her loss of
blood when she miscarried has lowered her resistance
to bad humours. She needs good nursing and constant
prayer, Crowner. We can supply both, though it would
not come amiss if you went on your knees more often
yourself on her behalf.'

When he went back in to Nesta, to softly tell her all
his news of the journey to Winchester, she seemed
attentive enough, but hardly spoke. Yet he felt that her
mood had improved since before he went away, and
she seemed slyly amused about something, but would
not tell him what it was. He put a hand on her brow

and felt the unhealthy warmth and saw a prickle of sweat on her upper lip.

'You are warm, my love, but Dame Madge says you are in no danger,' he said, diplomatically slanting the infirmarian's comments. 'You need the best attention, which I'm sure you get in this blessed place.'

Again the half-smile as she nodded slightly and reached for his hand.

'I'm glad the long journey went safely, John. The roads can be dangerous places.'

He avoided telling her that he was soon likely to face considerably more danger in confronting the outlaws and turned the conversation on to more innocent paths, such as Thomas's nostalgic ramblings around Winchester.

As he left her little room, he stared down the corridor of the infirmary and thought he just caught sight of a familiar figure stepping quickly into a doorway.

'No change there, Crowner,' said a voice from behind him, and he turned to meet the prioress.

'She still refuses to talk to me?'

Dame Margaret nodded sadly. 'I doubt you'll ever bring her round, sir. She seems set on staying here, though the time for a decision as to taking her vows is still a long way off. But she has a natural talent for nursing – the infirmary seems to suit her well.'

John recollected how Matilda had looked after him with such grim efficiency when he had broken his leg earlier in the year.

'I hope she finds happiness here, lady. But I would like to speak with her, just to say how sorry I am that I have brought her to this condition. Please intercede for me, when you get the opportunity.'

The prioress nodded. 'I'll do my best, but she seems firm in her intentions at present.'

With that he had to be content and, climbing up on

to weary, patient Odin, he set off on the last lap of his journey to Martin's Lane. Here Mary was pleased to see him home, soon setting out some clean clothes to replace the dust-laden ones that had crossed half of southern England. After he had doused himself with a bucket of cold water in the yard, he dressed and sat down to a good meal hurriedly put together by the faithful maid. Later than evening, he went up to Rougemont and sought out the constable to tell him of recent developments. He found Ralph Morin not in the keep, but closeted with Brother Roger, the castle chaplain. They were in the tiny sacristy of St Mary's chapel, just inside the inner ward – not engaged in any devotions, but covertly sharing a stone jar of good Anjou wine.

'I'm keeping out of the way of the bloody sheriff,' complained Ralph. 'He pesters me ten times a day as to whether you've returned from Winchester and what action is to be taken.'

The amiable Roger produced another earthenware cup and poured John a liberal dose of the rich French wine. 'This is a better drink than the sips of watered vinegar I'm used to handing out at Mass,' he said with a twinkle in his eye.

They waited expectantly for John to regale them with details of his journey. The castellan was entitled to know and, as usual, the chaplain was consumed with curiosity.

'Hubert Walter was very cooperative, thank God,' he began.

'Is he providing some troops?' was Ralph's first question.

'Yes. The two Ferrars and their men left Winchester for Southampton, with authority to collect sixty men-at-arms and archers, who were waiting to cross to Harfleur. The Justiciar said that though they were intended for Richard's army, they could delay for a few weeks and come down here. He placed them under your command, Ralph, to do whatever you think necessary.'

Morin's bushy eyebrows lifted almost into his hairline.

'Me? Not the sheriff?'

De Wolfe took a sip of his wine and explained.

'De Revelle is in bad odour with the Justiciar, though he can't get rid of him just yet because of his influential allies. But Hubert has given me a coroner's Royal Commission to use whatever means I wish to sort out this mess in the forest. That includes using these troops under your direct command.'

The constable looked delirious with joy. 'God's teeth, that's marvellous! But will the sheriff let you get away with it? He's supposed to be the King's man in the county.'

'I have letters from the Justiciar, speaking for the Curia Regis, which confirms the Commission. They strictly forbid de Revelle from countermanding my activities, as well as stopping him from becoming Warden.'

The man with the forked beard beamed. 'Anything else?'

'Another parchment gives me the power to arrest any forest officer whom I consider to be guilty of an offence, irrespective of forest law. As the Royal Forests *are* royal, they can hardly oppose a direct order on behalf of the King!'

'Is there anything you can't do?' asked the portly chaplain.

'You're safe enough, being a man of the cloth,' replied John. 'I've no mandate to do anything against clerics or any ecclesiastical or monastic establishments. So I can't act against this damned Father Edmund, apart from handing him over to the Church authorities, which would probably be a waste of time.'

Ralph Morin was already imagining himself in command of a small army. 'When do these soldiers get here?' he demanded.

'As soon as Ferrars can march them from Southampton – they should be halfway here by now. You'll have to find some accommodation for them somewhere.'

The constable swallowed the rest of his wine and jumped to his feet.

'I'd better get started – tents and shelters to put up in the outer ward and extra victuals to get in. The sheriff will have apoplexy when he hears, not least when he realises the cost of feeding these men!'

At the door of the sacristy, he turned to John,

'Please, let me come with you when you tell the bastard about all this. I wouldn't want to miss seeing his face at the news!'

John decided that there was no time like the present, and they walked across the bailey to the keep, smugly anticipating the violent reaction of de Revelle when he heard how he was being sidelined. But the man was not there, and from the furtive looks and feeble excuses of his chamber servant, John suspected that he had some dubious assignation in some backstreet of the city.

'Delay increases the anticipation of good things,' he told Ralph philosophically. 'We'll ruin his day by telling him first thing in the morning.'

As he walked through the gatehouse arch on his way home, Sergeant Gabriel bobbed out of the guardroom to intercept him.

'Crowner, Gwyn sent a message up by a lad a few minutes ago. He said to meet him as soon as you can just above the Saracen, but not to go inside.'

John stared at the grizzled soldier, unsure of the meaning of this cryptic message.

'Any idea what it's about?

'No idea, sir, but it was from Gwyn all right – I questioned the boy and he said it was a giant with red hair who gave him a quarter penny to run with the message!'

For Gwyn to be so generous for such a small task must surely mean something important, thought John.

'That Saracen's an evil place, Crowner. Would you like me to come with you, in case there's any rough stuff?'

The old soldier was obviously curious, as well as trying to be helpful, so John accepted his offer and they set off at a quick march for the lower town. The tavern of ill repute was at the top of Stepcote Hill, leading down to the West Gate, and ten minutes later they were within sight of the low thatched building, with dirty yellow-plastered walls displaying a crude painting of a Musselman over the door.

In the rays of the setting sun, they saw Gwyn lurking fifty paces short of the ale house, trying unsuccessfully to look inconspicuous in the doorway of the last house in Smythen Street. They walked cautiously up to him, as he peered down towards the hill.

'What the devil's going on, Gwyn? Are you spying on someone?'

He pointed a forefinger the size of a blood sausage towards the Saracen. 'He's in there! I didn't want to scare him off before you came.'

The Cornishman was in one of his exasperatingly obscure moods.

'Who, for Christ's sake?' snarled de Wolfe.

Gwyn looked as his master in surprise, as if he should already know.

'Stephen Cruch, of course! I was going to the Bush along Idle Lane when I spotted him creeping down here. I followed him and saw him going into the tavern.'

'After that affair in the forest near Ashburton, it's a wonder he'd show his face within miles of the city,' observed Gabriel.

'Maybe he didn't know about it – though every one else in Exeter does,' replied de Wolfe.

'From the way he was skulking along, I think he's well aware of the danger,' said Gwyn. 'Perhaps he left something in the Saracen last time he stayed there, which he urgently needs before making a run for it, out of the county.'

De Wolfe stared down the street, keeping the door of the tavern in view.

'If we seized him, it might help when the troops arrive. He can probably tell us where the various outlaw camps are placed. The one you saw, Gwyn – that must be only one of many.'

The big man's huge moustache lifted as he grinned. 'I'm sure he can "probably" tell us, crowner. Especially if I lean on him a little. He's only a small fellow!'

'How are we going to do it?' asked Gabriel.

'Just march in and grab him!' said John bluntly. 'Though I've got the King's Commission to do almost anything I like, he's already due for a hanging for consorting with outlaws – which I saw with my own eyes!'

'A good bargaining point!' chuckled Gabriel. 'Let's go.'

The taking of the horse-dealer was simplicity itself. The three men, two unusually large and the third in a military tunic, brandishing a sword, burst into the taproom of the tavern. There was a stunned silence from all the patrons, a rough-looking bunch with a sprinkling of resident harlots. As John and his friends scanned the room for Stephen Cruch, the silence was broken by the landlord, a grossly fat man called Willem the Fleming, with whom John had often had dealings, usually unpleasant.

'What the hell do you want!' he shouted.

Gwyn spotted Cruch sliding behind the fat innkeeper, trying to make for the back door. With a roar, he charged forward, brushed Willem aside and grabbed the horse-trader by his greasy hair. As he dragged the smaller man back towards the entrance, pandemonium broke out and the patrons surged forward, but Gabriel swished his sword back and forth in warning as he and de Wolfe retreated to the door and left.

Outside, their captive was writhing in Gwyn's grasp, now with a massive arm locked around his neck, cutting off most of the oaths and blasphemies that he was trying to scream. They dragged him across to Idle Lane, where beyond the Bush on waste ground were a few scrubby trees. From the pocket of his jerkin, Gwyn produced a short length of stout twine and, pushing Cruch back against the trunk of an elder, he tied his wrists behind it, then stepped back.

The three men stood around him, regarding him grimly.

'Your life is already forfeit, Cruch,' said John harshly. 'You have been seen not once but twice dealing with Robert Winter's scum.'

The leathery features of the dealer contorted as he babbled his innocence, but the faces of his accusers remained implacable.

'You will hang, unless the justices decide you should be mutilated, blinded and castrated,' said de Wolfe. At this, Cruch sagged against the tree, almost fainting with terror.

'There is one possible chance for you, if you can persuade me to be lenient.'

'Anything, anything, Crowner! I had no part in the

attack on you last week,' croaked Stephen. 'It was Winter who sent his men to deal with whoever was spying on them. We had no idea it was you.'

When de Wolfe put his questions to the man, he was so eager to reply that his words fell out in an almost incomprehensible gabble.

They learned that he admitted to being a messenger between Father Edmund and Robert Winter. This had arisen as an offshoot of his legitimate trading with Buckfast. Some months before, Treipas had paid him to seek out the outlaws, who were known to creep back into towns and villages for clandestine drinking and whoring. Cruch had provided ponies for the outlaws, paid for by the priest, then sent purses to them for reasons which Cruch claimed he knew nothing about.

'There were slips of parchment with the money, which Robert Winter alone could read, for I could not. I keep my accounts on tally sticks.'

Even Gwyn's heavy hands squeezing his neck until his eyes bulged and his tongue protruded failed to get the man to admit any more, and John was eventually satisfied that they had learned all they could for the moment.

'We'll keep you in the cells in Rougemont for now,' he said. 'When we move against Winter's gang, we will need you to show us the various places where you met him in the forest. If you comply, then maybe I will turn my back at the end of it all and forget that you are a prisoner – understand?'

Cruch nodded his understanding, well aware that with hard men like the coroner and his officer, his life hung by a thread. Gabriel and Gwyn agreed to take the man back to Rougemont and deliver him to the care of Stigand the gaoler, while John went home to a well-earned rest. As they began to frog-march him away, de Wolfe called a last warning to the horse-trader.

'I hear it rumoured that you yourself are already an escaped outlaw. If you have any sense, if we do let you go at the end of this you'll either take ship out of England – or at least hide yourself in Yorkshire or Norfolk, well away from here!'

With a wry grin at Cruch's abject terror, the coroner set off for home and bed.

The interview with the sheriff next morning, which Ralph Morin had been anticipating with such delight, came fully up to his expectations. He marched into de Revelle's chamber behind the coroner, a forbidding figure in his long mailed hauberk, wearing a round iron helmet and a sword dangling from his hip, as if ready to do battle that very moment.

De Wolfe's armament was less obvious, but even more potent. He carried three rolls of parchment, from which dangled the red seals of both the Chief Justiciar and one of the lesser seals of King Richard, which had been entrusted to Hubert Walter during the monarch's absence abroad.

John threw these down on to the sheriff's desk with a flourish. Though he could not read them himself, he knew every word by heart, thanks to Thomas's translation.

'Read those first, before you even open your mouth to protest!' he snarled to his brother-in-law, a more literate man than himself. The coroner's triumphant tone stifled Richard's tirade before it began and he rapidly scanned through the unambiguous Commissions that the Justiciar had issued. His appreciative audience watched the sheriff's narrow face tighten with horror, indignation and finally anger as the import of the documents sank in.

'This is intolerable – outrageous!' he fumed, as he threw the rolls back across the table towards John. 'I am the supreme authority in this county. You can't usurp the shrievalty with something penned on a piece of parchment!'

De Wolfe leered at him, delighted at this further opportunity to pay Richard back for all the sneers and slights he had inflicted in the past – especially his spitefulness in telling Matilda of Nesta's pregnancy.

'That smacks of outright treason, brother-in-law!' he responded. 'See those seals? They are those of your king and the man to whom he has entrusted his kingdom. The king who, misguided as he may have been, made you sheriff. Are you now saying you dispute those orders or intend to disobey them?'

De Revelle's mouth opened and closed like that of a stranded fish, as his face flushed like a beetroot. He was desperate to protest, but afraid that any rash words would brand him openly as a rebel or traitor. The coroner went through the main provisions of the Commission, ticking off the points on his fingers. When he came to the matter of the Wardenship, he took particular delight in demolishing de Revelle's ambitions.

'You are specifically excluded from putting yourself forward as Warden of the Forests, in the unlikely event of Nicholas de Bosco giving up that office. And unless you tread very carefully indeed, Richard, you may well be deprived of the office you now hold. It was only thanks to our sovereign's good nature – some would say folly – that he failed to crack down on all the supporters of John's rebellion.'

It was a fact that when the Lionheart had been released from his incarceration in Germany he had been extraordinarily lenient with those who had plotted to steal his throne in his absence – he even forgave the ringleader, his brother John, and restored many of his possessions.

The sheriff began some stuttering condemnation of this latest humiliation, but his past record of flirting with the rebels left him too vulnerable to make any effective argument against John's new-found supremacy.

'We are going to march against these outlaws and bring these forester friends of yours to account,' declared the coroner. 'And I doubt that your verderer protégé Philip le Strete will have his appointment ratified when the matter next comes before the County Court!'

At that moment the door burst open and Guy Ferrars and his son strode in, ignoring the attempts of the guard on the door to announce them.

'You've told him already, then?' barked the irascible baron. 'We arrived from Portsmouth last night. The foot soldiers should be here by this evening.'

Richard de Revelle, his nerves now twanging like a bow-string, stared at the new arrivals as if they had come from the moon.

'What soldiers? What are you talking about?'

'I'd not got around to that yet, Richard,' snapped de Wolfe. 'You explain, Ralph – they're your troops.'

The castle constable gleefully told the sheriff that he had been put in command of a company of men-at-arms destined for the King's army, to flush out the outlaws and other undesirables from the most troublesome part of the forest.

'This is intolerable!' gibbered de Revelle. 'I am sheriff and they should be placed under my control. So don't expect me to cooperate with you. I want nothing to do with this madness.'

'You won't be asked to take part, Richard,' growled

de Wolfe. 'In fact, as Commissioner, I won't have you anywhere near this operation. I don't trust you.'

De Revelle ranted and raved for a few more minutes, being repeatedly rebuffed by the others. Finally, an irate Guy Ferrars leaned over his table and thrust his face close to that of the sheriff.

'Listen, de Revelle! You're lucky to be allowed to sit safely in this chamber while better men go off to clear up the chaos you helped to foment. But I tell you, though the friends you have among certain barons and churchmen may have protected you so far, your time is fast running out!'

He drew back and stalked to the door, his son and the coroner following him. As he jerked it open, Ferrars made one last threat.

'I shall devote myself to getting rid of you as sheriff of this county. We need someone trustworthy, like Henry de Furnellis, to sit there in your place!'

After his visitors had stormed out, Richard de Revelle picked up a pottery ink bottle from his table and with a scream of ill temper hurled it at the opposite wall. The missile exploded and black fluid ran down the stones like blood leaking from his wounded heart.

The men-at-arms from Portsmouth spent the next two days resting from their long march and getting their equipment ready for the fray on Monday. During this time, the coroner was called out to a fatal accident in the small town of Crediton, where a wall around a cattle pound had collapsed on top of a wood-turner, crushing him under a pile of stones. The wall had been declared unsafe beforehand by many of the local people, and John attached the manor bailiff to the next Eyre, to appear to answer a charge of negligence. He did this with poorly hidden satisfaction, as the manor was one of many belonging to Bishop Marshal. He would have to pay any fine and compensation, which was likely to be substantial, as the turner was a craftsman with a wife and five children to support. John was sorry that he could not have declared the wall a deodand, as it was the instrument of death, but the value of a heap of stones confiscated on behalf of the widow was negligible.

This episode took much of the day, as he held the inquest as soon as he had inspected the scene and the corpse, so it was early evening before he made his daily visit to Nesta at Polsloe Priory. She still had a slight fever, but Dame Madge seemed satisfied that it had not become worse.

John sat by her bed and regaled her with a monologue about the day's events and the sheriff's discomfiture at having his authority usurped by his brother-in-law. His mistress listened quietly, holding his hand in hers, until he came to speak of the campaign planned against the outlaws in two days' time.

Then she struggled more upright on her bed and turned a pale and anxious face towards him.

'Be careful, John, please! For God's sake, don't risk your life again. You were nearly killed by them but a few days ago!'

She sank back, even the effort to rise exhausting her. He gave a lopsided grin, meant to be reassuring.

'Don't fret, there'll be almost a hundred others there too – a few knights and scores of men-at-arms, as well as Ferrars, de Courcy and their men.'

Nesta looked up at him, fearful of losing him after all that she had gone through lately. 'All the men in England can't stop a stray arrow striking you, John!' she whispered.

Anxious to stop this preying on her mind, he changed the subject.

'Have you seen any sign of Matilda?' he asked. 'She

still refuses to speak to me, though I've glimpsed her in the distance once or twice.'

Nesta gave a slight nod. 'She's passed by once or twice.'

She seemed unwilling to elaborate and John, suspecting that she had been ignored by his wife or even vilified, hesitated to probe further. There was no sign of Matilda when he left, and as the prioress was also nowhere to be seen he hauled himself on to Odin and took himself home, feeling that a good battle in the forest was preferable to trying to understand women.

Early on Sunday evening, a meeting was held in Rougemont of all those who were to be involved in directing the campaign the next day. To keep clear of the sheriff, they met in the Shire Hall in the inner bailey, using the benches and trestles on the platform of the bare courthouse for their conference.

The two Ferrars, de Courcy, Ralph Morin, John de Wolfe and Gwyn were joined by three Hampshire knights who had accompanied the foot soldiers from Portsmouth. Only Thomas de Peyne was absent, as John felt his timid presence would be no asset in a battle.

On a large piece of slate, fallen from some roof around the castle, the constable scratched a crude map with a lump of limestone. Like John, he was unable to read or write, but had a good sense of orientation and could draw a useful plan.

'Here's Ashburton – and up here is Moreton-hampstead,' he boomed. 'Between them, and to the west, is a tract of forest where it seems most likely that Winter's gang is camping at present.'

'How can you know that?' grunted Guy Ferrars.

'Two reeves came in this afternoon, as arranged. They have been spying out the situation for a couple of days on my orders. Several of Winter's men have been seen in alehouses along the road between these two towns – and they vanished into the forest west of the road.'

'Does this knave have any useful information?' asked Hugh Ferrars, jerking a thumb down towards the hall, where Sergeant Gabriel held the shoulder of a dishevelled Stephen Cruch, brought over in manacles from the cells under the keep.

Morin beckoned and Gabriel prodded the horse-dealer nearer the raised dais. 'How many camps do these brigands have in that part of the forest?' he demanded.

Cruch, very conscious of the fact that his life and liberty depended on his cooperation, stuttered out all he knew on the matter.

'I've been to three, sire, but there may be more that I've never seen.'

At a sign, the sergeant dragged his prisoner up on to the platform and propelled him over to the table.

'Point to where you think they might be!' commanded the elder Ferrars. Lifting his chained wrists together, Cruch took the chalk lump and added some marks to the slate.

'This one's on the slope of the high moor about here.'

'That's the one I visited,' cut in Gwyn.

The horse-trader pointed out two other sites and gave some directions as to how they could be reached.

'Take him back to the keep until tomorrow,' ordered Morin. 'He can come with us to show us the paths to these places – and woe betide him if he's trying to fool us!'

Guy Ferrars and Reginald de Courcy, some years older than John, had seen plenty of fighting in their time and were well-acquainted with campaign tactics.

'I say we should divide the men into two groups and push into the forest from both ends, starting from Ashburton and Moreton,' said Ferrars.

'And also have a few men moving up and down the road between them, in case they break out of the middle and vanish across into the woods on the eastern side,' added de Courcy.

They discussed variations on this plan for a while, with the coroner quietly hoping that they would be lucky enough to find any of Winter's gang. From past experience, he knew how difficult it could be to find men in dense forest. However, late that evening they had some good fortune which allayed John's fears about missing the outlaws altogether. A messenger from the bailiff in Lustleigh rode in on a lathered horse with the news that a group of twenty outlaws had been seen by a shepherd late that afternoon. They were crossing the old clapper bridge on the Bovey river, westwards into the forest between Manaton and North Bovey. This at least reduced the large area in which to search for some of them – and it was not far from one of the camps that Cruch had indicated, on the slopes of Easdon Tor.

Soon after dawn, the small army set out, the northern party under Ferrars and de Courcy marching for Moretonhampstead, together with Hugh Ferrars and a score of local men, who would patrol the road. They took Stephen Cruch with them, his wrists loosely tied and an archer stationed near him with orders to shoot him if he tried to escape.

Ralph Morin, de Wolfe and Gwyn took the remainder of the men south-westward to Bovey Tracey, as with the news of the latest position of Winter's men it was now unnecessary to go as far south as Ashburton.

Both groups were accompanied by the few mounted

knights and their esquires who had brought the troop from Portsmouth.

All set off at a marching pace, the riders walking their mounts behind the foot soldiers. At that speed it took until early afternoon to get into position, and after eating the rations they carried, the two arms of Morin's pincer movement moved towards each other, their target being Easdon Down.

De Wolfe and Gwyn rode alongside the constable, feeling an exhilaration born of memories of many a campaign in years gone by. Even Odin, who was too young to have been in combat before, snorted his excitement as he stepped out along the track, and John had to keep him reined in so as not to pull away from the column of men walking behind.

It was six miles between Bovey and Moreton, with Lustleigh just off the track about halfway between them. Before they reached Lustleigh, Ralph Morin called a halt, and when the thirty men-at-arms had all caught up, he gave orders for them to put on their armour.

The hauberks had been carried in two ox-carts at the back of the column, as it was impractical for the men to march the fifteen miles from Exeter in hot summer weather wearing knee-length chain mail. The hauberks each had a pole thrust through their sleeves and were hung on two rails fixed in the carts. Each man helped a comrade to get the cumbersome garment over his head, then adjust the mailed aventail which hung from their basin-shaped helmets down to their shoulders. Morin and de Wolfe did the same, as although they had great horses to carry the weight, neither wanted to sit in a hauberk for four hours in the July heat. Gwyn always refused to wear mail, relying on an extra-thick jerkin of boiled leather, which he now put on, but he did condescend to jam a round helmet on his wild red hair, the long nasal guard having been bent up a little to accommodate his bulbous nose.

When all was ready, the ox-carts were left on the track in the care of their civilian drivers and the posse turned off into the woods, heading for the narrow valley of the Bovey to the north-west. Four archers, not wearing armour, were sent on ahead as scouts. When all reached the river, they crossed and carried on steadily up the right bank, where the trees were less of an impediment to the mounted men than on the valley slopes. For an hour they saw nothing but greenery and the shimmer of the small river. There was an occasional glimpse of a startled deer and the distant crash of a boar as it hurried out of their path.

They passed through an area which a local Lustleigh guide said was called Water Cleave and then curved below Manaton, though it was invisible, being high up to their left and a mile away. The guide advised the constable that to aim for Easdon Tor they should begin to bear west, as the ground flattened out a little from the thickly wooded valley. Soon after they had moved away from the river, two of the archers came running back.

'More than a dozen men, camped in a clearing, five hundred paces ahead,' panted one.

Quickly, Morin divided his force into two and took half up the slope to the left, leaving de Wolfe to take the rest along the flatter ground to the right. Silently, his score of soldiers padded between the trees, one of the archers out ahead. A few moments later the scout held up his hand and the men slunk forward carefully. Another archer stood immobile, near the body of a young outlaw with an arrow sticking out of his chest, obviously a sentinel who had paid with his life for his inattention. The bowman pointed forward and John saw thin smoke rising from above some bushes where the sunlight was brighter in a gap in the trees. He gestured to the men-at-arms to spread out and then waved them on as he advanced, Gwyn at his side.

John was uncertain when to attack, as he did not know whether Ralph's force was in position yet on the other side, but his dilemma was soon solved as there was a sudden yelling and crashing from ahead.

'Come on, men!' he screamed, his pulse suddenly racing with the prospect of battle. The line of soldiers dashed forward towards the clearing, straight into the remnants of the panic-stricken outlaw band, who were fleeing from Morin's assault from the other side.

The action lasted no more than a couple of minutes and was more of a massacre than a combat. The two archers dropped the first pair of fugitives, then the rest careered blindly into the line of soldiers, to be cut down with sword and hand-axe. Every man was killed on the spot, which solved one problem for de Wolfe, as he was in no position to waste men on guarding prisoners.

A hoarse shouting from the clearing was a warning from Morin and his force that they were not to be mistaken for more adversaries, and seconds later the big constable lumbered up to John, still swinging a ball-mace threateningly.

'Any of yours left?' he demanded, looking at the still corpses scattered between the trees.

'All dead. None of them lifted so much as a finger against us,' grunted Gwyn, in disgust. As a fight it was a non-event as far as he was concerned.

'Like butchering sheep in the shambles,' confirmed de Wolfe. 'I don't think many of them even had time to pick up a sword before they fled.'

Ralph Morin stood counting the bodies. 'We put down eight – one ran away and it's not worth wasting time chasing him. So that makes fourteen exterminated so far.'

He called the scattered men-at-arms together and they began their march again, after a cursory look at the outlaw camp. There was little there, apart from some rude shelters made of boughs and canvas and some food and utensils around the fire.

'No sign of either Robert Winter or his lieutenant, this Martin Angot?'

De Wolfe addressed this to Gwyn, as he was the only one who knew them by sight. The Cornishman shook his head. 'Never seen any of this bunch before. They weren't in that camp down towards Buckland.'

'I wonder if there are still some ruffians down there,' mused Morin.

'It's a long way south of here, but if we don't find the ringleaders at this Easdon Tor place, then I suppose we'll have to go back there,' answered John.

They set off northwards again, wary of any further surprise contacts, leaving the bodies scattered where they had fallen. The four archers went on ahead as before, and gradually the ground flattened off, though it was still densely wooded. Where a fallen tree or a small clearing gave a glimpse to the north-west, now and then they could see the bare outline of the higher moor, with misshapen rocks sometimes crowning the skyline. The man Ferrars had given them as a guide from his manor at Lustleigh dropped back and touched his floppy woollen cap to the coroner.

'Sir, if we are going to Easdon Down, then soon we have either to cut left across country past Langstone or go on up the river to the clapper bridge, then take the track westwards.'

'Which is quickest?'

'Past Langstone, Crowner. No more than a mile, I'd say.'

They decided on the direct route and started climbing rising ground, still thick with trees. The few houses and fields of Langstone were off somewhere to their right as they crossed the lower slopes of Easdon Tor.

'What do we do if some of these bloody thieves throw up their hands without a fight?' asked Morin.

John was wondering that himself and hoped the matter would not arise. Perhaps they had been lucky back in the valley, where all the outlaws had blundered on to swords and axes.

'By definition, they are outside the law and don't exist in any legal sense,' he answered. 'Anyone can kill them at will – and get a bounty for it!'

'So we kill them all, even if they have their hands up in the air in surrender?' queried Morin.

'It sounds difficult, I know,' replied John. 'But if we take them back to Exeter they will be hanged without trial, as judgement has already been passed on them in declaring them outlaw. So it seems pointless to delay their deaths. They know this and may well try to flee as their only hope, in which case we can kill them with an easier conscience.'

'What about this Robert Winter himself? Does the same apply to him?'

De Wolfe considered this as they trudged diagonally across the steepening slope. 'He will die, one way or the other. But as the leader he might have information that could be useful, perhaps about the people behind this conspiracy.'

There was a soft call from ahead as one of the scouts turned back to warn them that the trees were thinning out ahead. They came to halt just inside the edge of the woods and saw that bare moor, with patches of bracken and bramble, rose up ahead to a jumble of rocks high above. To the right, the tree line curved around into the distance.

'That's Easdon Tor above – and the down runs right around its foot,' explained the guide.

The posse stopped for rest, while Morin and the coroner conferred.

'We don't know where this camp is supposed to be. The other party has got Cruch with them to pinpoint it.'

'And we don't know where they are at the moment,' growled Gwyn.

'They had a shorter distance to march than we, so they should be in position somewhere near by.'

'Surely the outlaws wouldn't make camp out in the open up there,' muttered Morin. 'They'd stick to the trees.'

'The place I saw was out of the trees, but they had a little nook in some rocks,' Gwyn told them.

De Wolfe turned to the guide. 'Is there anywhere like that up towards the tor?'

'Not really, sir. There are some ancient old hut ruins around the other side of the tor, but I wouldn't call that Easdon Down.'

'That damned Cruch was pretty vague about where the camps were, though he only had a lump of chalk and slate to work with. It could be that way, I suppose.'

They decided to send their scouts in both directions, working along inside the tree line to see whether they could find Guy Ferrars and his men. The whole area in question was no more than a quarter-mile across so they had to be somewhere near. Settling back against a tree trunk, Morin signalled the perspiring men to rest, and they sank to the ground to take the weight of their hauberks from their shoulders.

Ten minutes later, a pair of archers came silently back from their left side, with news of the rest of the squadron.

'Lord Ferrars and his men are concealed about five

hundred paces to the west, Crowner. They were waiting for us, as they have sighted a large group of outlaws further up the hill, camped in some old ruins.'

'Those are the tumbled huts I told of, ' said the guide. 'They were built by the ancient men of the moor, God knows how long ago.'

In no mood to consider history now, John waved all the men to their feet and, demanding complete silence from now on, led the way with Ralph along the edge of the forest towards the other half of the posse.

Within a few minutes they were reunited and the leaders quietly discussed tactics.

'There're a lot of men up there, you can see them moving about. I can't see any lookouts posted, the useless scum,' growled Guy Ferrars. 'But it's all open ground between us here in the trees and those heaps of stones that they're using to shelter their camp.'

John and Ralph Morin moved cautiously to the edge of the wood to look up the slope of Easdon Tor. It was a double hill, with a higher, rugged silhouette on the left and a lower, smoother mound on the right. The ruined huts were much lower down on a small, flatter part of the hill.

'They can't escape uphill, it's too steep. We must attack them in a broad arc, to stop them running down into the trees,' advised Ralph Morin. The other leaders agreed and the soldiers were spread out in a single line three hundred paces long, each behind a tree until the signal was given.

'If they see all of us they'll scatter and run for it, so let's entice them down here first,' advised de Wolfe. 'Keep the men-at-arms out of sight for the moment.'

With Gwyn and several of the roughly dressed men from Lustleigh, the coroner stepped boldly out of the trees and began walking up towards the little plateau that carried the tumbled stones, partly covered with grass.

'Slowly does it, Gwyn,' muttered John.'We don't want to be too far away from the men behind when they catch sight of us.'

As if the outlaws had heard him, there were some distant yells from above and a dozen heads appeared to stare down the slope at them. Then, with yells of derision and anger, a crowd of men surged from between the stones and began running down at them, waving swords, staves and maces. At least a score of ruffians came storming down the hillside, and the men from Lustleigh faltered at the prospect of being massacred.

But just at the right moment, thanks to the timing of old campaigner Guy Ferrars, the whole force of mailed soldiers burst out of the trees and began running in an unbroken line towards the outlaws, the ends of the line curving around in a constricting arc.

At the sudden appearance of three times their number of mailed soldiers, the men from the camp skidded to a halt and desperately looked for a way of escape. Some who had just come out of the old ruins turned around and vanished uphill, but the men lower down had nowhere to go except into the arms of the rapidly closing troops.

It was almost a repeat of the earlier blood-bath, as the men-at-arms had been told to give no quarter and the outlaws knew that the only alternative to escape was death. The ragtag crowd, with not a single piece of armour between them, fought furiously but were no match for the mailed and helmeted troops. The four archers stood slightly to the rear, and whenever a clear target presented itself they shot with deadly accuracy.

Within ten minutes it was all over. Four of the outlaws managed to evade both the soldiers and their arrows and, being fleet of foot, fled across the scrub-covered ground and vanished into the trees. The rest lay dead among the scrubby vegetation of Easdon Down. Gwyn had dispatched two himself, crushing one man's head with his mace and hacking the neck of another. De Wolfe, at the spearhead of the attackers, also accounted for two, running one through the chest with his sword and stabbing another in the throat with his dagger, after the man had wrapped the chain of his mace around John's sword-hilt.

He looked around at the scene of mayhem, with twenty-seven corpses lying on the ground. In the battles in the Holy Land, especially at Acre, and to a lesser extent in Ireland and France, he had seen ten times that number of dead in one engagement. Still, this was Devon, and he had a momentary twinge of conscience until he again recognised that any survivors would have been either beheaded or hanged.

The only casualty among the attackers turned out to be Hugh Ferrars, who had received a hacking blow on his left arm. The sleeve of his hauberk had saved him, but he had a large bruise spreading from elbow to wrist. He seemed mightily pleased with it, as a token of his first wound in combat. Although well trained by his father and his squires, Hugh had been short of a war in which to fight, and now had something to boast about to his drinking friends.

Gabriel was prowling with his sword amongst the defeated men, giving the *coup-de grâce* to one or two who still twitched, until all was still.

Morin called back the soldiers to rest on the grass, then came over to where the Ferrars and de Courcy were talking to John de Wolfe.

'Are there any more left?' he demanded. 'I suspect that any who stayed up in those ruins made a quick getaway across the shoulder of the tor. They'll be a mile away by now.'

Guy Ferrars, his rugged face redder than usual with the exertion and excitement, leaned on his long sword. 'We'll take a walk up there in a moment to see. What about this lot? Did we get the leaders?'

They scanned the crumpled bodies lying among the ferns and long grass.

'Gwyn is the only one who can recognise them now,' said de Wolfe. True to his promise, he had let Stephen Cruch loose back in the tree line and the horse-dealer had vanished like a puff of smoke.

Gwyn ambled among the dead, turning some face up with his foot. After a while, he gave a shout. 'This one's Martin Angot, the fellow I saw with Cruch in the alehouse,' he called. He looked at all the rest, then shook his head.

'Robert Winter's not among them. We've missed the leader, but now he has no one to lead.'

Ralph Morin stared around at the corpses strewn around.

'What are we to do with these? They'll be stinking by tomorrow!'

The guide and two of his fellows from Lustleigh deferentially tugged at their floppy caps, before making a suggestion.

'We can get a bounty for each of these, sir. If we undertake to bury them all back in the wood there, can we take the heads and claim the bounty?'

Ralph and John roared with laughter, even at such a macabre suggestion. The thought of Richard de Revelle's face, when an ox-cart trundled up to Exeter Castle filled with amputated heads, was too good to deny.

'You do that, good man! And add those from the last camp to your collection for the sheriff. If he refuses to pay you, let me know.'

As the local men went enthusiastically about their business, the coroner decided that he would like to see what was in the camp up above.

The leaders of the expedition, together with Gabriel and two of the bowmen, began to walk up the slope towards the grassy platform where the ruined foundations lay. As they neared the edge, they became cautious, in case any surviving outlaws were laying in wait. The archers tensed their bow-strings and the others gripped their weapons, but all was quiet as they stepped between the mossy piles of stones, barely recognisable as the bases of old round huts.

In the centre of the jumble of rocks was a fire, a radiating ring of logs still smouldering. Some cooking pots and pottery mugs lay round about and the half-eaten carcass of a deer was spread on a large flat stone.

A few of the hut remnants had been partially and crudely rebuilt and roofed over with branches to make a couple of shelters, high enough for men to crawl inside.

'What a way to live!' said Reginald de Courcy in disgust. 'Even animals fare better than this.'

'Do you think we've wiped most of them out?' asked Morin. 'We've missed this man Winter – maybe he's with another nest of the serpents somewhere?'

'There can be very few of his gang left,' replied de Wolfe. 'Together with the ones we killed on the way, this accounts for most of those who the villagers allege were plaguing the countryside.'

'We had better call at that camp Gwyn saw, down towards Ashburton,' advised the constable. 'I'll take a dozen men and go that way back to Exeter.'

'You'd best go with him, Gwyn,' said the coroner. 'You know exactly how to find it.'

But the Cornishman failed to respond. He had walked a little way from the group and was standing with his head cocked on one side, listening intently. Then tucking the handle of his mace into his belt, he slid out his sword and quietly advanced on one of the brush-covered shelters.

Bending down, he looked inside, and with a roar tore off one of the branches that straddled the stone walls.

'Look what we've got here, Crowner!' he yelled exultantly, waving his blade dangerously back and forth in the entrance of the shelter.

The others dashed over and Gabriel helped Gwyn drag off more of the crude roofing. Cowering inside the tunnel-like bivouac were four men, crouched against the end wall in a desperate effort to remain hidden.

'Get out, blast you! Come out of there!' yelled Gwyn, stabbing down with his sword to encourage the quartet to stumble out into the open.

De Wolfe stared in amazement when he saw who they had found.

'God's bowels! It's the bloody foresters and their tame monkeys!'

With expressions of mixed fear and defiance, William Lupus and Michael Crespin came out of the shelter, followed by the ugly Henry Smok and another burly man, who John assumed was Crespin's page.

Guy Ferrars was beside himself with rage, waving his fists in the air as he yelled at the foresters.

'You'll hang for this, you bastards! Consorting with outlaws, caught red handed in their very camp!'

Crespin looked desperately at his colleague, hoping for some deliverance. William Lupus glowered around at the leaders of the posse, racking his brains for an excuse.

'We were taken prisoner by Winter and his men,' he proclaimed. 'Thank God you've come. They would have killed us.'

De Courcy gave Lupus a hard shove in the chest. 'You bloody liar! If you were prisoners, how is it that you've still got your daggers in your belt and that lout there even has his mace?'

Lupus continued to bluster in an effort to regain the initiative.

'What right have you to be here? This is Royal Forest, you have no power here! Where's the sheriff? I want to talk to him.'

John stood right in front of the arrogant forester, his hooked nose almost touching his.

'You can forget all that nonsense about Royal Forests! I've just returned from Winchester with a King's Commission to clear up this anarchy and the sheriff is no part of it. We know about your dealings with Robert Winter – and Cruch the horse-dealer has confessed everything, including his priestly master.'

The surly forester seemed to slump with dismay at the coroner's revelations, but de Wolfe had not finished.

'Finding you skulking in Winter's camp is the final touch. But I also want you in connection with several previous deaths and for refusing to attend my inquests.'

He stepped back and motioned to Gabriel and Gwyn.

'Bind these men's wrists and rope them together – and take those weapons from them. They're coming back to Exeter with us, for a spell in Stigand's jail in Rougemont.'

'But only until we hang them!' added Ferrars viciously.

Getting back to Exeter was a complicated operation, as John's party had to return to the carts to shed their armour, collect the horses, then go on to Moreton-hampstead to meet up with Ferrars' group. By now it was too late to start out for the city, so the men camped overnight in the field where the sheep market was held. The town was scoured for enough food to last fifty men until morning, though at least Gwyn's huge appetite was missing, as he had gone with Morin and some soldiers down to the southern campsite and would meet them in Exeter on the morrow.

CHAPTER FOURTEEN

*In which Crowner John completes
his commission*

By noon the following day they had all assembled back
in Rougemont. John had travelled so much in the past
week that he had to work out that it was now Tuesday.
The borrowed men-at-arms went to their billets in the
outer ward, to rest until they began the long tramp
back to Portsmouth the next day, while the local leaders
adjourned to the hall of the keep for refreshment and
discussion about the whole forest affair. John, Ralph
Morin, de Courcy and Guy Ferrars and his son sat at
a trestle table, with Gwyn, Thomas, Gabriel and the
ubiquitous Brother Roger sitting at the end, eager to
hear what was decided. While castle servants scurried
to fetch them ale and cider to wash down cold meats,
bread and cheese, the coroner began the proceedings.

'What about the damned sheriff? He must know
we're back, but he's conspicuous by his absence.' John
looked across at the door to Richard's chamber, which
was firmly closed.

'To hell with him,' growled the baron. 'I have a
feeling his days are numbered as the King's man in
this county. I'll be in London in a week or two, when
I'm going to have a few strong words with some friends
on the Curia – and be damned to de Revelle's powerful
patrons.'

Between the steady champing of jaws and slurping of ale, the discussion went on.

'We've broken the back of the main outlaw band, though there's scores more of the bastards in the forest,' said Ralph.

'But they're a disorganised ragtag, with no object other than stealing chickens and holding up travellers for their purses,' said Reginald de Courcy.

'A pity we didn't get that Winter fellow,' said Hugh Ferrars, in one of his rare utterances. 'Where is he now? I wonder.'

'Without his second-in-command, that Martin Angot, and with most of his men slain, he's lost all his power,' replied John. 'Unless he can rebuild a gang out of the remaining villains that lurk in those woods, he's no longer of any consequence.'

'I suspect that Winter's already fled from these parts, either up to Exmoor or across into Cornwall,' grunted Guy Ferrars. 'Without the support of Prince John's mob, we can forget him.'

The portly castle chaplain leaned forward to speak to de Wolfe, a quart of ale in one hand. 'Crowner, yesterday, while you we all away, I met John de Alençon after a service in the cathedral. He asked me to tell you something interesting.'

John suppressed some mild irritation. This priest, amiable as he was, seemed to have his nose into everything. 'What was that?' he grunted.

'The archdeacon said that John of Exeter, our revered cathedral Treasurer, had told him privately that in the last few months, some considerable sums of money had come into the bishop's palace. The purses were dealt with by Henry Marshal's clerks, but had never appeared on any diocesan accounts and seemed to vanish equally mysteriously.'

There were raised eyebrows and meaningful looks

around the table. John of Exeter, unlike some of the senior canons, was a staunch supporter of the King and sided with the archdeacon and coroner when it came to opposing the Prince John faction.

'Had the Treasurer no explanation of this?' asked Lord Ferrars.

'It seems not. He had no dealings himself with the money, but came across the matter by chance. It would appear that the funds were merely passing through the bishop's custody, destined for somewhere else.'

'Perhaps they were collected by a Cistercian monk?' suggested Reginald de Courcy, with heavy sarcasm.

'I wonder what's happened to that fellow?' queried Ralph. 'Is it worth rattling the abbey at Buckfast to see if we could shake him out?'

'Ah, I can also tell you something of that,' said Brother Roger, beaming at his own erudition. De Wolfe groaned under his breath – this priest was a one-man spy ring. 'A vicar-choral of my acquaintance told me that Father Edmund Treipas spent one night last week in the guest house in the palace.'

Thomas de Peyne plucked up the nerve to butt into the discussion.

'I heard the same tale from a secondary in my lodgings. The father had a large pack behind his saddle and apparently was on his way back to Coventry, where he came from in the first place.'

De Wolfe slapped the bench in delight. 'We've scared the fellow off! He must have heard of Stephen Cruch's arrest and the bishop and his abbot have sent him packing, to save themselves any awkward questions.'

Ralph brought the talk around to current problems.

'What are you going to do about these damned foresters and their accomplices? The soldiering part is over. Now it's down to you and the law.'

'Hang the swine out of hand!' snarled Ferrars, still smarting at the loss of his woodward and his deer. 'Surely conspiring with outlaws is a felony? They were caught red handed.'

De Wolfe shook his head. 'They're not declared outlaws – and they are still King's officers. They will have to have a trial before the royal judges. I can't advocate one sort of justice for some then hang others without trial.'

Ferrars made noises that suggested that it was all a waste of time and effort, but de Courcy agreed with John.

'Have your trial, as long as it doesn't go to the Shire Court, where the damned sheriff would probably not only acquit them but give them a few marks from the poor box for the inconvenience they suffered!'

The coroner used his teeth to strip the meat from a capon's leg while he considered the matter.

'Later today we must interrogate them down below.' He pointed with his chicken bone at the floor, below which the prisoners were incarcerated in the undercroft. 'The Warden of the Forest should be present, as well as this new verderer, de Strete. They are the seniors of these miscreants, they should hear what they have to say.'

Guy Ferrars nodded reluctant acceptance of this alternative to a quick hanging.

'We'd better have de Revelle there, too, whether he likes it or not. I want to see him squirm when he sees his accomplices confess.'

'As he's still the sheriff, however much we resent it, he surely must fulfil his responsibilities as the enforcer of the King's peace in the county,' added Reginald, always a stickler for convention.

They agreed to assemble in the gaol after the bell for Compline, late in the afternoon. As John was fretting to get away to Polsloe, he left Ralph Morin to inveigle Richard de Revelle into attending in the under-croft.

When John arrived at the priory, he found Nesta slightly better than when he had last visited, a couple of days ago. She still had a slight fever and her pallor was not improved, but she seemed more cheerful and had lost the haunted look that had so worried him over the past two weeks. When he complimented her on the improvement, she managed a smile that was almost like her old self.

'It's the nursing, John, they are so kind to me that I cannot fail to get better every day. If only this fever would leave me, I'm sure I could go home.'

'You stay here until you are really well, my love,' he admonished. 'You can't struggle up that ladder in the Bush in your condition – and I can't always be there to carry you up myself!'

They talked for a little while, with John as usual relating all his recent adventures. Nesta was overjoyed that he had not suffered any injury this time. He avoided asking her whether she had seen Matilda, as last time this seemed to have caused her to give him some odd looks, but on his way out Dame Madge materialised in the corridor. She demanded once again that he display his wound for her inspection, and while he bared his hip he asked whether there was any change in his wife's resolution to ignore him. The bony midwife for once seemed oddly reluctant to answer him, saying that he had better talk to the prioress about such matters. When she had satisfied herself that his rapidly healing wound needed no further attention, he dropped his raised tunic and thanked her for her devoted care of Nesta.

'She is a sweet woman, Crowner,' said Dame Madge. 'We are all very fond of her.' Her tone suggested that

Nesta deserved better than to be wasted on an adulterer like John de Wolfe, but she did not elaborate.

When he sought out Dame Margaret in her parlour, the nun who acted as her secretary told him that the prioress was at prayer in the new chapel and could not be disturbed. With a vague sense of foreboding, he climbed aboard Odin and set off for home, his mind divided between the problems of the foresters and of the women in his life.

Soon after the distant bell in the cathedral tower rang for Compline, men began gathering in the gloomy vault under the castle keep. Even in the dry heat of midsummer, the grey walls and low arches of the ceiling were dank and slimed with mould – a fitting location for the misery and torment that often took place there.

The four prisoners who were led out of the rusted iron door by the grotesque jailer were subdued and apprehensive even before they faced their accusers.

Though they had been in the squalid cells only since that morning, they were already dirty and tousled. The green tunics of the two foresters and the leather jerkins of their pages were streaked with grime, wisps of dirty straw adhering to their hair and hose.

With Sergeant Gabriel at one end and the obese Stigand at the other, they were prodded into a ragged line, clanking the heavy irons that secured their ankles. Their belts and weapons were laid out near by on the dried mud of the floor, and off to one side Stigand had helpfully set out a brazier, with branding irons stuck into the glowing coals.

Facing them were the men responsible for their capture, together with Nicholas de Bosco, the Warden of the Forests, Philip de Strete, the new veriderer, and Brother Roger, who, as castle chaplain, now had a legitimate reason for being present, as a priest was required at such events in case a prisoner died during the Ordeal or torture. Thomas was also there, squatting on a keg, with his writing materials before him on a crate, ready to record any confessions.

'All we need now is the damned sheriff!' bellowed Guy Ferrars.

'I thought you said he had promised to come?' demanded Reginald de Courcy of the constable.

Before Ralph Morin could reply, a shadow darkened the light coming through the small entrance at the foot of the steps leading down from the inner ward. It was Richard de Revelle, scowling like thunder and obviously making a point by arriving last. He had a light mantle tightly wrapped around his body, as if to insulate himself from the others in the undercroft. The faces of the foresters brightened slightly when they saw him, as if they expected him to save them from this nightmare.

'About time, de Revelle,' barked the elder Ferrars. 'This is something you should have done long ago.'

The sheriff glowered, but made no response, standing apart from the others as if he had no interest in the proceedings.

John de Wolfe bent to Thomas's makeshift table and picked up the rolls of his Commission, which he brandished at the prisoners.

'These are signed by the Chief Justiciar himself, on behalf of our sovereign lord King Richard!' he announced. 'So let no one here try to dispute my right to proceed as I think fit.'

He handed the parchments back to his clerk, then took a step nearer the foresters, his fists planted aggressively on his belt.

'You, William Lupus – and you, Michael Crespin. I summoned you both to attend my inquests on the tanner, Elias Necke, and Edward of Manaton. You refused to attend and are already in mercy for that. Why did you not come?'

The elder of the two foresters appeared to have regained some of his former arrogance, perhaps emboldened by the presence of the sheriff and the verderer, who he assumed would be on his side.

'You had no right to interfere in forest affairs. They are regulated by the forest law,' he growled.

'Nonsense. The king's peace covers the whole of England, including his own forests,' snapped de Wolfe. 'The forest laws deal only with matters of vert and venison.'

'You had no Royal Commission when you summoned them, de Wolfe,' snarled the sheriff, opening his mouth for the first time.

'I needed no special commission to attach witnesses for an inquest,' said the coroner, testily. 'That power was granted by the Crown in Article Twenty of the General Eyre held in Kent last September.'

He turned back to Lupus. 'You and your accomplices have perpetrated a reign of terror and extortion in that bailiwick of the forest of Devon. You have closed forges, forced alehouses to take your own product, destroyed a tannery and caused the deaths of at least three people.'

'I've killed no one. Those outlaws did the deeds,' shouted Lupus violently. 'You can prove nothing against us. We did what we were told in the matter of commerce, like brewing and forges.'

'Told by whom?' demanded Ferrars, determined to play a part in the coroner's inquiry.

Lupus looked furtively at Crespin, then at de Strete.

'By the previous verderer, Humphrey le Bonde.'

There was a snort of derision from several throats at this.

'You damned liar!' shouted de Courcy. 'Very convenient to blame him, now that he can't contradict you.
No doubt he was killed because he tried to moderate
your evil schemes.'

'Which one of you put an arrow in his back?'
demanded Ralph Morin.

'It was an outlaw, some footpad who wanted to steal
his purse.'

'Strange that every penny was still inside it when he
was found,' said de Wolfe, with heavy sarcasm. He
turned to the elderly Warden, who had been standing
with a grim expression on his lined face.

'De Bosco, what do you make of all this?'

'It saddens me to think that forest officers, who on
their appointment swore loyalty to the King, should
have degenerated into little better than outlaws themselves. Whatever else happens to them, they are not fit
to wear the horn badge of a forester, and I hereby
dismiss them, as from this moment!'

'I doubt you have that power, Warden,' objected de
Strete. The verderer sounded hesitant, as if afraid to
commit himself to one side or the other. 'You certainly
cannot dismiss a verderer. I am nominated by the
sheriff, elected by the County Court and responsible
only to the King.'

Richard de Revelle supported his protégé, his voice
high pitched and pompous. 'The Warden can nominate foresters, but my recent researches show that he
cannot dismiss them – once appointed, they are royal
officers.'

John de Wolfe lost patience with this bickering. He
grabbed the parchment roll from Thomas once more
and brandished it in the face of the sheriff and the
verderer.

'Must I tell you again, damn it?' he shouted. 'This is
all the authority I need to do as I see fit! I speak now,

not as the county coroner, but as a Royal Commissioner.'

He waved the roll again at Philip de Strete. 'The first action I take under these powers is to dismiss you from your office.'

The podgy verderer found enough courage to protest. 'You can't do that. I was nominated under a writ from the sheriff here!'

De Revelle also snarled a contradiction at his brother-in-law.

'And he was duly elected by the County Court!'

John dropped the roll back on to Thomas's packing case.

'The appointment has to be ratified by the Curia or their Justiciar – and I can assure you, Hubert Walter had no hesitation in annulling that confirmation.'

Philip de Strete, now the ex-verderer, responded by walking out of the undercroft, giving the sheriff a look of bitter recrimination on the way.

'Let's get on with the business, de Wolfe,' rasped Guy Ferrars. 'What are you going to do with these rascals, if you won't send them to be hanged straight away?'

'I want some answers from them, for a start. I'm declaring this to be the continued inquests on Elias Necke, Edward of Manaton and William Gurnon, a woodward of Lustleigh. Put that on your record, Thomas.'

His eyes moved slowly along the line of men opposite, his face like thunder.

'Who killed Elias the tanner? Was it you, Crespin – or you, Lupus? Or did you send one of these louts you call pages to do it for you?'

The so-called pages, bullies usually full of swagger, seemed to have crumpled after a few hours manacled in the cells and now faced with the implements of physical persuasion. The ugly Henry Smok had a haunted, fearful look on his face and was the one who answered the coroner, the words tumbling out.

'None of us, sir, certainly not me! It was those men belonging to Winter. They came down from the edge of the woods and put a torch to the place.'

'You seem to know a lot about it, you rogue,' rasped de Courcy. 'So tell us who gave them the orders – and who paid them.'

Smok caught a poisonous look from his master, William Lupus, and avoided an answer, mumbling that he did not know.

'Then who killed Edward, the poacher from Manaton?' demanded de Wolfe. The four men looked at each other warily, but all shook their heads.

'Right, it seems that your memories need jogging,' snapped the coroner. He had identified Henry Smok as the weakest link, though the other page, who was called Miles, also looked as if he would betray anyone if it could save his neck. John crooked a finger at Stigand, who was waiting expectantly a few yards away. The finger moved to point at Smok and the gaoler waddled across to grab the page. The man struggled violently, but Gabriel and Gwyn seized his arms and dragged him across to the brazier. Stigand pulled an iron rod from the glowing charcoal and spat on the small cross-piece at the end. There was a hiss of steam as the gobbet vaporised and an almost simultaneous scream of fear from Henry Smok.

'It was Crespin, he fired the arrow!' he yelled in terror.

'Into the back of Edward?' persisted de Wolfe.

'Yes. The poacher was running away, but he said he'd teach the bastard a lesson,' gabbled the page.

There was a roar of denial from Michael Crespin, but Lupus was silent. If it had not been Crespin, then he would have had to take the blame.

Lord Ferrars felt he had been silent for too long.

'Who directed you to start all this upheaval in the forest, eh?'

He took a step forward and glared at Lupus and then Crespin, his nose almost touching theirs. 'Where did you get your orders?'

There was a sullen silence, then Lupus growled that there were no orders, they had done it for their own purposes, to make more money for themselves and the verderer.

'So you killed three men, burned down a tannery and consorted with a gang of outlaws, all on your own initiative?' snarled Ferrars. 'A likely story!' He turned to the gaoler, who stood hopefully in his filthy leather apron, spotted with burns and what looked like dried bloodstains.

'Carry on, Stigand, see if you can restore the page's memory – then we'll try this other lout, before moving on to the men in green.'

The grossly fat gaoler stuck the first iron back into the fire to reheat and pulled out another, the end of which glowed a dull red. Advancing on the cringing Smok, he reached out and ripped down the neck of his tunic to expose a broad, hairy chest. The page wriggled violently in the grip of the men holding him and screamed out in a last attempt to avoid the branding.

'I don't know, I'm just a servant!' he howled. 'I suppose it must have been that horse-dealer – he was always bringing purses of money and whispering into the foresters' ears!'

The hot iron was now near enough to start singeing the hairs on Smok's chest, but the coroner waved Stigand back, much to the sadistic gaoler's disappointment. John accepted that the page was not privy to any important information, so he turned back to the foresters.

'And what can you two fine men tell me about it?' he asked ominously. 'There's plenty of charcoal to keep the fire going, remember.'

'You wouldn't dare torture us, we're officers of the King,' Crespin said defiantly.

'No, you're not any longer! Didn't you hear the Warden dismiss you just now?' snapped de Wolfe. 'And if he hadn't, I would have, under the terms of my Commission. You're just common men now, subject to the law like anyone else.'

He turned to face the elder man. 'Who was behind all this, Lupus? We know Stephen Cruch instructed and paid you, but he was just a messenger.'

'Stop beating about the bush, de Wolfe! Was the Count of Mortain behind all this, Lupus?' Ferrars seemed permanently angry, but today he was even more pugnacious than usual.

The granite-faced forester looked stonily at the coroner. 'The Prince's name was never mentioned. I know nothing of politics, I did what I was asked and was paid for it, that's all.'

'Were you also asked to stab William Gurnon to death at the deer-leap – or was that your idea?' growled Ferrars, still smarting at the loss of some roe buck and his servant.

'We were told to get Winter's men to dig the salta-torium – but I killed no one afterwards,' said Lupus stonily.

De Wolfe pointed to the men's weapons lying on the floor.

'Are those your daggers?' he demanded, motioning to Gwyn to bring them across. He held the belts up for them to see.

'Which is yours and which belongs to Crespin?'

Sullenly, the men confirmed which was their property. John slid the knife belonging to Michael Crespin from its sheath and looked at the intact blade. He laid it on Thomas's writing desk, then pulled out the weapon belonging to William Lupus. Dropping the belt to the floor, he used his free hand to feel in his waist pouch, pulling out a shrivelled green leaf. His fingers freed a shining triangle of steel and, wordlessly, he held the dagger up for all to see. As he displayed the broken tip, he showed how the fragment from his pouch fitted exactly.

'I took that scrap of metal from the body of William Gurnon. Does any one here need better proof?'

There was silence, broken only by the footsteps of Richard de Revelle, as he followed the example of Philip de Strete and walked out of the undercroft without another word.

John went home to his empty house for a meal. He could have gone to the Bush, where he had eaten so often in the past, for the cook-maid was providing the same good fare as before Nesta had been taken to Polsloe. However, with his mistress absent, he had no urge to sit at their table by the hearth without her and preferred to eat in his own hall. Mary kept him company for a while, as she brought him various dishes from her shack in the back yard. As he tackled the ham-and-bean stew and the boiled knuckle of lamb with cabbage and onions, she sat across the table, her handsome dark head supported on her fist, listening to his account of the past few days. When she came back with bread, butter and cheese, she raised the subject of Matilda, her worries about the future still nagging away.

'I'm going up to Polsloe later this evening,' said John, with a reassuring tone that failed to convince her. 'Gwyn and Thomas have asked if they can come with me, as they've not seen Nesta for some time, with all this commotion in the forest.'

He paused to cut a thick slice from the loaf with his knife.

'This time I'll insist on seeing my wife. It's ridiculous that I can't get some kind of answer from her about her intentions, one way or the other.'

'Lucille is even more concerned than I am,' said Mary. 'At least for me there's always the house and the cooking to be attended to – but without a mistress, what use is a mistress's maid? I don't like the girl, I'll admit – but I'm sorry for her, being so uncertain about her future.'

Once more, John promised to discover what he could that evening, and when his meal was finished he walked the few yards across the cathedral Close to the house of his friend, the archdeacon.

The evening period after Compline was the most restful time for the clergy, as this was the last of the nine canonical hours, the services that occupied most of the ecclesiastical day. There was free time now until Matins at midnight, when priests could pray, read, sleep, eat or gossip.

John found the archdeacon in his usual place at that hour, sitting in his austere room, reading a book, with a flask of good wine on the table in front of him. He greeted his namesake with a smile and set another cup before him. Though de Wolfe rarely made formal confession, it was to the Archdeacon he came when that was necessary – but more often he unburdened himself to him as friend to friend, over a measure of wine.

This was how it was tonight, as he unfolded the whole story of his visit to Winchester and the subsequent escapade in the forest.

De Alençon listened intently, crossing himself when the coroner described the extermination of the outlaws. 'It seems brutal, John, but as the law stands they would have died one way or the other, with every man's hand against them,' he said soberly.

'They had burned the tanner alive, shot the verderer in the back and inflicted many other miseries on the forest dwellers,' pointed out de Wolfe. 'I have no stain on my conscience about them.'

'What about these two foresters and their pages?'

The coroner shrugged and took another sip of the excellent wine.

'Crespin was denounced as a killer by Lupus's brute – and I showed clearly that it was Lupus who stuck his dagger into the back of Ferrars' woodward. Our impatient baron wanted them hanged straight away, but I have attached them to the next visit of the Commissioners of Gaol Delivery, who will undoubtedly send them to the gallows.'

'And the pages, what about them?'

'They are stupid louts, but I will do likewise with them and let the Commissioners decide on their fate.'

The archdeacon drummed his fingers lightly on the leather cover of his book.

'And your dear brother-in-law? How is he to come out of this?'

John gave one of his rare lopsided grins. 'The sheriff's reputation, such as it was, is in tatters. Hubert Walter is well aware of the situation in Devon and I am sure he will begin maneuvering within the Curia to get rid of de Revelle. But you know as well as I that our sheriff is supported by some powerful names, both by barons and those in the Church.'

'Some no more than a few hundred paces from here!' agreed de Alençon, dryly. 'Speaking of that, did you get my message about that monk from Buckfast?'

The coroner nodded. 'And I also hear that he has left for Coventry, for good, it seems.'

'He's gone back to that nest of insurrection built by Bishop Hugh. We'll hear no more of him in these parts. The Cistercians will close ranks, as they have no love for this king, but have high hopes of who they think will be the next.'

They sat silently for a moment, both thinking of the injustices that the division between Church and state could throw up.

Then the archdeacon roused himself to broach another subject.

'I have done some research into canon law on your behalf, John,' he said rather diffidently. 'I fear I can find no precedent for annulling a marriage because the wife has entered a monastic order. It would require an appeal to the Holy Father in Rome, and even then I doubt whether it would succeed.'

John de Wolfe nodded glumly. 'I had expected that would be the answer. I don't know what's going to happen there. She still refuses to speak to me. I've only clapped eyes on her once since she left – and that at a distance in the priory.'

He threw down the rest of his wine and stood up.

'I'm going up to Polsloe now, to see how Nesta is faring. According to Dame Madge, she came near to death from blood loss when she miscarried and is still far from well.'

With the concerns of his friend and promises of his prayers in his ears, de Wolfe took his leave and walked up to Martin's Lane in the evening warmth to fetch Odin from the stables. Gwyn and Thomas were waiting patiently for him on their mounts at the East Gate, and half an hour later they were at the gate in the wall of St Katherine's.

'We'll wait here until you have finished your visit, Crowner, then slip in one at a time to pay our respects to Nesta,' said Gwyn with uncharacteristic tact, having been primed previously by the more sensitive Thomas.

John strode to the door of the little infirmary and went inside. He had visited often enough now, not to seek one of the nuns to admit him, and he walked the few steps to Nesta's cell, the first in the short corridor.

The door was ajar and he pushed it open. His usual greeting died on his lips as he was confronted by a familiar broad back, bending over Nesta's low bed.

It was Matilda, and her hands were on his mistress's throat.

For a second, John was frozen from the shock of seeing both Matilda and what she might be doing to his lover. Before he could throw himself at his wife and drag her off, he caught sight of Nesta's face looking up at him. It bore an almost roguish smile of guilty amusement. Matilda saw it as well and swung round in surprise, holding her hands open before her, the fingers sticky with a mixture of goose grease and wintergreen.

'Oh, it's you, is it?' she snapped, her square face glowering at him.

She turned back to the bed and laid a folded length of flannel around Nesta's throat, tucking the ends gently behind her neck. Then she stood erect and rubbed her greasy hands on the apron that covered the front of her black habit.

'She's had a sore throat since last night, but this salve will help to ease it.' Without looking her speechless husband in the eye, she swept out of the room and vanished down the corridor.

'That is a truly Christian woman,' came a voice from behind him and, turning, his battered senses recognized Dame Madge hovering in the doorway.

'Matilda has been nursing me this past ten days, John!' said Nesta from the bed, her voice a little husky from both soreness and emotion.

'And a more caring and gentle nurse could not be found in the kingdom!' boomed the gaunt nun. 'She is a saint and we shall be sorry to lose her.'

She approached the bed to put a hand on Nesta's brow and smooth the red hair that streamed across the pillow, while John managed to find his voice again.

'Lose her? What do you mean?' he managed to croak.

'She will tell you herself after you've finished here, Crowner. I'll leave you two alone, but be brief. Nesta has a phlegmatous throat.'

She loped off and John, bewildered by the vagaries of womankind, knelt alongside Nesta and took her hand.

'I don't understand, dear girl! When I came in, I thought she was trying to strangle you!'

Nesta gave a husky laugh, which ended in a cough, though a hint of her old roguishness returned in spite of her continuing weakness.

'She has shown no signs of wanting to throttle me, though I would understand it if she did.'

'What's this that Dame Madge said about losing Matilda? Why wouldn't she tell me?'

'I honestly don't know, John. I'd miss her ministrations if she did, You must ask her yourself, as the nun commanded.'

John climbed to his feet, puzzled, anxious and impatient. 'I'll do that right now, then come back to see you.'

He squeezed her hand and went to seek his wife.

As soon as Thomas saw his master striding out of the infirmary door and making for the parlour of the prioress, he limped across to visit Nesta himself. Gwyn had already ambled over to the kitchen to wheedle a pastry or two from the lay sisters who did the cooking, before taking his turn at seeing the invalid.

Thomas was glad to see a genuine smile on the face of the patient, as he automatically crossed himself and held up his fingers in benediction.

'You look better today, dear lady,' he said, his thin face creased with pleasure. The pretty innkeeper beckoned him closer.

'I feel more at ease with life, Thomas – though I've got this soreness of my throat,' she said quietly, with a slight rasp in her voice.

'Have all your desperate thoughts of self-destruction fled?' he asked solicitously.

She nodded and crooked a pale hand to bring him even nearer.

'Let me tell you quickly, before John returns. The secret that I told you about the father of my child has leaked out a little, but your master must still never know, it might destroy the bond between us.'

'It never leaked from my lips!' protested Thomas, his eyes widening.

'No, no, of course not! But Dame Madge knew straight away the age of the unborn babe – and she must have inadvertently let it slip to Matilda de Wolfe. The dame would have no reason to know it was so significant.'

Realisation began to dawn on the little clerk. 'Then Matilda worked out for herself that her husband could not be the father?'

Nesta looked furtively across at the door to make sure that John was not barging in again. 'Yes. She came to me ten days ago and told me that she was now aware that John was not responsible. She was very gruff at first, and I think she wanted to insult me. But when she saw how poorly I was, she began to attend to me – and since, has been kindness itself.'

Thomas gaped at this unusual vision of Matilda, as the woman had never made any secret of the fact that she despised him as a misshapen rapist and renegade priest.

'But surely she will tell him that she knows the babe was not his?'

Nesta gave a little shrug. 'I just don't know, dear Thomas. She has it in her power to wound him badly, as he was so proud of the prospect of becoming a father, even to a bastard.'

The clerk clutched her hand in reassurance. 'The truth will never come from me, whatever happens elsewhere.'

John stalked about, looking for his wife, but failed to find her. When he reached the door into the West Range, he found Dame Madge waiting for him. She imperiously beckoned him inside and tapped on the door of the parlour, where they found the prioress sitting at her table. Dame Margaret was not one to beat about the bush.

'Sir John, you have several times asked to speak to your wife about her intentions. Well, now we can put your mind at rest. Matilda wishes to leave our care and return home to her wifely duties.'

De Wolfe's senses had received a battering during the past ten minutes and this final piece of news needed some assimilation.

'Coming home?' he croaked. 'You mean, this very minute?'

The prioress shook her head, an amused smile on

her plump face. 'Not quite, Crowner. But within a day or so, no doubt.'

John rubbed his chin in agitation. 'But why has she decided to leave? I thought she was firmly set upon taking the veil.'

Dame Margaret looked across at her colleague with a wry smile.

'We both thought from the outset that your wife's taking refuge here was more an act of protest and indignation than true devotion. There's no doubt that she is a deeply religious woman, but the simplicity of life here could never be to her taste. She has made her point now and has said that, grateful as she is to us, she cannot see her future within these confining walls.'

John needed time to know whether he was glad or sorry. The prospect of divorce or annulment had already been quashed and his daydreams about running off to Wales with Nesta to start a new life were not really a practical option. He had come to hate his empty house and his lonely table and secretly missed Matilda's pugnacious presence, much as it often infuriated him. He was confused and uncertain whether he was devastated or relieved.

'May I talk to her now?' was all he could think of saying.

The Prioress raised her hands, palms up. 'It depends on whether she yet wishes to speak to you. That is her choice, but Dame Madge will seek her out and ask her. Is there anything else, Sir John?'

'Just one matter, Dame Margaret,' he said in a low voice. 'The child – my only child. What happened to it?'

The nun's eyes flicked across to Dame Madge and for a moment she looked uneasy.

'It was buried in our cemetery, Crowner. Though it was tiny, it was still one of God's flock and was laid to rest with due ceremony.'

'May I just see the place, please?'

'Dame Madge will show you the spot.'

Again an uneasy glance passed between them before the raw-boned nun showed him out and took him around the back of the new church dedicated to Becket, another penitent gesture by one of Thomas's killers. Here there was a small cemetery plot, with a dozen plain crosses marking the resting places of the sisters who had passed away during the past thirty-eight years since the priory had been founded.

Dame Madge led him across to the far corner, almost against the boundary wall. Here a tiny mound of fresh earth, no larger than a mole-hill, was surmounted by a little wooden cross small enough to lie on the palm of his hand. At its foot lay a posy of daisies and buttercups, plucked from the surrounding pasture.

'There it is, Sir John,' said the dame gently. 'I'll leave you in peace.'

She walked away, and John stood staring down at the dimple of reddish earth, his thoughts rolling forward to what might have been.

He heard a footstep behind him and, turning, saw his wife. She still wore a white apron, soiled with salve from his mistress's throat. Coming near, she stood alongside him, but avoided any contact. He turned back to the tiny grave and stared down at it. Suddenly his throat seemed to tighten and his sight blurred with moisture.

'There's part of me under that soil, Matilda,' he said, with a break in his voice.

'Yes, John. But come away now. I'll be home before long.'

She took his arm and steered him back across the grass.

POCKET
BOOKS

THE TINNER'S CORPSE

Bernard Knight

When Crowner John is summoned to the bleak
Devonshire moors to investigate the murder of
a tin miner, he has little idea how difficult this
new investigation will prove to be. The victim
worked for Devon's most powerful mine owner,
Walter Knapman. There seems to be only one
possible motive – to sabotage Walter's business.

But the tinners have their own laws, and they
are none too pleased at Crowner John's inter-
ference. And then Walter Knapman disappears.

A decapitated body, a missing tinner, a disgruntled band of miners and a mad Saxon intent on
destroying all things Norman. Only Gwyn,
Crowner John's indispensable right-hand man
seems to be of any help at all – until he is
arrested for murder and put on trial for his life.

PRICE £5.99

ISBN 0 671 02966 5

THE GRIM REAPER

Bernard Knight

May 1195, and Sir John de Wolfe is summoned at dawn to inspect a corpse which has been discovered in Exeter's cathedral precinct. Aaron of Salisbury, a Jewish money-lender, has been found dead, his head enveloped in a brown leather money-bag, a scrap of folded parchment clutched in his fingers.

This is just the start of a strange series of murders in which an appropriate biblical text is left at the scene of the crime. Setting out to track down a literate and Bible-learned killer, Sir John deduces that he is looking for a homicidal priest.

But with at least twenty-five parish churches in Exeter, the killer could be any one of more than a hundred clerics . . .

PRICE £6.99

ISBN 0 671 02967 3

**POCKET
BOOKS**

This book and other **Simon & Schuster** titles are available from your book shop or can be ordered direct from the publisher.

Guenevere:

0 671 01812 4 **The Queen of the Summer Country**	Rosalind Miles	£6.99
0 671 01813 2 **The Knight of the Sacred Lake**	Rosalind Miles	£6.99
0 671 01814 0 **The Child of the Holy Grail**	Rosalind Miles	£6.99
0 671 03721 8 **Isolde**	Rosalind Miles	£6.99

The Stone of Light:

0 671 77371 2 **Nefer the Silent**	Christian Jacq	£6.99
0 671 77374 7 **The Wise Woman**	Christian Jacq	£6.99
0 671 77375 5 **Paneb the Ardent**	Christian Jacq	£6.99
0 671 77376 3 **The Place of Truth**	Christian Jacq	£6.99

0 671 51673 6 **The Sanctuary Seeker**	Bernard Knight	£5.99
0 671 51674 4 **The Poisoned Chalice**	Bernard Knight	£5.99
0 671 51675 2 **Crowner's Quest**	Bernard Knight	£5.99
0 671 02965 7 **The Awful Secret**	Bernard Knight	£5.99
0 671 02966 5 **The Tinner's Corpse**	Bernard Knight	£5.99
0 671 02967 3 **The Grim Reaper**	Bernard Knight	£6.99

Please send cheque or postal order for the value of the book, free postage and packing within the UK; OVERSEAS including Republic of Ireland £1 per book.

OR: Please debit this amount from my

VISA/ACCESS/MASTERCARD ....

CARD NO: ....

EXPIRY DATE ....

AMOUNT £ ....

NAME ....

ADDRESS ....

....

SIGNATURE ....

Send orders to SIMON & SCHUSTER CASH SALES
PO Box 29, Douglas Isle of Man, IM99 1BQ
Tel: 01624 836000, Fax: 01624 670923
www.bookpost.co.uk
Please allow 14 days for delivery. Prices and availability
subject to change without notice